More praise for
Lee Smith and *Oral History*

"Deft and assured . . . Miss Smith's seemingly effortless work is a considerable feat."

—*The New York Times Book Review*

"Brings the storytelling gift off the porch swing and onto the printed page with an often breathtaking vitality . . . A writer of rare talent."

—*Publishers Weekly*

"A spellbinding storyteller."

—*Newsday*

By Lee Smith

Oral History

LEE SMITH

Ballantine Books • New York

Copyright © 1983 by Lee Smith

All rights reserved under International and Pan-American Copyright Conven-tions. Published in the United States by Ballantine Books, a division of Random House, Inc., New York, and distributed in Canada by Random House of Canada Limited, Toronto.

This book, or parts thereof, may not be reproduced in any form without permission.

http://www.randomhouse.com

Library of Congress Catalog Card Number: 96-96632

ISBN: 0-345-41028-9

Manufactured in the United States of America

This edition published by arrangement with G. P. Putnam's Sons

First Ballantine Books Mass Market Edition: August 1984
First Ballantine Books Trade Paperback Edition: July 1993

10   9   8   7   6

Author's Note

For information about early Appalachia, I have found these books to be invaluable: *Our Southern Highlanders* by Horace Kephart (New York: Macmillan Co., 1922) and *The Southern Highlander and His Homeland* by John C. Campbell (New York: Russell Sage Foundation, 1921). Other source books I used include the following: the *Foxfire* books, edited by Eliot Wigginton (Garden City: Anchor Press/Doubleday); *What My Heart Wants to Tell* by Verna Mae Slone (Washington, D.C.: New Republic Books, 1979); Vol. I of *North Carolina Folklore* (Durham, N.C.: Duke University Press, 1952); *Looking Back One Hundred Years, A Brief Story of Buchanan County and Its People* by Hannibal Albert Compton; *Tales of the Hills* by Arthur Ratliff, Jr.; *Old Town and the Covered Bridge* and *People of the Horseshoe* by Dan Crowe. The anecdote that Parrot Blankenship tells at the hog-killing is closely based upon an anecdote told by Vance Randolph, from *Folk-Say, A Regional Miscellany: 1931*, edited by B. A. Botkin, pp. 86–93. Copyright 1931, by B. A. Botkin, Norman: University of Oklahoma Press. This tale was later included in Bantam's paperback edition of *A Treasury of American Folklore*, edited by B. A. Botkin, which is where I ran across it.

I want to thank, in particular, the following people, who have given me songs, tales and stories, ideas for sources, good lines (the "phone call from Hell" is Dorothy's, for instance), and all kinds of support in general during the writing of this novel: Ann Moss, Dorothy Hill, Bland Simpson, Lou Crabtree, Louis and Eva Rubin, Charlotte Ross, Hal Crowther, Tom Huey, Cece Conway, Katherine Kearns and Grady Ballenger, Glenn and Gertrude Kiser, Mrs. V. C. Smith, Mrs. Ruth Dennis Scott, Martha and Wilton Mason, Ava McClanahan, and especially Ernest L. Smith. Thanks to Peggy Ellis for her help in manuscript typing and preparation; to Faith Sale, the editor; and to Liz Darhansoff, my agent.

For Josh and Page

Fair and Tender Ladies

Come all you fair and tender ladies
Be careful how you court young men.
They're like a star in a summer's morning,
First appear and then they're gone.

If I'd a-knowed afore I courted
That love, it was such a killin' crime,
I'd a-locked my heart in a box of golden
and tied it up with a silver line.

Oral History

Little Luther Wade just sits out there in the porch swing, swaying back and forth with his new suspenders on, a little bitty old shriveled-up man so short that his feet in the cowboy boots can't even touch the floor. He's got one leg shorter than the other, anyhow. And he's the oldest thing you ever saw. Every now and then he strums a little bit on his dulcimer. Every now and then when he slows down, he sticks one foot out, jerks himself forward and pushes off from a flowerpot, which sets him to swaying again. He's wearing his Western shirt with the flowers on it, too. He knows how cute he is. "It's time she was a-gettin' back now," he says, looking up at Hoot Owl Mountain. "What time is it anyway?" he asks a while after that, but nobody will pay him any mind. Old Ora Mae sits in her chair making a brown and yellow afghan in the star pattern, her fingers busy, busy, busy, without her even looking down at her hands. She's looking off to the side yard where two of her grandsons, Al's children, have tied string on some june bugs they are swinging around and around through the hot evening air.

Ora Mae gives a long sigh. She sits as big and shapeless as a rock in her green easy chair, pushed up against the house wall. This is Ora Mae's all-time favorite chair; they moved it out of her house for her and brought it down to put on the porch when she and Little Luther moved in here with Al and his family because their own house up in Hoot Owl Holler was haunted. But it is not a porch chair, never was. Al's wife Debra will not have it in the house, though, because it doesn't go with her and Al's living room suite, which is Mediterranean.

"I went down to the Saint James Infirmary, I saw my sweetheart there. All stretched out on a long white table, so cold—so sweet—so fair," Little Luther sings in a high bluegrass falsetto, strumming. Ora Mae sighs again: old fool.

She feels a heaviness in her bosom which means that some-thing bad is going to happen.

Debra comes out of the house wearing pink knit slacks, tight, and a black T-shirt with "Foxy Lady" written on it in silver glitter. Debra has curled up her long yellow hair like a movie star. She sits down on the steps and paints her finger-nails silver and then waves them around in the air to dry. Once, Debra was Miss Tug Valley. Now she has three chil-dren like stairsteps, and all of them blond as you please. "Suzy Q!" Debra hollers. "Come over here, honey. Come sit down here a minute and let Mama do your nails." Suzy Q, five, comes running and sits down next to Debra and spreads her fingers out pudgy and wide. "Hold still, now," Debra says. Out in the yard, Roscoe and Troy throw down their june bugs with a whoop and head toward the house.

"It's time for Magnum," *Roscoe says.*

"You Roscoe! Watch out for Daddy's cord!" Debra yells. Roscoe and Troy just miss tripping over it, thick and black where it curls out the front door like a blacksnake.

"Let her go, let her go, God bless her," Little Luther sings, "wherever she may be. She can look this whole wide world over and never find a man sweet as me." Debra gives one of Suzy's fat white hands a little smack. "I said hold still," *she says. "Anybody else want to watch* Magnum?" *Roscoe yells out the front room window. Roscoe likes TV so much he could watch it all day, he even likes the game shows. That's why he's so smart. Ora Mae sighs and wipes one eye, where a tear comes trickling out. "I just don't like it," she says.*

"Well, why did you say she could go up the mountain, then?" Debra is always right down to earth.

"I never," Ora Mae says, nodding her head at Little Luther. "He done it. He done it all by hisself."

Little Luther gives his famous cackle. "Now honey," he says.

"Now blow on them," Debra tells Suzy, and leaves the child sitting on the steps blowing on her little silver nails while she gets up, pulls down her T-shirt, and follows the black cord out to the van. Al is inside, putting orange shag

carpet all over the place. He's got that cord out here because he's been doing something electrical, and also because he's got a high-intensity light in there to work by. Al—that's short for Almarine—is a big, heavy, blond-haired man, six-three, with a streak of the devil in him. He made All-State Guard in high school football. He used to have a concrete business in Black Rock, before he and Debra got into AmWay. Now they do AmWay full time. Al has three kids, a van and a bass boat and his parents living with them, and he can handle all of it. Al has never been one to stand in the way of progress. He carries a calculator around all the time, for instance. He is a member of the Lions Club too, as well as the Junior Toastmasters Club.

"C'mere a minute, honey," he calls to Debra from inside the van. "We've got all this carpet here left over. I think what I'll do is just put it right up the sides like this." Debra sticks her head in to look.

"I said c'mere," Almarine says, but when she climbs inside the van he grabs her and sticks his hand up the T-shirt to feel of her breasts in the pointy bra.

Debra starts giggling.

Back on the porch, Ora Mae stands up slowly, holding onto the arm of her chair. She goes and stands by the steps and looks up at Hoot Owl Mountain, shading her eyes with her hand. It's getting dark now, down here by Grassy Creek, but high up in Hoot Owl Holler it's still light. There's sun in the tops of the trees. Ora Mae sees the house up there with the grass grown high all around it, her flowers gone to seed by the fence. She sees the cedar trees and the outhouse, the steep and weeded slope where the garden grew. But Jennifer is coming down the path now, thank God, stopping along the way to write things down in her notebook. Ora Mae feels old. She has a heaviness in her bosom like the end of the world, so she goes inside for a Rolaid.

Jennifer picks her way down the mountain with beggar's-lice stuck to her jeans. All the weeds are so high and they grab at her. Jennifer thinks it is just beautiful in this holler, so peaceful, like being in a time machine. She can't understand why her father never would let her come here *when it is so plainly wonderful, when it was her real mother's home, after all. And these people are so sweet, so simple, so kind . . . they are not backward at all! And Little Luther, what a character.*

The salt of the earth, *Jennifer writes in her notebook. Then she stops.* Please pass the salt of the earth, *she writes, which will be even better if she can work it in. Dr. Ripman is bound to love it; she knows she'll make an A for the course. When Jennifer thinks of Dr. Ripman, her heart does a little jump. He has opened up new worlds for her— whole new worlds! Even though he came to the community college from Miami, Florida, Dr. Ripman is still a Yankee. He talks real fast, and jumps around, and he has frizzy black hair and horn-rim glasses. Jennifer was nothing when she signed up for his Oral History course. She didn't know a thing. All her life, she looked down on her real mother's family, the way she was taught by her father and her step- mother, Martha, who might as well have been her mother anyway for all practical purposes, since she's the only mother Jennifer remembers. Jennifer knows she lived up here in Hoot Owl Holler once, when she was little, but she can't remember anything about it.*

Jennifer's stepmother Martha is the president of an ama- teur drama group which is rehearsing right now for Our Town *by Thornton Wilder. Jennifer's father is an uphol- sterer, quite successful. He has his own business in Abing- don, about fifty miles east of this holler. He is a dim sweet man who has never discussed Jennifer's real mother with her in all her life. "The subject is closed," he used to say when she asked him, but now Jennifer hasn't asked for years. She grew up loved and petted, sensitive and nervous and "artistic," a shy little girl with bronchial asthma and a collection of forty-two dolls from foreign countries and a giant dollhouse that her father made himself, with tiny little upholstered chairs in it. Her father has given Jennifer every advantage all along, in fact, including—for her birthday— that baby blue Toyota which is parked right now beside Al's van. Looking down, Jennifer can see it, see the van and the* ranch-style house and the garden behind it, and over Black Rock Mountain, she knows, is where her Aunt Sally lives with her husband Roy. Another uncle, Lewis Ray, lives near here too. It's weird to think of her kin, strangers, sprinkled out like salt over Appalachia. Jennifer doesn't know any of them. She sees her grandfather like a tiny little doll in the front-porch swing. The van and the Toyota look like toys.

Jennifer wonders what her father will say if he finds out she has driven over here. But what can he say? It's a free country. Besides, Jennifer never would have thought of this if she hadn't happened to overhear Martha telling a couple they played bridge with, over a bridge game, how backward his first wife's people were and how of course they've lost contact with them now, but listen, this is really a riot, the last Martha heard, her parents had moved out of their house because it was haunted. Haunted! In this day and age! Martha's shrill theatrical laughter had pealed out over the bridge table, over the gin and tonic and chips and dip. "Now Martha," Jennifer's father had said in his quiet-quiet voice. "I really think . . ."

But that was two years ago, and now Jennifer can't remember any longer exactly what it was that her father had really thought. It doesn't matter. What matters is that Dr. Bernie Ripman unexpectedly invited Jennifer to have a beer with him after class one day—her, out of all those girls! What matters is that the class had been talking about common superstitions that day, and that when Jennifer told him—laughing, to show she was embarrassed because she was even so slightly related to people like that—about her real mother's family and their haunted house in Hoot Owl Holler near Grassy Creek, Dr. Ripman's eyes lit up like big Miami stars. "No kiddink!" he had said. "No kiddink!" So here she is now, halfway down the mountain, and behind her, in the empty old house on the hill, the tape recorder is set to record for one hour. Jennifer finds a flat rock like a table and sits on it. The rock surprises her, it's still so warm from the sun. She can feel its heat through her jeans. She *looks back up the mountain where she has come from, and then back down at Al and Debra's house. She opens her notebook and writes:*

Impressions

The picturesque old homeplace sits so high on the hill that it leaves one with the aftertaste of judgment in his or her mouth. Looking out from its porch, one sees the panorama of the whole valley spread out like a picture, with all its varied terrain (garden, pasture, etc.) stitched together by split-oak fences resembling nothing so much as a green-hued quilt. It is not as humid up here on the mountain, one notes, and one is led to wonder if that or perhaps other reasons led my ancestors (yes, mine!) to build up here, so high above the lush quiltlike valley with its gaily roaring creek.

The porch steps of the old homestead sag and the porch itself is falling in, rotting, with ivy climbing sensuously up through the floorboards. Yet this old place appears in no way haunted as in the stereotyped versions of haunted houses one sees perhaps on late-night TV. The door slid open with a somewhat melo-dramatic creaking effect when I turned the key in the lock. It did sag inward as if exhausted also. But the parlor inside was empty of theatrical cobwebs or any other stirring items. It resembled nothing so much as a house before someone moves in. Empty—not evil! True, dust was spread like an even lacy carpet on the floor. True, the handmade rocker I had heard about sat forlornly before the blackly yawning fireplace, in the place where I had been told it would be, but it resembled nothing so much as some old dilapidated relic left behind in the hustle and bustle of someone's Moving Day. It certainly did not look significant. I wandered all through the six-room house. Originally it was but a cabin—you can see where they have paneled over the old logs, where they have added on. The kitchen, of which little remains, must have been *primitive!*, but it was very difficult for me to visualize my real mother as a little child gaily playing in these rooms, or her cousin Billy (the ghost?) or Al or Lewis Ray and Sally whose acquaintance I have not even made.

I turned the tape recorder on and left it beside the fireplace, near the rocking chair. I looked back at it from the doorway as I was leaving, at its plastic spools silently spinning in the empty room, where it resembled nothing so much as a conscious anachronism in some kind of folklore film on ETV. As I stood there in the doorway, I received a chill which caused me to pull my sweater around my shoulders. Yet was this a premonition, or the real chilliness that comes in these mountains even in June as the sun dramatically sets, spraying its brilliant hues across the western sky?

I cannot say.

Meandering back down the rocky hillside, I come upon a strand of green glass beads shining in the weeds. I pick the beads up, turning them this way and that in my hands, letting the sun play over them, before letting them drop again to earth. They are cheap, half broken. Suddenly they seem to me symbolic of this whole enterprise which strikes me as silly, a fool's errand, even though my grandfather told me in such detail on the telephone about the rocking chair, the terrible banging noises and rushing winds and ghostly laughter that began every day at sundown, driving them at last from their home. One feels that the true benefits of this trip may derive not from what is recorded or not recorded by the tape now spinning in that empty room above me, but from my new knowledge of my heritage and a new appreciation of these colorful, interesting folk. My roots.

I think this is why Dr. Bernie Ripman urged me from the beginning to choose this as my oral history project: he wanted me to expand my consciousness, my tolerance, my depth. I wonder how I shall ever be able to repay him for the new frontiers of self-knowledge I have crossed.

I stray. From where I now sit, with the warmth of

this sun-warmed old primeval stone soaking into my body, I feel nothing so much as an outpouring of consciousness with every pore newly alive. I shall descend now, to be with them as they go about their evening chores.

Jennifer shuts the notebook and picks her way down the hill. But when she reaches her uncle's house, nobody is doing any chores. Everything from dinner has been put away. Even the smell of fried chicken has disappeared. The big old woman who is her grandmother, Ora Mae, has gone from her easy chair on the porch. Little Luther has fallen asleep with his head cocked over on his shoulder like a bird. TV sirens shrill out the open front door. Little Suzy, dragging a Charlie's Angel doll by the hair, stands crying in front of the closed van with its ornate custom painting job—maroon palm trees, golden waves, a black death's head on the back. Every now and then Suzy bangs her dolly on the closed door of the van. Her crying is like a cat mewing, and it's getting dark already down here, and lightning bugs are coming up everywhere out of the grass. You can hear the creek from out of the darkness beyond the yard.

Then Ora Mae comes out of the house, huge and pastel and shapeless in her housedress, and gets Suzy by the hand because it's bedtime.

"Can I help you with anything?" Jennifer asks, standing by a tire full of blooming begonias in the yard. "That dinner was so good—I know you must be tired."

Ora Mae stands still in the yard, breathing hard, while Suzy pushes crying against her legs. Ora Mae stares at Jennifer. "I don't reckon," she says.

"Good night, Suzy," Jennifer says, reaching for the little girl's hand, but Suzy just cries and pulls away. With a start, Jennifer sees Suzy's fingernails shining up at her, phosphorescent silver in the dusk. Ora Mae takes Suzy into the house while Jennifer stands in the yard by the tire. "You can set on the porch if you want," Ora Mae says back to her from the door. Ora Mae thinks Jennifer is a lot like her mother Pearl, even though Jennifer has been raised by

strangers. *Pearl never knew what to do with herself either. Jennifer even looks like Pearl, pale blond hair and white skin, slight, with too-big blue eyes and the kind of face that asks a question all the time. Jennifer goes and sits on the porch and listens to her grandfather snore, a soft rattling noise. Resembling nothing so much, Jennifer thinks, as the wind blowing through a tree full of autumn's dead leaves. She sits in an aluminum chair on the porch and writes that down. After a while Ora Mae comes back out to sit in her easy chair. She takes up her yarn again. The boys watch TV and Little Luther sleeps, all dressed up. Up on the mountain, that tape rolls on in the empty house.*

"How can you see to work?" *Jennifer asks, trying to start a conversation. It enters her head that her grandmother is not as friendly as someone might have supposed. She doesn't seem pleased at all to have a new-found granddaughter turn up after so many years.*

"Don't need to see much," *Ora Mae says, but she has some light anyway from the front-room window behind her. Her fingers, large and twisted, move in the light, but Jennifer can't see her face.*

"I think it's just wonderful the way all of you still live right here in this valley and help each other out," *Jennifer says.* "It's remarkable. Not many people live that way any more." *Extended family situation, she thinks, but it's too dark to write in the notebook.*

Ora Mae says nothing.

"I was wondering," *Jennifer says after some time has passed and the boys have switched the channel,* "if you could give me a little more precise information. Now, Grandfather told me all about the rocking and the laughter and the wind. And of course I know how my mother came back here when I was little, after she and my father separated, and then she got pneumonia and went to the hospital and died. But it must have been about that time too that my uncle Billy died, wasn't it, if I've got it all straight in my head. Uncle Billy was murdered by a mentally ill teen-ager, isn't that right? An escapee from a home of some kind? At least that was the information I got from Little Luther—your* husband," *Jennifer adds crazily, since her grandmother is giving no sign of even hearing her, just moving the brown and yellow yarn in and out of her fingers. "Grandfather said that Uncle Billy was killed in the rocking chair because that's where he sat all the time after my mother died and even before. So I was wondering if you could tell me some more about that time, which must have been very difficult for you, coming so soon after the death of my mother. Maybe you can tell me something about what Billy was like as a child, so I could gain some insight into why he sat in the chair for so long." Jennifer is all out of breath when she finishes, but Ora Mae doesn't say a word. The silence stretches out. Jennifer squints at her watch: 7:30, only one half hour to go. Ora Mae works the yarn. Jennifer wishes she was back at the college, or back in her father's house watching* Masterpiece Theater *with Martha or making popcorn for her little sisters.*

But then Little Luther wakes up with a jerk. "Why hello *there, honey!" he almost hollers. "Just catching a catnap myself. That's all, just a little catnap. Listen now. Listen here. I bet you've never heard this one." Little Luther grabs up his dulcimer and starts in on the cabbage-head song which, sure enough, Jennifer has never heard, and after a while she is joining in on the chorus. Jennifer has a sweet, pure little voice with no feeling in it at all. Little Luther does "Fox on the Run." He is a real treasure. The boys turn up the TV louder so they can hear it. Al and Debra's whole house is loud and happy except for Ora Mae, who sits like a pile of dough in her green easy chair. Then the door of the van opens, to Jennifer's complete surprise, and here come Al and Debra, who must have been in there working on the carpet all along! Debra runs right up on the porch and starts clogging even in her thong sandals, and Al leans up against the porch post and sings along with his dad. Al has a deep, rich boom-boom kind of a voice, which goes fine with his daddy's high thin one: they sound great together, in fact.*

"Listen here," Little Luther says. "I bet you've never heard this one."

He and Al sing, "Mama, don't whup little Buford, Mama

don't pound on his head, Mama don't whup little Buford, I think you should shoot him instead," and Debra clogs too in front of the bright screen door.

Jennifer claps her hands when it is over. "You all are just wonderful," she says.

"Al ain't so wonderful," Little Luther says. "That Al there, he was so ugly when he was a boy, I had to tie a pork chop around his neck to get the dog to play with him."

"Why, shoot, Daddy!" Al takes it up, grinning, "there ain't no truth in you. Why, you're so ugly yourself that one time when we put your picture out in the field, the crows brought back corn they stole four years ago."

Then they started singing "Wildwood Flower" and it is all so fine, it is just like Jennifer hoped it would be, until Ora Mae stands up all of a sudden and ruins it.

"It's time," she says.

Jennifer stands up too. "Have you all got a flashlight I could borrow?" she asks. "I'll just run up and get the tape recorder and then I've got to go."

"She can't go up there," Ora Mae says.

"Well, you can count me out!" Debra says, shaking her curls. "I wouldn't go up there for a million dollars."

"Oh, I don't mind," Jennifer says. It's her honors project, after all.

"No," says Ora Mae. She stands up by her chair like an old white rock.

"OK, Mama, I'll do it," Al says, and he gets his flashlight and takes off up the trail, so big and strong that nothing— man or ghost, either one—would want to mess with him. While he's gone, Little Luther plays and sings some more and Debra goes inside to get the boys to bed. "Come on Mama, just let us see what's coming on next," Roscoe wails, but Debra hushes him up and cuts off the TV. Little Luther sings "Wise County Jail," which Jennifer has never heard before either. She hopes she will be able to remember all these concrete details. She hums along.

Al comes bursting out of the darkness carrying the tape recorder and hollering at the top of his lungs, something you can't understand. "Mama!" he says. "Lord God! Mama!"

*She opens her arms and wraps him up in them, big old man
that he is.*

*Al lets the tape recorder drop on the steps by Jennifer. She
jumps up. "What happened?" she asks. "What happened?
Did you see something? Did you hear anything?"*

*"Lord God! Lord God!" Al whoops. He has to sit down
on the porch steps and light a cigarette. After one drag,
though, he takes it out of his mouth and flings it off into the
grass. "Lord God!" Al says. He runs his big hand through
his hair.*

"Did you hear something?" Jennifer asks.

Al sits still and looks right at her.

*"Shit," Al says. "Hear something? Hear something?" he
mimics. Al gets up then and goes into the house, yelling for
Debra. The screen door slams.*

*Little Luther tries to say something, but he's all wrought
up and the words come out crazy, you can't make out what
he means.*

*"You hush now," Ora Mae tells him, and he does, and
Ora Mae goes and stands out in the yard. "Storm coming
on—" she says this out loud, to nobody. Ora Mae stands
completely still, like she's waiting for something or like she's
listening. Jennifer sits on the steps clutching the tape recorder, watching Ora Mae, who is nothing now but a tall
white shape in the night. Tree frogs sing out in the darkness;
lightning bugs blink in the darker dark of the shade trees.
The sycamore tree looms white. The heat is lifting some
now, so a little wind comes up from the creek and ruffles the
hem of Ora Mae's dress. It ruffles the leaves of the shade
trees, sighing, rising stronger now up from the creek and
blowing across the yard, it's sighing up the holler toward
Hoot Owl Mountain, moaning around the house. It has
voices in it, and thunder coming, and Jennifer on the steps
and Ora Mae in the yard incline their heads in the wind like
they're listening.*

I

Granny Younger

From his cabin door, Almarine Cantrell owns all the land he sees. He's not but twenty-two years old now. Young, then—you could call him young for owning this much land and that's a fact, but they's other ways Almarine is not young now and never was young atall. He growed up right here, right on this place. Nobody ever knowed what he was up to.

Where's Almarine? they allus said, and who told the answer to that? Not his mama, nor his daddy, nor yet those sorry brothers of hisn, nor even me over here where I live on the south side of Hurricane Mountain where I have been a-living praise God for more years than I could tell you if I was to sit down and try to count them which I won't. I been here a long time. Years. I know what I know. I know moren most folks and that's a fact, you can ask anybody. I know moren I want to tell you, and moren you want to know. And if I never knowed exactly where Almarine was when he was little, I could of give you a good idea.

He'd be down on Grassy Creek all by hisself most likely, seeing how the water ran over the rocks and how cold it kept even in summer, or he'd be up in the crook of the biggest sycamore there at the bend afore the trace starts down through the spruce-pines, a-setting up there still as a little old owl for hours and hours just waiting to see if anybody ever come up the trace, which nobody ever did, or he was out back in the dugout where they kept the meat all winter on the cold dirt floor, and potatoes and onions down in the straw in the grabbling holes, but him not a-grabbling neither, just sitting there still as you please and breathing that musky salty smell in there, a dark smell like something too old to figure whatever it mought have been.

Well, that was Almarine. Almarine fell down between the cracks in the family like some children will.

In spite of him being so pretty, with all that pale-gold hair, in spite of him being no trouble to a living soul. Almarine was said to spend nights in the laurel slick over by Frenchman's Cave, nights by hisself out there when he was not but nine or ten. Now that's the wild side of Black Rock Mountain. And Almarine knowed where Grassy Creek starts, away up high on Hurricane behind this land of mine, away up there where it comes a-bubbling and a-snorting like a regular fountain right out of the ferny ground. Almarine went beyond that spring, too, straight up the rocky clift where the trees won't grow and this little fine green grass grows all around in a perfect circle. A lot of folks won't go up there. But Almarine went and lived to tell it and went again, and nobody marked his comings or goings in particular, or cared how he could scream in the night like a painter until the painters all around were screaming back. Almarine trained a crow one time, till it could talk. It could say about fifteen words when his brother Riley kilt it with a rifle, out of spite. That's how Riley was. But Almarine! Almarine had the lightest, biggest eyes when he was a little child. It seemed like he never blinked. He liked to look out on some distance.

Almarine didn't need nobody, is what it was, and there's folks won't take to a child like that. Still and all, he was sweet when nobody else in that family was, so this was a part of it too. People don't like somebody to be so sweet it makes them look bad, that's a fact. Which he was. I mean he was that sweet. In fact Almarine was that kind of sweet moony child who'll likely end up without a thing in this or any other world, without a pot to piss in.

How Almarine ended up with all this land is a curious thing.

His daddy, Charles Vance Cantrell, was a big old man as mean as a snake and hard on women and children. He had him one gold tooth in the front. Charles Vance Cantrell was Irish or so he said at one time. He had him a long gold chain with a big watch on it that had some dates and "Dublin"

carved into the back, but don't you know he lost it in a poker
game at old man Joe Johnson's store like he lost those mules
and everything else he owned sooner or later except his land,
and Lord knows it's surprising how he never lost that too.
He never put up his land. Anyway, Charles Vance Cantrell—they called him Van—was a fat old man who gambled
a lot and would just as soon strike you as speak. He come by
ship, he said, and then by wagon, and they was religion
mixed up in it someway, but of course you couldn't never
prove it by Van Cantrell. He brung that wife of hisn, that
Nell, from Ireland with him, or so we thought, although
wasn't nobody sure since she was so ashy-pale and she never
said a word until Van went off to fight in the war after which
she perked up considerable. It would of been all right with
me if she had not, now that's the truth. I never give a fig for
that Nell.

Anyway, Van went off through Indian Grave Gap, over
Snowman Mountain and down into West Virginia, where he
joined up with the Union. Nobody knowed if he joined with
the Union out of principle or because, what I thought, it was
the quickest army to get to, and Van Cantrell ever loved a
fight. Now some men hereabouts took up on one side, and
some the other. They was nary a slave in the county. So
they done what they felt to do. It split some families down
the middle, I'll tell you that. Churches too. They is a church
in Abingdon that to this day has got one door for those who
stood with the Union in the war and one door for Johnny
Reb, and this is true, and I'll swear it. To this day.

Van Cantrell stayed with the army as long as he could,
and lost one leg above the knee afore he come home. Things
was different when he got back, he found out right away.
Old Nell Cantrell, who had not done a thing but lay in the
bed having a sick headache since the day he carried her in
that wagon up the trace, Old Nell was up and farming! She
had planted her some cabbage and some corn; she had three
hogs on the side of Hurricane Mountain. She never got back
in the bed neither. She didn't have to, since Van was laid up
hisself and couldn't get around like he used to do. Thank
God! is what she thought. But she needed some help of

course, and so she had them three boys right in a row—stairstep boys, with Almarine in the middle. The other two, Riley and Shelby Dick, took after their daddy, and they growed up a-fighting and a-fussing just like him. They would throw your wash off the line, I've seed it, they tromped on their mama's beans. It was clear from the beginning that they would kill each other or get kilt theirselves before they was through, which is nearabout what they did.

But this happened first. Van Cantrell's leg started up oozing a clear liquid where it had been cut off and healed over. It was a clear smelly liquid, not like pus, which seemed to ooze right out of the very skin without no break that you could find atall. You never saw the beat of it. They called me, of course, and I done what I knowed, but nothing I knowed done any good. The first thing I done was lay me a spider web acrost it, hold it on with soot and lard. Now this had no effect. The next thing I done was what my mama showed me and which I am knowed for everywhere in these parts, what I do to stop bleeding. They will call me anytime, day or night, and when I hear who it is I start saying the words even afore I get my bonnet on, I start saying the words which I know by heart from my mama, and when I get there, most times, the bleeding's already stopped. It is Ezekiel 16, sixth verse, what I say. I done this for Van Cantrell too, done it two days running with nary result. But it is for bleeding, like I said, and not for no smelly old ooze.

"Hit ain't going to work," I told Nell when the sun come up. Then she sent Riley off for old Doc Story, but by the time he got acrost Black Rock Mountain, Van was dead. We had to burn sulfur in there for two weeks to get the smell outen the cabin.

Anyway, without no old man to keep him in line, Riley got hisself in trouble over a girl and had to leave this county fastern squat. This left Shelby Dick, who was the youngest, and Almarine, but him and Almarine fell out someway over a knife and whose it was, or who knows what it was they fell out about, but pretty soon Almarine was gone too, leaving Shelby Dick to farm with his mama. Now this was fine with Shelby Dick and with old Nell Cantrell too. Nobody took much to Almarine as I have said, and even when he was there it was like he wasn't really there so twerent much difference atall with him gone. Almarine allus wanted something—who knows what?—and that's why he kept staring out beyond them hills.

He was gone almost five years. And whatever happened to him in between, that's his story. He never did tell a word. Almarine went off sweet and shy and distant, like I said. He come back all of them things—not changed in any way you could put your finger on—but with another set to his jaw and a hard look sometimes around his eyes. He appeared tired. He appeared oldern he should have been, for his age. Old man Joe Johnson said he heard that Almarine had been in prison someplace, and the way Almarine looked, you could feature it. Of course folks'll say anything but it's true, a man is his father's son. Anyway it was clear that they had been some hard times, even if we never knowed what they was, just like when Almarine was a little boy and you couldn't guess what he was up to.

So I am telling how Almarine come back one day in August 1902, a-walking up the trace in mincy shoes and a snow-white shirt without one thin dime to his name. He just missed burying his mama, who had died about five days prior. His face never changed a bit when he found this out, but I for one couldn't fault him on it since the sweetness and goodness you find in most women were not present, it has to be said, in old Nell Cantrell. Not at the first when she was young and laying in the bed so sickly and down in the mouth, nor yet later when she took to farming herself and smoked that pipe. I smoke a pipe too and you know it. The pipe's not the point. It was the way she gone about everything, like she was too smart for this world, like she couldn't be bothered to smile. She sulled around all the time. A decent woman, folks said. Hard-working, could hoe her corn like a man. But any sweetness in the family, it went straight to Almarine. I see I have forgot to mention Shelby Dick. He died in a whorehouse fire in Roseann, West Virginia, two years before Almarine come a-walking up the trace in that soft white shirt.

Shelby Dick broke his mama's heart.

So Almarine got it all.

And Almarine sits now in the cabin door in his daddy's chair, and he owns all the land he sees. Truly this holler is so much a part of Almarine that he doesn't even think of owning it, not any moren a man would think of owning his arm nor yet one of his legs. The whole time Almarine was gone, most of him stayed right here. He wasn't nothing but a half-boy, a half-man I guess you'd say, but now he's come back here with all of them dead as stumps and he won't have to leave again, he won't have to go noplace, ever again. Almarine's soul swells out over this whole holler. He rolls a cigarette outen rabbit tobaccy and gets up and goes in to the fire and lights it and comes back out. Dragging the smoke in deep, he tilts hisself back in the chair and runs his hand through his long light hair. Then he blows smoke out the cabin door, smoke so blue it gets lost in that blue haze that comes creeping up the holler of an evening, like right now.

Leave him be.

Let Almarine set awhile. He's not but twenty-two years old, and look at what-all he owns. Hoot Owl Holler is the prettiest holler on God's green earth, the way this creek runs through. Most hollers don't have no creek. And Almarine's cabin sets high, high up in the head of the holler, it gives him a view. Most hollers don't have no view. Almarine's daddy mought of been a son of a bitch, but he was a strong man and he knowed how to build a cabin. This cabin is here to stay. It's got a puncheon floor instead of pure dirt, which most don't. A front room, a back room, a lean-to and a big high loft where old Nell's beans have been strung into leather-britches since July, a-drying against the winter, alongside her strings of apples and peppers, pears and tobaccy twists. She's saved the seed in gourds, there at the back. She's got them lined up on the farthest wall. A fireplace in the front room, little old jumping fire. Beds with corn-husk ticks on them, quilts. Jacob's Ladder, Poplar Leaf, Bear Paw, Star. The quilts is real pretty and bright in the lights and shadows throwed up by that little fire. One of the beds has got a down tick on it, and that one will be Almarine's. Many's the time he held the goose while Old Nell plucked the down— and got bit, too, over and over, for all his trouble—but never has he slept on down his whole life long.

So let him. It's his house.

Let him look out the door past the ash-hopper nailed on the tree, where they ran their lye, out past the big black kettle on the tripod, where Old Nell boiled her clothes. It's all hisn, now. It's all hisn including Hoot Owl Mountain behind the cabin, them apple trees and pear trees at the foot of it, the burying ground up on top. Old Nell's up there already, along with the other two. He owns that mountain now. He owns a strip on the side of Hurricane Mountain too, that strip running next to me where the dogwood's so thick in the spring. He owns the garden on the other side, and starting up Snowman Mountain, he owns them blackberry bushes all in a tangle there where the garden stops and the mountain starts. Now these three mountains is all different, let me say, Hoot Owl and Hurricane and Snowman, with Hoot Owl Holler smack in the middle of them three like a play-pretty cotched in the hand of God.

Hoot Owl Mountain looks like how it sounds, laurel so thick you can't hardly climb it atall, in fact you plumb can't do it iffen you don't know the way. They's not but one trail up Hoot Owl Mountain and it goes on to the burying ground. So you start up that trail through the laurel and it's so dark in there you can't hardly see your way. You get through that laurel and then you're climbing, see, but climbing slow—it's a big mountain, and the trail goes round and round. They's trees up Hoot Owl biggern you ever saw in your life, they's ferns nigh as tall as a man. On up, they's caves in the rocky clift and one cave a man got lost in, so they say. They say you can hear him holler. Now the burying ground on the top of the mountain is a flat grassy bald, and it's real pretty. They's a wind that blows all the time. I like that burying ground. But I mislike Hoot Owl Mountain myself and don't go up it lessen I have to, but you can find yellowroot there, and ginger, heartleaf and pennyrile, red coon for poison ivy. What I need. Hoot Owl Mountain is a

dark mountain though, maybe it's all them pines, and it
don't get hardly no sun. Fog will hang on the north side all
day long, with that blue mist spread over the top. Moss
grows everywhere under them pines, moss thick enough to
sleep on if you cared to. Not me, mind you. They is something about Hoot Owl Mountain makes a body lose heart. If
you laid down to sleep on that pretty moss, you mought
never wake up again in this world. It's no telling where
you'd wake up. They was never anybody knowed to court
on Hoot Owl neither, you see for why. I keep a buckeye in
my pocket, traveling Hoot Owl. I get right along.

But up on Hurricane, where I live, now that's as pretty a
place as you please. Grassy Creek running down it, all them
little falls, why it is music to your ears just a-walking up
Grassy Creek. It is pussywillow and Indian paint, Queen
Anne's lace and black-eyed Susan. It is swimming holes
with water so clear you can see straight down to the bottom.
They never was any water bettern Grassy Creek. Then you
get on up, you've got your oak, your chestnut, your tulip
tree. Big old trees all spreaded out which lets the sun shine
through. The mast under these trees is so good it's what they
call hog heaven up here on Hurricane Mountain, everybody
lets their hogs run here. Hurricane Mountain is a fine
mountain and they's other folks lives here too, you can see
for why. Now I've got my own holler, mind. Nobody ever
lived in it but me and mama, and mama's dead. But I've got
my neighbors up here on Hurricane, not like Almarine.
They's a bunch of Horns, been here forever, and some Justices, some Rameys, Davenports. They is one-eyed Jesse
Waldron lives all by hisself in the Paw Paw Gap. Rhoda
Hibbitts not far from me with them two ugly mealy-mouth
daughters of hern, and no man in sight. That wouldn't
bother me none if I was Rhoda. I'd not put up with a regular
man if you paid me. But it grieves Rhoda considerable. Take
'em to town, I says. Well, that's another story.

And Snowman, over on the other side of Hoot Owl
Holler, why Snowman's the biggest of all. They's a rocky
clift the other side of Snowman, looking down into West

Virginia, that's the spitting image of a man, and that rocky clift is so high that snow will stay on it nigh into April sometimes, why they call it Snowman. If you want to go to West Virginia, you follow the trace over Indian Grave Gap and down Coon Branch and into Roseann where the lumber company's at. It'll take you a day and a half to get over Snowman from here if you walk it steady. Mought be it'll take you two days. And they's folks all over Snowman—Ratliffs and Presleys, Ashes, Stacys, and Skeens. There's moren I know including lately them foreigners come in with the lumber trade.

This is not to mention old Isom Charles nor yet Old Isom's red-headed Emmy up there on Snowman Mountain, that same red-headed Emmy who's to be the ruination and the end of Almarine. I'll get to them. Nobody knows them anyway, half-crazy a-living way off up there under the Raven Clifts. I'll get to them in my own sweet time.

Anyway here's Almarine, not knowing any of that. Almarine a-looking out the door of his cabin where the creek goes down the holler, and down, and down again in front of the cabin until it turkey-tails out in the bottom and runs along flat down there so far you can't hardly see it, beyond that stand of sycamores where it flows on through the spruce-pines and from there down the Meeting House branch and into the Dismal River at Tug, where the store is.

Almarine looks past the creek and the dropping-off holler, Almarine looks out on space. Away acrost his valley he sees Black Mountain rising jagged to the sky—county seat beyond it, Black Rock where the courthouse is—and if he looks to the left on past it, he sees all the furtherest ranges, line on line. Purple and blue and blue again and smoky until you can't tell the mountains apart from the sky. Lord, it'll make a man think something, seeing that. It'll make a man think deep.

And Almarine is thinking, I seed him from the trace. Tilted back and thinking, a-smoking that cigarette, with night coming on like it does.

"Well Almarine," I says.

And Almarine says, "Granny."

Then he says, "Come and set with me, Granny," and I was proud to do it. I set in the chair and Almarine hunkered down in the doorway smoking, he hunkered down there just like he used to do as a little set-along child. It seemed like no time since he was borned. But he had growed up into the finest-looking man you ever laid your eyes on, that's a fact. All that pale gold hair and them light blue eyes, and so tall and so straight. Everbody else around here is mostly dark complected and mostly slighter than Almarine.

"Air ye going to stay now?" I asked him, and Almarine said he was.

He said he was home for good.

That did not surprise me none, as Almarine was made for this holler and it for him, iffen he left it or no. I could see how he knowed it for home.

We set out there while the fog rolled up in the bottom and the lightning bugs commenced to rise all along the banks of the creek. "Ever thick fog in August means a heavy snow come winter," I says, and Almarine grins. It was getting so dark I couldn't hardly see him, white tooth-shine in the dark.

"Old Granny," he said. "I misremember all of that."

"Don't make no differ," I said. "Old woman like me." I stands up to go. "What you need is a girl," I says to Almarine. "What you need around here is some children on this land, and a woman's touch in the house. You better find you a girl," I says.

Then I left, off up Hurricane, how I go.

Later, I wished I'd of bit off my tongue.

Sometimes I know the future in my breast. Sometimes I see the future coming out like a picture show, acrost the trail ahead. But that night I never seed nothing atall. If I had, it would of been graves and dying, it would of been blood on the moon. And I never saw a blessed thing in the night but them lightning bugs a-rising from the sally grass along by Grassy Creek.

Because of course Almarine went right out and done it, what I said. Everbody does what I say. Almarine went a-

courting. He courted on Hurricane, he courted over in Black
Rock. He courted until he run acrost Isom's red-headed
Emmy, and that was the end of him. I'll tell it all
directly.

I'll tell it all, but don't you forget it is Almarine's story.
Almarine's, and Pricey Jane's, and Lord yes, it's that red-
headed Emmy's. Mought be it's her story moren the rest.
Iffen twas my story, I never would tell it at all. There's tales
I'll tell, and tales I won't. And iffen twas my story, why I'd
be all hemmed in by the facts of it like Hoot Owl Holler is
hemmed in by them three mountains. I couldn't move no
way but forward. And often in my traveling over these hills
I have seed that what you want the most, you find offen the
beaten path. I never find nothing I need on the trace, for an
instance. I never find ary a thing. But I am an old, old
woman, and I have traveled a lot in these parts. I have seed
folks come and I have seed them go. I have cotched more
babies than I can name you; I have put the burying quilts
around many a soul. I said I know moren you know and
mought be I'll tell you moren you want to hear. I'll tell you a
story that's truer than true, and nothing so true is so pretty.
It's blood on the moon, as I said. The way I tell a story is the
way I want to, and iffen you mislike it, you don't have to
hear.

Now it was late in the year for courting. Most folks court
in the spring. But they had a working over here on Hurricane for the eldest Ramey boy, Peter Paul, and that young
wife of hisn, and Almarine attended. This was in September, little old nip in the air. I love a good working myself. All
the womenfolks and gals had brung the food and laid it out
on a piecey-cloth right down on the ground. So they was a-
sitting and a-talking and keeping the dogs away, and watching this big old fire, and the littlunses running ever which
way and playing fox and geese, and the biggerunses—girls, I
mean, playing pretty girl station. Boys had to help on the
cabin. And the biggest gals was all of them looking at Almarine. I done said he was something to see. One thing
being how he was so much biggern all the rest, just purely

and strictly the size of him, another thing being how he was always so easy to laugh. Nobody had seed him for five years, and he was a sight for sore eyes. And Lord, he was strong as a ox! When it come time to roll the ridge-pole up them rolling-logs, there it goes easy as pie. And Almarine just a-laughing.

Dinnertime comes and all the menfolks and the boys eat first. Womenfolks and the gals carries the cookpots around. Now you won't catch me a-carrying no cookpots. But I have borned my share of these folks, and I am an old, old woman, and I aim to do as I please. There is food at a working to last you up near a week. It's coming on for dark now, big old fire and the fat-pine torches stuck in the grassy ground. Cabin done excepting the shingles and the outside chimley, save for another day. Crackling bread, fried chicken, shucky beans, sweet potatoes, and a big old pot of corn, fried eggs and buttermilk and liquor, what you want. I like a little liquor myself. The gals comes around with the food, and one of these gals comes right frequent to Almarine. She's a pretty little girl with curly black hair. Almarine just a-grinning, you could see he was taking it in.

"Did you make this?" he asks her, when she brung him a fried apple pie.

"I did," she says right back, all peart, and never once drapped her eyes.

"Mought be hit were your mama," Almarine says, and she says, "It was not," and flounced off. But a little while later she comes back around with another fried pie right outen the fire and draps it smack in his hand.

"Now what you want to do that fer," Almarine says, seeing as how this hurt, but she just laughed a little laugh and flounced on away. Her name was Nancy Wiley.

"Sweeten you up," she says over her shoulder, and everybody laughed at Almarine. So when old Joe Johnson takes out his fiddle, you know who Almarine takes by the hand, and you see how sassy she is. Then they go around and around. Old Joe Johnson waggles his head when he fiddles, I wish you could see him, he's got a big old beard and a belly

as round as a tick and those little stick legs. Old Joe Johnson
sings,

> Rattlesnake, oh rattlesnake,
> What makes your teeth so white?
> I've laid in the bottom all my life
> An' I ain't done nuthin' but bite
> > bite
> > > bite
> I ain't done nuthin' but bite.

Joe Johnson is a sight, you wouldn't think it to see him of a
day in that store. Old Mrs. Virgie Justice is leaving now—
she don't hold with dancing—and taking Hassell Justice
with her, a-looking back over his shoulder. Time was when
Hassell could cut a rug, afore he got tangled up with that
Virgie.

Oh it was a frolic time all right, at Peter Paul Ramey's
new cabin on Hurricane Mountain, and Hester Little was
there to call the steps. Old Joe done Shady Grove and Cumberland Gap and then he done Cindy. *I been to the East and
I been to the West, I been to the jaybird's altar. But the
prettiest gal I ever seed was Jimmy Sherlock's daughter.*
Now that don't make no sense. And oftentimes, courting
don't neither. But it don't make a lick of difference. Almarine and Nancy Wiley went around and around with
their faces giving back the light of the fire and him so tall,
and her so little and dark. Her mama was watching her like a
hawk-bird. Her mama had this real long nose.

"Where do you live at?" Almarine asked, and Nancy
Wiley said, "Who wants to know?" Little bits of her hair
bounced out from under her cap, and all the gals were giggling behind their hands.

Almarine just grinned. Whatever he had been up to those
five years, you could see it had not been courting.

I traveled back home acrost the ridge just a-grinning myself. I had a full belly but I was light on my feet as everly. I
don't need no light to show me where I'm going, nor a body

to lead me the way. I know all the ways there is on Hurricane Mountain. Traveling light that night through the pure dark I grinned to myself, as I said, to consider Almarine courting.

Once when I stopped to light my pipe I heard me a big old *thunk* when a blacksnake fell out of a tree. Then I heard that little rustle-rustle they make in the leaves when they slip away. Now a blacksnake can climb up a tree, but he can't never climb back down. He has got to fall out like a log. It tickled me, hearing that blacksnake fall. I likened it to Almarine in my mind. The biggest falls the hardest, what I said.

Well the upshot of the working was, Almarine come back over here on Hurricane Mountain and started courting that Nancy Wiley. I have to say this did not last long. It was clear almost from the word go that Nancy Wiley's daddy was in the bed and not going to be getting up from it anytime soon, and Nancy Wiley's mama as much as said that if Nancy was to move over to Hoot Owl Holler, why they thought they mought all of them come. This is Nancy's stove-up daddy, her hawk-nosed mama, and some several littluns besides. It taken Almarine aback when she said it. Almarine got up and went over and looked outen the window and said he had to go out and see to his horse. He was on it and gone afore you could say squat, with Nancy hollering holy hell at her mama while Almarine rode away. And there was not a thing in the world they could do about it neither. Things had not progressed that far to where he was bound for good. Nor could their daddy have got up outen the bed if it come to that. So Almarine got home free, that time.

The next time was over in Black Rock where Almarine had found him a town girl named Judy Lynn Long. He saw this girl in the five and dime, what it was, and follered her home. Judy Lynn Long was a sweet thing but she took a lot after her mama who put on airs, and her elder sister Louise who was even worse. They kept doilies on their chairbacks in that house. Still, Almarine took her a-walking. She had a dimple beside of her mouth. Almarine taken her to talk by the Dismal River and kissed her lips. She had something on them which tasted sweet, and Almarine loved that. For all his size and all his land, remember, Almarine was nought but a country boy, come to town to court. In the end it was the sister caused all the trouble. She taken a shine to Almarine herself, and then she started a-crying and wouldn't eat. They said she wouldn't touch a bite. "I am distraught," their mama said, and Almarine mounted that horse again while the getting was good.

Hog killing, Christmastime—come and went. Almarine bided his time. It was coming spring when he set off again, down toward Roseann over Snowman Mountain. It was a cold, cold day with a pale bright sun and the ground still froze where you placed your feet. Almarine stepped along right smartly. He had his gun, and he had his dog, and he had him some new boots he had bought offen a man in Black Rock, new boots for to do his courting in. Them boots crunches down on the moss, still froze, and the little slivers of frozen ground. But some of the birds was back, he saw, and the redbud was fixing to show. Almarine walked along the trace a-whistling and then all of a sudden he stopped. He couldn't have said why he stopped whistling, nor what passed over the day. It was like it all growed brighter, that kind of a shining day you get sometimes at the tail end of winter.

All of a sudden a redbird flew right up in front of his face.

"Ho redbird," Almarine said.

Seeing a redbird gives you a wish, you mought know what Almarine's was. As for whether he got it or not, I'm never the one to say.

"Ho redbird," Almarine said again, for the redbird had never flew away. In fact it hopped right along the trace ahead of Almarine's new black boots.

"Sic em, Duck," Almarine said to his dog—the name of his dog was Duck—but Duck never moved a foot. Duck cocked his head at that redbird and whined, and the hair rose up all along his back. Seeing this made Almarine grap his rifle and hold it closer, and look all around the mountain. Now Almarine was on the wild side of Snowman, as I said. Nobody much lives over there. They's a stretch of the trace goes down from the Stiltner place to the county line and it runs over rocky ground—they is big old white rocks strewed off down the side of the mountain—and this is the stretch he was passing through. The rocks is funny here. Some of them so big-like, and laying in funny forms. Like they was throwed out agin the side of the mountain. You can't see how they got where they are. They is no rocks like it anyplace else on any of these three mountains.

The little redbird is singing to beat the band, and Almarine stares all around. Duck is growling and backing up with every hair on his back standing right straight up. The sun shines white offen all those rocks, so they take on a diamond glow and shine in that bright cold sun. The air itself is so fresh and cold it's like it beats on your face almost, it's like you can't get no breath. And Almarine, big old man that he is, Almarine feels all light-headed. He sees these bright white shapes, looks a lot like snowflakes, in front of his eyes. Only there ain't no snowflakes. This is when Duck commences to growling, then to barking, and then takes off lickety-split back over the trace.

"I be damned," says Almarine.

This little redbird now is still a-hopping along the ground, and Almarine kind of follering. This little redbird sings the prettiest song a body has ever heard. The little song is so sweet and so sad it brings tears into Almarine's eyes, or mought be it's only the cold. But it makes a pull on Almarine's heart. He knows he is going to foller it whether or no. The little bird flies up in the crook of a tree, offen the down side of Snowman Mountain. Almarine follers it offen the trace without even considering what he's about or where it might lead him. He don't have a choice in the world. There goes that redbird and there goes Almarine. He is surefire surprised to see how a trail opens up where there never was one before, and how his boots travel right along it.

So Almarine goes off down Snowman Mountain a-follering the redbird with the day all shiny around him. Little freshets of water is busting outen the rocks all around, the way they do in the spring of the year. Every year this happens, along about the time of the thaw, waterfalls springing where they wasn't no water before, and running along down to the creeks. This water is the coldest and the best you ever put in your mouth because it comes from the driven snow. Almarine stops where a freshet has bubbled into a rocky pocket in one of them rocks, and takes him a long cold drink. It wasn't like water atall. It was like liquor the way it run straight to his heart, and the way it made his hands and his feet set to tingling. Almarine is feeling light-headed now, and he's starting to grin. On he goes, down he goes, on the path between them big white rocks with the redbird a-leading the way. He stops one time and looks all around, just to get his bearings. But he don't know from noplace where he is. The rocks above and below is a-shining so white in that so-bright sun, and the water coming down off them is a-shining too, and tinkling as it runs off down the mountain. The sky up above is a fine deep blue, blue as a robin's egg, without no cloud in sight. Right by his boot is a little yaller flower that Almarine has not seed the likes of before, in all his years running these mountains. So Almarine leans over and picks it. This is a pretty little flower what resembles a rose. It has sprung straight up from the rocky ground on a pale green stalk without nary a leaf. Almarine studies the flower awhile and then the redbird starts up again all of a sudden, and he quits studying it and looks ahead, down the mountain.

What Almarine sees sets a stamp on the rest of his life. The streams had all flowed into a pool which was set in a little circle of rocks at the bottom of the mountain. This was a deep pool, too, plumb full of that crystal-clear water, so you know how cold it was, and a woman was kneeling before it a-washing herself. Almarine come upon her from the back. She was down on her knees leaning forward, dipping up the water in her hands. She was naked from the waist up. Her black skirt was pulled down around her hips and her shirt-waist was throwed on the ground. The skin of her back showed the whitest white that Almarine ever seed, and her hair fell all down her back to her waist. And that hair! Lord it was the reddest red, a red so dark it was nigh to purple, red like the leaves on the dogwood tree in the fall. And the red-

bird perched on a rock to the side of the pool and directly he
started to sing.

The woman whirled around. She stood. Now everything
that happened, happened real fast of course, but for Almarine it was like it taken a hundred years. She seemed to
turn so slow, and her hair whirled out slow as she turned,
like a red rain of water around her head. In his mind he
would see her again and again, the way she stood up so slow
and how she turned.

"Git outen here," she said.

But she made no move to cover her glory and Almarine
looked his fill. She was a woman as big as he was, a woman
nearabout six feet tall. Her eyes was as black as night and
her nose was long and thin. Her mouth was as red as a cut on
her face and the color flamed out in her cheeks. It was a long
face. Bony. But Almarine thought she was beautiful. Her
hair hung all down her back like one of them waterfall freshets along the path and her breasts were big and white with
her nipples springing out on them red as blood.

"My name is Almarine Cantrell," he said, "and I aim to
take you home."

When he said that, it was like a shadow crossed her face.
She looked sadder for a minute than a body has ever looked.
She looked like all the sadness in the world was in her heart.
She knowed it couldn't happen, that is why. Because this
was old Isom's red-headed Emmy who could never have a
mortal man in all her days. She belonged to the devil is why.
Her daddy had done pledged her years before. And all those
years she had fucked with the devil and not give a fig for a
regular man. But she had never seed a man like Almarine
neither. It was like she knowed for the first time what it was
she couldn't have. It was like it pained her so bad in her true
heart's core—iffen a witch has a heart, that is, which I don't
rightly know to this day. Anyway she looked at Almarine a
long time with that woebegone face of hern, while all around
them it was bright and still there on Snowman Mountain.

Now Almarine didn't know none of that, about Red
Emmy being a witch. All Almarine knowed was that he had
follered a path and come upon a woman he had to have and

there she was, standing well-nigh naked before him in the middle of the morning. And she didn't try to cover herself neither. And that look on her face gone straight to his heart, for they was never a young man yet who don't want to go out and right a wrong, or kill a man, or have to do *something* to earn his right to what is there for the taking, all along. Only he don't think he can ask, nor take, without earning it. Without no pain. Oftener than not, a young man's a regular fool.

Red Emmy throws back her head and a new look, tight and closed-up, comes over her face. A darkness comes into her eyes. Still looking hard at Almarine, she stoops over quick and graceful, her breasts a-swinging, and picks up her shirtwaist offen the rocks.

"Would ye kindly turn yer head fer a minute?" Red Emmy asks most polite, and Almarine looks to the side.

She's gone when he looks back.

Almarine screams like a painter and plunges ahead down the trail to the little pool. He runs off in the woods to the left, and yet again to the right. He runs all over the place a-hollering, but he can't find his red-headed woman again, nor has she left any sign. She has gone as quick as ever she come, like firesmoke up into thin air. Almarine sits on a rock and cries and then he stands up and swears to find her. He fires his gun off once, straight up in the air. It echoes off all them rocks. Almarine puts that yaller flower in his pocket, starts for home. He has forgot all about the courting trip he had planned, to Roseann, West Virginia. He has forgot everything he ever knowed nearabout except for that red-headed Emmy.

Almarine come over to ask me about her, but I daren't tell him a thing. I was churning the time he come.

"You better go back over to Black Rock," I says. "Find you a sweet God-fearing town girl, what I say."

"My mind is set," Almarine says. "Ye could help me if ye would, old granny."

"I will not," I says. "I don't know a thing."

"I'll find her whether ye help me or no," Almarine says. "I don't give a damn fer yer notions." And then he turned on his heel and left. I watched him walking off down my holler a-swinging his arms. I would swear in my soul he was whistling. A young man like that, he don't have ary idea what he's fooling with, and not afeard of a thing. Well, I went back to my churn but the butter never come that day, I can't say twere ary surprise. I was lying through my teeth to Almarine, and butter won't come on a lie.

I had not set eyes on Isom fer thirty, mought be twere forty years. Isom kept to his doings, me to mine. They was a time when we was children, we was friends. We both growed up right here on the side of Hurricane, but then Isom's maw died and his daddy beat him so bad that he took to the other side of the mountains. A mountain man, old Isom was. He used to come down to Joe Johnson's store at Tug with them bags of ginseng—you could get five dollar a pound for it, even back then, you get eight dollar a pound for it now—and trade for supplies and then hightail it back up on Snowman Mountain. Then he started a-sending that Emmy. As for Emmy, I'll get to her in a minute. Old Isom is what I want to study, for a spell. Because it's a funny thing how I had not seed him for years, and yet in a way I felt like I knowed him bettern I ever knowed ary a soul. They was a time once when me and Isom—but Lord, that's another story. Isom had done gone his way, I'd went mine. For Isom was evil clear through. He kilt his brother and beat his paw before ever he took to the mountain, or so they say. Myself I knowed Isom, albeit I hadn't seed him, like I knowed the back of my hand.

But didn't nobody know how he got that gal. Some says he had him a wife and he kilt her, and others says he just drempt Emmy up outen the black air by the Raven Clifts. Others says he stole him a baby from West Virginia.

Abednego White swears Isom has got them ravens trained to cotch him chickens and bring them up there. He says those chickens is a-flapping their wings all the way, with the ravens a-carrying them. Abednego tells it for a fact. But anyway Isom got him a girl someway, and then he pledged her to the devil, as I said. She growed up with ravens, in caves. She was a fair sight oldern Almarine, too, Red Emmy, she

must of been forty when Almarine happened upon her. I'd
say she was forty if she was a day. But a witch don't show
age like a regular gal, her body's too full of blood.

So I never said a word while Almarine searched, and
searched, and searched all over Snowman Mountain. He
tried and tried to find that path again, leading down from
them old white rocks, that path and the little pool, but it was
like it had plumb disappeared. Try as he would, Almarine
never could find it again. Nor could he spot the little redbird, nor find that yaller flower he thought he'd put so careful in his pocket, nor any other flowers like it. It was like it
was all in his mind. Iffen it was or iffen it wasn't, twerent up
to me to say, but I'll say this—iffen a body searches for so
long, he's bound to find something, that's a fact. And soon he
come upon her up there by her daddy's cave, a-cooking out
over a fire. It was fixing to get dark that evening, and the
smoke swirled all around.

Almarine stood right there and viewed her through the
smoke.

"How are you called?" he said. Then he started walking
toward the fire.

She looked at him through that smoke like she didn't want
to speak, and then at last she said, "Emmy." Her voice
seemed to come from a distance. "You better git on away
from hyar," she said, but then her daddy come a-running all
wild-haired outen the cave and knocked her to the ground
and fired a pistol at Almarine's head. He had already killed
him two or three, it was said, who'd come around courting
his Emmy. Of course, they said too that he and Emmy were
moren a hundred years old, or old as the hills or older.
Folks'll say anything.

But Almarine had him no gun at the time and so he was
forced to leave. The ravens were squealing and calling out in
the night, twas like they were laughing him home. Almarine
grit his teeth and he swore he would kill her paw.

But as it turned out, he never had to. Old Isom just up and
died. Or that is how Red Emmy gave it out—but you know
in your heart she kilt him. Kilt him for Almarine. Well and
be that as it may, old Isom fell offen a rocky clift and died,

and the ravens ate out his eyes. They'll do that, it's natural. They'll eat the eyes outen a deer or anything. But nobody knows iffen Isom's death were a natural death or not, him a-falling offen a rocky clift he'd lived on for all of his life. Red Emmy buried him herself. Then she packed all she owned in a poke—it was precious little—and set out a-walking in the light of the moon for Hoot Owl Holler.

It was right at midnight when she come, Almarine asleep on the down tick beside the fire. Duck stood out in the yard a-howling, but she spoke a word and it hushed him. Red Emmy pushed open the door with her foot and walked in the front room. She laid her poke in the corner. Then she walked over and looked down at Almarine where he laid in heavy sleep, his light hair splayed out on the piller.

Lord! What could have went on in that Emmy's head? She knowed she could never be no man's wife. She knowed how her daddy had raised her. She knowed too what her own needs was and how she had to fill them. But just right then, for a minute, when Emmy looked down at Almarine sleeping, it was like she was the one bewitched. She wanted to be a witch and a regular gal both, is what she wanted. But mainly she wanted Almarine, and her powers were considerable.

"Almarine Cantrell," she said.

Almarine sat bolt upright and rubbed his eyes. At first he thought twas a dream come into his own house on Hoot Owl Holler. She stood as tall and straight as a Indian with her head wrapped up in a big dark shawl.

"Take that off," he says, and he watched while Emmy reached up and unwound the shawl and then pulled pins all outen her long red hair.

"Now do ye know me," she says, and Almarine nodded his head and reached over and opened her dress and pulled it down and pulled off her underthings too and there she stood in the wavy light of the fire, that fire as red as her hair and her mouth, and she moaned when he pulled her down.

Well, there's Almarine laying with Red Emmy at last, and Duck a-howling bloody murder out in the yard.

Of course Almarine knowed better! By then he had heard

those stories too, by then he knowed moren you do. He knowed he was playing with fire. Now you yourself mought know what that's about, or it mought be that you do not. Iffen that be the case I am sorry for you, there ain't no way I can say it in all the world. It's like you want something so bad, you're all et up with the wanting. It's like the ground opens up all of a sudden under your feet and there ain't no end to your falling. If you're bound and determined to play with fire, you'll do it whether or no—you'll play till it burns you up, or the other one up, or the both of you, or mought be till it burns out.

Almarine and Red Emmy stayed in that bed for two days solid. At the end of those two days she got up and cooked some beans and Almarine went out to feed his horse and his dog. Now what was Emmy up to, a-cooking beans? It was like she was a little child with a new play-pretty, and that play-pretty was Almarine. She was just a-playing house, is all, until her true nature come out.

But before that happened, and it happened soon enough, they had them a spell of what I call froze-time on Hoot Owl Holler. Everthing stood still. Almarine took care of his chickens and his mules and he even planted. It was planting time. But he moved like a man set under a spell, which is what he was. Almarine moved along so slow with a little grin on his face so constant it was like it was slapped there for good. He moved like a man in a dream. And that Emmy? Lord, she was a-dusting, and a-sweeping, and a-cooking and milking the cow. As I said she was playing house. She looked real young and real pretty—her red hair just a-bouncing all down her back as she walked. You know a woman orter bind up her hair. But Emmy did not. It was the only way you could tell by looking that she differed from other womenfolks, but Almarine liked it that way and asked her to wear it loose down her back and she done it. Now this was all in froze-time when they were so happy. But twerent natural, no moren a snow in July.

And of course nobody would venture nigh that cabin on a bet. Folks turned their heads a-hurrying along past the mouth of Hoot Owl Holler, they well-nigh run through them sprucey-pines. Rhoda Hibbitts who had spoke so favorable of Almarine—she had them two ugly daughters of hern, remember, a-trying to find them a man—why, Rhoda would not speak his name. Harve Justice swore he ventured up that way squirrel-hunting, and a big black raven flew outen a sprucey-pine and aimed straight at his head. Harve said that raven had eyes so big they looked like a human's and it made a sound like a baby screaming. Peter Paul Ramey's new baby took to colicking when his mama carried him past, and he colicked so bad he liked to kilt her afore he was through. I walked that baby half a day myself, with him just a-spitting up and a-hollering, so his mama could get her some sleep. She was just a young girl, and dead for sleep.

Well, they is stories and stories.

But the point is Almarine was bewitched, and twerent none of us could holp him. Everbody that had liked him so good, turned their back now. You don't want no truck with a witch.

I seed them one time myself. It was when one of them Stacy babies over on Snowman had the thrash and I was heading over there acrost the mouth of Hoot Owl Holler on my way, when something pulled at my heart. I believe I'll just go up there and see that Almarine, I says to myself. I would like to set eyes on his face. Now I loved him as a baby, you recall. I said he was always so sweet. So I started traveling up Hoot Owl Holler on the trace alongside the creek. It all seemed natural to me right then, I couldn't feel no witchery in the air, nor nothing wrong atall on the trace nor around that cabin when I got to it. Almarine's chickens come a-running and a-scratching, and that witch had her wash strung out on the line like anybody. Can you feature a witch a-washing? She must of wanted so bad to be natural, what I think. She must of tried hard for a while. Anyway I hollered out one time for Almarine, but wasn't no reply, so I went around the side of the holler to where the garden was, and sure enough they was out there a-planting. Something made me stop then, and stand stock-still behind them two cedar trees. That was the first time I remarked how it was coming on a storm—they'll come up in these mountains real sudden-like.

Well, Almarine was a-plowing with a bull-tongue plow hitched onto one of his mules. He was a-follering along behind the mule, guiding the plow, and you know how hard it is guiding a bull-tongue plow in the rocky ground. Red Emmy walked behind him with corn in her apron, drapping it down where he plowed. Now you plant your corn when the oak leaves is about as big as squirrel-paws, so this was about the right time. And I have to say that Almarine and Red Emmy looked like regular folks, going along down the side of the hill with their planting. The dogwood trees were a-blooming white and pink all around the field, and the purple judas behind it. The wind was all the time rising. It blowed that Emmy's red hair all around and she was so pretty, I could see how he was bewitched. But something kept me from a-stepping out from where I stood behind them trees. All I want to do, I says to myself, is see how Almarine is a-doing. That's all I want, I says. I says I'll look my fill, and then I'll be traveling directly.

I watched while the storm come on.

Thunder rolls, then comes lightning, over on Black Rock Mountain. The wind is a-whipping the trees and the ash leaves is showing their silver backsides. Almarine keeps on plowing as long as he can with her right along behind him. Most womenfolks would of run for the house, but you know Red Emmy don't fear no storm. Well, the rain comes falling in big old draps makes a splash in the dirt like a silver dollar, and Almarine's mule commences a-neighing and raising up in the trace. Almarine lays down the plow and turns, and Emmy is twisting up the rest of the corn in her apron. She raises her face up to him and now she's wet and her hair is dark and like it's stuck flat to the side of her face. Her skin shows real bright in that crazy light that comes in a early-spring storm. This was the firstest thunderstorm of the year. Almarine draps that plow, and turns, and looks at her, and she moves toward him and him toward her and they go to kissing, right there in that half-plowed field in the wind and the rain. By then I knowed bettern to come out, I wouldn't of come out for the world. So there they are kissing, with Almarine's mule a-rearing and a-hollering, and ever time it lightnings, their faces comes plain in the sudden dark.

You never saw such kissing in all your life! Made me feel like I had not felt for years and if that surprises you, you ain't got no sense. Now a person mought get old, and their body mought go on them, but that thing does not wear out. No it don't. And anyway they was kissing, and I was a-watching, and then still holding on.tight to each other they start for the cabin acrost the field. They had plumb forgot that poor mule. Well, I never said a word but when they passed by where I was, Red Emmy done something made me see she had knowed I was there all along. Of course she knowed it! Child of the devil. But I had like to forgot it, that day.

Red Emmy turned her head away from her kissing one time, once only, and looked at me directly where I was hid. The lightning flashes right then and I see her face and it is old, old. It is older and meanern time. Red Emmy stares me right in the eye and she spits one time on the rainy ground. Almarine never seed a thing.

Well as soon as she spits, I get a pain in my side liked to bend me double, it is all I can do to get outen that holler that day and get over on Snowman Mountain where I belongs to be curing the thrash, stead of going spying on a witch and her business. That pain bent me double for seven days, wouldn't nothing cure it. I learnt me a lesson for sure, and all during the froze-time, I never went up there no more.

So I never knowed exactly when things commenced to change, and Red Emmy's true nature come out. Which it'll do ever time, you mind me. The devil mought loan out his daughter, but comes a time when he'll take her back. Almarine must of knowed this too, somewhere in the back of his mind. When she turned to evil for good, he must not of been that surprised. The first I heered of it myself, was old man Joe Johnson down at the store says Almarine is looking puny. He says Almarine come by for some coffee, all white-faced and thin as a rail.

"That boy don't look good, Granny," Joe Johnson says. Joe Johnson has got this big white beard stands out in a circle around his face. I was getting me some salt as I recall. "That boy looks plumb tuckered out. You orter go up there and see him, Granny. I tell you, they's something wrong."

"I ain't going up there," I says. Joe Johnson always gives me some tobaccy for my pipe and gives it free.

"You ort to go," Joe Johnson says. He shakes his head back and forth like he is grieving. "Now that were one fine boy."

"Iffen a body don't want no holp, I can't holp em," I says, and Joe Johnson allowed that was so. I took my tobaccy and left.

But I kept Almarine in my mind. I knowed what was happening, of course. A witch will ride a man in the night while he sleeps, she'll ride him to death if she can. She can't holp it, it is her nature to do so. The same way she'll run a horse in the ground, and she done that too before long. Now Almarine had set a big store by that horse, and twerent another month till it was dead. She had run it to death, the same way she was doing to Almarine. Witches'll leave their bodies in the night, you know, and slip into somebody else's. They'll do it while you're asleep and they'll drive you all night long with nary a speck of rest. They can take on any form. Sometimes they'll go into a cat, or a cow, or a horse, or a rabbit, or a hoot owl out in the night. They leave their bodies in the bed and out they go. All that being so nice in the daytime was moren Red Emmy could take, what I think. She had to go hell for leather all night to make up for them long sweet days. Almarine was wore out all the time, of course. He laid in the bed and slept most of the time while she worked his farm and then she'd come in and get in the bed. He was servicing her, that's all, while she liked to rode him to death. Red Emmy, she worked all day and she rode all night and she never slept. But a witch don't need no sleep.

Things went on like that into the summer. It was hot as fire, I recall, the day I crossed the mouth of the holler heading for Tug. It was a full moon coming on that night, which meant it'd be Marylou Harkins' time for sure by the time I got there. They is nothing like a full moon to bring on a baby. I was stepping on the stones acrost Grassy Creek when I heerd my name.

"Granny." He was hunkered down by the side of the creek, throwing little old rocks in the water. He looked awful.

"Ho Almarine," I says.

I keep on stepping from rock to rock.

"I been hoping to see you," he says. Almarine's eyes that used to be so blue had turned pale and runny. His collarbone showed through his shirt. His hair, that used to be so beautiful, looked just like old dry straw and that's a fact.

I was talking to a man bewitched.

"Granny, I got to do something," Almarine says.

"You'll up and die if you don't," I says.

I sit down on the grass where he'd hunkered, and bees buzzes all around us. It was the prettiest day.

"You got to holp me," Almarine says.

"I can't do nothing," I tell him, "even iffen I would. You're under a spell and you've got to break it yourself," I says.

"What must I do?" he asks.

"You've got to throw her out," I says. "You've got to make the mark of the cross on her breast and her forehead with ashes, and throw her out the door and say the name of the Father and the Son and the Holy Ghost as loud as ever you can."

"What iffen that don't work?" Almarine looks down at the ground.

"Then you've got to cut her," I said, "and make the mark of the cross with her blood."

Almarine turns whiter yet and shakes his head. "I'll not do that, Granny," he said.

"Do what you will," I says.

"I couldn't cut her," says Almarine. Then he busts out crying as hard as he can, and it is one of the awfulest sounds I ever did hear. Almarine loved her, is what it was. You know a man can love something he don't even like, and Al-

marine loved her as much as he disgusted her, and scared as
he was. I had seed them kiss in the rain and I knowed it. He
loved her iffen she were a witch or no. Almarine put his head
in my apron and cried, big old man that he was.

"Now you get up," I said, when I thought this had lasted
long enough, but he did not.

"They's something else," he said.

"They's always something else," I said. "Well, let's hear
it. What is it?" I asked.

"She's gonner have a baby," Almarine says. He cries
down into his hands.

"Good God in heaven," I say. "It won't be no baby like
none of us-uns ever seed, I'll tell you that. You get rid of her,
Almarine," what I told him, "afore you get you a passel of
witch-children up there."

Almarine stood up. I'll swear it was the prettiest day, full
June, bees a-buzzing and butterflies flitting all over the
creek. Queen Anne's lace ever place you look. Almarine
rubbed at his eyes like he couldn't see.

"I come back here a free man," he says. "I served my time.
I growed up here, Granny."

"I knowed you," I says.

"I love this holler," he says.

"That's so," I told him.

"I ain't a-going to lose it," he says. Then he looks down at
me and grins. Despite of him being so thin, he looks like
himself now in the face, around the eyes. "I won't have no
witch-children in my holler," Almarine says. "I don't know
what come over me," he says.

"Holp a old woman up," I says, and Almarine done so.

Then he puts his hands on his sticking-out hipbones and
laughs so loud it comes back from the rocky clifts.

"I still need a wife," he says.

"I reckon you do," I told him, "and I reckon I'll be traveling on down to Tug now. I got me a baby to cotch."

Almarine stood tall by Grassy Creek just a-grinning, and
watched me on my way.

Marylou Harkins had a britches-baby, taken it two days
to come. End of that, and I went around to the store, and

what-all I hear from Joe Johnson is mighty good news. They was some several folks in there as I recall, and all of them dead to tell it. Harve Justice was in there, and One-Eyed Jesse Waldron from the Paw Paw Gap, and Luther Wade sat picking on the porch. He can play a guitar as sweet as you ever heard. I sets down on the porch to rest my bones.

"How's that baby?" Joe Johnson hollers out, and I holler back it is fine.

"Hit's a little girl," I say. "They ain't named her yet."

"I reckon ye could use a little of this," Joe Johnson hollers, and he sends his girl out with some liquor in a glass.

"I reckon I could," I allows.

They was all of them a-watching me real careful while I takes me a sip.

"What air you all up to?" I asks, I see how they're watching so close, and Harve Justice slaps his leg and laughs real loud.

"Boy, you sound like a mule," I said, which was true, and all of them starts in laughing then. Joe Johnson's girl is catching june bugs in front of the porch.

"I guess you ain't heerd it, then," Harve says. He is a big old skinny feller can rile you to death without even trying. No use to rush him neither. So I sit here on the porch with Luther a-picking, and all of us sipping a little, and that Stacy boy rides up with the mail and folks starts to come from all over. It's getting on for afternoon by then. That Stacy boy thinks he is something on a stick, got him a leather pouch says the U.S. Mail. Joe Johnson gives his girl a string and so she's swinging that june bug around in the air, just a-whizzing him, flash of greeny gold. Marylou Harkins' mama come over after a time and brung me a apple stack-cake for my sweet-tooth, she says, and I thanks her kindly. I love a apple stack-cake. I was feeling real good a-setting there on the porch, and by the by it all come out like I knowed it would.

Almarine had up and got rid of Red Emmy, was the long and short of it.

He had throwed her outen the door and she had left. Mrs. Davenport had told Harve that she seed Red Emmy going

off up the trace toward Snowman Mountain where she come
from, all bent over and moving slow. Mrs. Davenport said
she seen her face and it looked like a old, old woman. All of
this had put such a scare into Mrs. Davenport that she went
straight home and got in the bed and wouldn't cook no dinner, Harve said. Harve said he bet she's there yet. Luther
Wade said he had run into Bill Horn—now Bill Horn works
over in Roseann for the lumber company, comes home
whenever he takes a mind to—and Bill Horn said he was
crossing Snowman on the trace and heard the awfulest hollering and laughing you ever heard, coming down from the
Raven Clift. He said it made his horse shy and the hair on
his arms stand straight up. They was all laughing over Mrs.
Davenport down in the bed and Bill Horn taking a fright.

I sat there a-sipping and never laughed or said ary a word.

I was a-looking out the valley there—it's real pretty where
Joe Johnson's store is—over toward Black Rock Mountain
off in the sky, and all of a sudden it was like a thundercloud
rolls acrost my eyes and it all turns dark and I'll swear I can
hear her laughing. Then I rubs my eyes and takes another
sip and it's all gone, Joe Johnson's girl is whizzing that bug
around my head.

"You ought not to laugh," I says. "We ain't seed the end
of it yet."

"Now, Granny." Joe Johnson comes out and puts his
hand on my shoulder. "Now, Granny," he says. "Almarine
took up with a crazy girl, and now he has run her off. There
ain't a man among us mought not of done it nor worse. That
gal and her daddy was crazy as coots."

But I can't get what I seed and heard outen my head. I
stands up slow. "You mark my words," I say, and I take up
my stack-cake real careful, and set off a-traveling for home.

"Crazy old woman," that Stacy boy says, and I hear him
alright, but I never look back nor give any sign. Thinks he is
a power with the U.S. Mail.

I walk the trace for home and after a time the moon comes
up to light me on my way. Now this is a big full yaller
moon, and no harm in it. I cross Grassy on the stepping
stones at the mouth of Hoot Owl Holler, and the water is all

shiny from that moon. There's a little wind through the sprucey-pines, sounds like a song. I look up Hoot Owl Holler and I can't see a thing, but I don't feel nothing neither. It feels real calm and pleasant now in Hoot Owl Holler, and I lean down and get me a drink outen Grassy Creek and I heads upstream for home.

So Almarine gets shed of Red Emmy, and it's not two months before he has got him a wife for sure. And this time he done hisself proud.

He was over in Black Rock on a Saturday as I recall, to buy him a new mule and shoe his horse, when a wagon comes in all burdened down with goods and children and womenfolks walking along. They was not but one man, a little old bent-over man said he was bound for Kentucky and how far was it, and set down there where Squirrel Waldron's forge is, a-wiping his face.

Squirrel looks up from shoeing Almarine's horse and says, "You have got you a mess of family, ain't you?"

The man wipes his face again and says, "Lord, Lord."

It don't look to anybody like he'll make it to Kentucky the rate he's going. Then the womenfolks—twere his wife and her sister, if I recall—they go down to Poole's store to buy them some food, and the children start running all over the place a-banging Squirrel Waldron's tools. Squirrel being real particular about his tools. Almarine is just standing there a-watching it all, and they's other folks too have come out to see. There hadn't been such a commotion in Black Rock for a while.

This old man wipes his face and says "Lord, Lord," and then he whoops at two of his biggest boys to get him something. He whooped in a foreign language. So they go to rummaging around in that wagon, spilling goods all over the road, and then they come up with the fanciest saddle you ever saw, silver tracings all over it. They brung it over to the old man and lays it down in the road. By this time a considerable bunch has gathered around to look.

His wife and her sister has come up too now, all babbling and crying they ain't got enough money for food.

"How much you gimme?" he says.

"Well now, that depends," Squirrel says. He wipes his hands on his apron and comes around closer to look. What the foreigner don't know is how much store Squirrel sets by his trading. So they commence to trading—it takes a while—and while they is at it, a gal jumps outen the back of the wagon and runs around the side to look, too. Almarine seed her right off, he slips through the folks to her side.

Everbody said it and I'll say it too—this was about the prettiest gal you ever laid eyes on. She was slight and just as dauncy as a little fancy-doll, the smallest, whitest hands and the littlest ankles. She had that blue-black hair they all had, excepting hern was all in curls, and a face like a heart, with them big blue eyes. She sees Almarine coming and blushes, and looks down at the ground.

"Whar you all headed?" Almarine asks real polite, and she says, "Kentucky." She has a low voice what reminds Almarine somehow of a dove.

"Ye reckon to make it?" He grins that big grin and she goes to giggling.

"I don't keer iffen we make it or not," she says. She shakes her curls at Almarine and when she done so, he sees a flash of gold at her ear. She's got real gold earrings, they come from her mother who died, and this foreigner is nought but her uncle—but Lord, I'm ahead of myself. Anyway she shakes her head at Almarine and stomps her little foot. "I'm tired of traveling," she says.

"Let's take us a little walk, then," says Almarine.

So he taken her by the arm and off they go toward the Dismal River. They do make a picture, him so big and fair, and her so dark. She goes with a spring in her step, she goes with those curls a-bouncing. Now half of the people is watching them two walk off, and a-shaking their heads, and the other half is watching Squirrel Waldron trade with the foreigner.

Almarine and the gal come back in about a hour.

Squirrel has got him a new saddle by that time, and the mules is fed, and they've got some food, and two of those little children is laying asleep under that sycamore in the front

of Squirrel Waldron's place. When Almarine and the gal
comes in view, the women start hollering out for her to
hurry and get on in the wagon. But she don't hurry. She and
Almarine walks along slow and they're holding hands.

"Get in the wagon," the man says to the gal, but he looks
like he don't give a damn. He looks plumb wore out.

Almarine and the gal walks up to him and stops. Everbody is drawing around now, you can tell that something
is up.

"How far you aiming to get with them mules?" Almarine
says, and everbody turns around to consider the mules. Now
the mules was the only thing that hadn't come in question all
that day, but they was sorry. One of them was the sorriest.

The man looked at Almarine through his little old runny
tired eyes.

"I'll get whar I need to," he says.

"Hit's a long way," Almarine says. "You gotta go on
through the Breaks and up the Big Sandy before you get
anyplace atall."

"Git in the wagon," the man says to the gal, but not taking
his eyes offen Almarine. The gal don't move but the red
comes up in her cheeks.

One of them foreign women sets to crying and throws her
shawl up over her face.

"Now, Almarine," Squirrel says.

"I just got me a new mule," Almarine says. "Hit's over
there." Everbody looks where he's got it hitched in front of
Mr. Poole's store.

"What I purpose is this," says Almarine. "I'll give you
that mule scot-free, hit's a good mule, and you let Pricey
Jane stay here with me."

Lord, everbody sets to talking at once! and Squirrel, he is
trying to talk Almarine out of it. But Almarine don't give a
inch. He stands there staring down at that little old man,
stands tall with the sun shining offen his yaller hair. It don't
take long. The man looks at that mule, then he looks at Almarine, and then he nods his head one time. His boys give a
whoop and one of them runs over and gets the mule and
hitches it on behind the wagon and the man gets in the

wagon seat. "Giddyup," he says, and he clicks his tongue,
and off they go. That's the last anybody ever seed them in
this world, going off through Black Rock a-raising the dust,
that man a-driving and looking straight ahead like there ain't
nobody even with him, all those kids a-scampering ever
which way around the wagon and them two women walking
behind crying and holding on to each other and dragging
their skirts in the dust. There they went, and it ain't a one of
them ever come back.

Almarine give a whoop and picked up the gal and swung
her around and around, both of them laughing to beat the
band, and everbody is running off to be the first to tell it
iffen they can.

Except for Miss Lucille Aston. Now she's real important.

Miss Lucille Aston is the sister of old Judge Aston and she
come from Richmond to keep house for him when his wife
died and he started going blind. She puts on airs all over
Black Rock and she would up and die rathern set one foot in
the hollers. Miss Lucille Aston hires women to come in and
clean her house and she keeps everything just so. She had
her some fancy long curtains made in Richmond and
shipped into Roseann on the lumber train, and she makes
them women what works for her polish the silver all the
time. She mought as well live in New York City, what I say.
Wearing them hats with the feathers downtown. Well, Miss
Lucille Aston was out doing her shopping that day, had her
a parasol and a little boy along to carry whatever she found
that was fitten to buy. And so it was that Miss Lucille Aston
just happens along in front of Squirrel Waldron's place with
her parasol and her little old loaded-up boy at the very time
Almarine was a-trading to get him a wife. She stood right
still and watched it all, pig-eyes a-flashing fire.

"I saw that, boy!" she hollers out at Almarine, who is
whooping it up in the road, as I said.

He never paid her no mind.

"I said I saw that, boy!" she hollers out even louder, and
Almarine sets the gal back down on her feet and turns
around.

"Air you a-talking to me, ma'am?" he asks real polite.

The feathers on her hat is shaking she's so mad and all of her chins is a-shaking too. Her mouth is drawed up in a bow.

"You can't trade a mule for a girl, boy," she says. "I never heard of such a thing in all my days. I don't know where you've been, but I tell you it can't be done here, not in this town, not in this day and age," says Miss Lucille Aston.

Almarine starts laughing, which flusters her up even more. She pokes her parasol out at the gal.

"How old are you?" she asks in that way she has, but the gal bows her head and giggles. "I'll bet you're not even sixteen." Miss Lucille Aston squints her little pig-eyes, but the gal draws up close to Almarine and won't say ary a word. "I'm going to speak to the sheriff about this," she says.

Now that tickles Almarine good. Everbody knows the sheriff, old Cord Ballew, who has daddied more children than ary other man in these hills. You can feature what he'll have to say.

"Why don't you do that?" Almarine says. "Hit ain't any of his business, lady, meaning no disrespect now, and hit ain't any of your business neither."

That little boy was so surprised he drapped all of Miss Lucille's packages down in the road and had to go scrabbling to get them.

"Well!" she says. "Well!" She is flapping around like a chicken with its head cut off. Then she stands stock still.

"I hope you're planning to marry her, at least," she says.

"Oh, yes ma'am," Almarine grins. But you know it hadn't yet entered his head, most likely. Young folks just gets them a roof and moves under it and when the circuit rider comes around he makes it legal by saying the words, or they don't fool with it one way or the other. It's nothing but words, what I say.

"Then you come right along with me," Miss Lucille Aston snaps out, and Almarine is so surprised, he done it. He and that gal follers Miss Lucille right down the road to the judge's fancy house, Almarine a-waving to folks along the way like he's one big parade. They goes in the door and walks on blue-flowered carpet straight up the stairs and in the bedroom where old Judge Aston is a-laying in the bed with the curtains drawed. He's blind, don't know iffen it's night nor day.

"Lucille?" Almarine said the judge had a voice like a little old woman's.

"I've brought two young people up here and I want you to marry them," Miss Lucille says, and they all stand there in the dark while Miss Lucille and the judge argues about it until of course she gets her way. You know Miss Lucille is bound to get her way. So old Judge Aston lays in the bed and says they are man and wife. Don't know iffen it's legal or not, ain't nobody ever heard of him marrying folks before. What it is, he's scared of his sister. They's a spirit lamp in the corner, spraying camphor all out in the dark. When he says the words, you can't hardly hear his little old voice for that hissing lamp. And of course you can't see him nohow.

"Now leave this house," says Miss Lucille, and they do it while Miss Lucille stands in the doorway under the fancy fanlight and cries, and cries like her heart will break, and don't nobody ever know why.

So this is how Almarine traded a mule for a wife while that foreigner greened out Squirrel Waldron—the silver in the saddle being nothing but shiny metal, which you mought of knowed. But Almarine got him a bargain. She come without nothing, but she didn't need nothing. Almarine had it all. She rode behind him on his horse back to Hoot Owl Holler, horse's new shoes ringing like bells when he hit a rock. This was right in the early fall, potato-digging time, and punkins a-coming on. She walked in the cabin door and it was home.

Her name was Pricey Jane. She weren't a foreigner neither, or leastaways not as much of one as them others was, her having lived most all her life around Matewan. Her mama had died right about the time when her aunt and her uncle was passing through and so she just up and come on with them, wasn't nothing left for her there around Matewan. She was glad enough to stop and glad to stay. In fact Pricey Jane was pure glad about everything, she was a girl like a summer day. And work! Lord, she turned that cabin upside down and sideways cleaning it, she was a-drying apples on the shed roof, she churned butter so light it'd melt in your mouth. And it was a sight the way she follered Almarine around, and how she'd reach right out and touch him whenever they passed in the house. Almarine was like a different man. Or I'll tell it—he was like he used to be. He was like the sweet boy he was before he run off and got tangled up in foolishness and darkness, before he got hisself bewitched. It done my heart good just to pass by the mouth of the holler and look up that way, see clothes out on the line and Almarine a-working his land. I recall how once I passed there in the snow and it looked plumb like a picture, cabin closed agin the snow, icicles hanging from the shakes, cedar trees full of snow and smoke a-rising from the chimley to the sky.

Almarine had him a hog-killing that year and folks come from all around to see his gypsy-gal wife, what they called her, only of course she werent no gypsy. She was a good girl, Pricey Jane. All that was gypsy about her was them big gold hoops in her ears. Everbody liked her fine. I recall how folks was a-milling around in the yard while they biled the hog and Uncle Roy Estep had his dulcimore acrost his lap. He has got a game leg, you know. But when Uncle Roy done that one about "Who's gonna shoe your pretty little foot and who's gonna glove your hand? Who's gonna kiss your ruby red lips? Who's gonna be your man?" I seen how Almarine looked at Pricey Jane. He was not bewitched no more, it was a clear-eyed look, I'll tell you, the way a man don't often look nor often love. She was already big then, and she had that baby she was carrying come spring.

And had a powerful hard time of it, too. I said she was frail, and she was. She bled a long time after and she taken a long time a-getting her strength back. She never complained one time neither, and you would of thought the sun rose and set in that baby. Named him Eli. Almarine used to set with him by the hour.

Now there was another baby I had heard tell of too, but I never breathed ary a word. I travel these mountains up and down, I've got my ways of knowing. And I had heard it told

how Red Emmy had had that baby of hern all alone where
she lived in the Raven Clift, and how she had nursed it at her
breast three days and then had flung it straight into the fire. I
had heard it told for a fact. Ever now and then somebody'd
swear they had seed her—or say they *mought* of seed her,
moren likely—and said she was a-running through the
woods talking all to herself and laughing, and you couldn't
get nary a word. They said her hair stringing down her back
was all gray now with red showing through it like streaky
paint. I was afeared for Almarine and Pricey Jane, hearing
them stories, but Red Emmy kept her distance. She never
come down, as far as I knowed, offen the wild side of Snowman Mountain. She never left them caves and rocky clifts,
not even to trade in Joe Johnson's store at Tug. Some folks
said she had died up there, but I knowed she had never died.
And meantime Almarine and Pricey Jane was so happy, and
this went on for three years.

Three years of summers coming and going, and snow on
the ground in the cold, and I'm still traveling my mountains
but I know it in my heart I'm slowing down. I can tell how
I'm getting old. Some days I'll set by my fire all day, and
think back on things that was, and them things is ever as
clear to me as the here and now. Some days I swear I can't
tell no difference between them, and I tell you, I don't give a
damn.

But Almarine wanted me there, he said, when it come
Pricey Jane's time again. So he comes a-knocking on my
door real early, and I got up my things and off I went. I got
up my scissors, got my strippy cloth, what all I need. I
knowed it was the lastest time I'd ever birth a baby in this
world.

"Come on, Granny," Almarine said. He was a-poking me
and a-pushing me down the path alongside of Grassy, and it
so early twerent even full light. Some little birds, back early,
was a-rustling along the way, I reckon they thought we was
fools. It was early February before the thaw.

"Is Rhoda over thar yet?" I asks him, and he says yes.
Rhoda Hibbitts has got to where she has about took over

from me in birthing babies. Almarine says Mrs. Crouse is over there too. So we go along as fast as I'm able, with Almarine holding my arm. "You're about to break hit," I tell him, and he leaves off holding so tight. Well, we get there directly, and I goes in, and I see Rhoda and Mrs. Crouse has put the old quilt on the bed and Pricey Jane is twisting and turning on it and crying out. When she sees me, she gives a little smile like the ghost of a smile.

"Hello, Granny," she says, and I feel of the baby, which has drapped, and I say, "Honey, hit won't be long." I puts Rhoda Hibbitts on one side of the bed and Mrs. Crouse on the other, for her to hold onto. "Where's Eli?" I say, and Rhoda says he is down there with her girls and I say fine. Almarine stands in the doorway looking like he's the one a-having this baby instead of Pricey Jane.

"Git out of here," I tell him. "Now go on. Git," but he never moves. "Go chop us some wood," I tells him, even iffen I know he's got wood chopped to last him a month. "Git in or out," I says, and then he goes and then I can hear him a-chopping. He is worrit because of how it was with Eli, and I'm just as worrit as he is. Only it don't do to show it. But I'm expecting trouble in my bones, and looking down at Pricey Jane don't do a thing to ease my mind. She's not as big as a minute, narrow in the hips. And her face is so white and she's sweating moren I like, a unnatural sweat I thinks to myself. Them women has pinned back her hair but she's thrashing so that it's all come down and it's dripping wet all around her face. She's got big purple shadows looks like bruises under her eyes. Them earrings is shiny with sweat but she won't take them off, she's never took them outen her ears ever since she got them, what she says. She wouldn't take them off with her firstborn neither. So I am expecting the worst.

It don't happen, I'm proud to say. Pricey Jane gives out a little scream and I push down, and out pops that baby as easy as pie. I'll swear it didn't take a half hour, it was the easiest baby I ever birthed. It was so easy it like to got me spooked, and I'll admit it. As I said I expected the worst. They is something special about this baby, I says to myself, and sure enough she was the prettiest baby girl I have ever seed before or since, come out with a full head of pale yaller hair like Almarine, not a mark on her noplace. She screws up her little mouth till it looks like a bow and then she cries out real healthy-like. Pricey Jane smiled the sweetest smile.

"Let me have my baby, Granny," she said, and I did.

And it were a funny thing. Even how twas the easiest baby I ever birthed, I was plumb wore out. I cut the cord and tied the strippy cloths and let Rhoda and Mrs. Crouse get on with it. I sets myself down by the fire to rest, and I set there the whole time while the rest of them was a-carrying on and finishing.

Here's what they do—you ring your bell, and Almarine done it, and all the womenfolks and gals comes from all over, carrying food. There's no little girls can come, nor yet no singular women. They'll eat and they'll drink, and Almarine has got some corn liquor there ready, along with ginger-bread Pricey Jane made herself when she figured her time was nigh, and directly they'll dust the baby with dust from between the chimley-rocks, for luck, and then they'll take the ax outen under the bed where you put it to cut the pain.

And then they'll take it and chop up the man's hat iffen they can find it—and Almarine had left his a-laying right out in plain view he was that worrit. And then they'll take and bury the borning quilt and then they'll go on home, and they done all of it, me watching it all like a dream. I couldn't make no difference twixt dream and day.

"Poor old Granny," Pricey Jane said when they left. The firelight was a-jumping everwhere and it seemed like her voice was a song. I could see them gold earrings a-shining. Almarine was right up there on the bed-tick by her, and Eli had him a bunch of dried cobs on the floor, a-building a house of his own.

"Come on and sleep here," Pricey Jane says, but she should of knowed I won't. I don't sleep noplace but my own bed in my own house on Hurricane Mountain. I knowed it was time to go.

Once I stood up I felt good on my feet, and my feet was ready to travel. I looked back at them all from the door. The

firelight flowed all over everbody casting such a glow. The
new baby was sound asleep in that cradle what Almarine
made, and her hair shined out in that light.

"Wait, Granny," says Almarine. "What ought we to call
the baby?"

I says, "Name her Dory. Hit means gold."

Pricey Jane

It's full summer now, July and close to dog days, and Almarine has been gone for three days over to Black Rock,
trading. Pricey Jane sits on the front porch nursing Dory
and feeling his absence like a live thing, a real presence there
with them on the porch, in the cabin, in the yard. Pricey
Jane loves Almarine so much it's like she made him up out of
her own head, the perfect only man for her to love.

Mooning, her mama used to say, and send her out looking
for eggs. *No point in all the time mooning*, her mama said.
Her mama's face was white and thin and grainy, and she
never said a word about love. She just wouldn't answer Pricey Jane. And then she was always so tired. If you asked her
about love, her eyes would glaze over like she couldn't remember how it felt or what it meant or even recognize the
word spoken right out loud like that, in air. Or she'd act like
there was something shameful in it, something Pricey Jane
ought not to know.

In some of the songs, love was described as a game, with
dosey-do and curtsy and funny responses. In others it was
like a sickness. Pricey Jane remembered the song about the
two sisters and one of them had drowned herself in a mill-
pond, out of love. It was like a sickness unto death. In any
case, Pricey Jane's mother had died before she ever gave any

answer, if she had any answer to give. Instead, her mother had given her these earrings, pressing them into her hand. But where had they come from anyway, these beautiful earrings, with the roses traced in gold around the loops? Who had made them, in what faraway country, and when? Was it her father—or was he even the one who gave them to her mother, all those years ago? And where had he come from anyway, to speak the way he spoke—oh, she knew well enough where he had got to, the grave beyond the pond. But what of her brother, or those sisters, all of them gone or almost gone before Pricey Jane was even born, and all of them disappeared beyond this rim of hills, beyond the glaze that had come to her mother's eye? Questions upon questions, like the mountains close by and the mountains beyond them.

Pricey Jane's still mooning, as you see. The world beyond Hoot Owl Holler seems a swirling place, and full of wind. The people who brought her to Black Rock—her family, or her father's, or so they said—had traveled to her out of nothing, then returned. She came with them because there was nothing else to do, because the men were there with the paper to claim the land, and the preacher-man from Matewan had said, "Take her on, then," when her father's people came up in the wagon and said who they were. Or she thought that's what he had said. The journey seems a dream. Them crying out in a foreign tongue, the gruntings in the night, and how the boys had tried to touch her while she slept. They had made her sleep out on the ground. One night she had awakened suddenly and sat straight up to find the boy so close to her face with his eyes shining out in the dark, she could smell his breath, and she pushed him away and the man hit him and the woman cried. But when she first awakened she had been dreaming, a dream that she thought was true perhaps, of her own mother singing a song. She could not understand the words. Her mother's hair was loose and dark and drifting as she whirled, she was dancing, singing a song for Pricey Jane. Her mother had leaned over and kissed her and Pricey Jane had been caught fast in the tent of her mother's long dark hair. What was the song she sang? Singing, and smiling as she had never smiled in the real time Pricey Jane remembers.

But Pricey Jane remembers it now, the truth or the dream, it doesn't matter which, and sings a song without words as she nurses Dory. The steady pull on her nipple is like a chain somehow, linking her to Dory and more than that to Almarine, gone off trading. It's like a chain that closes her in and holds her here, a chain of her own choosing or dreaming.

Since Almarine brought her to his holler three years back, she has never left it. There's not any reason to leave, and no-place to go if she went. None of the womenfolks do much traveling. Oh, she's been to Granny Younger's, and over to Rhoda's cabin on Hurricane, and down to Joe Johnson's store in Tug, and to meeting when Brother Lucius comes and holds it beneath the big sycamore down at the mouth of Grassy, and other places. But mostly Pricey Jane stays home, and Almarine brings it all back. Wild roses from along the creekbed, storebought shoes from Roseann, a cardinal feather, an ironstone platter with a yellow house painted on it he got from a woman in Black Rock. Pricey Jane knows he's not like other men. The way he brings her things, how sweet he is, how sometimes he'll cry in the night and when she wakes him she'll feel his wild heart in his chest when he pulls her close. What's he afraid of, Almarine? Of losing her, he says. Pricey Jane laughs to think it. She laughs, nursing Dory, and puts her up on her shoulder and turns to wipe the milky drool off her little mouth. Dory is fast asleep. Pricey Jane takes her in the cabin and puts her in the cradle Almarine made, and then she pokes up the fire. Almarine says he's going to buy them a stove, might be what he's trading for now. Pricey Jane can't imagine how he will ever get it up the holler if he does.

"Eli," she calls from the cabin door, and Eli comes around the side of the cabin riding that stick he calls his horsey. "Giddyap," Eli says. He is as dark as Dory is fair, with bright black eyes and a nose that turns up like Pricey Jane's.

"Let's get us some water," she says, and Eli says, "Gid-

dyap" again and she takes the buckets. They go to the
spring. It's back of the cabin at the treeline, and Eli makes a
mule-noise to himself as they go along. The spring comes
right up out of the ground. Almarine has built a little house
over top of it, and ferns grow all around. Two dragonflies
mate in the shimmering air above the springhouse, blue in
the sun. They fly together, a single enormous glittering
dragonfly, and Pricey Jane smiles. *"Hit's a woman's duty
and her burden," Rhoda said.* Pricey Jane smiles and fills
her buckets at the spring. Almarine couldn't drink the water
down below, he said, down at the lumber camp. He kept re-
membering his spring up here, he said, but he won't ever say
anything more about that time or what-all he did in the lumber camp. Pricey Jane doesn't care. Eli makes leaf-boats and
sails them where the spring comes out of the springhouse
and goes off down the mountain toward Grassy Creek.

The buckets are heavy and Pricey Jane has to stop, and
stop again to rest. Eli is crying because he wanted to stay at
the springhouse, and when she finally gets back, Pricey Jane
lays him down for a nap with a little molassey-tit to suck
himself to sleep, and then she pours one bucket of water into
the pot on the fire and sweeps out her house while the children sleep. She has a sedge-broom that Harve Justice made.
Then she sweeps the yard, too, making graceful circles in
the dust, a pattern of swirls all over the yard, and it looks
real pretty, and Pricey Jane wishes Almarine would get back
in time to see it. She puts her sedge-broom back where it
goes by the chimney and puts her hand to her side—she gets
a little catch in her side every now and then—but it's time to
shoo up the cow and so she goes down the holler to find her
and bring her home. The cow is a skinny old cow, but
they're lucky to have her. Not many folks has a cow, thinks
Pricey Jane, finding her finally in the cow-stomp where she
ought not to be, Granny said. Said milk is better made in the
sun. But the cow knocked down the fencerail and got back
there anyway, in the cool shade, and Pricey Jane can't much
blame her. Pricey Jane drives her back with a switch and
milks her into the same bucket she poured water out of. The

milk foams up in the bucket and she can hear Eli hollering in the cabin while she milks.

"Come on here," she cries out to him, and he comes dragging his blanket that Mrs. Ramey brought him when he was born. "Whar's your cup?" Pricey Jane says, and he gets it, a little old hollowed-out gourd, and she scoops him up some foamy milk and he drinks and she dips him some more and then finishes milking. The long purple shadows are slanting now from the cedars across the yard. "Hit's coming on fer dinnertime," Pricey Jane says, and picks up the bucket and hits the cow. "Git on," she says.

But the cow won't go. Pricey Jane hits her again. "Git on," she says. The cow stumbles sideways on the rocky ground and turns and looks at Pricey Jane with its big doubtful eyes that have a kind of filmy blue cloud, she sees, across them.

"Git, git," Eli cries, and swats at the cow, but Pricey Jane sweeps him back and away from the hooves. The cow hangs her head and stumbles. She makes a sound she has never made before. Pricey Jane can't get her to go and so she takes the bucket finally, and hauls it back to the cabin, and Eli comes along behind her with his thumb stuck fast in his mouth.

"Don't get on my yard, now," Pricey Jane says, but it's too late, and Eli has tracked the swirls. You can't keep nothing nice, thinks Pricey Jane, but she doesn't really believe it. In a month, she will turn eighteen.

The chickens are coming up to the back of the cabin now, and she sends Eli around with a panful of dried corn to scatter while she sets Dory up on a pallet in the floor and makes some cornbread and cuts some sidemeat off the piece of it hanging there by the chimney and fries it. She nurses Dory again. When Eli comes in, she feeds him and then she eats too, cornbread and sidemeat, and drinks some milk. Dory plays with the wooden clothespins in front of the fire, turning them in her hands. When Eli was Dory's age, he was creeping everywhere, but Dory sits still and looks at her play-pretties one by one and smiles right back when you speak. Then Pricey Jane pours her milk in a jar and puts a clean cloth over the top of it and sets the jar in the corner to clabber. She'll churn first thing in the morning. She sits up with Eli until he falls asleep and then she gets some more wood and puts in on the fire for the night. *Where is Almarine anyway, what can he be doing, away off down the trace?*

Pricey Jane can barely remember Black Rock. She recalls the blacksmith's sooty mustache, and purple feathers in the lady's hat. *What can he be doing, to take him so long?* Yet Pricey Jane smiles. She goes out on the porch to set for a spell. Her breasts hurt, full of milk, and she opens the front of her dress and fans herself with her hand. Rhoda said it's time to ease up some now, and wean her to a cup. Don't never wake them up to feed them, Rhoda said. A cool breeze comes up from noplace and her breasts leak a little. She wipes at the watery milk with her hand and tastes it experimentally, giggles, and makes a face. Too sweet. But the throbbing hurt in her breasts has stopped. Pricey Jane sits on the porch while the dark comes on, until the cedar trees are just a blacker patch against the black of the night all around the cabin. No moon yet. And the air is cool; it's always cool up here, even now in dog days. *Down below they're burning up*, thinks Pricey Jane. Away across the long valley she can see two fires on the side of Black Rock Mountain. Might be hunters out there. Might be Paris Blankenship's place, she knows he lives that way, Almarine said so. Almarine and Paris growed up as friends. But Pricey Jane has never laid eyes on Paris, nor has she crossed back over that mountain since Almarine brought her here.

Tree frogs and crickets call out in the night; she likes the way they sound. A little wind comes up and sighs through the cedar trees. She likes this sound, too. Pricey Jane sits surrounded by Hoot Owl Holler like the fall of her mother's hair; and after a while, the moon comes sailing out of the clouds over Snowman Mountain, a slip of a moon like one of Eli's leaf-boats, sailing in and out of the puffy silver clouds. Pricey Jane stands up and goes in the cabin, closing out the night noises of Hoot Owl Holler and the long strange sound of the cow. *Oh he'll be home tomorrow*, she knows he will. But Pricey Jane feels weak suddenly, and kind of sick-like, as she bolts the heavy door and goes to bed.

Almarine

It was nearly noon the next day when Almarine's heavily laden horse came picking its slow accustomed way up the trace to Hoot Owl Holler, picking its careful way with Almarine slouched over and dozing. Duck ran along by his side. Almarine had been up all night playing a little poker with the boys at Joe Johnson's store. That's as far as he'd got and no farther, on his way coming home from Black Rock. They were in the back room dealing when he came in. Even then he might not have stayed, in spite of his skill at the game, even then he would have come on home to Pricey Jane if Harve Justice had not started riding him the way they all did about the way it was with him and Pricey Jane. Harve asked if his gypsy-girl had put him on a leash or maybe under a spell, or maybe he was still under a spell from the first one. Now nobody ever mentioned *her*. Harve had been drinking some or he would not have said it, and Almarine had been drinking too or he would not have let it get by; in another mood, or in later years when he had darkened so much because of what was to come, Almarine would have simply killed him. But he sat down at the table instead, and the cards came his way as he knew they would, as everything came his way lately, and he wouldn't quit until he had taken every cent Harve had on him.

"Cleaned his plow," said Luther Wade, standing with Almarine on the porch of the store that morning in the pearly faint dawn watching Harve stumble off down the trail toward Hurricane and that sharp-tongued woman of his and all those gals and that wall-eyed son. Almarine grinned, watching Harve go.

"Jack of diamonds, jack of diamonds, I knowed you of old. You done robbed my pockets of silver and gold," Luther sang out to the morning. But Harve never turned around. Luther mounted his horse and rode off then, and Almarine stretched and yawned. It was like he could feel the light cool dew coating his face. He guessed he had taught Harve a lesson after all. But he ought to be on his way.

Almarine packed up his horse and left without waking Joe, the store wide open behind him in the early slanting sun. He was pleased with what he carried in his packs—white sugar, coffee, tobacco, scissors, a new razor, a hammer, sweet-smelling store-bought soap for the baby and Pricey Jane, a string of rosy beads for Pricey Jane. And newspapers, too, a magazine—he liked to watch how she'd look through them, pointing at the pictures, making those soft clucking sounds in her throat and giggling to beat the band. Then she'd make her a flour paste and put them up so careful on the wall, it tickled Almarine how she kept everything just so. Anytime the papers got sooty, why down they'd come, and he'd better have some others there to take their place.

Now Almarine's head bobs up and down as the horse picks its way up the rocky trace. Luther's voice goes along in his mind. *Jack of diamonds, jack of diamonds, I knowed you so well, you lost me my woman and done sent my soul to hell.* Almarine grins, dozing.

She's never suspecting no rosy beads.

But he sits up straight as he passes through the stand of pine trees, as he hears his cow for the first time.

"Lord God," Almarine says, kicking hard, urging his horse ahead. When they break out of the pines, galloping now along the short level space at the mouth of the creek, that's when he sees the buzzards wheeling in their circles overhead, black wings outstretched and never moving, flying circles over his holler. No smoke comes from his chimney. "Lord God," he says again. But getting up there takes forever—there's no way to hurry that trail.

Finally he comes to the cow, lying on her side with her belly distended and her large brown eyes already gone filmy and blank. She's still breathing, he sees, but that's all. Sometimes she makes that sound. Duck circles her, barking, the hair on his back standing up.

Almarine gives a whoop so loud it come back from all three mountains. "Pricey Jane!" he hollers. "Pricey Jane!"

Insects buzz through the hot yellow day and a black and yellow butterfly settles for a second on the cow's belly.

"Eli!" Almarine hollers, and he hears nothing, and then he's back up on that horse and gone ahead and finally he hears the baby crying in a way she's never cried, a thin little wail like a mewling cat.

"Pricey Jane!" he yells. The cabin door is still bolted from inside so he kicks it open, his heart banging hard in his chest and all of this happening, it seems to him, in some clear awful light that renders it both real and not real, happening but not to him, not to him and Pricey Jane and their family, and not in Hoot Owl Holler.

The air in here is foul. She lies on her back on the tick by the fire with one thin arm extended out and dropping beside the bed, her fingers open, her head turned a bit to the side as if in sleep, her body curled on the star-flower quilt. Purple flowers, yellow stars. *She must of gotten up, she must of pulled up the quilt, she must of gone and laid back down.* He sees the churn where she pulled it out, where she started churning before she lay back down.

"Pricey Jane." Almarine kneels by the bed and pulls her to him, shaking her frail shoulders, but her head rolls over to the side and her mouth drops open and slack. Her breath smells like something dead. But anyway she's still breathing, and a faint blue pulse in her temple beats on when he smooths back the hair from her wild white face. Dark circles ring her eyes. Finally she opens them. She cannot speak but something seems to show there, for an instant, in her eyes. He thinks she knows him. Almarine lays her back gently and whirls toward the other bed, but Eli lies so still there, and the skin of his cheeks has gone cold. Dory's crying fills the cabin. The smell is everywhere. Almarine grabs Dory up out of the cradle, wraps her in her quilt like an Indian baby, and holding her tight he runs back out of the cabin. Throwing his packs to the ground he rides one-armed holding Dory, faster than anybody has ever ridden down that trace before, and off on the trail toward Hurricane Mountain. He hollers it out to everybody he sees. Dory is crying and crying. Miraculously, the sun shines still; and it's still summer, it's still afternoon.

Later Almarine will not remember how he almost rode his horse to death until bloody-mouthed and foam-flecked it buckled to its knees not thirty feet from where he was headed, Granny Younger's cabin on Hurricane Mountain. He will not remember how Granny lay in the bed with her face turned toward the wall, or how Rhoda Hibbitts told him to get on back, that Granny was sick and maybe dying, or how Rhoda took a second look at him and jumped up and then Granny Younger looked too and got up out of her sickbed and took off the white socks she had put on for dying, her burial socks, and put on her boots instead, to go back to Hoot Owl Holler with Almarine. He will not remember how Rhoda rang and rang the bell, summoning Bill Horn to take Dory over to Peter Paul Ramey's cabin for a spell so she can get some titty off Peter Paul's wife who is nursing a baby herself, or how they sent a Justice boy hell-for-leather toward Black Rock for young Doc Story, or how the Davenports came and strapped a bed-tick onto a little sled and strapped Granny on top of that, hitching up their mule to pull her along, three Davenport men and a bunch of children running behind, and the smoke from Granny's pipe floating out blue behind them in the hot still air. Rhoda Hibbitts and her daughters came last. They marched along carrying everything they could think of; they looked like they meant to stay.

Almarine remembered none of that as he rode a Davenport mule ahead of them all, holding fast in his mind's eye to the scene that lay before him, or behind him, the scene that would never leave him again: the look that came into Pricey Jane's eyes when she saw who he was, the way her head drooped slack to the side, the feel of his boy's cold cheek,

how the dog barked and how the buzzards, slow and graceful, made those awful circles in the blue sky over his holler.

He beat them all back by nearly an hour, and nothing had
changed. She was still alive.

The Davenports paused with the sled to let Granny ob-
serve the cow.

Granny's eyes squinched tight together, her mouth
bunched around her pipe.

"Dew pizen," she said. "I knowed as much."

Granny closed her eyes and lay back against the bed-tick.
"Giddyap," said the Davenports.

"How much farther is it?" asked the older Hibbitts girl,
Rose, and the younger one said she was so tired she was
about to die. All the little Davenport children had stopped
following them back at the Hurricane turn-off. "I wisht I'd
of gone back too," the younger one, Louella, said.

"Hush your mouth," said their mother, picking up her
skirts as she walked a wide circle around the dying cow,
with both of them following behind. Rhoda lowered her
head and prayed, approaching Almarine's cabin. She
knew—they all knew—about dew poison, and they all knew
it had no cure. Either you lived through it or you died.
Rhoda had had an uncle to die of it, over in West Virginia.
This was why you had to watch where a milk-cow grazed,
keep her out of cow-stomps and shady swamps and ferny
places so she wouldn't get took milk-sick like this one did.
Anybody who drank off a milk-sick cow, or ate her butter,
would die too.

Granny had had the Davenports drag the churn out on the
porch by the time Rhoda got up to the cabin; Granny was
lifting the dasher to see. The milk, silver-black, dripped
down from the wooden dasher and would not foam. "Lord
sweet Jesus," Rhoda prayed, but Granny threw the dasher
down in the churn and stomped back inside chewing her
pipe. "Git me some water and bile it," she yelled back out to
Rhoda, who had to do it herself because her daughters were
crying out in the yard. They were not good for a thing! The
eldest Davenport sat on the porch and commenced whittling
while the other ones fed the stock. Across the long valley,

over Black Rock Mountain, the sun rode low in the sky and when the Hibbitts girls had stopped crying, they remarked on how good the view was from up here, how pretty the sunset looked. The Hibbitts girls had mousy-pale hair and pock-marks all over their faces. Rhoda set them to peeling sweet potatoes; she had a lot of folks to feed, and a long hard evening ahead.

"Cool up here," the eldest Davenport said, whittling.

"Wouldn't never know twas dog days," the youngest one said, and they looked at each other then, thinking the same thing, how blood won't clot in dog days, or a sore heal up, or a bone mend.

"Rock of ages, cleft for me, let me hide my soul in thee," Rhoda sang at the door, to nobody in particular, and then she said, "You-unses come eat." Rhoda was a big woman, running to fat but sturdy, a bosom like a shelf beneath her face. Nobody messed with Rhoda. The Davenports all stood up, and she fed them—sweet potatoes and sallet and side-meat—and she tried to feed Almarine too who wouldn't eat or leave the bedside of Pricey Jane. Louella and Rose stared down hard at Almarine there by Pricey Jane's bed-tick as they came past, but he never raised his head or looked their way. Louella and Rose stared as hard as they could at his fair hair spread on the bed-tick, at the heave of his shoulders, as if they knew somehow already that this was as close to passion as they would ever come; their pale eyes watered as they stared. When the men had finished eating, Rhoda and the girls ate.

Almarine wouldn't touch a bite.

Neither would Granny Younger, out in the lean-to laying out Eli. Sometimes the rest of them heard her murmuring voice out there, and looked quickly away from each other's faces. Who knew what Granny was saying, or worse yet, what-all she did?

Nobody went to sleep.

Finally Granny came around from the lean-to like a little old bent-up straw doll in the night. They could barely see her.

"Davenports!" she cried, and the Davenports got up off

the porch and went with her and then in a while they brought Eli back around, laid out on his own little bed-tick, hands crossed over his sunken chest. The Davenports carried him to the front porch and put him down.

"Don't he look pretty," Louella said, but Rose started crying.

"I need me some silver money, Almarine," Granny called, hobbling after, and Almarine got up from his wife's bed and came to the cabin door and stood there, looking out. The Hibbitts girls and Rhoda sat on the porch rustling their skirts and bending back and forth in the darkness like big dark flowers. They wanted to see it all. Then the Davenports went and stood in the yard, all three, and Granny Younger stood by Eli, laid out on his little bed-tick on the porch.

"Air you got any silver money?" Granny said.

Almarine stood in the door.

"Yessum," he said, and he reached into his pocket and held out his hand to her, and she put a dime on each of Eli's closed eyes. Eli looked like a big doll laid out on the porch.

Almarine stood in the door thinking about how he had been playing poker at Joe Johnson's store, that was why he had the money and more money besides, how this might not have happened if he had come straight home. He was sure it would not have happened if he'd come on home. He said it to Granny Younger, who snorted.

"Hit ain't got nothing to do with yer poker," she said. "Hit all has to do with the cow."

"That cow has eat in the holler before," Almarine said. "Hit ain't never took sick."

The yellow light from the fire came out through the open door to light the porch, and Eli's body, and Granny Younger's face.

"Now that's a pure fact." Almarine stood dark against the door. "Hit ain't never took sick before, and neither has none of yourn, and every one of you-unses knows it."

They stood like that, all quiet, until a hoot owl started up steady in the pines right behind the cabin and a little sliver of moon skidded out from behind Snowman Mountain and hung there blood-red in the sky.

"Like a killing knife," said Rose—she was the fanciful one—and Rhoda shook her head at her daughter but it was too late.

Almarine said something low and strangled and took off running down the trace as fast as his legs would carry him. "Lord sweet Jesus," Rhoda prayed out loud. The Davenports pissed in the yard. Five shots rang out directly, echoing off the mountains, and Granny nodded. She bunched her mouth. She knew he had cut out the cow's heart and fired in the light of the moon. *What he orter do. You have to cut out the heart still beating and shoot it five times.* Granny lit her pipe and they all waited for him to come back, but he never came. That little moon slipped across the sky. They sat up with Eli's body all night long while Pricey Jane moaned in sleep beside the fire and Almarine ran through the night toward Snowman Mountain screaming out like a crazy man, or like a man bewitched.

Rose Hibbitts

Lord! It was awful. *He* was awful. I will hate him now to the day I die, and that's a fact, I don't care if it's not Christian. I don't care what Mama says neither. I'm not one to go throwing myself on a man, all I was trying to do was help out. But the whole time I was over there at Almarine's, I felt so funny and weak-like, I just couldn't do a thing. And cry! I never cried so many tears in all my days, and never a reason for it. Of course I have ever been the sensitive one. I have a good heart. And of course I missed Mama and Louella. And it truly was sad and all, that little Eli dying and then Pricey

Jane, but it wasn't like Mama had died, nor Louella, and I still don't know why I took on so. I just couldn't do a thing! I could feel it coming on and I'd have to run right out to the springhouse or the cedar trees to cry in peace. And it made me feel so funny in my stomach and around the tops of my legs, like I was coming down with the ague. Lord! I never would of stayed over there if it hadn't been my Christian duty, neither. If Mama hadn't said. I'm not one to throw myself on a man, I'd never of done it for sure. And it was awful. Sometimes I thought I'd die iffen he looked at me, other times I thought I'd die iffen he failed to.

Which made nary bit of difference, that's a fact.

Almarine looked, but he never saw. He never minded nothing, and this went on for the longest kind of time, for days and days. They brung Dory back home from Margie Ramey's by and by, after Margie had got her weaned to a cup, and I took care of her and kept the house as best I could. Lord! That Dory was the sweetest thing. It would just make you cry. But Almarine wouldn't have nothing to do with her neither, oh not for the longest time. All he did was set on the porch like he was sleeping, or he'd set inside by the fire. Everbody came over and cut his corn or he would of let it rot, and I'll swear it. He would of let it rot in the field. He never minded a thing. It was so sad how he set with his face all still, and never a flicker in them blue eyes.

"Almarine?" I'd say, coming up behind him. I'd say, "Almarine?" But he never said a thing, and then that would start me off crying again, and I'd have to run out to the spring.

One time I remember I woke up way in the night and sat smack up in the middle of the bed. I thought I had heard him speak. It was dark as pitch in the cabin, little tiny fire nearabout out. But I thought I had heard him speak. "Almarine?" I said out loud before I could stop myself. I said, "Almarine?" I don't know what I would of said if he had answered, or what I would of done. I swear it to this day I just don't know, and him so hateful. My heart was a-beating, beating to beat the band, while he slept away there so sound.

It was like all the blood rushed up to my head then, and made me cry, but still he slept on and on.

The way he slept and the way he done nothing but sit, you couldn't hardly remember how he had carried on at her passing, the way he had ranted and raved. Why Lord, it scared Louella and me to hear him! He come back all tore up covered in blood and said his dog had been kilt in a fight. And the dog never come back neither. But we knowed the truth of course, that he had gone to that witch and kilt her and I'll swear it made goosebumps all over my arms. I'll swear it made goosebumps come. We all knowed what he had done.

By the time he come back it was morning, and Pricey Jane had passed on. Granny had her in the lean-to, laying her out, and when Mama told Almarine the news, he give a big holler and kicked in the lean-to door and told Granny he'd do it hisself. You see how hateful he is.

"Hit ain't fitten," Granny told him, and Mama too, but he was wild. He wouldn't do a thing they said. He kept his gun by his side, couldn't nobody change his mind.

So Almarine was laying her out hisself and Mama was a-praying and Granny was mad as a wet hen when all the rest of them finally got there, Harve Justice with the pine to make the boxes, and old Joe Johnson, and Luther Wade and Hester Little, and all the Rameys and the Justices, Ratliffs and Horns and Skeens, and one-eyed Jesse Waldron hauled the liquor up there on a sled, the same way they had hauled Granny. They had come across Doc Story at the creek and sent him back.

It took considerable doing to get Pricey Jane in the box that evening when they had finished it, considerable doing. They had to hold Almarine back, I forget how many it took to do it. But after they done it, and after Harve nailed her shut, it was like all the fire went out of Almarine directly. It was like he had done give up. He slept finally, that night, and early in the morning they carried her and Eli up Hoot Owl to the burying ground and put them down.

I didn't go up there myself. Mama made me and Louella

stay and clean out the cabin while they was all gone a-bury-
ing. We cleaned and swept and beat out the bed-ticks in the
yard. I'll tell you, we worked like dogs!

And all for naught, which I'll get to directly.

I recall how Mama pulled me over when we was finished,
and set me down out there on the little bench he'd built for
her under the cedar trees. "Now listen here, Rose," Mama
said. Mama can lay down the law when she wants to. "After
this burying, we are all of us going on home. Excepting me, I
mought go on to Granny Younger's. Her time is coming on
and I can tell. But we are all fixing to go off from here and
leave you to take keer of Almarine."

"Now Mama," I said. I never knowed what she had in
mind till right then.

"They'll be bringing that baby back up here directly,"
Mama said. "Almarine is in no shape to keer for her neither,
as ye see, and so I'll be a-leaving ye here to do it fer him.
Somebody has got to stay fer a while, and that's a fact. He
ain't got no people in the world."

Well Lord! My heart was just a-thumping in my breast. I
knowed what she was up to.

"Mama," I said.

But Mama looked right hard at me and pushed back my
hair and said, "Hush your mouth." Then she said it was my
Christian duty, but I knowed.

My mind went back to a time years and years ago when I
was naught but a girl and already I knowed, even then, how
I looked and how boys turned away. Even if folks tries to
hide it, you allus know. Well, it was early spring right after
the thaw and I woke up before light and I heard it raining
and I slipped out. If you wet your face in the first spring rain
it'll make you beautiful, Granny said. So I was a-standing
out there in the yard, in the rain, when it got light at last and
Mama opened the cabin door and said, "Oh Rose. Oh Rose,
come back inside." I was soaked clear through to the skin.
"Oh Rose," Mama said and she held me so close and she
cried.

This all went through my mind when she said stay.

"Let Louella," I said, but she took ahold of my shoulders and shook them till my teeth like to left my head.

"You're the eldest," Mama said. "Don't be a fool," she said.

But I was a pure-tee fool for Almarine, till I saw how hateful he is.

And he wouldn't never look, nor never speak. Oh I felt so sorry for him, it like to broke my heart when they come back with the tales of the burying and how Almarine had built a little lattice burying-house above her grave to keep out wolves, and how Joe Johnson who had the learning and the skill had carved her name PRICEY JANE CANTRELL on a slab of fine-grained oak he brung from home a-purpose and nailed it over the door. They said it almost kilt old Joe to climb Hoot Owl Mountain. Nobody thought he'd make it, but he did. Nobody preached at the burying, of course, that was still to come. When the circuit rider comes around he does all the funerals and marrying which has built up over time, since last he came. But you've got to go ahead and get them in the ground, all the same. They say Hester Little played the harmonica over her grave. What with all that building and digging and so on, it was full dark when they come back down and went their own ways home. I guess they was glad to leave, the Davenports in particular.

I stayed on.

And he never paid me no mind atall, nor even spoke to Dory when they brung her back, until three weeks or more had gone by and he started coming out of it. All of a sudden I could tell. He picked Dory up, that was the first sign, and then the next day he turned to watch me pass as I come in with water from the spring. I could feel his eyes in my back as I passed.

"I'm Rose," I said, and Almarine said, "I know who you are." I cotched up my apron and started to cry, I'll say it— oh Lord! I was such a fool. I won't even say what I thought then, or what I hoped.

Well, it went on this way into October, and one rainy cold

morning early when he was out feeding the stock, come a knock at the door.

I opened it.

A woman who looks like she might be part Indian is a-standing there, and a little old girl behind her a-holding her skirts. This is a skinny little girl with great big eyes. Now this gives me a surprise because where that cabin is, don't nobody much get all the way up there without you knowing it, and I never heard a thing. Dory starts to holler then and I turn to get her, and this half-breed woman just walks right in. She sighs and puts her sack down on the floor. That little girl is peeping out behind her skirts, and both of them dripping wet.

"Can you spare me a bite to eat?" the woman says, and I get her a cornpone and she eats it and gives the little girl half. She is a tall woman with thick shiny black hair, dark complected, of course, and a big strong nose and a wide mouth and big dark eyes. She made me feel puny a-standing there. The rain had made beads on her shiny black hair.

"I've come a long way," she said. Nothing moved in her face when she talked, old Indian poker-face is what I told Mama later. Of course I would not have given her the time of day if I had met her in the road, and there she walked right into Almarine's house.

I never said a thing.

"I'm looking for Almarine Cantrell," she said. "Air you his wife?"

"No, she ain't," Almarine said from the door and I started crying and run past him out that door into the rain, he was hateful just like I said.

By the time I come back, she had clean took over. She was the kind of woman to do that—just like I am the kind, I reckon, to have such a tender heart. Oh she was hateful, and he was too. She was making coffee and frying eggs and her little girl was holding Dory on her lap. This was Riley's wife, I found out—that brother who ran away, and now he had died, and she came looking to find his people. Her name was Vashti Cantrell, she said, and her daughter was called Ora Mae. She said it all in a low flat voice, just like an In-

dian, and her face never moved atall. By then she was
sweeping his floor. Almarine was just a-sitting there blowing
on his coffee and nodding his head and watching what-all
she did.

"You might as well stay for a spell," he said, "since it's
raining."

Lord! I went and packed all my things in a poke and said I
was leaving, but he never made nary a move to stop me, after
all I'd done. He sat there watching that half-breed work. He
did say I orter take a mule to get home on and he would
come get it later, but I said I never wanted no mule of hisn.
Then he said he wanted to pay me something for my trouble, and I'm proud to say I throwed it down on the floor. I
was not such a fool as he thought!

By the time I got home, I was wet clear through and
coughing. I take a cold really easy, allus have. I'm the delicate one. I had liked to fell in the creek a-trying to cross it at
the bottom of Hoot Owl Holler. It was all swole up from the
rain. I never got home till after noon, and the rain had paled
to a little old fine cold drizzle by then. Mama saw me coming
and run out the door.

"Rose!" she said. "Why honey." I could tell she was mad
at me for coming back and that started me crying again, to
have your own mother rile on you for coming home.

"Hit ain't my fault," I said. "Hit ain't my fault atall. He
ast me to stay but I won't," I said. "He ast me to git married
and I turned him down. Hit's a curse on the whole holler," I
said, "and I ain't having any part of it. Almarine has done
tole me hisself. That witch, she put it on before he kilt her,
and I ain't staying there, Mama, you couldn't pay me to
stay." These words come out of my mouth just as smooth as
glass, and I liked to have died when I heard it. I had never
knowed what I would say till I opened my mouth.

"That holler is hanted," I said.

"What kind of a curse?" Now this is Louella, asking out in
the rain from the cabin door.

"Never you mind," I says, "but I'm not having no part of
it myself, I'll tell you that."

"Oh Rose," Mama said in the funniest voice, so I couldn't

tell if she credited me or not, but then she put her arm around my waist and pulled me toward the door and said, "Why honey, you're wet clear through, you poor thing, come in and we'll make you some pennyrile tea. You poor thing," Mama said, and I thought just for a minute about the time I sat up in the bed and called his name, and about what would have happened if he had come, and I was crying then with the rain on my face and I remembered that other time I went out in it to get beautiful. Lord! I wouldn't of stayed over there in that hanted holler if you had paid me.

At the Burying-Ground

The funeral of Pricey Jane Cantrell was preached two years after her death, in July, upon the arrival of Brother Lucius Basnight, the circuit rider, and his son. The funeral honored the memory of old Nan Cantrell, of Pricey Jane Cantrell, Eli Cantrell, and Granny Younger, who had asked before her death to be buried in the Cantrell family plot on the top of Hoot Owl Mountain. "I likes the wind up there," she had said to Almarine, "iffen ye'll have me," and Almarine had smiled and said he would. He had buried her himself, near Pricey Jane, at the edge of the grassy bald nearest the precipice, over the gorge that the wind rose from.

It took them all morning to climb the mountain, with Almarine leading the way. Almarine walked straight ahead up the path carrying his walking stick, to beat the bushes for snakes, and the others followed behind, stopping often to talk or to rest. Nobody had traveled this path since spring, and yet the path itself was clear. "Weeds won't grow in the way of death," Rhoda said, clutching her side, and the Justice boys looked at each other and rolled their eyes. "Mama, you sound like Granny Younger," Louella said, and one of

the older Wade girls said she had heard how when Granny
died, all the doors in all the cabins on Hurricane Mountain
flew open. Was that a fact? the Wade girl asked. The Wade
girls were pretty, with dimples in their cheeks and sandy
hair. "Yes, it is," Rose Hibbitts said, and Louella turned to
stare hard at her sister.

Rose had changed so much in the last several years.
Louella had seen the children teasing Rose sometimes,
lately, and she had heard the littlest Skeens girls jumping
rope to the chant: "Rose, Rose, runny nose." Louella
couldn't remember the rest of the chant. Rose's blotched
complexion had grown blotchier than ever, with scaling
sores that appeared often now on her cheeks, impervious to
all her mother's medications. Her pale hair, always thin, had
fallen out gradually so that now it was possible, sometimes,
to see the pale blue rift of Rose's scalp when she pulled it
back. But the way she looked was not the worst of it, to
Louella's mind: Rose had taken to crying suddenly, inex-
plicably, at the most inappropriate moments. Louella shook
her head. They were passing through a laurel slick, so dark
as to be nearly impenetrable to the bright July sun which
still shone, Louella knew, someplace. The air up here was
chilly, the path steep. Louella climbed. Behind her, Rose
sobbed. Ahead, their mother gasped in a long rattling intake
of breath. She was determined to get up this mountain, she
had said, if it killed her. And it might, Louella thought.
Ahead of them walked Paris Blankenship, Luther Wade,
Harve Justice, all the Davenports and the Rameys and some
of their wives. Behind them walked more wives, and older
children, and behind them still more children, skittering in
and out along the trail like bugs on the surface of water.
Children never get tired, Louella thought. Every time is a
big time.

Then Louella thought of the time not really so long past
when she and Rose were children together, when they had
drawn a bear in the dirt with the point of a stick and then an
angel. They made towers with smooth bright creek-stones.
This time seemed so long ago. Louella bit her lip. Almarine
was so far ahead on the trail that nobody could actually see

him, the children so far behind. The trail wound up and up through rocky dimness; Rhoda clutched at her side. "Lord, Lord," Rose cried, and Louella had a moment of sudden awful clarity where she saw them getting old this way, all of them, and dying. Louella bit her lip; she thought she saw them dying.

The big boys carried sticks, too, and hoped for snakes.

"Hoop snake'll run like a hoop," Wall Johnson said. "Roll fastern you can run."

"That's nuthin'," said Billy Skeens. "You ever seed a joint snake?"

"Ain't no such thing," said Wall, whose daddy was back at Tug dying.

Both boys beat the bushes alongside the path as they climbed.

"Is too," Billy said. "You hit 'em and they fall all apart, then you turn yer back and they runs together again."

"Liar," Wall said, whacking Billy on the leg with his snake stick, and Billy hit him on the side of the head and the two boys rolled off the path and into the laurel, fighting. Nobody told them to stop. The big girls giggled, passing, to see the fight.

"Come on, come on," the big girls said, dragging the little ones on. The little ones giggled and stumbled and came, and sometimes they had to be carried, and everybody wanted to carry Dory. Ora Mae walked by herself, a bit removed from the other children though she was only six or so, but already she looked older, with that smooth closed face like her mother's and that way they both had of looking away when they spoke. The path was dark and hard and Ora Mae hated it as much as she hated everything else since they had come to live here: Almarine, and Dory, and Hoot Owl Holler. *Hanted*, Rose Hibbitts had said, her bleary eyes holding fast to Ora Mae's making her see her face. *You live over there in a hanted place, and all of ye've got a curse.* Rose's eyes had watered in tears that coursed slowly over her pitted face. Ora Mae climbed steadily.

Behind them all came a bunch of Davenports arguing.

"I tell you he kilt her," the eldest said. "You was there too and you seed him come back. You seed the blood."

"I don't know if I seed it or not," the youngest said.

"Well, you was right there as sure as you're a-living," the eldest yelled out. "What ails you, boy?"

"Never kilt her," another one said. "Bill Horn has seed her in West Virginia on the streets of Williamson, I tell you, right out on the street a-whoring. And he said she looked pretty good."

"Ast Almarine iffen he kilt her or not, an' you credit me," the eldest said, but the others said, "Hoo! Not me!" and "I'll not ast Almarine nothin'!"

The Davenports stopped to roll cigarettes and smoke.

The group ahead moved out of the laurel and into the bright full sun on the grassy bald at the top of the mountain. The little girls broke in a bunch to play "frog in the middle." "Ye can hold my hand," Rose Hibbitts said to Ora Mae, who stood silently watching them, but Ora Mae gave Rose such a look and ran up ahead to her mother, to hold to her mother's skirts. "Frog in the middle can't get out," the little girls chanted until Margie Ramey went back to swat them. Ora Mae held tight to her mother's skirts and finally Rose Hibbitts walked on. "I tell you she ain't dead," said the youngest Davenport. "If she was dead, then whar's the body? Answer me that," he said. "You know old Cord looked high and low and never come up with no body."

Almarine moved ahead of them all across the grassy bald to his burying ground. The sun fell thick as a blanket; trees won't grow on a grassy bald. The peak was the highest for miles and miles around: crowned by the windswept field, it fell off in sheer cliffs on three sides.

And now they are here; it is time; the men go to form one group and the women another. The littlest children play back by the trees. The preaching starts. Brother Lucius goes until he gives out and has to be helped to sit down. He sits right there on the windswept grass wearing his black hat and coat, with his legs stuck straight out ahead like a child's. Brother Lucius's son takes it up, and then old Hester Little,

who will preach whenever anybody will let him, whenever
he gets half a chance. Some of the men leave the group for a
little drink or a hand of cards down in the woods; the women
move back and forth tending to children. Old Lucius fans his
face with his hat, and wonders why in tarnation they always
have to bury them up so high. He thinks he will leave off
riding, perhaps this fall. But then he'd have to stay home
with Bess. Hester Little goes on and on. Lucius Basnight's
son, Milton, his part of the funeral over with, goes off down
the mountain a piece, pursuing a Ramey girl.

Immediately beyond the black stick figure of Brother
Lucius, who sits as if painted there on the yellow grass, lies
the Cantrell burying-ground itself with its burying-houses
sagging now in disrepair, its few straggling wooden crosses,
its several unmarked graves. Nobody knows who lies in
those. The only legible name is Pricey Jane's. The graves,
and there look to be about a dozen or so, meander in an un-
even line across the grassy bald, with Pricey Jane's and Eli's
and Granny Younger's separate from the rest. All the graves
face the rising sun. The women and men talk among themselves as Hester Little goes on and on, and the sun moves
across the blue sky. You have to come to a funeral but you
don't have to listen too close, it ain't expected, it ain't like
meeting. These folks have been dead a while.

Almarine stares out over the graves and beyond them,
across the deep gorge named the Breaks and beyond it, into
Kentucky. They say the soil is richer over there. They say
it's black as coal. Almarine looks at her little burying-house
which he made himself out of white oak staves, weaving
them into lattice for the sides. The white oak has turned
darker now, but the house still holds. She likes to stay home,
Pricey Jane does, but she'll need some air. The air up here is
fresh and clean and cold even now, in summer. She likes it.
Granny likes it too. But he made Pricey Jane that lattice for
the air. A steady wind rises from the gorge far below, where
the Big Sandy River flows through the Breaks, too far down
to hear or to see. But the wind comes up. It blows across this
grassy bald, this burial ground, in every weather, a steady
wind, so the grass lies flat as if it had been grown that way

on purpose, trained like that, long flat yellow grass like you never see down below.

The July sky is a deep, brilliant blue. A hawk circles lazily, slowly, over Kentucky. She could see that hawk iffen she could see. Almarine's face has changed in the past two years: what was sharp and vital once, has grown hard and cold. His prominent nose and his cheekbones and chin look flinty. He rarely grins these days. His blue eyes are stern and flat. Almarine stands shoulder to shoulder with the other men and looks at that hawk circling and thinks or tries to think of his old friend Joe Johnson who carved her name and is not here now because he too is dying, coughing blood. The next one we'll bury is Joe. But what Almarine feels is not pity or loss, it's nothing really, or nothing more than a sense of the void which opened up when Harve nailed Pricey Jane into the box. Nothing, Almarine thinks. Just nary a thing. He remembers Joe Johnson carefully—squirrel hunts, poker, all the years—but he feels nothing. He considers how Joe Johnson's eldest, Wall, will run the store, in time, as his own sons will work his land. A man's got to have him some sons. Almarine's mouth tightens. He remembers meeting Emmy at the spring, and how she turned. He remembers Pricey Jane: the delicate line of her cheek, the luster of her long black curls, the little squeal she had when she laughed sometimes. Hester goes on, chanting now and punctuating his chant with an occasional sharp loud intake of breath, while the wind blows steadily across the grassy bald and the people talk under their breaths until at last it appears he is through. Luther Wade takes off his hat and starts singing then, and others join, Rose and Louella Hibbitts' clear voices soaring away above them toward the sky. "Bright morning stars are rising, bright morning stars are rising, bright morning stars are rising, day is breaking in my soul." They're helping old Brother Lucius up to his feet now. His face has a yellowish, lost look to it, as at last he stands, supported by Rameys. He'd hate it at home with Bess. "Oh where are our dear loved ones, oh where are our dear loved ones, oh where are our dear loved ones, day is breaking in my soul." Luther's voice rings out deep and true over the burying-houses and the silky blowing grass: out over the whole burying-ground and into the far hazy distance beyond it, the mountains of Kentucky. Rose and Louella sing rings in and out of his voice. "They have gone to heaven a-shoutin, they have gone to heaven a-shoutin, they have gone to heaven a-shoutin, day is breaking in my soul." Funny how two ugly girls can sing so sweet. "Let me hold her now," a Skeens girl says, and Susie Ramey hands her over. Dory's earrings catch the sun as she cocks her head, for all the world as if she can understand the words of the song. "I wish you'd look at that!" the Skeens girl says. "A coachwhip snake'll ride a horse to death," Wall Johnson says. "I seen 'em a hunnert times." Almarine does not join in the singing but stands like a man asleep or a man in a trance perhaps, staring off into long blue distance. "Hit's hanted back where we live," Ora Mae tells the little Wade girls playing at the treeline. "I live in a hanted house," says Ora Mae, and the little Wades giggle and give her their hands and they all go off to play follow-the-leader. "Oh where are our dear mamas oh where are our dear papas oh where is our dear Jesus day is coming Jesus in my soul." Rose Hibbitts can't help but cry. Rhoda is praying out loud. Vashti, singing, loosens her dress to give Almarine's son Isadore some titty and he hushes and sucks as singing they leave the burying ground and the grassy windswept bald on the top of Hoot Owl Mountain.

Pricey Jane   +   Almarine Cantrell

                   ⌐ Eli — 1899
                   ⌐ Dory — 1902

Vashti Cantrell   +   Almarine Cantrell
⌐ Ora Mae – 1895   ⌐ Isadore – 1903

II

Richard Burlage: His Journal,
Fall 1923

September 5th

After so strange a journey as I have completed, I find it difficult to marshall my confused impressions into any form which even approximates coherence. Dear God! What a vast and awe-inspiring country we live in; what a wild and various state is Virginia herself, this mountainous region a stranger land than Richmond can conceive of. But first: I intend for this journal to be a valid record of what I regard as essentially a pilgrimage, a simple geographical pilgrimage, yes, but also a pilgrimage back through time, a pilgrimage to a simpler era, back—dare I hope it—to the very roots of consciousness and belief. I make this pilgrimage fully aware of the august company I hereby join: all those pilgrims of yore who have sought, through their travels, a system of belief—who have, at the final destination, found also themselves. I seek no less. *I seek no less*, I say, even though Victor's slurred denouncements still ring derisively in my ears.

It was twilight a week ago—though it seems a month! Victor sat in one of the great velvet wing chairs, which he had pulled to the French window overlooking the garden. The high curved back of the chair made a somber elegant shadow against the lingering light, Victor having left the library, as always, in darkness. His words came at me out of this shadow, a disembodied voice which told my strongest doubts. "How many times do I have to tell you?" The question was rhetorical. "This is it, this is it, and this is *all there is to it*. You might as well stay here and join the firm."

I crossed the room to stand beside his chair. Below us, in

the garden, I could barely make out the dim figure of
Mother, her pastel dress an ethereal blur against the box-
wood as she bent, stood, bent and stood, clipping roses. I
could not hear the snip of the silver shears. All I saw was her
fading ghostly form as she bent and stood, handing the cut
flowers to Mary (Mother's eternal shadow), Mary who
stood silently there behind her on the garden path as she has
stood silently behind Mother, "waiting on" her, ever since
they were both young girls growing up at Lightsey Planta-
tion, near Gloucester. Mary held a basket. She received the
flowers. Mary and Mother did not speak. Mother bent and
stood. Mary held the basket. Yet by infinitesimal degrees, it
seemed, they moved together up the garden path, progress-
ing as if by some magical process slower than any possible
human movement, flowing softly together in their ancient
symbiosis beyond the trellis and off into the fragrant August
dusk.

The garden lay shadowed before us, Mother's pale dress a
ghostly blur, the white marble forms of the statues gleaming
faintly at intervals through the somehow luminous dusk.
The scent of the flowers floated upward to Victor and me by
the open window. From somewhere, beyond our walled
garden, came the unmistakable tinny beat of a jazz piano, a
Victrola recording no doubt, just audible. Mother and Mary
had passed beyond sight. Father, I recall, had not returned
that evening for dinner. Victor raised his ever-present glass
from the Moroccan brass table to his lips, ice tinkling eerily
in the darkness.

"Cheers, Richard," he said.

I was overcome, I confess, by the sadness and beauty of
that moment, a moment rendered even more poignant by
my consciousness that it was to be my last evening at home
for many months to come. "My God," I choked, or something to that effect, the strong emotions smiting my chest
like a fist. Beauty, sadness, *decadence:* Mother and Mary
gathering the last of the flowers as night falls over the garden, Victor drinking alone in the library, sequestered by the
enveloping velvet wings of his antique chair. (Huge white
columns support that house—Grecian columns. It is a house

supported by the past, and the past, as we all know, is dead. Yet we perpetuate its anguish, preserve its romance, and appreciate, by God, its beauty.) My consciousness of these things produced in me again that claustrophobia which has caused me, finally, to flee.

"Listen." Victor turned suddenly and clasped my arm, squeezing it until I could bear it no longer.

I cried out in protest.

"That's it," Victor said. He released my arm. "That's all there is. There is pain, and the absence of pain. Remember."

Victor lost his soul in the war, I say, somewhere in France, no doubt, along with his leg, along with certain ideas of conscience and decency I hold dear. And yet I am his brother, and I confess I have had my visions too, my own intuitions of nothing beyond this very day, my own fear of nothing at the core. I realize that Victor is far from unique; a pervasive loss of meaning may have been the cost of our winning the war. (Strange how I can transcribe in this journal the words which I have never dared to voice.)

"I intend to find out the truth of the matter," I told Victor then. "I hope to prove you wrong."

Victor laughed. Although I could not see his face at that moment, I knew it; I know it now as well as I know my own (in fact, it resembles my own)—the lazy slanting hazel eyes; the high pale forehead; the prominent, almost painful jut of the cheekbones; the aquiline nose; the curling, sensitive mouth.

"Richard," he said. "Little Richard, going forth to slay the dragon, that dragon which in all probability he will not recognize even when he finds it. You know," Victor continued—and this was perhaps the unkindest cut of all—"you know, Richard, I wish you well. God knows I do. And the thing that bothers me most about this so-called pilgrimage of yours is that I'm afraid you will fail through sheer assiduousness."

"How's that?" I asked him.

"Your expectations are so high," Victor said. "They're ridiculous. And furthermore, your tendency is to catalogue a thing to death. Your awareness of experiencing any emotion is likely to get in the way of the emotion itself, so that you think about feeling rather than feel. Do you understand what I'm saying, Richard?"

"Good evening," I said.

I left him there, in the midst of his drunken philosophizing, aware that his words cut all too close to the bone. Yet, hurt as I was, I resolved to turn even this criticism to my own advantage, to extract and digest that kernel of unfortunate truth which I knew his drunken remark contained.

"Richard!" Victor called out to me as I quit the library, passed through the hall, and started up the wide curving stairs. "Shit," he said to himself. "Richard!" he called again.

Mother bustled into the hallway then, making those soothing clucking sounds in her familiar fashion, flashing on the electric lights. "Why, goodness!" I heard her exclaim to Victor. "Why, whatever are you doing here, darling, in the dark? And close that window, for heaven's sake!" Mother holds tenaciously to her idea that night air is dangerous, bringing Negro illnesses into the house.

I went to my room without further ado, leaving Victor to his loneliness, Mother to the terrible solicitude which Victor so resents, and Father to the enjoyment of Mrs. Sidley, the mistress he keeps across town.

In the morning, I bade them all *adieu*. I kissed Mother on her soft white cheek, shook Father's hand, and had extended my own hand to Victor when he pushed it aside to clasp me suddenly in his arms and hug me fiercely. "Take care," he said. Mother sobbed. Father shook his head and made a gravelly noise in his throat. They stood on the front stoop as Thomas brought the automobile around and loaded my bags. I entered the car, he started the engine, and we were off! I looked back, waving, to see the three of them there like a frieze, like a lovely and lifelike frieze on the façade of the Burlage mansion, I thought. Thomas accelerated around the corner onto Ampthill Road; a new chapter in the book of my life had begun.

I was familiar with the Broad Street train station, of course, having passed through its lofty portals so often in my many trips to and from Charlottesville, trips made—I thought then, in my naiveté—in order to acquire a "gentleman's education." God knows, in point of fact, what I actually acquired there: a passing acquaintance with the classics, I suppose, a haphazard knowledge of Latin and French; some sense of history; a love of literature; and last, but by no means least, how to hold my liquor, look a man in the eye, and play—I confess it!—the ukelele. Beneath its great frescoed dome, the train station was filled with youths as shallow as I now perceived myself to have been only several months prior. They sported cardigans, carried books, and bore their fresh and animated faces like so many gifts. Girls clung to their arms saying good-bye, perhaps, or boarding the train too for Sweetbriar or Hollins. Blond curls, wet red lips, those lovely darting eyes and the way some of them have of staring so boldly, promising all. And giving it, I reminded myself: giving it, but not to me. The war had changed so many things. I was sorry to have missed it, in a way.

I stood beneath the vast dome of the train station with a sudden sense of irrevocable loss: the happy, close family of my youth, gone; my college days, which now seemed a mere exercise in frivolity, nevertheless gone; Melissa, the girl I had hoped to marry, engaged to another man; my religious faith and the sanguine equanimity with which I had been wont to face the world, gone. The train station seethed with mounting activity as two great engines pulled up on the tracks beyond, roaring. Fiery cinders shot out beneath their giant wheels. Thomas had turned my bags over to the porter and now stood before me, turning his cap in his hands, a dark grinning gargoyle-like reminder of the life I had to leave before I could assume it. In that moment, I felt as lonely as it is possible to feel, I think, utterly cast off from humanity's moorings, adrift. The travelers' echoing voices reverberated around my head, a hum as meaningless as my life appeared to me at that crucial moment before departure.

"Thass yo train, suh," Thomas said.

It was so. There was no way to proceed but forward, no course but "All aboard!"

I gave Thomas some money and shook his hand. Then I

rushed out to the platform, my heart thudding as that acrid and exciting smell of cinders reached my nose. I swung up, onto the trembling platform; the whistle sounded; the journey had begun.

And a fascinating one it proved to be!

I settled myself in a coach toward the rear of the train, two coaches distant from the dining car. No one took the seat next to mine, but the seat facing me was soon occupied by a young college girl—a schoolgirl, at least, and clearly an incipient vamp—her eyes ringed with some dark substance and her full red lips in a pout. She settled herself with a flourish, pulled a compact from her purse, and powdered her nose. After this pointless exercise in vanity, she treated me to a brilliant meaningless red smile before turning her attention to a fashion magazine. I felt that I was nothing more than an object to her, unworthy of respect or even proper notice. This rankled.

I was secretly pleased when a cumbersome old country woman with myriad paper parcels claimed the seat next to hers, considerably jostling and discommoding that young fashion plate as she settled herself with difficulty, appropriating well over half the seat. This woman, about sixty-five years in age, gave off a faint, peculiarly musty odor, which appeared to emanate naturally from the great quantity of clothes she wore, all of them discolored and faded to an indeterminate kind of gray. Her lined face was kindly, however, and a large goiter stuck out from her neck. The young lady glanced sideways at this goiter, and shuddered. I smiled. The old woman folded her wrinkled grayish hands primly on her lap, leaned back, and closed her eyes. Was she praying? I wondered. Or sleeping? Never mind. The point seemed clear.

I had before me an object lesson, I thought: two ways to face the world. One way as embodied by this old woman— simple, unassuming, a kind of peasant dignity, a naturalness inherent in her every move. The other, exemplified by the girl—smartness, sophistication, veneer without substance. I was conscious that I have now opted for the old woman's way, have thrown in my lot with a creature I would have jeered at a year ago. My present trip to the mountains is indeed a trip to that wellspring of naturalness she symbolized. And I admired my choice: the correct choice, the only choice for a sensitive and moral man in my dilemma.

But oh! The girl's very presence across from me brought up so many unwonted images of Melissa: Melissa stamping her little foot and tossing her yellow curls in anger; Melissa with gin on her breath pressing her whole warm trembling body into mine as we stood in the moonlight by the Colonnade; jet beads flying as Melissa danced till dawn, as I stood near the door in misery and watched her. A creature of frivolity, of sensation, and yet—oh, the manly passion she had aroused in me as I held her in my arms! *Carpe diem*, that was Melissa's philosophy, yet she threw me over for a man ten years my senior, a man who had served with distinction in the war, a man who had made his fortune early in tobacco. Who could blame her? We had never been formally engaged. And yet—and yet ... a hint of the girl's perfume reached my nostrils, bringing with it such pain that I stood abruptly, resolved to go into the dining car or out upon the rear platform until I had fully conquered my emotions.

"Excuse me." I stood, nodded curtly, and withdrew. The girl's eyelids merely flickered; a vein in her temple throbbed blue. The old woman slept on.

I made my way through two cars to the rear platform, where I stood rocking with the movement of the train, watching as the town of my birth receded behind me. Richmond: I saw only the rag-tag remnants—those sad little houses, row upon row, where fat men sit out on the stoops in their undershirts and the dingy wash flaps on the line. Then the tarpaper Negro shacks, the unpaved streets, and so variously peopled: huge black women with their heads wound in bright-patterned fabric, thin old black men bent over and shuffling along, the giggling high-hipped bronze girls with their jutting breasts, the immaculately fashionable swaggering gent with the yellow hat; and all those dark barefooted children who stood by the tracks to see us pass, impassive as stones with their huge round dark eyes as we came and went. Beyond all this lay the part of Richmond I would see now only in my mind's eye: Monument Avenue, the wide calm street with those wonderful statues, all that upright Confederate bravery, and the lovely flying hooves. And the intricate grillwork atop the garden walls, the generous wax-leaved magnolias within, the huge columned houses themselves with their shining beveled windows, their wide cypress halls, their glittering chandeliers. Ah yes, I thought. All that. I felt relieved, increasingly relieved, my spirit somehow lightened, as we clattered through the bedraggled edges of Richmond and passed into the flat open country beyond.

The fields stretched green and endless then, shimmering on either side, Negroes working the cotton, an occasional imposing farmhouse set back up a long driveway, surrounded by shade trees, the dusty country court-towns where we stopped just long enough to toss a mail pouch out and take on parcels. Powhatan, Midlothian, Cumberland.

In the dining car, I treated myself to a fine, lingering lunch. I nodded to my fellow diners, but spoke to no one. I wondered how I must appear to them—student, young father, man of the cloth? But in those bland faces, I could find no clue. The apple pie was excellent. Virginia rolled past slowly, as a green and fertile dream.

The girl disembarked at Lynchburg, met by a tall earnest young man who clearly worshiped her. I pitied him as I watched the two of them walk away, fingers entwined, he the willing recipient now of all her baggage. I went back to my seat, napped, and read a bit. The afternoon slowly passed as we rolled westward into the setting sun. My companion slept on. It crossed my mind several times that perhaps she had died, a circumstance which would place me in an undeniably awkward position, but she stirred in sleep just often enough to assure me of her continuing mortality.

The landscape was changing now before my eyes, flatland to mountains, and I found myself enthralled by the passing view. The Valley of Virginia, as it is called, is unbelievably, breathtakingly beautiful. The mountains rise like improbable monoliths to brood over the broad sweeping valleys, producing a landscape of such texture and hue that merely to see it is to thank God. Such beauty cannot but proceed, one feels, from the Divine. Darkness fell. I dined upon roast pork and candied apples. Easily making my way back to the seat, I remarked upon how I had accustomed myself to the bucking, rolling motion of the train. The lights were dimmed; the man brought around some pillows. Sleeping thus was profoundly uncomfortable and I wished I had acceded to my mother's desire to purchase a sleeping-coach ticket, yet it had seemed a foolish extravagance, inasmuch as we should reach my stop before morning. I instructed the man to wake me, turned my face to the window, that impenetrable rolling darkness, and slept. Roanoke: a lengthy stop. Christiansburg. I never fully woke, nor fully slept.

I awakened in the dead of night, understanding immediately what this oft-encountered phrase actually meant: the dead of night! My heartbeat seemed loud and irregular. Our engine was straining as we proceeded slowly on an upward grade. The mountains! at last. Something akin to panic clutched at my throat. As we attained the summit, I pressed my forehead to the cool glass. Pale moonlight fell on a stretch of landscape which reminded me of the storm-whipped surface of the sea: the mountaintops were whitened by moonlight like the crests of waves. I had never seen a view so cold, or strange, or beautiful. I felt a sense of awe and wonder, and then of foreboding as we plunged down through a stand of trees and the light was gone, that lovely land torn as if by magic from my sight.

"Here. Get ye a chicken leg."

The voice was old and soft, with a true sweetness; nevertheless, I confess I jumped in fright as she spoke.

I turned from the window to view my companion—old priestess of the realm of Lethe, as I had dubbed her in my mind. Amazingly, she had spread a huge repast upon her seat, and ate hungrily. "Here's ye a chicken leg," she said.

I was too startled to answer. The interior light was so dim that I doubted my eyes; it was as if this whole encounter were taking place in a badly-made moving picture. It must have been four o'clock in the morning. Everyone else in the coach slept on. And yet this was the time which the strange old woman had chosen for her repast. And I had eaten two large meals within the past twelve hours. "No, thank you," I started to say, but I found to my amazement that I was suddenly ravenous.

"You are very kind," I found myself saying instead. I accepted the proffered chicken leg and a good deal of other food besides. Of course, this was a most peculiar response on my part: while never finicky, I am nonetheless a regular and somewhat disciplined partaker of both food and drink. Yet I joined the old woman in her unorthodox spread without the slightest hesitation. She was going back home, she told me. She had been to stay with her sister in Richmond, who was sick. She would not say much more than that. Ours was a brief and difficult conversation, in fact; she volunteered nothing. The track was rougher now, the coach swayed, and cinders flew out in the night. I ate chicken, pound cake, deviled eggs, dried peaches. "That's right," she crooned, "you'll need it. A young man like you, traveling. You'll need it," she said. A chill went through me at her words, but I shook it off directly. I have always been too prone to the workings of the imagination, a tendency I am well aware of. We finished our strange repast in silence as gray light grew in the windows of our car. My man came to wake me. He looked surprised and somehow disapproving when he found me thus engaged; he withdrew quickly.

The bell clanged once. "Mar-i-on!" the conductor shouted. The train ground to a jolting halt. I gathered my belongings furiously, jumped into the aisle so burdened, and turned to thank my companion again. But it was as if our breakfast party had never occurred. All the papers and bones and scraps had been swept into some bag or other, apparently, and she had folded her hands again and closed her eyes. Had I dreamed the whole thing, in my overwrought state—had she ever spread that huge meal out upon the seat and bade me join? She slept.

The conductor deposited me rudely upon the platform at Marion, Va. Some bags of mail and some parcels were exchanged in the cold gray light of dawn; a man laughed, a cock crowed, a dog barked furiously. Then, with a huge gushing rattle, the train, like some lumbering medieval monster, moved on. Marion, Va. It was colder here. I put on my coat and entered the tiny station, where a lone bald-headed man in shirtsleeves sat behind the ticket-counter. Several people, inert folded forms, slept on the long hard benches. It was an old marble floor, tobacco-stained. My footsteps echoed hollowly when I walked.

The ticket-taker looked up over his wire-rimmed spectacles, observing my approach. "Now where are you bound for, sir?" he asked. "Can I send you to Price's Hotel?"

"No," I said. "No thank you. I'm going on to Black Rock," I told him, "and I understand I must make connections here for a smaller-gauge lumber train."

His eyebrows shot up several inches. "Black Rock!" he exclaimed in a dubious voice which sent my heart plummeting down to my feet. "You don't say!" he squinted at me.

"I'm going to teach school," I said.

"Are you now?" The fellow grinned odiously; I thought perhaps he was dim-witted, yet his evident responsibilities appeared to settle the question. "Ralph!" he yelled suddenly; I confess I jumped! Ralph, a grizzled, portly old fellow, appeared in due course, and a lengthy conversation ensued. I could ride the lumber train *part way*, it developed. I could ride the lumber train to a town named Claypool Hill, which was probably the best thing to do, and then I should have to hire an automobile and a driver, or—more reliable, because of the roads—catch a ride on a mule wagon across the mountains to Black Rock. In any case it would be nearly dark again before I attained my destination. The man named Ralph was chewing tobacco. He spat on the floor as we spoke, several times, dark "splats" which resembled stars. It grew light, people awakened, the doors to the station opened and closed; at length I went up to Price's Hotel for some coffee, leaving my baggage with Ralph. Now Ralph was not the sort of person with whom one would normally entrust one's belongings, any more than the old woman on the train was the sort of woman I am accustomed to dine with. But I confess that I never thought twice—at the time—in either case. (Perhaps my education has already begun?)

At length I boarded the narrow-gauge line, which originated at our station.

It stopped at every crossroads, it seemed, and every store; the two passenger coaches were soon packed beyond capacity with mountaineers carrying everything from babies to live flapping chickens. Their stench rapidly became overpowering, yet I was so fascinated by their physiognomy that the long day's journey passed swiftly. The men were tall, lanky, with not a spare ounce among them. Most were all dressed up for the occasion of traveling in their best dark suits, which gave them the appearance of a convention of pastors; a few, poorer men, I imagine, wore faded clean overalls. They spoke little, mostly to each other and rarely to the wives who accompanied them—if, in fact, they deign to call these women wives! The women were a sad, downtrodden species, from what I could tell. They appeared to be quite subservient to the men, speaking only when spoken to. Some of the girls were remarkably pretty, and yet it was apparent that they age quickly here—the men appearing, by and large, much less the worse for wear. These solemn mountaineers were interspersed with an occasional flashily dressed salesman, or "drummer" as they're called here, hauling his shoddy case of samples into the hills.

And the hills themselves: I have never seen such impenetrable terrain. The mountains here are not grand and rolling, as they are around Lynchburg and Roanoke. They are steep, straight up and down, with rocky cliffs and vertical gorges. It astounds me that anyone ever thought to settle here in the first place! Viewing this virtually inaccessible land from the jolting train, I was struck forcibly with a thought: seeing this, who would choose to live here? And yet there is an inescapable appeal, I find, in the very strangeness, the very inaccessibility. As our little train jolted ever farther into the rough terrain, I realized that, unwittingly, I had probably picked the most remote area still left in these United States; certainly I could not have felt more a stranger had I just entered India. My few attempts at conversation were promptly repulsed, and I sat in silence until the squeal of metal on metal and a violent bumping and grinding stop nearly threw me into the floor. "What's happening?" I asked wildly. When no one answered, I made my way through the dirty children to the platform between cars and looked out.

A tiny old man stood in the mud by the side of the track, head flung back, mouth open. An extravagantly dressed younger man, wielding some sort of pincers, had him in a kind of stranglehold with the pincers, and indeed, his whole hand, thrust inside the old man's gaping mouth. Several of the trainsmen stood about the pair, commenting and laughing.

"What's the matter?" I asked. "What's going on?"

"This old man here flagged us down," one of the trainsmen said. "Says he knowed we'd got Doc Winter on this train. Says he has got a toothache what's killing him, and Doc Winter has got to pull the tooth. Says if he don't do hit, he'll up and throw hisself beneath the train. You think he would've, Rip?"

"Sure! He'd do it in a minute," said the man who was obviously Rip.

"Aha! You rascal!" Doc Winter shouted, holding aloft the infamous tooth.

I turned away.

The "doctor"—who resembled no doctor I have ever seen, neither in dress nor manner nor mien—regained the train, the little old man left, grinning his wide, bloody, gap-toothed grin, and we shuddered into motion again. I considered trying to find the "doctor" in the next car in order to speak with him, yet riding conditions in our car had become such that I could not bear to press myself through the throng.

"Clay-pool Hill!" The cry finally came.

I disembarked to find myself in the middle of Main Street. It was a town resembling a stage set for a motion picture: plank sidewalks, badly paved road, horses and mule teams tied up along the way, although some automobiles were parked, too, in front of the buildings. As I stood blinking in the harsh mid-morning light, trying to breathe despite the dust raised by the passing vehicles, a man stepped out from the crowd and approached me.

"Mr. Burlage?" he asked.

"Yes?" I turned to look at him. He was well over six feet tall, with a bushy red beard and a wide, free smile. He stuck out his hand.

"I'm Wall Johnson," he said, "over here trading, and they said I was to look for you and bring you on back with me if you was to come on this train. Mr. Perkins said I was to git you if you was to come." I nodded, amazed by his diction, which I attempt to record faithfully here. Mr. Perkins is the local superintendent of schools, with whom I had corresponded.

Wall Johnson smiled then, a huge young giant of evident good will, and I relaxed.

"Splendid!" I said, and we loaded all my bags into the back of his rattletrap truck. A young girl sat back there too, wrapped up against the weather.

"Doesn't she want to sit up here with us?" I asked. "Won't she be cold during this long ride?"

"Nope," Wall Johnson said. "Ain't that far nohow."

He started the engine. Turning in my seat, I looked back past his rifle in the gun rack and through the cracked glass window. The girl sat among the boxes of foodstuffs and hardware, with her face turned away from us, watching the dust we raised, I suppose, with our passage. Her hair was curly and abundant, a warm vibrant brown. As I could elicit no conversation from the grinning imbecile beside me in the truck, I fell to fancying, idly, the girl's face—giving her all Melissa's most attractive attributes, yet correcting Melissa's flaws—in my mind's eye I created for this unknown girl a Grecian nose rather than Melissa's shallow little upturned snout, for instance. The road we traveled, which is indeed the only artery into this remote area, is terrible. At times it is so narrow that one conveyance must stop in order to let an oncoming vehicle pass. At other times, the ground falls away beside the road in what appears to be a sheer drop. The grade is often unbelievably steep. From the windows I could

glimpse the many small cabins, set up on hillsides so sheer
that I believe for the first time my great-uncle Aston's anecdote about the mountaineer who fell out of his cornfield and
broke his leg. The mountains rise steeply here to their high
and often rocky crests. An occasional gray outcropping of
rock can be glimpsed.

The lovely trees, beginning now to sport their bright fall
colors, often meet to form a lovely canopy over the road.
Several times we rounded a dangerous curve to be rewarded
by a remarkable, sweeping vista. Wall Johnson appeared to
be entirely engrossed in his driving, however, and in the cigarettes he smoked one after the other, rolling them expertly
between the yellowed fingers of his right hand. I could not
tell his age: 25? 30? 35? I wondered whether the girl in the
back of the truck were his daughter or his wife. Thus occupied, I passed the ride in a trancelike state of speculation,
and wonderment at the beauties of nature unrolling before
my eyes. At length we crossed a particularly frightening
mountain and jolted down into town.

Black Rock appeared to conform in every particular to my
great-aunt's and uncle's descriptions of it, a fairly well-kept
if ramshackle little village, houses and stores which run the
length of Main Street, pleasant trees at intervals, two
churches, a fairly new stone courthouse with a kind of tower
and a clock, and the broad deep river which runs along beside everything and then rounds the bend out of sight. The
river is full of logs. So beautiful this little town, like a town
of fifty years ago, an idealized kind of town. A person could
live here, certainly. A person could more than make do. I
imagined box suppers, bingo games, hoedowns, the hearty
jolly peasantry of these hills.

"I said I'll be seeing you." My driver startled me. He
stood beside his truck, having dumped my luggage rather
unceremoniously there in the dirt by the raised plank sidewalk, right in the middle of town.

I must have shown my surprise.

"Yer school," the huge idiot grinned. "Hit's over thar in
the holler whar we-unses is. I reckon I'll see you," he said,

and I said, "I reckon so," all the time wondering why in the devil he had kept this information to himself so long. A kind of perversity, a cunning? He had known who I was all along! Yet he had seemed open and friendly enough, in his rather opaque fashion. He jumped back in his truck and rattled away, and as I turned to watch him go, I received the greatest shock of my journey thus far. The girl in the back of the truck, whose beauty I had occupied myself in imagining all that torturous last leg of my trip, this girl looked up at me then, and grinned. She was hideous. A purple birthmark covered nearly half of her face, and her left eye, somewhat larger than her right, wandered off to focus on something beyond me, yet the right eye stayed fixed on mine. "Bye-bye!" she called, waving childishly. I could but feebly respond. Was she his daughter, sister, wife? I could form no clear conjecture. I watched the truck traverse the length of Main Street and head off into the hinterlands beyond, those remote and unimaginable hinterlands which I shall come to know so soon myself.

I put up here, at the Smith Hotel, which is nothing more than a glorified—and only slightly glorified, at that—boardinghouse, run by a widow, the blowsy Mrs. Justine Poole, a plumpish woman with a disconcertingly loud laugh. "We eat at six," she said, leading me up to my room. "You look plumb tuckered out," she said, and with a start, I realized that it was so. And why not? precious little sleep, and this long uncomfortable journey. I unpacked my belongings, actually placing shirts and underwear in the bureau drawers provided. *I mean to do this; I mean to stay.* It is difficult for me to believe. The bed is lumpy, with rumpled unprepossessing sheets. There is one bare hanging lightbulb, and another lamp which springs like a ghastly glass clamshell from the wall. Neither of these two—or even combined—affords adequate light for reading. I have resolved to ask for a table lamp, the table here in the corner being sturdy and adequate, actually, for all the writing I shall expect to do. A small wavy mirror hangs on the wall, above the shaving stand upon which has been placed the requisite bowl and a pitcher of water. Plumbing, one presumes, exists. I must go down the hall, however, and share the facilities with the other boarders of the Smith Hotel. Primitive! I imagine, for a second, Melissa—*here!* Impossible. Yet I suppose I am lucky. For when the term begins and I go to board with the parents of my students, I shall encounter homes with out-houses or even—according to Aunt Lucille, who devoted her last years to the County Health—homes where the inhabi-tants freely use the nearby woods and have never known any sanitary facilities at all! So I have resolved to keep this room, however unpromising it may appear at this moment, in the knowledge that worse is probably in store, and I shall need a restorative haven, a refuge, in the months to come. Perhaps Mrs. Poole can find me a bookcase. . . .

Enough, enough. I have written away the end of the after-noon. From my window I look down upon the sleepy town square surrounded as it is by these harsh mountains. I see the shopkeepers locking up now and heading home, an occa-sional bright leaf spiraling downward to land unnoticed upon a sober dark hat, a somber coat. Why do I want to weep? Earlier today Mrs. Poole said I look "plumb tuckered out," and yet my nerves feel so jangled that I am certain I shall never sleep again. I have the sense of standing upon some precipitous verge which will alter the course of my life. I believe in God, yes—Victor notwithstanding. I believe in the Father, Son, and Holy Ghost. I believe that nothing happens at random, that we all of us fill a role in His master plan. Each act, each occurrence in our lives has its signifi-cance: at least I *want* to believe these things. Thus I am sty-mied and puzzled by these "signs" which I have recorded herein. I refer to the old woman whose meal I shared on the train in that magical dead-of-night, to the bloody-mouthed old fellow receiving such rudimentary dental care there by the tracks, and to the deformed girl who smiled and waved at me so enthusiastically from the back of the storekeeper's truck. Are these, indeed, portents? What do they signify? But I am suddenly weary of portents and of significance. I want no more portents. As someone said, "Bring on the bear!" Yet even as I write these words, I know them to be uncharacteristic. What is happening to me? Whatever it is has already begun. I hear laughter below, voices rising. A dinnerbell clangs. I stand and don my coat. Yet still I see them in my mind's eye: that old woman, that horrible girl. The wallpaper in this room bears a repeated pattern of faded violets gathered up into a kind of corsage, tied with a bow. These sprigs recur, and recur, and recur. God knows when they were put here, or by whom.

I shall descend for the evening meal.

September 18th

I am all but overcome at the impossibility of the task which lies ahead. I make this entry in the lovely late afternoon, in my one-room "schoolhouse," as it is called, after my "students" have left for home. Following tradition, I am boarding, this month, with a local family, the Justices. At the weekend, I return to Black Rock, to my dim yet increasingly well-appreciated room at the Smith Hotel, to a hot (and weekly!) bath, and to Mrs. Poole's delicious, as it turns out, rice pudding. I make this entry here, I repeat, in the schoolhouse, because I can find no privacy at all in the Justice cabin, where, according to long-standing custom, everyone sleeps in one room. This is the home of Harve Justice, mountain farmer, cabinet- and coffin-maker and whittler *par excellence*, his silent scrawny wife, Hildy, and their three sons.

The food there is abominable: boiled beef, tough as brogans; thick flat peas; sticky yams with an acrid, burned taste; green beans cooked to death in a kind of greasy gruel; and the ubiquitous cornbread which appears at every meal. More like some kind of seed-cake than like a raised bread, made from the ground corn they have grown themselves, this is the family staple in these hills. No wonder that these people, often handsome and hardy in youth, sicken and die so soon! Their diet is not only inedible but appalling from a nutritional standpoint (sanitary precautions being, of course, unknown . . .).

Last Wednesday afternoon I entered the cabin to find a particularly vile odor rampant in the close air. "What's that I smell?" I inquired of Mrs. Justice, who started violently (these mountain women are unused to conversations with men) before replying: "Hit's sallet!" she said. Salad! I thought. At last! I could all but taste the crisp green lettuce on my tongue, when reason again took over. "Salad!" I cried. "How wonderful! But what's that I smell?" "Hit's sallet," she said again, and set her mouth, and refused to answer any more questions. So the peculiar odor remained a nauseating mystery until Harve and the boys returned from squirrel-hunting and she served us our dinner, which turned out to be, as prophesied, "sallet" indeed: a rank oniony collection of mountain greenery collected on the slopes and cooked to death with a piece of pork. "Hit's creasy-greens," Harve said, and mentioned several other unfamiliar names. Despite the Justices' great hospitality—hospitality being, indeed, the rule among these people, who never pass each other on the trail without an invitation to "come along home"—despite it, I say, I am resolved to obtain a bed-tick and a few other items of convenience and sleep right here in this school room during the school week, largely in order to fend off my own imminent starvation!

Also, I feel that in so doing, I shall be better able to keep in mind the rather lofty ideals and desires which brought me here in the first place. Good intentions so easily disappear, I find, when they come face to face with the exigencies of comfort. And I have been brought here, I repeat, by more than mere "good intentions," a phrase too wish-washy to have any meaning within these four rough walls.

My "schoolhouse": a "puncheon" floor, as it's called, logs split halfway, laid side by side; rough log walls, with the mud "chinking" in need of some repair before winter comes; a squat black woodstove which reminds me, for some reason, of a funny little foreign man; a chalkboard; a beautiful oak desk made by hand by Harve Justice, my erstwhile host; and the roughly built benches on either side of the center aisles, and the long wooden tables covered with carvings put there by several generations of schoolchildren. Schoolchildren! the very term conjures up a vision of happy youth, and although some of the children conform to this ideal, most of these "students" emphatically do not, resembling, instead, wizened and already woebegone grownups who expect nothing more from life than the subsistence their parents have torn from these mountains. I have no children at all over the age of ten or eleven, although I encounter plenty of older school-age children as I come and go, to and from the Justice cabin to the schoolhouse, or back to Black Rock at the weekend. The eleven- and twelve-year-olds are judged to have had "enough schooling," most of them, unless they are considered exceptionally "smart," in which case they are sent over to Black Rock to board and attend school there—the only upper school in the county. But most of them quit at about age eleven. The girls are put to work in house and field for a year or two until they marry, which they do at appallingly tender ages. The boys go to work on the farms or in the last few of the lumber camps which have denuded this virgin forest of all its best and mightiest trees, or they are sent down into the coal mines where often their small size allows them to chisel out the dark ore from the lowest, the smallest and most dangerous seams. Union regulations prohibit child labor, of course, yet these are small nonunion mines, the mountaineers here being, it is said, too cantankerous to organize! But also it is true that the large coal mines are all across the neighboring state lines, in Kentucky and West Virginia. This is a poor, poor land, where even the sketchy soil holds no rich secret. Oh, it is a black life I picture, and yet, in all honesty, I have to admit that the brightest often do go on to school. From boarding in Black Rock and attending the high school there, some of them have traveled on to colleges and then to distinguished careers in varied professions throughout the state, and indeed, the country. Few, it is sad to say, choose to return. And among my boys and girls I can already pick out the few who will go on perhaps, and the many others who will stay. It breaks my heart! It breaks my heart to read aloud to them, for instance, as I did today—we are reading, together, aloud, *Robinson Crusoe*—and see the light which comes to their quick little eyes and know how soon, for how many, it will be extinguished. (I have been thinking today how images of light have for so long been associated with learning, with religion, and with love. . . .) ·

Oh, they are an intriguing and exasperating lot! A quick, humorous anecdote before the light fades: I have been attempting, by hook or crook, to interest the Skeens boys, Merle and Harlan, in the fashioning of complete sentences. Not only did they first appear to see no reason for learning this task at all, but they also displayed absolutely no aptitude for distinguishing the subject from the verb, or for having both of these elements present in their rudimentary written "sentences." At last, through casual conversation, I elicited the fact that the highest point in their lives, thus far, had come when their uncle took them out of the county last summer, all the way to Cincinnati, where they saw a major league baseball game! Aha, thought I. I began to fashion sentences employing baseball terms, and their interest rose dramatically. My little experiment was so successful that I decided to have them "show off" for Mr. Perkins when he paid us a visit last week—to see whether I am still alive, I suppose, as we far-flung teachers in the one-room schoolhouses have no real official contact with him or the School Board all year long. At any rate, Mr. Perkins came for a visit, wearing a bowler hat. He is a slight man, waxy-faced, with drooping mustaches. I bade him sit down. I introduced our two prospective scholars, Merle and Harlan Skeens, who grinned and blushed, exactly as if they were actors playing the part of idiots in a play. I outlined their difficulty with the creation of complete sentences, and told Mr. Perkins that I had, however, through the use of baseball as subject, found a way around the problem. Mr. Perkins, well aware that, as he had told me earlier, "Some people cannot be taught anything," cleared his throat and looked askance. Undaunted, I proceeded to write "The home run" on the board. Then I asked Merle to use this term as the subject of a complete sentence. Merle rubbed his freckles and giggled. Then he appeared to frame a sentence in his mind; in fact, he moved his lips. He sidled up to the chalkboard and very carefully, very laboriously, he wrote "away," and then made a huge round period. Here, then, was Merle's complete sentence: "The home run away." I could feel my face flushing warmer and warmer. Mr. Perkins stared at the chalkboard without comment for a while, and then his weak chin began to quiver spasmodically and he broke forth into his peculiar whooping laugh. "Whoo! Whoo!" he laughed, wiping at his eyes. Merle Skeens, poor thing, grinned in pleasurable incomprehension until I excused him, excused both the Skeens boys, in fact. Only when they had left the schoolhouse did I permit myself a chuckle of my own.

September 29th—Important!

I have a funny little fellow in my class named Jink Cantrell. This is a child of ten or so years, exceptionally bright and able. So bright, indeed, that I had sent a note home to his parents volunteering to tutor him and one or two others in Latin, after regular school hours, one or two days a week. This was on Monday. Tuesday came, and Jink was absent. He was absent again today—Wednesday—and as I straightened up the schoolroom I could not help but wonder whether I had overstepped my bounds, perhaps, and offended . . . I clapped the erasers together, raising chalk dust which hung dreamily in the shafts of sunlight that came in the windows.

It was then that she came; it was then she appeared, and stood in the door.

I must say without preamble that she is the most beautiful woman I have ever seen, with an ethereal, timeless, otherworldly quality about her. Her alabaster face is framed by the finespun golden curls, almost like a frizz, about her head—hair like a Botticelli! Her eyes are deep, limitless violet. Her lips are red and full. When she smiles, a blush and a dimple grace her smooth fair cheeks. Her rough attire—a dark green wool skirt, brown handmade sweater, tan, nondescript coat—served only to accentuate the delicacy of her beauty. The sun streamed in the schoolhouse door behind her, turning her curls into a flaming gold halo around her head.

"Yes?" I said. "Yes? What is it?" I put down the erasers, moved toward her. "Yes?" I said. I felt as if something in my life were decided at that very moment, or resolved. An image springs to mind, although it makes no sense: I felt as if I were Jesus, and the stone door to my tomb was rolled away!

She smiled. "I'm Jink Cantrell's sister," she said, "And Daddy, he sent me over here to tell you Jink don't need no special school. He said Jink can take what the rest of 'em gets, and hit'll be moren enough."

"I don't understand," I said.

"My daddy said he won't be beholden." The girl looked me full in the face, and I understood.

"Tell your father," I said, picking my words carefully, "tell your father that I did not mean to offend him, nor to suggest that Jink needs extra help. Tell him that I think your brother is very smart, that's all, unusually intelligent, and I wanted to give him some additional tools to use when he goes on to high school."

"He ain't going on," she said. "He won't need no tools." She wandered into the schoolhouse and stood fingering the fountain pen on my desk. "Pretty," she said.

"He's very bright," I said.

"Well, he ain't a-going on," she repeated. "Daddy ain't a-going to let him. Ora Mae has quit already, and I'm through with it, and Isadore quit, and Bill and Nun. And Mary's poorly. Ain't none of us-uns gone on, and anyway, whar'd we go if we was to do it?"

"To high school," I said. "In Black Rock. Listen . . ." I found myself growing terribly agitated, a problem I have had at intervals of course throughout my life. She was so lovely—a girl from another world. "Who are those others?" I asked finally. "Isadore, and . . ."

"Bill and Nun," she said. "They work with Daddy," she said, and a strange closed look passed over her face. "Mary's too sickly," she said.

"Tell him to let Jink come to school," I said. "I am not going to try to take him away. He will not need to stay after school for the special class so long as he can come at all," I said. "The more he learns, the more he can help your father," I said. "Tell him that." She stood by my desk, fingering the silver pen which I had inherited from great-uncle Aston.

"Hit's so pretty," she said.

"Take it!" I leaped forward in my eagerness—having lost, I repeat, control—and in my eagerness I nearly knocked her over. "Take it!" I said. "It's yours! I want you to have it," I cried.

"Hit ain't mine," she said in a quiet, reasonable voice, looking at me curiously. "Hit's yourn. And Daddy'd whup me up one side and down t'other if I was to come home with something like this."

"Oh." I was so near to her I could scarcely breathe. "Well, don't take it then," I said. "It's nothing, anyway. Nothing!" I said. I flung the fountain pen violently from me; it hit the wall and fell to the floor, rolling several feet before it came to a stop lodged against a bench.

She stared, following the progress of the fountain pen. Then she turned her slow and blindingly beautiful gaze to my face. I can't think how I must have appeared to her then.

"I swan!" she said. "You do beat all." And then she began to laugh, a lovely musical sound, and she laughed so hard—at me!—that at length I found her laughter irresistible and joined in, laughing and laughing. I leaned against the wall and held my stomach, laughing at myself.

Finally she wiped her eyes and made as if to straighten her curls, which she wears, as I say, in the most remarkably artistic disarray. "Lord!" she said. She turned to go.

"Wait!" I rushed up and clasped her from behind, the tiny waist. She spun around.

"Where do you live?" I asked. "I must see you again."

"I live on Hoot Owl Holler," she told me, "and you'd best

not come up there atall." She slipped from my grasp.

"Wait!" I called from the door. "I don't even know your name. Who are you?" I called.

She stood on the swinging bridge that crosses Meeting House Branch here in front of the school, swaying gently in the autumn air. Behind her, the woods were aflame with color.

"My name is Dory," she said then. "Hit means gold."

I know, I thought. I know.

October 14th

During the past two weekends I have undertaken a conscious effort to make the acquaintance of the more genteel citizens of Black Rock, and during the busy weeks of teaching I have attempted to lose myself in my work.

To no avail.

Her image remains constantly before me, as she stood on the swinging bridge, as she laughed in the schoolroom with myself the occasion of her mirth—she stands, I say, front and center in my mind, and all else happens in some nether region of consciousness where I appear to function quite adequately without concerning myself unduly. I have now dined with my "boss," Mr. Perkins, the local superintendent of schools whom I mentioned earlier in this account. Again I have turned down his offer of a post in classics at the high school in Black Rock. I *do* intend to serve in the hinterlands and I have, I feel, at last made that clear to him. Perkins is a weak little figure of a man, his mustache contrasting oddly with his baldness. His large and imposing wife, Ruella, gives piano lessons at their home and directs the local choir. She is a woman with a high, strained speaking voice and tremulous lips; she appears to be eternally in the grip of some unknown angst (I like that phrase!), and eternally upon the verge of tears. I am resolved to keep my distance from this family, but Mrs. Perkins has set her cap for me, I fear. I think that is the expression.

For the Perkinses are in the unfortunate possession of a marriageable daughter—an attractive girl, indeed, this Ca-

milla: dead-white skin; soft, very fair hair; a kind of listless
beauty; a slow grace. Perhaps Camilla is even lovely; it is
difficult to imagine what will become of her here. I cannot
say. But there came a moment when Camilla and I were
alone in the Perkins' parlor, a moment when I stood by the
piano turning the pages of her sheet music as she played,
brilliantly, and sang the bittersweet "Mighty Lak a Rose."
Her voice is pure and sweet. But for me, Camilla can be but
a faint shadow of that other I have seen, my mountain girl,
my Dory.

In addition to the Perkins family from whom I had best
keep my distance, I judge, I have called upon the Rev.
Aldous Rife, who was a friend of my great-uncle's—an aging
and embittered Methodist minister who has lived here for
thirty years and "buried two wives, thank God," as he says,
in the process! As a young man, he was a circuit rider. Now
he ministers to the congregation of the little gray stone
church in Black Rock, the only congregation here which
does not thrive. And no wonder! He is a wild, white-haired
old man, as stern as Jehovah himself. He does not "hold
with," as he puts it, revivals and snake-handling and foot-
washing and speaking in tongues. He does not hold with
total immersion in the river, as practiced by the Primitive
Baptists and the Apostolics and other denominations back in
the hollers with such names as Church of Christ and Church
of God Comming (sic) Soon. He does not hold with what
he calls "carnival emotionalism." (He, too, was educated at
the University, perhaps fifty years ago.) And yet he is
clearly fascinated by these practices and by these mountain
people. He showed me an entire desk containing "notes" he
has made over the years. They say his own preaching is dry
and somber; no wonder his congregation has almost gone.
Soon they will all die, as will he. It is difficult to imagine
what keeps him at it, what perverse desire to continue what
is clearly a failure, to continue it, and draw it out to last as
long as it possibly can. I judge him a misfit!

We were having sherry in his drawing room, as I recall;
beyond the heavy draperies, certain noises intruded from

the street: yelling, laughter, and an occasional shot. It was "Court Day," regarded as a great spectacle by the entire region, many of whom "come to court" to jeer and disport themselves, considering this the highest form of entertainment. After court they stayed on, to drink and carouse in the streets. Fist-fights of course occur. If I had not previously arranged to keep my room at the Smith Hotel, I should have been unable to find a bed in the whole of the town—or perhaps not!!! For I detect a certain twinkle in the eye of Mrs. Justine Poole!

But *first:* the Rev. Aldous Rife smiled at my assertions that I have come here to make some contribution, however slight, to the cause of civilization, that I wish to find in Nature the source of that religious impulse which has been stifled rather than nurtured by the rigid disciplines of the Episcopal Church, the church of my youth. He laughed drily, I say, and offered me more sherry; when I declined, he poured himself another glassful and tossed it off as if it were water.

"God help you, then," he said, and from his tone I could not tell whether he meant those words in irony or good will.

I reentered the Smith Hotel to find Mrs. Justine Poole a bit tipsy, flinging her soft form against mine in a kind of spurious "accident" as I bade her good evening and passed through the hall. I lay in bed that evening rigid, my eyes and loins burning, as I listened to shouts and laughter out in the street and to the rhythmic thumping of the bed in the room above mine, a noise punctuated at intervals by a man's soft curses and a woman's (*Mrs. Justine Poole's?*) ecstatic cries. I could not see the repetition of violets. For some reason I held my hand outstretched before me; I could see nothing. But I felt my fingers tremble in the dark.

I saw her hair, her face; I heard her voice. The woman above me screamed. I imagined the high solitude of Hoot Owl Holler, the clean purity of her barren life. I am resolved to go there, this week. I am resolved to find her.

As the days drag past until the coming Saturday, I find myself turning again and again to this poem in the collection

I so luckily brought along. It is Christopher Marlowe's "The Passionate Shepherd to His Love," which I set down here:

> Come live with me and be my love,
> And we will all the pleasures prove
> That valleys, groves, hills, and fields,
> Woods, or steepy mountain yields.
>
> And we will sit upon the rocks,
> Seeing the shepherds feed their flocks,
> By shallow rivers to whose falls
> Melodious birds sing madrigals.
>
> And I will make thee beds of roses
> And a thousand fragrant posies,
> A cap of flowers, and a kirtle
> Embroidered all with leaves of myrtle;
>
> A gown made of the finest wool
> Which from our pretty lambs we pull;
> Fair-lined slippers for the cold,
> With buckles of the purest gold;
>
> A belt of straw and ivy buds,
> With coral clasps and amber studs:
> And if these pleasures may thee move,
> Come live with me, and be my love.
>
> The shepherds' swains shall dance and sing
> For thy delight each May morning:
> If these delights thy mind may move,
> Then live with me and be my love.

I cannot adequately express the exaltation this poem arouses in my heart, when I read it aloud to myself, accompanied as it always is by the most vivid mental image of Dory Cantrell. The words seem to dance in the air! I begin to think that I myself may begin to write, and it occurs to me that this extreme sensitivity which has always been my curse may in the end prove to be my salvation. We shall see.

October 19th

I set out this morning—Saturday—for Hoot Owl Holler (rather than Black Rock, my accustomed direction of a weekend, these days), filled with a well-nigh unbearable mixture of elation, apprehension, and excitement, emotions which seem, now in retrospect, prophetic. It is a long walk, though very beautiful, from Meeting House Branch, where this schoolhouse is, to Hoot Owl Holler. I stopped at the store in Tug to pass the time of day and buy a soda, some hoop cheese and crackers. I have never yet entered this store—run, of course, by the afore-mentioned Wall Johnson with the help of his malformed wife—I have never entered it, I say, when a poker game is not in progress in the back room! They say it has been going on for forty years. Although Wall Johnson treats me with uniform deference—I do quite a bit of shopping here, now that I am sleeping at the schoolhouse—we are not easy with one another. For I am what they call a "foreigner." As they use it, this term does not necessarily refer to someone from another country, or even from another state, but simply to *anybody* who was not born in this area of the county. Their insularity astounds. At any rate, I purchased my lunch in Wall Johnson's store and munched meditatively as I paced the trail, or "trace" as they say, proceeding to Hoot Owl Holler. The autumn foliage is at its loveliest, and I must say the beauty of the area quite took my breath away. The trace is well-traveled until one attains the "mouth" of the "holler"; there, in a gloomy group of pines, the paths diverged. I forded the lovely creek and took the steeper, rockier grade—the "path less traveled"!!!— which runs for the most part along that same creek while climbing swiftly. I looked back at each turn, to find the panoramic vista below me more and more beautiful. Yet it was, too, unspeakably remote, and somehow alien and sad. There is, according to Mrs. Justine Poole, some witch-tale told about this holler; yet that is true, I'm sure, of more than half the county. I could see, however, that a place so dramatically remote and glamorous would naturally give rise to legends of this sort, just as fog would cling to its coves, and mists obscure its mountaintops. I had begun to feel quite uneasy when the sight of woodsmoke rising up into the fair blue sky set my mind partially at ease. I rounded the last sharp turn and happened suddenly upon a large young woman coming down the same path I was ascending. It was not Dory. This young woman, obviously older, bore a broad impassive face with dark, somehow almost burning eyes. She looked to be, perhaps, part Indian.

"Good morning," I said cheerily.

To my utter astonishment, she cast her apron up over her head and emitted three loud piercing shrieks! Then she turned and raced back up the path whence she had come, each of her long strides covering as much ground as a man's. The cool wind, which had been frittering away at my heels all morning, picked up considerably at this point and began to blow in earnest, moaning through the trees. I grew conscious of a certain hostility in the environment. Somewhere ahead, I heard voices; a dog began to bark. Yet the steep path was empty of all save the brilliant, blowing leaves. I squared my shoulders, somewhat unnerved, and continued on. At length I attained the cabin, which sits in a high indentation among the three mountains, commanding a truly dazzling prospect, an awesome vista, below.

A large woman, both imposing and imperious, appeared in the door, with a frail child behind her, clinging to her legs. I could see immediately the resemblance between this woman and the girl I had encountered on the path: no mother and daughter were ever more alike.

She stared at me.

I removed my hat and bowed.

"God almighty," a masculine voice spoke, and I turned to see a tall muscular young man—evidently one of those "brothers" Dory mentioned—who materialized now at the side of the cabin and stood there stock-still in that curiously

impending way of mountain men. Then he smiled. It was
not a friendly smile.

"Allow me to introduce myself," I said with as much
forthrightness as I could muster. "I'm Richard Burlage, the
new schoolteacher down at the Meeting House Branch.
Jink's teacher," I said, smiling, and yet the woman at the
door—now joined by her look-alike daughter—continued to
stare impassively.

"I'm attempting to determine whether or not all the eligi-
ble children in my district are in fact enrolled in school," I
said. "This little girl, for instance. What is your name,
dear?"

"Mary," she said immediately, to my immense relief.

"Mary," I said. "Should she not be in school, along with
Jink?"

Nobody answered. But the child named Mary smiled and
came to stand in front of her mother. She was so thin that
the delicate white bones were almost visible in her face, a
face, I should add, of nearly unbearable sweetness.

"She's got fits," the daughter said finally.

The young man laughed.

Mary smiled sweetly, staring.

All of them stared.

I stood my ground, more nervous by the moment. I had
not the faintest idea how to proceed—it all being mostly a
ruse, of course, to see *her*, and yet having found myself so
strangely touched by the poor sick child in this hostile environment. I don't know what I would have done had not a
commanding figure appeared, riding up on horseback from
somewhere in the mountains behind the cabin. It had to be
Almarine Cantrell. He was followed by a younger man, un-
doubtedly another of his sons. We had all turned to watch
his approach—myself, with growing dread. Never have I
seen a figure more forbidding, more remote. Pale, chiseled
features like the angel of death himself. Piercing blue eyes. A
large, spare, athletic physique. He wore a black coat and one
of those shapeless dark hats favored by mountain men,
pulled down low across his face.

"What's going on here?" he asked—I should say "growled"—swinging down from his mount.

"Hit's naught but the schoolteacher," the woman said. "He's wanting Mary to go to school."

Almarine Cantrell sat his horse and regarded me sternly.

Then, as luck would have it, *she* came around the house carrying a bucket of water in each hand, quite flushed by her exertions. She set the buckets down immediately. "Why, Mr. Burlage!" she said. She was even lovelier than I had remembered, a beautiful flower growing among these weeds.

I addressed her father. "If Mary is too ill to come to school," I said, "perhaps I could send some things to her from time to time, and Jink or someone could help her learn."

"Oh, I can!" Dory said immediately. "Oh please, Daddy, say yes!"

Mr. Cantrell looked at Dory and his countenance softened in a way I cannot describe. For a moment he appeared to be a thoroughly different kind of man. His high regard for his beautiful daughter was abundantly clear. He turned then to look at me: in retrospect, I am amazed that I withstood so well the rigors of that gaze. Then, apparently satisfied with whatever he saw, he nodded brusquely, swung up on his horse again, and rode away. The woman took Mary by the hand, pulling her back, and shut the door. The young man grinned and spat in the dirt near my feet.

"This here's my brother Nun," Dory said.

"Howdy," Nun said, his temporary civility another testament to Dory's position in her family. Of course, they would love her, I thought. Of course. "Be seeing you," said Nun, regarding me darkly before he went off in the direction his father and brother had gone.

"Well." Suddenly I felt completely drained, totally exhausted. "Well." I looked at her. The October sunlight fanned through her hair and it seemed truly golden; I noticed, for the first time, the golden hoops at her ears. The cool brisk wind had reddened her cheeks and seemed to make her eyes appear, if possible, a deeper blue, as if, in fact, she were a part of "October's bright blue weather." She smiled. I recalled my ostensible purpose: "Here," I said, reaching into my bag for the books I had brought. "These are for Mary. You can read them to her." I don't know how I knew that Dory would be able to read, how I intuited that she alone among all those children was the only one whom Almarine Cantrell had allowed to complete the "education," such as it was, offered in the elementary schoolhouse at Tug. And yet I discerned this truth immediately, as though we had known each other for hundreds—no, thousands!—of years.

This, I see now, is the sense I had when first she appeared at the schoolhouse: that knowledge of inevitability, that feeling of recognition. She took the books and turned—as I say, inevitably—to accompany me as I retraced my steps back down the mountain trail. She matched her pace to mine, so that we descended even that rocky trail as one, flawlessly. I confess I breathed more easily the more distance we put between ourselves and that strangely forbidding cabin! We spoke as we walked, but her hair blew forward and I could not always see her face. We spoke so easily, as if we were old confidants; even our vastly different manners of speech seemed to meet and blend together into some single tongue we share, as the many instruments in the orchestra produce the symphony.

We talked. I say we talked, and yet I cannot now retain the continuity of our conversation. The whole afternoon seems to me like a multifaceted jewel-hung pendant on a golden chain, a jewel whch flashes and turns and offers its multitudinous secret gleams of light.

"Is your family always so unfriendly to strangers?" I remember asking, and I recall how she laughed in response.

"I told you not to come up here," she said. "Didn't I tell you that? Ain't nobody comes up here much, you can see fer why."

"But are you happy?" I asked—I think I asked—desperately. "Stuck way up here with your family, so many of you in that house? What do you do all day?" I paused, and she looked at me as if I were crazy.

"Do?" she said. "Lord, they's a-plenty to do!" She giggled

then, but I couldn't see her face behind the shining screen of her hair.

"But what will happen to you?" I asked in a kind of frenzy. "You can't stay up here like this forever. Why don't you move over to Black Rock, finish school? or get a job?"

"I reckon I'll git married sometime," she said. "I reckon I'll stay till I do."

This jolted me. I grabbed her arm, rather more roughly than I had intended.

"Is it anyone particular?" I asked. "Are you engaged?"

"Engaged?"

"Spoken for," I said. "Well, are you?"

"I ain't," she said simply, and how my heart leapt at these words! "They's one boy, Little Luther Wade he is, what wouldn't mind, I guess, but so far I ain't been too interested. Why do you reckon not?" she asked suddenly, looking at me, and I saw myself then in her eyes as some superior being from another place, with a fund of "knowledge" beyond her ken. Thus I realized how I seem to her. I understood my position and my responsibility.

"Oh, I don't know," I answered easily, although what I felt at that moment was more chagrin than ease. "I wouldn't worry about it."

"What about you?" she asked, showing more initiative than I had thought she possessed. "Are you engaged?" And I noted how quickly she had picked up the new word.

"No," I said. "I'm not." I made this admission for the first time with relief and not regret.

"Looky here," she said suddenly, leaning down to pluck a large brown and black caterpillar from the scudding leaves. She allowed it to crawl across her upraised palm. "See how wooly it is?" she said. "Hit's a hard winter coming ahead."

This remark jolted me, revealing as it did such a profound simplicity, such a oneness with the natural things of the earth. We had reached the end of the holler path, the point where one must ford the creek. The wind rose steadily and acorns fell at our feet. Leaves whirled around us. She turned to go, and I was filled with an instantaneous and total despair. I realized that any emotion I thought I had felt for any girl, before this time, had been nothing: counterfeit. This was, as they say, the real thing!

I grabbed her shoulder and turned her around so that, for the first time that afternoon, we stood face to face. Her beauty was breathtaking. Then all our differences, all the exigencies of fate, seemed to rise up between us like a shield, cutting us apart entirely, and I became desperate. I resolved to clear up the mysteries.

"Listen," I blurted. "Listen. What's going on up there? What did that girl—that woman—"

"You mean Ora Mae," she said.

"Ora Mae, then. Why did she scream out like that when I came upon her on the mountain? You know the way she screamed?"

Dory threw back her head and laughed. "I would of done it too," she said, "iffen you'd come upon me. You shouldn't of come up here by yourself. You got to come up here with people we know."

"Buy *why?*" I asked, tightening my grip on her shoulders.

Dory smiled out of her eyes. "Hit ain't nothing personal," she said. "Now I've got to get on back."

"But what's the big secret?" I asked. "I worry about you, living away up here."

She smiled mischievously. "Maybe hit's all hanted, this whole holler. Ain't you heard about that?"

"About what?" I wanted to draw her out.

"Nuthin'," she said, and as she spoke, the antic wind blew harder, lifting her hair.

"Those are beautiful earrings," I said. "May I see one? The tracings on them remind me of a design which I once saw, if I recall correctly, in Florence." As soon as I spoke I was mortified, afraid she would think I was "putting on airs," as they say here, and realizing too that she could have no concept of where Florence might be. "May I see one?" I asked again, quickly, to cover my embarrassment.

But instead of handing one of the earrings over, as I had expected her to do, she stepped even closer to me and put up both hands to lift her hair up off her neck, inclining her head slightly to the side.

"There," she said.

I was intoxicated, I was overcome by her nearness!

With trembling fingers I pretended to examine the ear-ring, and then suddenly I found myself pressing her against me urgently, covering her neck, her hair, her cheek with kisses. I couldn't stop myself!

"Dory," I said hoarsely.

She turned her face to me then and I kissed her full red lips. I stroked her amazing hair, which sprang up under my fingers like something alive. She broke away then, and looked all around—but there was nobody!—and shivered slightly. Then, as if somehow reassured, she came back into my arms and pressed herself against me; I could feel the softness of her breasts. Sensing that I was about to lose my self-control, I clasped her hands together firmly and kissed them, then stepped back.

"I'll go then," I said. "I shall hope to see you again."

Something—perhaps the very phrasing of this sentence—caused her to break into giggles, and still giggling, she turned from me and ran back up the trail until her flying hair was lost in the golden woods.

I cannot now recall the long tramp home.

In desperate need of a confidant I settled (perhaps fool-ishly!) upon Aldous Rife, old misanthrope though he is, and told him of my infatuation with Dory Cantrell and the strange welcome I received upon the occasion of my visit to her home. Aldous Rife listened to my recital with raised eyebrows, running his hand occasionally through his wild white hair. As I continued my recital he began to mumble, shaking his head back and forth, staring down into his glass.

"Sit down, boy," he said at length, and once I had seated myself upon the black horsehair sofa before his fire, he began to talk in his rumbling, sonorous voice, apprising me of the following (chilling!) facts:

Ora Mae's strange crying out—those three shrieks—are the universal indicator for "foreigners" in these mountains, a known sign meant to convey to moonshiners ("blockaders," they are termed here) that a stranger is on the way. For I might have been a revenuer, searching out liquor stills. I listened to old Aldous in complete astonishment, his interpretation of the girl's behavior having never even occurred to me. This, then, is why Dory said she would have "done it" too, if I had surprised her instead of Ora Mae! This is why Mr. Cantrell himself emerged from the woods on horseback, to assure himself of my purpose and to validate my identity. For Almarine Cantrell and his "boys," according to Aldous Rife, manufacture a great deal of corn liquor, in partnership with a man named Paris Blankenship.

I drew in my breath with horror and dismay. "A criminal, then," I said immediately. "A common criminal, and to involve his own family in these activities . . ."

Old Aldous poked up the fire. "I wouldn't be so fast to judge, young fellow, if I was you," he surprised me by saying. "Now you've been up that holler, and you've seen how many folks Almarine Cantrell has got to feed."

"That's so," I said.

"And you seen the land up there, and the hardships, and the way they have to live." (Aldous has been among these people so long that when he becomes agitated he reflects their manner of speech.)

"That's so," I said once again.

"Well, you can just figger for yourself how much a man can earn by selling his corn at the mill, versus how much that same man can earn if he takes that selfsame corn and lets it sprout a while, and then grinds it up in a mash and pours him in a little boiling water and lets it stand. . . ." Aldous broke off, observing me shrewdly. "Do you see what I'm getting at?" he asked. "It's a hard life up there."

"Yessir," I said. I was struck by the truth in his words. I mentioned that Prohibition, too, must have greatly increased the demand for the product.

"Increased both the demand and the danger," he said. "It's a desperate life. There's the revenuers, and then there's the competition and bickering among blockaders. And I'll tell you something else. No man engages in such a business unless he is a desperate man. Almarine Cantrell is a man who would just as soon kill you as look at you, son, I can tell you that for a fact. Since the death of his first wife, Pricey Jane—who was Dory's mother—since her death, he has become one of the hardest and meanest individuals in the entire region. A man's nature is dual, you know"—Aldous stared into the fire—"part angel and part devil, with the body as the battleground . . . part evil, part good. . . . We are created this way, and we engage ourselves in the struggle until we die. But when a man who has been a good man becomes embittered by fate and turns to evil, that good man, I tell you, is worse, is more dangerous to society, than the man who has been committed to ill and followed that path without deviation all along. This convert, though: he will turn guilt to cruelty and act with no compunction, I tell you, with a total lack of compassion, I tell you—" Aldous turned to me. For an instant I had a sense of the preacher he could have been if he'd tried, or if he'd cared to, and the irony of this entire situation came to me with the force of a thunderbolt: how one ruined man can offer an accurate insight into another.

"You must forget her," he said then, the note of true finality clearly present in his fine old voice. "You have no choice. She is not suitable. She is not your equal. You are a sojourner here, and the least you will do is to create longings in that girl which her life can never fill. That is the least you can do. The worst you can do is far graver. As your uncle's friend, I counsel you most solemnly, Richard, to have nothing further to do with this girl. Her father is a dangerous man, a criminal, as you say, and he dotes on her. You must break this attachment, Richard, and break it at once."

I was quite shaken by the vehemence of this reaction. When I stood to go, old Aldous stood up too, and grasped my hands. "Let us pray," he said, and I was further shaken to see this side of him emerge. Standing then on the worn blue rug before his little fire, I bowed my head.

"Almighty Father," he prayed, "please give this young man the strength to do Thy will, Lord, to forgo the temptations of the flesh and to cleave to the purity of Thy spirit, Lord, though he be shaken round by doubts, Lord, in Thy Holy Name we pray. A-men."

"Amen," I repeated, very uncomfortable. He released my hands. He picked up his glass, offered it to me, and I without considering the strangeness of this action, took it and drank. I blinked and bit my tongue; the glass proved to contain what I judged to be a fiery brandy.

"That's Cantrell liquor," he said.

Tears came to my eyes, whether from the burning liquor I had swallowed, or from the knowledge that I must renounce her, or from the pathetic irony of this drunken old man of God who rails against a species of that which has brought him low.

Directly I took my leave.

I looked back once, on my way up the sidewalk to the Smith Hotel, to find him still there at the door, looking after my retreating form with a blankness on his face which suggested he saw, in fact, nothing, and I marveled at the vehemence of his advice. When had his "call" come, I wondered, and how, and what had brought him here? Stranger still, what kept him? A thousand questions occurred.

Yet we human beings are all, I reflect, like planets which revolve throughout the great darkness of the universe. Sometimes our orbits bring us perilously close to one another; other times, we collide with a great explosion of sparks; but more often than that, we simply spin on in ignorance, through the vast globy blackness of space.

Reasons for pursuing Miss Dory Cantrell:

1. As previously noted elsewhere in this journal, I have never been so strongly attracted to a member of the female sex in all my life. All other emotions felt or *imagined felt* for others, including Miss Melissa Hamilton, now seem as *bagatelles.*

2. Her beauty and fresh purity have a salubrious effect upon my spirits: elevating, it seems, my capacity to appreciate beauty and to respond to the world around me—a capacity which has been all too near extinction in recent months. My intellect *trembles with my body* as I consider, again and again, that kiss . . .

3. (Not unrelated to #2) I have the sense that her contin-

uing presence in my life would keep me attuned to my soul, would prevent my sinking again in the depths of nervous despair which have been my *environs* from time to time . . .

4. She appears to encourage my pursuit, and furthermore, she is unattached.

5. She possesses an innate sense of the finer things of life—a sense which I could encourage, enhance, and mold; I could enrich her life.

Reasons to forget Miss Cantrell entirely:
1. She is not of the same social class.

2. She is ignorant and largely uneducated; such a gap exists between us that it could never be truly bridged, not even by any attempt on my part to educate her.

3. To encourage her affections might be to make the remainder of her life too bleak to be borne, such a life as I know she is destined to live (*Aldous Rife).

4. It would be immoral to take advantage of her innocence, and impossible not to do so.

5. My preoccupation with her is drawing me away from my original intentions in coming to this place: to make my separate peace with God, to do my part in trying to educate these poor children, and to delineate my future plans—in which, it is becoming increasingly clear to me as I set down this list, Miss Cantrell can play *no* part!

6. Her father and her brothers would kill me.

I therefore resolve:
1. Attend to the state of my soul.

2. Throw myself into my teaching. Schedule a holiday pageant, perhaps?

3. Exercise regularly.

4. Socialize in the town, but

5. Do not encourage Mrs. Justine Poole either.

Notes on the state of my soul
Five weeks have passed since last I saw Dory Cantrell. I have occupied my intellect primarily in an assiduous attempt to clarify, for myself, my religious values. Aldous Rife

has been surprisingly helpful. He understands my decision not to attend his own church, that sad staid little building which appropriately faces the courthouse in the middle of town. In fact it was he who nudged me in the direction of the Freewill Followers at the mouth of Grassy, near Tug, and in fact quite close to this schoolhouse which has become my second home.

I wanted, I repeat, to find a form of worship free of those Catholic constraints imposed upon the spirit by the Episcopal Church.

I have found it.

The Freewill Followers, who number no more than forty in all, meet in a cabin set in a lovely, lush little meadow by the side of Grassy Creek. Save for the "old rugged cross" attached to the roofbeam, this cabin could well be a schoolhouse; in fact, it may have so served in the past. Indoors, the rough-hewn benches are arranged on two sides of the room—one side for men, and one for women. A rough boxlike pulpit in the front houses Brother Autry Lily, who comes here by mule from Roseann to "bring the message," as they say, every second Sunday, and the lay leaders, like the ancient but actually quite effective Hester Little, who come forth from the congregation to bring their own interpretations of the Word.

I have served as altar boy at St. Stephen's Church, Richmond.

I have worshiped at Notre Dame.

I have worshiped at Chartres!

Yet never have I experienced the sense of majesty and trepidation—of awe at the literal presence of God—which I have found within these mud-chinked walls. It is as if we travel back through time, back through the centuries. Let me describe a typical service.

It is any Sunday morning, let us say late fall, let us say November, 10 A.M. No church bells ring. These mountaineers have bells, indeed, but they ring them to herald events: a baby's birth, a death, an accident.

I repeat—no church bells ring.

The ever-present blue mist, which hugs the hollers and

valleys all night long, begins to rise as the sun appears above Black Rock Mountain. At first the sun has no delineation at all, is nothing but a shapeless spectral brightness behind the mist. But the mist rises, and the sun burns it off by degrees, and degree by degree that sun appears until now at length it shines full over all this wild landscape, the sky blue and cold, the wind whipping through the skeletons of the trees and rattling the half-frozen leaves on the ground along the path, frisking those leaves across the path of those who are venturing forth to church, or to "meeting," as they say. They come from their cabins here around Tug, from homeplaces all along Grassy Creek and Meeting House Branch and even farther, from the three mountains.

They come on foot and on mules or horses, traveling these paths, and as I stand before the meeting house to watch their approach I know, although they do not, that I am here at the end of something, that these days soon shall pass from the face of the earth and that these people and all their kind shall pass as well. Construction of roads throughout the remote areas of this county will soon commence—is slated, in fact, for spring. The men who keep their cars and trucks now at Wall Johnson's store will drive them straight up to their own doors. These mountains will open up, and much will be gained perhaps, but from the viewpoint of this sojourner, much will be lost as well. Within three years, I predict, rural electrification will proceed even here to Tug, and soon after, each cabin will boast a radio. And what a change will then be wrought! when news becomes actuality rather than week-old newsprint, or rumors spread mouth-to-mouth, enhanced and transmogrified in the telling . . .

I do digress.

I stand by the door as they come, and no bells ring, and yet they all converge as one. This coming to church is a happy thing—as witness the skipping children along the path, the timid smiles on the worn faces of these hard-working home-bound women, the proud silence of the men. Meeting brings not only respite from work, but also affords one of the few opportunities available for socializing.

On my first day here, they indeed looked askance, but the

Justices greeted me warmly, or at any rate as warmly as I imagine they will ever greet anybody, and several of the schoolchildren came up to take my hand and giggle (it is strange how the innate warmth and friendliness of these little children appears to change so drastically, and suddenly, into the poker-faced taciturnity of the adults), and after that first service, the venerable Mrs. Rhoda Hibbitts (Granny Hibbitts) came up to squint nearsightedly at me and ask me whether I had "not got nuthin' better to do on a Sunday," and when I smiled and said no, I had not, she flashed her toothless jack-o'-lantern grin at me and said she "reckoned," then, that I might as well "come on back."

The women take one side and the men the other, as I said. The Hibbitts "girls"—Louella and the other one who is "tetched" but nonetheless boasts a lovely voice—begin the song, some old traditional hymn like "Washed in the blood of the lamb" or "Bringing in the sheaves" or "There is a green hill far away," singing in the high nasal mountain manner, with sometimes the accompaniment of dulcimer or mandolin, as played by old man Luther Wade or his son Little Luther Wade (a partially crippled young man whom, you may be sure, I have carefully observed!) or, perhaps, old Hester Little. The message, such as it is when "brought" by the sweating red-faced apoplectic Autry Lily, is usually no more than gibberish, concentrating upon the evils and rigors of Hell, pictured in great and gruesome detail, and the availability of "salvation" through the "blood of Jesus Christ." Gore and violence are the order of the day in these sermons, which Autry Lily delivers in a high-pitched kind of shriek, punctuated by the traditional sharp intake of breath, these two noises combining upon occasion to produce a sort of incantatory rhythm broken by such remarks as "Tell it, Autry!" and "Lord, Lord!" shouted out by the congregation, men and women alike. For here is a phenomenon: this most expressionless of people, who pride themselves—even my schoolchildren—in showing neither hunger, nor pain, nor grief—these people certainly "let go" in church. At length the women begin rocking back and forth, there is a kind of collective sobbing, and often someone will rush forward at the invitation to be "saved from the fiery pit of hell and them little old licking flames," as Autry Lily pictures it in his characteristic language. On my third visit to meeting, one of the Ramey boys, a thin anemic-looking teen-aged fellow who goes by the peculiar nomenclature of Peter Junior, leapt forward sobbing, and this service was followed by the entire congregation's pilgrimage down to Meeting House Branch where Brother Lily baptized Peter Junior on the spot, beneath the icy rushing waters of the creek. He came up white as a sheet and shivering violently—his being "saved," I presume, the ultimate consolation in the face of that pneumonia which I was quite sure he would contract as a result of his salvation.

A further word about salvation: it has to do *only* with one's emotional sense of "being saved." It has nothing to do, apparently, with any notion of living a "good life," as I was brought up to believe a Christian ought to do: hence, all the apparent contradictions. The most evil man imaginable could, theoretically, be "saved" on his deathbed. What one does in this world "don't hold a candle to Jesus's blood" (!) as Autry Lily put it in one of his stranger images. Only occasionally does the concept of salvation have anything to do with the reality of daily life: once a Blankenship was "preached" from this pulpit for his public drunkenness. But rarely do the two coincide.

In some meetings, I am told, people speak in tongues. Some meetings use a snake to determine "true faith," allowing it to twine about the entire congregation. No one who "believes" will be bitten! Aldous Rife has told me that he witnessed one camp meeting at which a woman actually bared her breast to the snake (which did not bite it). At any rate, I understand that this is a "foot-washing" congregation, although this ceremony has not been practiced yet in my presence, due possibly to that very presence. I am still a foreigner here. But I expect that foot-washing will occur if I persevere, which I continue to do, the only detriment to my presence being the somewhat "off" daughter of Granny Hibbitts. She has begun to stare at me so strangely, muttering under her breath, and yet when I met her on the path to

Tug last Tuesday A.M. and said "Good morning," she burst
into tears and raced away! She bothers me. It bothers me
that she is a member of this congregation. In every other respect, however, I feel I am making progress.

Now. I was describing a typical Sunday service—any
Sunday in November. After the singing, and the praying
and the preaching and the moaning and the crying out, after
all this, when the meeting is concluded with everyone venturing back to their homes in what I would assume to be vast
trepidation that indeed He will come to "judge the quick
and the dead"—instead of the trepidation and apprehension
I would expect to be occasioned by such an awesome final
injunction, I see *joy*, real joy, upon the faces leaving this
meeting house. It is as if God's eraser has wiped each slate,
has smoothed each brow, has calmed each soul. Something
real is here at work, as I have reported to Aldous Rife, who
did not disagree. (Aldous appears to disagree with *nothing*,
however: to leave all his options distressingly open, or perhaps distressingly closed?)

But something real is here. I feel it as I stand in the wind
before the meeting house at the close of meeting, as I see the
people move forth once again into their lives. They are indeed, as they say, "sanctified." I do not understand it. I do
understand however that I, who have spent my life in "being
good," I who was christened in a long white gown in the
hallowed nave of St. Stephen's Church, Richmond, and who
was then baptized effetely in the Episcopal manner—I have
not been sanctified. Nor am I "saved." Rather am I a sojourner, as old Aldous referred to me, merely a sojourner
here, standing outside this little meeting-house in the biting
November wind at the close of worship. I am resolved to attempt to "open my soul to God" and "let him in," although I
face this decision with a great sense of inner trembling,
really with a kind of dread, for I deeply fear the loss of control. And yet I sense it to be a prerequisite for the kind of
emotional experience these people deem necessary to salvation, what they call "taking a great through."

And why not? I have eternity to gain and naught to lose!
A "revival" is to occur here shortly and I am resolved to at-

tend, to give myself over, insofar as possible, to these sentiments.

And so I leave the meeting-house a sojourner still, with my collar turned up and my hat pulled down against the wind, a sojourner not only in the symbolic sense, as are we all, caught here between birth and death, and doubt and belief, and evil and good, but a sojourner in the most literal sense of that term, as I am between places, between the meeting-house and my schoolroom-home, or between my schoolroom-home and my rented room in the Smith Hotel in Black Rock, or between the mountains and the flatlands whence I came, or—as the Cherokees said, and this applies to all this lovely hazy land—"between the mountains and the sky"!

My mind whirls, it churns and eddies like the angry brown floodtide which even now rips through the "holler" outside my schoolhouse with such abandon, carrying off stumps, logs, and—just a moment ago—a wooden crate with a hen on top, clucking wildly. Although the rain has ceased, the stream shows no sign of diminishing—water, I imagine, continues to gush down from the mountains into the freshets which feed the stream.

O God!!! Why do I go on—and on!—about "freshets which feed the stream"? O God.

This is what happened:

She came to me today, and we kissed, and we almost made love. *Would have so done*, in fact, but for the accident of rising water and her brothers coming to take her home!

It was the fourth straight day of rain. December rain here is bitterly cold and dismal, the low clouds creating a darkness which hangs on the land and changes it, to my mind, entirely—all the wild beauty stripped away and replaced by a frighteningly sombre flatness and grayness, a palpable depression. Needless to say, few children attended school. The Johnson boys from Tug, who live so near, the Justices, one or two of the Wade girls, two out of six Rameys, and Jink Cantrell, who had walked all that way in the drizzle primarily because I had promised him that when he had finished his pages of extra sums (he had done so), he should have a little copy of *Tom Sawyer* to keep for his own. He came in wet and grinning, hand already outstretched. Dory's charm can be read in his face, that charm which derives, I suppose, from the father, whose good looks were legendary in his youth, according to Aldous, who has for years been writing a kind of "history" of this region.

Lessons went well. It did seem strange, however, to have so few pupils: early December should be the peak season for school attendance, since the children are not needed for planting or harvesting, and the paralyzing snows which come in January and February have not yet begun. The gusting rain of the two days previous had fallen off to a faint, dull drizzle; inside, by the stove, we were warm and content. At lunchtime, I had planned a surprise for these few hardy souls who had braved such weather to come to school— Ovaltine!

But well before noon, we were interrupted by a rousing knock on the door—Wall Johnson, who had come in his wagon as far as the bend to get his sons and take them home, and who volunteered transportation to all the others as well.

"Creek's a-rising, Richard," he said. "Iffen you-all don't get out of here, hit's like to wash out the footbridge and then you'll be stuck fer sure, I reckon. You'll have to walk the long way round over Black Rock Mountain."

The children chirped like excited birds as they gathered their belongings together. Wall Johnson, wearing a wet black hat of a vaguely Western cut and a great dark coat, looked like a man out of a novel as he stood dripping just inside the schoolhouse door, his wet red whiskers clumped together in an almost comical way. "You'd best come on, yourself," he said. "You can stay with us fer a spell." But the idea of such close quarters with the unfortunate Mrs. Johnson made me demur.

"I thank you kindly," I said, and meant it. "But I'm all stocked up here, Wall, and I guess I'll just ride it out."

He nodded, gathered up the children, and left. As I stood in the door watching them cross the creek I saw that, indeed, it had risen almost unbelievably in the past two hours: it

rushed along now at a mere four or five feet beneath the
swinging bridge (or "footbridge" as the natives say). I stood
there enjoying the sudden contrast of warmth and chill—the
momentary excitement of this "flood"—and no sooner did
Wall Johnson and the children pass from sight, than she appeared!

She stepped suddenly out of the dark wet woods on the
far side of the rising creek, wrapped in a long blue coat and
wearing a scarf. Before I could call out—if, indeed, she could
have heard my voice over the sound of the rushing water—
she was running across the bridge which now seemed to
sway dangerously, perilously: my heart leaped into my
throat.

For I realized, in that instant, the truth.

I loved her, and no amount of reason, as supplied by
Aldous Rife, or "Mighty Lak a Rose" as supplied by Miss
Perkins, or silk stockings and manicured hands which await
me in Richmond, or even religious conviction (*what I know
to be right* vs. *what I know to be wrong*)—nothing at all can
change this. It was as if the six weeks since last we met had
never passed, as if all my efforts to forget her had not tran-
spired.

I stepped out into the rain and she ran right into my arms.

She lifted her face to mine, and I kissed her; I could not
have done otherwise! Then I drew her inside. She flung off
the scarf and pressed herself to me again and I kissed her
again. In some part of myself I was amazed, and yet there
was that sense of the inexorable, that inevitability which I
feel with her always.

"You never come," she said, making it not an accusation
but a statement. "I been waiting but you don't come."

"I will," I said. I think I moaned. "Or you can come here."

The instant I said it, I was appalled, but she looked
around the room and then took off her coat, laying it across a
desk. "I might ought to do that," she said. "Hit might be the
best if I did. You've cleaned it up," she said. "It looks all different from when Mr. Parrish was here." (Mr. Parrish was
the teacher who preceded me.)

"I'm living here most of the time now," I said, indicating

with a trembling gesture the corner I have made my own—
the blanket strung up on a length of rope, which affords me
my private "bedroom," and my desk, and my few cooking
utensils. And then it hit me, what she had said: *she expects to
see me. She is willing to come here!* My mind reeled.

"Where's all the kids?" she asked. "Where's Jink?"

"Wall Johnson came and got them all," I said. "They'll be
back at the store by now."

"Well, I reckon Nun'll get him, then," she said. "We come
down when we heard that the creeks was on the rise. We had
to go to the store anyway."

"You did," I said stupidly. I was conscious only of her
standing there before me in the room; but then she turned
from me abruptly and began to pace back and forth before
the stove, and I noticed for the first time that she appeared
agitated, even upset.

"You ought to've come," she said, facing me finally.

"I know it," I said. "I'm sorry."

"You ought to've sent me word," she said. "You can do it
by Jink or by Rhoda, and then you ought to've come—hit's
been awful," she said, and then to my dismay she burst into
tears!

I began to realize that there was more to this than met the
eye.

"What do you mean?" I asked, taking her hands.

"Air you my sweetheart or not?" she said.

Needless to say, I was stunned. But of course I could not
refuse her. I nodded, I think, too surprised to speak. Who
knows whatever goes on in the minds of girls! Her simplicity
touched my heart.

"What's been awful?" I finally asked.

"Daddy and Paris has fallen out," she said, "and hit's real
bad, and you never come—"

"But you told me not to come," I said logically; logic not
being, apparently, her strong suit, this set her to sobbing
again.

"Listen," I said. I enfolded her in my arms and attempted
to calm her, stroking her hair. But for once—for possibly the
first time in my life—*I found myself at a loss for words!*

So I stroked her hair.

We stood before the stove, we two, in this empty school-house, while rain fell steadily on the roof and the creek roared past outside. The schoolhouse was dim, warm. Dory's wet wool clothing gave off a peculiar kind of a smell—pleasant, really—which will stay in my mind for-ever. For once I had nothing to say. I held her close, I stroked her hair. And then I felt my manhood rising un-awares, and died of shame and a kind of glory as I realized she must feel it too, pressing against her body.

"Honey," she said. Who would have thought that anyone would ever address me so? She kissed me, opening her mouth.

"Dory." It was all I could say. Kissing we made our way to my bed in the corner where we sat, or fell, in a kind of a heat, and she leaned back and pulled me to her. I fumbled at her waist and finally succeeded in pulling up her blouse—to my surprise, she wears no brassiere! Or maybe none of these mountain girls do. Her breasts are the most perfect breasts which exist in all the world!

"Sit up. Sit up for a second," I said. "I want to see you," and she sat up and lifted her blouse to reveal them, two white orbs as round as apples, with the nipples aroused and pointed.

"Suck me," she said.

"What?" I could not believe my ears.

"Suck me," she said, and took my head and drew me to her breast, offering it up with her hand, and by now I was near delirium. While I sucked at her nipple she took my other hand and guided it up her thigh beneath her skirt and inside her panties until I could feel her wet warmth. She pushed my fingers inside; she began to move her hips. (A hasty parenthesis: this was a "far cry," as they say, from the coquettishness of Miss Melissa Hamilton—who, though her demeanor promised all, had given virtually nothing. *Vir-tu*ally: ha! For a second I envisioned—God knows why!—my father and Mrs. Sibley! For a second, too, I was dis-tressed, I confess it, by Dory's apparent knowledge of love-

making, but then I recalled her upbringing in that randy
cabin with all those boys, the animals around the mountain
farm, and I understood her desire to be a kind of purity:
everything is transparent with her. When she's hurt, or
worried, she cries. When she's happy, she laughs. When she
wants a man, she . . .)

Who knows what might have happened, had not her
brothers come?

We were there on that very bed-tick, behind the blanket,
me kissing her open lips and exploring her innermost parts,
my member about to burst my trousers, when guns were
fired into the air, repeatedly, across the creek.

Dory pushed me back and sat up.

"No," I said.

Gunshots rang out again.

"Hit's them," she said. "They mean for me to go," and
hastily she stood and tucked her blouse and donned her coat.
"Lord, no wonder," she said from the door. "Hit's almost up
to the foot-bridge"—meaning, of course, the water.

"But Dory, Dory—how can I see you? What must I do?"
I called out then but she was gone.

!!!!!!!!

I relieved myself by my own hand and stood for a long
time there at the door with the fire at my back, the chill
ahead. I was there when the creek rose that final foot and
brought a huge stump whirling down with it, destroying the
bridge. Now I am completely cut off, at least for the time
being, a circumstance which seems most in keeping with
everything else in my life. For what am I to do? Impossible
to "court" this girl in the approved mountain fashion; impossible to "take her home" to my family in Richmond—I
can see Victor's snide smirk even now, in my mind's eye—
and yet, impossible not to have her.

Smith Hotel, Black Rock, December 12th

Tonight, at dinner in the Smith Hotel, the table conversation centered around none other than Almarine Cantrell and

his "feud" with Paris Blankenship! (Mountaineers being of course famous for their feuds, which appear to offer vast amusement for everyone not involved, and violence being here the order of the day). The quarrel is over money, of course, and they say that Mr. Blankenship is "out" for Mr. Cantrell, whatever that means. (It certainly means I shall not set foot in that holler until this business is concluded!) Mrs. Justine Poole shook her blond curls back and forth as she spooned up the gravy, making a "tsk-tsk" disparaging noise. She wore large imitation-emerald earrings, and a great deal of rouge. Dinner concluded, we all stood up and most of us made for the new movie house where we watched and laughed at the humorous remarks which Big Harp Combs, a lawyer, addressed to the crowd throughout the feature. Mrs. Justine Poole, seated beside me, placed her hand on my knee; she sniffed grandly when it became clear I would not respond, and left the darkened movie house slightly before the rest of us—three drummers from out of town, an unscrupulous land speculator who goes about the country buying up mineral rights with something he calls a "broadform" deed, a lawyer from Claypool Hill here to settle a will, and yours truly. We were a disparate crew. We strolled back to the Smith Hotel through the clear cold air, smoking cigars.

I try to imagine taking Dory to a picture show, walking along a sidewalk with her, as we did tonight, yet she seems to exist for me only in that shadowy setting—those three mountains, that closed valley—whence she came.

Plans: I shall tell Granny Hibbitts to tell her to come to meeting: any night of the revival, I'll say.

Imagine my surprise when, after school today, one of the Johnson boys arrived to tell me that old Aldous Rife had driven his car from Black Rock to Tug and awaited me there at the store.

"You better come on," the Johnson boy said, and I came straightaway across Meeting House Branch over the sturdy new bridge which Harve Justice finished building only today.

Aldous stood on the front porch in his three-piece striped suit, overcoat open, smoking a cigarette. His wily old eyes narrowed when he saw me, and he smiled. "Richard," he said, and we shook hands. He suggested a walk, although the weather was far from clement—we're having quite a "cold snap," as they say—and we set off accordingly along the path that runs from the mouth of Grassy Creek, there by the store, to the point where Grassy merges with the Dismal River, around the bend. Ice had formed along the edges of the creek and our breath blossomed white in the air as we spoke. I expected him to open the discussion with the subject of Dory Cantrell: instead, he fooled me.

"You know why they call this Tug?" he asked.

"No," I said. "Why?"

"It was along about the end of the French and Indian war," he said, "that a patrol came through here, under the leadership of a man named Milligan, headed for Kentucky. They were down to almost nothing, in terms of rations, by the time they came through, and it was wintertime, but Milligan pushed them on. There wasn't nothing here then," Aldous said, staring around absent-mindedly. "No store, no nothing. This was all way back, mind you. There wasn't nothing here at all except for an old Indian woman had her a cabin back there where Wall's store is now. She used to buy hides off her people and tan 'em, and she had her some leather tugs out drying on a frame when they come back through, having been to Kentucky and back, and starving by now, and those men were so hungry they grabbed the leather tugs off that frame and ate them, that's how hungry they were."

"Did they make it back?" I asked.

"Some did and some didn't," he said.

Grassy Creek, before us, swirled and tinkled in the pale cold sun, the ice along its edges as brilliant as diamonds. Our breath hung in the chill air, like clouds over the creek. Impossible to imagine how this creek—how all the creeks—had looked, only several short days ago! I shivered, as much from the idea of the terrible hunger Aldous described as from the cold bite of the wind. We walked on.

"What do you want?" I asked him finally. "Why have you come?"

But instead of responding to my questions, he stared across the creek and into the trees on the other side. "Have you heard about the Baisden brothers?" he asked, and I said I had not.

"There were three brothers," he said, "John Henry, Harrison, and Bill, and they were among the meanest sons-of-bitches that ever walked these hills. They came from over around Pigeon Creek, and they would fight at the drop of a hat. When the Baisden boys came to town"—I assumed he meant Black Rock—"when the Baisdens came to town, decent people went inside and locked their doors. They killed five men at least, and maybe more. But nothing could be hung on them, nothing could be proved. Harrison had an ivory toothpick, I remember, on a gold chain, and shoulder-length black hair. And I remember when they were building the courthouse tower, the Baisdens rode into town and shot out the brand new clock, and no sooner did they get it replaced, about five months later—they had to send to Cincinnati for a new clock—than the Baisdens came back and shot that one out too. They cared nothing, Richard, nothing"—here, Aldous turned to look at me intently—"nothing for human life."

"What happened to them?" I asked.

"Bill eventually made the mistake of arguing with Bob Irons, a man as dangerous as he was. Bob hit him over the head with a revolver. Then John Henry and Harrison went to the hotel where Bob was staying, and shot him through the window as he was eating lunch. They shot him between the eyes and he fell forward into the chicken and dumplings." Aldous grinned, but I was of course appalled.

"Well, that time the law succeeded in rounding up Bill and John Henry, but it was an uneasy time, I'll tell you, with them over here in jail. Everybody was just sitting around waiting for Harrison to come and try to get them out. One time some horses got loose across the river, where the high school is now, and a rumor got out that it was Harrison Baisden coming to free his brothers, and everybody in town hid. The sheriff and his deputies locked themselves up in the vault."

"Is that true?" I demanded, cracking a sliver of ice with my foot. Aldous is, as I have said, a strange old bird.

"Yes," he answered. "Finally the two brothers were taken to jail, but on the way back here for the trial, Harrison ambushed the sheriff and his party and freed them single-handed. They took all the horses, tying up the sheriff and his men. So Harrison rode off on the sheriff's horse, or so it was said, along with his brothers, and nobody in these parts ever saw hide nor hair of the Baisden boys again."

"What hotel was it?" I asked. "The one where the Irons fellow was shot?"

"The Smith Hotel," Aldous said. We walked side by side down the path toward the mouth of Grassy.

"When was this?" I asked.

"Twenty, thirty years ago," he said. "The time doesn't really matter."

"Of course it matters. This could be a fact of history, or it could be a county myth, a folk tale," I said. "I know you collect them, and you know it too. I suspect you make some of them up."

"It doesn't matter," he said. "Nothing ever changes that much."

"I'd better get on back," I said, and at the widening creek we turned, and as we retraced our steps he said, "Listen, Richard. There is story upon story I could tell. I could tell you a more recent one, and more horrible, about the six Negroes lynched and shot while they hung in the air, until their bodies were full of holes, and this is true, and this was done by a vigilante posse to avenge the robbery of a drummer on the way between here and Claypool Hill, and not a one of those men was ever tried nor even caught."

I stared at him. But he kept his gaze straight ahead, walking, and it was impossible to tell his intent. "I can come closer still. I can tell you about how Paris Blankenship got him up a company here to go to war. Just formed his own

company right here on his own recognizance, in 1916 I guess
this was, and he had well over 200 men quartered over there
by the bend of Dismal, below town, and all of them armed,
and he'd come into town to requisition food, you know, or
supplies, and everybody was too afraid to say no. Mr.
Poole—that's Justine's ex-father-in-law, he's dead now—he
was the mayor then, and he went over there once to try to
get Paris to pay his grocery bill, and he had to go by two or
three armed guards, he said, until he got up with him. Paris
was in a tent having a foot-bath. And Mr. Poole kept asking
him about his money, and when was he going to get it, and
when was this-here company going to war, and so on, but all
Paris Blankenship would do was grin and say how fine his
feet felt. And then finally he said, 'Poole, you ever have any
trouble with your feet?' and when Mr. Poole allowed as how
he did, upon occasion, experience some difficulty with his
feet, Paris recommended this foot-bath highly. And the upshot of it all was, Mr. Poole ended up with his feet in the
foot-bath, and Paris Blankenship picked up Poole's shoes
and socks and walked away, and Poole never got his money
back nor any answer at all to his questions."

"What happened?"

"Eventually Paris's company was taken straight into the
Rainbow Division," Aldous said. "And the Army paid off
those bills. But they didn't take Paris himself, oddly enough,
or maybe they had too much sense. So Paris was in the
Coast Guard in Norfolk during the war, which landed him
in some kind of trouble what with everything that was naturally happening in Norfolk at the time, and then he spent
some time in prison before he came back here."

"And went into the liquor business," I said.

"And entered the liquor business with Almarine Cantrell," said Aldous. We had nearly reached the store by then;
he stuck out his hand.

"I know what you're up to," I said. "but you won't scare
me off."

I shook his hand then; we shook vigorously, as if a bargain
had been struck. Perhaps it has.

Strange Baptism

It was the fourth night of the revival, which I have been attending vigorously in hopes of meeting Dory there, and three "souls"—mine not among them—already had been "brought to Christ." The congregation, accustomed to my presence, appeared to have lost all restraint, or to have forgotten, at least, that initial constraint which they felt I placed upon them. Fainting had become commonplace, as had chattering wildly "in tongues." I had been accepted, I think, and yet, I remained a sojourner still. I sat among them, but near the back, still as much observer as participant, inwardly cursing my fate, that trait of character which has made me thus, and awaiting *her*.

The scene was intensely dramatic, rivaling anything, in terms of a scene guaranteed to produce nearly overwhelming emotion, I have ever seen. The wind howled fiercely outside, yet the stove in the corner kept us warm and cast its ruddy glow upon all those present, some twenty-five people, I should say, a glow augmented by the fat-pine flares which burned wildly at the front of the church, all of this firelight producing a kind of magical, intensely lyrical, special sense of being removed from the exigencies of time and place, a sense of being among the chosen, borne out by Autry Lily's text, "The Church Is the Body of Christ." I'm sorry to say that most of his message did not live up to the title or to the promise of such surroundings, being more of the same blood and gore. I'm sorry too to admit that I found myself listening to his (often comical!) grammatical errors rather than trying to grasp his intent. I found myself counting the flakes of dandruff on the back of Rupert Dodd's black coat, and wondering if she would come the following night, or if she would never come.

So when it came time for the invitational, as it is called, I was quite surprised to find myself somewhat moved. I could not tell whether the agitation I began to experience at that moment had to do with a true religious impulse, or with my anxiety over her, or whether I had simply been swept away by the strangeness and beauty of the scene. They sang it all together, that high wailing "Jesus says please, son, Jesus says please," with the Hibbitts women screeching like banshees, and before I knew "what had grabbed me," as Autry Lily would say, I was up on my feet and moving forward along with several others. And yet, even at this crucial moment, I remained a sojourner still—it pains me deeply to admit this—I was observing my actions even as I performed them. I moved forward and knelt at that crude altar, hoping for God knows (literally!) what: grace? immortality? love? Autry Lily embraced me. Even at that moment, the moment of my putative "salvation," I recoiled from the odor of his body: he stank. His breath stank too. Next to me was a pale skinny pubescent girl, a Wade, all flailing arms and legs, who kept yelling out, and the rest of the Wades had to come up to the altar to hold her down. Others came forward, too, to congratulate us, or welcome us into the fold, or whatever they call it, and then the whole congregation was moving forward. I felt as if I had been awarded the trophy for a race someone else had run. And yet, just for a moment, there had been . . .

A blast of cold air swept into the meeting house then and I looked back at the door. She had entered, red-cheeked and breathless: she paused, just there, her eyes seeking mine. I mumbled something or other to Autry Lily and those around me; then without further ado, I rushed straight out of the church!—leaving quite a commotion, needless to say, in my wake. Now everyone knows. By now they will have "told it up and down the holler," as they say. *I don't care.* For once I am living my life rather than watching it pass in review. I said I rushed out of the church.

This happened next: I took her hand and led her along the path to my schoolhouse. We did not speak. We entered; I bolted the door behind us; we did not speak. We went straight to my corner bed and made love as no mortals have ever made love before! She answered my passion with her own, taking me beyond all boundaries of physical sensation I had ever experienced or even imagined. And then, stretched body to body on my bed-tick, our legs interwined so that I could feel the sticky semen (mine!) all over her thighs, and only then she told me.

"Hit's over," she said. "Paris has kilt Daddy, he come in the late afternoon around milking time and catched him there by the gate."

"What do you mean?" I asked, clutching her frail shoulders so sharply that she recoiled. "What did he do?"

"Kilt him, shot him two times in the chest, shot him clear offen his horse."

"Jesus," I said, yet any thought of Jesus remained, I confess, far from my mind at that time. I fingered her smooth soft breast.

"Mamaw ran down there when she heard the shots, so she was the one who found him. She knelt down and put his head in her lap, and helt him like that till he died. She said he never woke up one time."

"I'm so sorry," I said, but Dory went on. "Mamaw has done saved that apron, and she brung it up to the house and showed it to the boys and she ain't never going to wash it, she says, till justice is done."

"By which she means . . ."

"By which she means till the boys kills Paris Blankenship, I reckon," Dory said.

"Will they do that?" I had the curious sense of having fallen completely—although I must say Aldous warned me—down the "rabbit hole," so to speak, of having entered another world. I could not even see this girl I lay with in the dark. I touched her abundant, springing hair; the delicate line of her cheekbone, her jaw; her nipples; the dimpled curve of her back; her buttocks. A strange phenomenon: we are almost exactly the same size, toe to toe. I felt as if she completed me, and I completed her, as if we were truly one.

"They'll kill him, all right," she said, and it was curious to me how she seemed, if not to want this outcome, at least to expect it. She reached for my penis then and I succumbed eagerly to her ministrations, entering her again before, toward dawn, she dressed and left, leaving me here exhausted yet too emotionally tense for sleep, leaving me here to write this account as the cold winter dawn creeps into the room at last, bringing me to my senses not at all—or: yes!! *Bringing me to my senses!* For this is exactly what she has done.

Merry Christmas

Dory and I spent Christmas here, in the schoolhouse, before this roaring fire in the little fat-bellied stove. We spent Christmas in bed, to be accurate; and I must say that never has a holiday passed so sweetly. The snow, which began three days ago, on Christmas Eve, has now piled up in drifts around our door. It has transformed all the landscape hereabouts. The pines on the other side of the creek are quite weighted down with it, and the little creek itself is a dark tinkling rift through the snow, a rift which changes its delineations almost daily as the wind changes the configuration of the snow. Long icicles hang from the cedar shakes of the roof. We are all enclosed here, as in God's womb (intriguing image!) surrounded by the rounded mounds of icy snow, by hillocks where no hillocks ever were, by icy sheets glistening like diamonds, tree to tree. It is a veritable new world! which corresponds, needless to say, with the state of my soul. If this is sin, then I am Christendom's worst (or best!) sinner. If I be damned, then let it be. But I think otherwise.

For I have found here all the grace I ever hope to see. To wake up in the night, in the close darkness lighted only faintly by the stove, and then to feel her body curving into mine. To wake up in the morning in that first pale pearly light, and watch her as she sleeps: rosy mouth slightly open on the pillow; her breath the faintest of whistles, in and out; the high lovely line of her cheekbone; the dark lashes curling against her cheek; and all that hair in a tangle like a golden halo across the pillow.

Night before last I heated the water and we took baths, or a kind of bath, I sponged her off all over, head to toe, and she sponged me, and again I had that curious sensation that she is not separate from me, that indeed we are truly one. We used, ironically enough, one of those washcloths Mother packed, that match the set of white towels with the embroidered border of green pine trees. In my mind I see the guest bathroom at the Ampthill house in Richmond, the house where I grew up, where these are used: I see the spotless white-tiled bathroom, the green rugs, these towels hung on wooden racks in descending order of size, the bath towels, then the regular towels, then the face towels, these washcloths—oh why do I go on and on? I see this white cloth with its pine-embroidered border, see it *there*, and then I see it here. I rub it across her pubic hair, between her legs. She is amused by my insistence upon these baths, used, as she is, to bathing seldom in Hoot Owl Holler. I soap her thighs, her knees, her feet, and she squeals and giggles . . .

I know it cannot last. I know it, and yet this knowledge renders here each moment doubly sweet. For it causes me to feel each moment twice with her, as it happens, as it goes —of course it cannot last. A knowledge rendered more poignant still by her ignorance of it. Each moment we spend together is a moment torn from time. And my supply of tinned food from Wall Johnson's store continues to dwindle before our eyes, and still I keep her here, they do not come.

"Richard," she says, "do you reckon they're going to like me?" She's standing by the window now, it is morning, she wears her handmade shift and one of my shirts. "Say. Do you reckon they will?"

"Sure they'll like you," I say. "Who would not?"

"Tell me about the train," she says, and I tell it again: how we will board the spur line at Claypool Hill, and how she will wear a hat, and how we shall disembark at Marion, and spend the night in a fine hotel and eat in the dining room, and how, the next day, we will take the train for Richmond, and how we will rumble across the whole state, and I tell her the names of the towns we'll pass through, Roanoke, Lynchburg *et al.*, and I tell her that there will be a rose in a silver bud vase on our linen-topped table in the dining car, and a little silver pitcher to hold the cream.

We do not speak of her brothers, or what they've done, or where they might be now. She has not mentioned them since she told me when she came three days ago, at the commencement of this snow, when she showed up across the creek and cried out to me and I rushed over the bridge to take the little bundle she had brought. Her coming thus has ended the six weeks which began at the revival, when first she came, six weeks which I confess I have passed in a kind of trance, it seems; I cannot now recall much of that time. I know she came to me, and I to her, I know that more than once at least we met and coupled like animals there in the woods, on the dark wet freezing ground, we rolled in the underbrush with no light to see by. I did not care. It grew increasingly difficult for me to keep my mind on my teaching position, on my work; I chucked my earlier plans for a Christmas pageant. But the huge package for my students arrived, which Mother had packed and sent, I do recall passing out the gingerbread men and the nonpareils and the chocolate stars and—wonder of wonders, for them—the fresh oranges! But more than once I was forced to dismiss my students early, I trembled to such an extent, and always in those days I smelled of sex, of her body, of our juices which flowed together into one. I thought everyone could smell it, all must know! In fact I recall particularly one excruciating evening when I dined with Aldous at the home of the Perkins family, I was dark with fear lest I should be discovered, but no one seemed to see or smell or seemed to know. Camilla played "We Three Kings of Orient Are" in a rousing manner upon the piano; "Whoo! Whoo!" Mr. Perkins laughed at some joke which I must have made, I cannot now remember.

I went always, in those days, in a state of grace, or dread perhaps, a state at any rate of a kind of emotional pointillism, with each nerve quite on edge. I felt fragile, I felt razor-thin, as if to be toppled by any breeze—and it is true of course that I was steadily losing weight, a matter remarked upon by both Aldous and Justine Poole. And meanwhile her brothers hunted Paris Blankenship down like a man might hunt a deer, and found him at last, she told me, on the wild side of Snowman Mountain, and shot him through the heart, and strapped his body to his horse and sent it home. I cannot seem to end a sentence today, nor see to my punctuation, these sentences just run on, I write while the sun shines so brightly, the snow is melting, Dory naps. Her brothers are murderers now—Isadore, Bill, and Nun. They are wanted men; there is a warrant for their arrest. But they have gone away, it is said they have gone to Ohio, and they do not come, and now it is Granny Hibbitts who comes, I see her across the creek, and Wall Johnson wrapped in that huge black coat, who has brought her, and Aldous of course who stands back by the trees with the faintest of smiles on his lips, and there are Vashti Cantrell and Ora Mae as fierce as eagles beneath their hats, they wear big dark boots like crones in a fairy tale, they have come, I see, they all are there like figurines in the snow, like porcelain figures in the crèche on the mantel at home which is appropriate is it not for this is a kind of nativity isn't it—the nativity of me!—they are all like little dolls, their breath little puffs in the air I cannot see them well for the blinding light from the sun on this snow, I won't say a word.

"Don't get up," I tell her, "and don't go to the door. They'll soon leave," I say, but she rises and dresses, I pen these words I cannot restrain her of course "I have to go home and pack," she says, "for the journey." She pulls her black wool stockings carefully up to her waist. She takes off my shirt and folds it so carefully, laying it flat back on the bed-tick, crossing the sleeves, then folding the shoulders back then tucking up the tail, she pulls on her blue wool dress and does all the buttons one by one up the front of the dress. She has three dresses to her name, does Dory, and they are shouting now and making their way through the snow across the footbridge, across the creek: the snow is so bright (like sun). She bends forward now to lace on her shoes and her fine curly hair falls forward springing to either side of her neck, hiding her earrings, her face, but I see the pale white nape of her neck oh how warm we are here it is cold and icy out there but we need never leave my love you need not answer their cries yet she says she must pack to go, perhaps as she says, she must pack, Wall Johnson is a big man and his sons are big too they will break in the door or they think they will. "Tell me about the train," she says, and

I tell her about the train, and about Thomas who will meet us with the car at the Broad Street Station she has seen a Negro only once in all her life it's so hard to write with the noise they make at the door they burst it open and she wonders if she should take her quilts from her hope chest of course I say if you hope it's a little joke I am easy with my beloved.

And now here I am again! With a decent light, with a warm soft bed, with good hot food and violets dancing on my wall and the welcome attentions of Justine Poole . . .

I have been quite ill, and time has passed, and on the morrow I shall depart. It is none too soon! About the trip from Tug here to Black Rock in Aldous's car, I quite frankly prefer not to think (that old muddled syntax again!). The Hibbitts woman, Rose, muttered that nonsense which seized hold of my mind in a peculiarly ruthless fashion, contributing in no small way to my fever and delirium. And yet what she said was so trite, really, was nothing that any reasonable man should credit: some wild information proceeding straight from her diseased brain, I'm sure (they say she runs through the hills baring her breasts to drummers!), to the effect that Hoot Owl Holler is haunted, and she recited those many deaths (quite chilling, in all truth, in kind as well as number: a horrible litany) and she said that Dory, too, was cursed, and that a "witch-woman" walks up and down Grassy Creek from Hoot Owl to Tug and over to Snowman Mountain, and I cannot now remember everything she said. I do recall—I shall never forget!—her countenance: the vehemence with which she spat her accursed words into my face, her rolling eyes, her red-pocked skin, her rotting teeth. "Shut up!" (I am told) I screamed. "Shut up!" and her mother, old Granny Hibbitts, restrained her at last and led her away. But the Hibbitts woman's raving came at a crucial time: all during that fever, she occupied my mind, and in the strangest ways. I saw her face, I heard her words, and yet sometimes I saw instead Dory's face, while I heard those accursed words, and stranger still, I would hear in the background the words of a hymn, and see before me a meeting in progress at my beloved little church—to which I can never now return!—and I would hear her laughing, until I began to fancy a woman's dark shape here, in this room, by my bed, a dark shape from which I shrank as if from death itself. It agitates me now to pen these thoughts.

And yet they passed, or mostly passed, though I must confess that something of that dark shape still remains, and always shall! But the fever is gone, and in its wake has come a vast and curious lassitude. Of course I am still in love. I love Dory Cantrell. I write these words and know them to be true, but at this moment I cannot even conceive of the passion—nay, obsession!—which held me for so many months so tightly in its grip, of the abandon with which I coupled, on wet pine-straw or scratchy bed-tick or puncheon floor, with my mountain love. It grieves me so, that I shall not be here in the springtime. For we were always cold, or wet, or "cooped up," as she said—always uncomfortable, and always in desperation—no time for leisurely love. No time for plans, for getting to know one another in any intellectual sense although I felt—I shall always feel—that no purer physical and spiritual union ever has or ever shall exist on earth. But ah! if only we could have had the spring.

And again these words recur, nay, echo, in my mind:

> Come live with me and be my love,
> And we will all the pleasure prove
> That valleys, groves, hills, and fields,
> Woods, or steepy mountain yields.
>
> And we will sit upon the rocks,
> Seeing the shepherds feed their flocks,
> By shallow rivers to whose falls
> Melodious birds sing madrigals.
>
> And I will make thee beds of roses
> And a thousand fragrant posies . . .

I so shake with sobs that I cannot write these words. For now it seems to me that it is she who speaks, calling out to me . . . I hear her soft sweet voice above the rush of Grassy Creek. The room spins, these violets dance . . .

And suddenly I am emboldened! The train leaves tomorrow night at eight o'clock sharp. And perhaps . . . perhaps those stories that I spun shall yet come true!

Granted, I have been quite ill. Granted, I have a weak constitution and a vivid imagination. Granted, granted, granted.

And yet suddenly I cannot grant that final admission, which Aldous has thrust so precipitously upon me while I have lain in this curious stupor day to day: that I must leave straightaway, and leave alone. He seems to imply that I have sown my wild oats, or something to that effect, and now that I've sufficiently recovered, I must go. And then of course there is the business of her brothers, still dangerously at large, and of Mr. Perkins' misunderstanding my situation, and my summary dismissal from my post. Yet it comes to me now, exactly what I must do.

Why *not* take her too? Such a sturdy mountain flower will surely flourish wherever she takes root . . . and if my family disowns me, why then, family be damned!

I feel that I have "seen through a glass darkly, and now face to face . . ."

Why must I give her up? My own voice echoes in my ear, as I described that journey I thought we should never take. I have my imperfections, of course, and my recent actions have perhaps demonstrated a certain lack of judgment—oh, I have my limitations, as have we all—but why should I be so punished? For I have passed beyond believing in retribution, beyond morality as I have known it, beyond belief in any God but that mountain God who traffics not in words and acts but in the heart. I take my fate in my own hands. I will write to her this instant, and send the note by one of the loafers below.

The rhythm of this train is an ongoing clackety-clack, a ceaseless rhythm which goes in time to the thoughts which run through my head in circles and cycles and never shall cease, even as I shall never sleep, enervated as I am by this ceaseless racket and these wild thoughts.

God knows when last I slept.

I wrote and told her to come; it seemed my only hope of salvation in all the world.

I lay in bed all that night, it seemed, imagining it, but I confess I could see her in no setting other than the lovely wilderness of her birth, against no background other than these high mountains which are her home. A failure of the imagination perhaps, or a presentiment of the sort which has characterized my journey since first it began.

In the morning came a gentle knock on the door, and Mrs. Justine Poole entered with my breakfast tray. I gather Aldous has assured her of some extra recompense for this service, which she has seemed but too glad to perform.

"Why honey," she said immediately, concern flooding her ruddy and good-natured face. "You had a real bad night, didn't you? Justine can tell you did." (Mrs. Poole has this annoying habit of referring to herself in the third person.)

I stammered something. In truth my nerves were so jangled that I welcomed her solicitude, and I suppose it showed on my face.

"You're just all wrought up, aren't you?" she said. "Well, Justine can set you straight."

Mrs. Poole set my tray on the table and then—before I had a moment to protest or even to realize what she was up to, even though of course in retrospect the signs have been clear all along—she unbuttoned her housecoat (made of some quilted, rosy material, oh why do I care about that? why do I go on and on?) and let it fall in a puffy cloud about her feet. And there stood Mrs. Justine Poole herself in the altogether, or thereabouts—she kept on her grayish panties— puffy in all her white flesh, as honest as the day is long, before me.

"I'll warm you up," she said, and flinging back the yellow chenille bedspread, hopped heavily into the bed.

I do not know how I would have responded, nor what I should have done (of course one hopes one would have performed manfully), but the fact of the matter is that no sooner had she leaped into bed than the doorknob began to turn, squeaking and creaking as is its wont, and she stopped her amorous assault upon my person and quite literally "froze"—head up, blond curls askew, and fingers splayed across my chest. I remember my own sharp gulp of air, as all my bodily functions seemed to cease in that moment of gross suspense. It is an old glass doorknob with a beveled circumference. It turned ever so slowly, creaking . . .

It was Ora Mae.

She seemed to me wholly and totally strange in that sunlit morning room, that warm coffee-smelling room with its frosty panes of glass and all the cold outside, Mrs. Poole's rosy robe in a comfortable heap on the pine-board floor and my own clothes in disarray, most of them packed in the two valises flung open on floor and table—and myself, of course, disporting with the buxom Justine Poole—Ora Mae stood in the doorway as dark-featured and still as the angel of death! or, to be more accurate, she stood as still as a great dark stone, as a piece of obsidian. Her thick black hair was pulled straight back from her hatchet-nosed face into the customary long braid (I presume, although in fact her hood hid most of her head: it's a sin for a girl to cut her hair before marriage, they say, but that's another story: oh why do I go on and on!) Over her shapeless long brown skirt and those ubiquitous black boots, she wore a sort of woolen pea-jacket (Navy issue), and did not lower its hood, so that her starkly dead-white face stood out in fearsome opposition to this frame. Have I ever described Ora Mae? Her eyes are large, black, and ringed with circles. Her black eyebrows are perfectly level; and her mouth is a thin level line. She has no color at all in her face. Hands thrust deep in her pockets, she silently stood and stared.

For the life of me, I could never have said a word.

Ora Mae, staring, suddenly seemed to me the embodiment of something timeless and mythical, something as old and uncompromising and unchanging and hard as these ancient mountains themselves. I viewed her over a heap of chenille bedspread, of course; in my immediate peripheral vision was a greenish star-shaped mole on the plump freckled shoulder of Justine Poole. And yet there by the door stood Ora Mae like a messenger from the timeless world of love, like a message in a bottle—no, not like that at all!

Ora Mae stood by the door.

And it came to me what I was doing, and I was flooded with longing for Dory, who leapt into my mind's eye then in all her beauty and all her clean, fresh youth. Oh, how I wanted Dory!

Ora Mae looked at me directly.

"She ain't comin'," Ora Mae said.

"What?" I would have leaped in agitation from the bed had I not been restrained by Justine Poole.

"She ain't comin' now, and she ain't comin' later, and she ain't never comin', and she don't want to see your face. She axed me to tell you that." Ora Mae turned and left then, shutting the door carefully, silently, behind her, and yet I winced as though she had slammed it. My vision darkened and blurred: all the violets seemed to be running, running or sliding off the walls. Justine Poole was shaking me vigorously.

"Well, I swan!" she declared, using that expression I have never quite understood. Then she got out of bed and picked up her robe and put it back on, shaking herself like a dog emerging from water, settling herself. She patted her brassy curls and stared about the room, humming a little tune. When her perusal of the room brought her back to me, abruptly she ceased her humming. She looked at me for a long moment.

"Well, goddammit," she said, in a voice as close to meditative as Justine Poole will ever get.

She left.

I left, too.

And so it is that I write these words in transit, as I pass back across Virginia the way I came. It seems years since I made this trip, and yet it has been a mere five months, though I feel that lifetimes and lifetimes have passed. It appears I am the only one awake in this whole car. The light is dim, nearly purple; the purple light and these shadows sway with the ongoing rhythm, that ceaseless clackety-clack.

Virginia rolls by me darkly, beyond the window. We pass through a tiny station at full speed. For a second, the station-master himself is visible on the lighted platform, hand raised in greeting, mouth frozen in a smile. Is this all there is, all there ever is? the moment of lighted clarity, and then the rushing dark?

And I am torn asunder by conflicting thoughts, each one as valid, it seems to me, as its opposite. I am a sinner, bound for hell; I am a saint, purified by love; I am only a fool. I shall regain my strength and then return to these mountains, I shall sweep her up and take her back to Richmond with me as my wife; I will come back here and marry her, we will raise a family, I shall do some sort of manual labor, leaving each day with my tools while she waits with her hair bound up in a bright blue scarf; I shall never marry, I shall become an artist, I will transform all of this into a novel. And meanwhile the train clacks on, bearing me back to Richmond, bearing me home, and yet ever and ever more clearly I see her again as I saw her first on the swinging bridge over Meeting House Branch, a girl so lovely as to take your breath away, and all the leaves of autumn swirling about her, red and orange and gold.

Pricey Jane   +   Almarine Cantrell
                    ┌ Eli — 1899
                    └ Dory — 1902

Vashti Cantrell   +   Almarine Cantrell
 └ Ora Mae—1895   ┌ Isadore—1903
                        ├ Bill—1904
                        ├ Nun—1906
                        ├ James—1914
                        └ Mary—1916

III

Little Luther Wade

I was out in the yard working on that old truck we got off of Giles Hogg when Daddy come back from town and come over there and told me what old man Rife had told him that morning. I'd been out there working on that truck since dinner nearabouts, and my hands had like to froze off. I had some gloves up at the house, but I didn't give a damn. That whole winter I was a fool for work, it seemed like I couldn't get enough, and I couldn't do nothing else. I couldn't sit in a chair. And I never played no music all that time. So I was under there working when Daddy come.

"Son!" Daddy hollered. "Get out from under that truck and mind what I'm telling you," Daddy hollered out in the yard.

"I done heard you the first time," I said.

"Then get out from under there," Daddy said, "and get on up to the house."

"I'll be there in a minute," I told him. "You go on."

"What?" Daddy hollered. His hearing is going bad.

"You go on," I hollered back. "I said I'll be up there directly."

I watched from under the truck where I could see his boots, which stayed right where they was for a while and then I could see he had done give up on me when he turned and left. I stayed under there for a while longer though, thinking things over, afore I come out myself. Thing was, I never knowed that Daddy knowed what I'd been projecting, until he said. So I was kindly surprised-like, that he knowed what I'd had in my mind, what I was fixing to do. Thing about Daddy is, he's so old and all, and he acts like he can't hear much, but I guess he hears what he wants to, like the rest of us. I guess he hears enough. Anyway I laid under there in the cold and I was sorry I wasn't going to do it, at first, and then I was glad, I guess, even though I was sorry too. If ever a man needed killing, that was the feller, and now he had done got away. I stayed under there and thought about it, I stayed till my face worked right.

Then I got out and got my tools and went up to the house and they was all in there, Mama and Daddy and Earl was, anyway, and Earl's little girl Blanche, and they was all acting like they was so goddamn busy, like they wasn't nothing atall going on.

I put the tools in the box and got the keys to the other truck and told them I'd see them after while.

"Hit's coming on for dark," Mama said. "I saved you some supper," she said next. "Why don't you just stay home?" Mama's the kind can drive you crazy without even trying.

"Let him be, Mary," Daddy said, and then he tells me there's a icy patch on the road at the Paw Paw Gap and to watch out for it.

"I ain't goin that way," I said. But seeing as how they already knew so goddamn much anyway, it looked like, I'd be damned if I'd give them any more satisfaction and say where I *was* going. I don't reckon I knew myself, until I got ahold of those keys, and then it come to me. All I wanted to do was drive over to where I could see the spur line, coming from Claypool Hill, and see that train pass by. Iffen he was on it, and Aldous said he was going to put him on it, why then I wanted to see it pass. It was a long way and a crazy idea and I knew I had better get going.

"Mama says Dory is ruint," Blanche said.

Blanche was holding the yarn up and Mama was winding a ball. I looked at Mama and she wouldn't look back, and then Blanche said, "What's *ruint*?"

"You shut your mouth," I said. Daddy was acting like he couldn't hear none of this. Then I got my rifle and my guitar and then I left. I know they was wondering what I wanted with all of that, and I was wondering too. It was like my head was a-spinning around. I throwed everthing in the truck and then I clumb in too, and pulled that thing what throws the seat forward—I have to sit way up, on account of my leg—and it come up so fast I knocked my gun in the floor, give me a big scare. It could of gone off and kilt *me*, and then wouldn't that be a sight? I got to grinning, thinking about it, cranking the truck. I hadn't grinned in such a while, it was like it was hurting my face. So I don't have to shoot nobody after all, I thought, not even myself. But still I wanted to see him pass.

I went by Wall Johnson's store and him and Merle and some other fellers was coming out the door and they tried to wave me down but I drove on, I wasn't stopping for nothing, and I drove on past Tug and through the Paw Paw Gap where they wasn't no ice atall, Daddy just made that up, and then I drove over the mountain to Claypool Hill and pulled off at that bend of the Levisa River where you can see the stretch where the railroad track comes when it goes out of town. It took me a hour or so to get there, and I still didn't have no gloves, I just wanted to see him pass.

By then it was dark for sure. I got my gun and got out of the truck and walked over there by the river so I could see better. It was cold, Lord! I blowed on my hands and stomped my feet, but didn't nothing help. I wondered if Dory knew he was leaving, too, if she was thinking about him. I wondered how she felt and what she thought. It was cold as a bitch that night and I got to wishing I'd of shot him anyway, then I wouldn't have to stand out here and wait no more. Then I got to whistling till my lips got too cold to whistle. First I'd feel alright, and then I'd feel awful. Things was confused in my mind. I thought how Mama had said Dory was ruint, which was just about what you could figure Mama'd say, but I knowed she weren't never ruint. I thought on Wall Johnson saying he wouldn't take no man's leftovers. Well by God I'll take what I can get, I thought all of a sudden. I'll take it and be damned, I thought, and then I heard it coming far away around Black Rock Mountain, and then I heard it coming closer. By and by I seen the light, coming around the bend, and then before I knowed it, here it was going by me kicking up the awfulest ruckus you ever heard way out here in the night. Steam pouring outen the engine, and you could see the men in there, stoking the fire,

one of them looked like Bill Horn's boy. They was not but
five cars and a caboose, and two of the cars looked to be
empty, from what I could tell in the dark. But I knowed in
my bones he was on it someplace, up there in the engine
with them or else in one of them other cars. I knowed he was
on that train. It went on with a great big roaring racket and
leaving smoke in the air. I pulled my gun up to my shoulder
then and sighted down it, just for the hell of it, at the swinging light on the back of the caboose. It swang back and forth,
back and forth, in and out of the sight, and then the train
was gone and him with it. I went back and got in the truck
and got my guitar and made up this song, my fingers was too
cold to pick, but anyway I made up this song.

> Darlin' Dory stands by the cabin door
> Standing with her Bible in her hands
> Darlin' Dory stands by the cabin door
> A-pinin' for her city man.
>
> You can throw that Bible down on the floor
> You can throw it out in the rain
> Prayin' for him all night long won't do no good
> For he ain't a-comin' back again.
>
> Well he ain't a-comin' back to the meetin'-house
> and he ain't a-comin' back to the school
> City feller gone with a head full of dreams
> Oh, why can't you see him for a fool?
>
> Dory let me dry those tears away
> Dory come back in and shut the door
> A month or two don't add up to a life
> A slip or two don't make you a whore.
>
> Dory come back to your own true love
> A month or two don't add up to life
> Dory let me dry them tears away
> Dory let me make you my wife.

It took me nearabout a hour to make it up. I knowed I wouldn't never sing it to nobody, least of all to her, but anyway I made it up and then I knowed what I was going to do and I felt good, I tell you, I got to feeling like myself again for the first time all winter. I laughed out loud in the dark and cranked up that old truck. She was my girl afore she was hisn, whether she knowed it or not. I allowed as how she was my girl now, whether she knowed it yet or not, either. I knowed then that she might not love me as much as I loved her, but that was all right with me too. She'd love me more than she thought. A girl needs a man she can depend on, and by God there's worse things than that. By God there is, I says to myself, gunning that truck back home, and she'll come to know it afore she's through. In a way I still wish he hadn't of left, though, I was going to shoot him dead as soon as he walked out of Justine Poole's no doubt about it. I had been laying for him. I wondered how Daddy knew. You have to get up mighty damn early to get ahead of Daddy. I rode along grinning, and it was cold as a witch's tit. But I tell you, it wouldn't have turned a hair on my head to shoot him, that's a fact.

Mrs. Ludie Davenport

Now I want to tell this the way it happened, and I want to tell you all the circumstances of it. For I believe it's been going on a long time, and it's high time you heard it out loud. It ain't gone do no good to tell it, I know that, nothing ain't gone to change in the telling, but leastways somebody can warn the younguns. The younguns orter be told.

Now you know me and how I love the Lord, you know I'd die before I'd tell a lie. So you can take every word of this as the Gospel. And anybody that loves the Lord as much as me, you know they fear the Devil too. You can't have one without the other any moren you can have the dark without the light. It don't make no sense if you leave out the other half, is what I'm a-saying, and I have knowed the Devil for real ever since the first time he appeared to me when I was not but eight years old at a church dinner on the ground, and told me to do something nasty. Not me, I said, you go on, old Devil, and find you somebody else! So he up and disappears, and it was not but five or ten minutes later that Mama's little chow dog, which was always so nice and sweet, come a-running out of the woods all wild-like, and bit Grandaddy on the knee right through his Sunday trousers! Old Devil had got into Mama's little chow dog. Now all this took place in Bluefield, W. Va., before I was brung here by Harp. And I have knowed the Devil, old Nick, nearabout as good as I have knowed God. And there ain't nothing he'll do, nor no way he'll work, to surprise me.

Anyway, I pick up on stuff. I know things afore they happen sometimes, I seen my daddy dead in a dream. I seen two black-headed babies in a dream and I had black-headed twins. It was me, you recall, way back—must of been twenty-five years ago—that seed the witch a-leaving after Almarine had throwed her out, that heard her laugh. It was old Nick in a woman's form and I'll swear it, just like he went into that chow dog. It put me to bed for a week. So you can talk about devils and witches all you want, and it ain't none of it news to me. I been in on this thing from the word Go.

Well I had put up pickle lilly the night before. Now nobody around here makes it as good as me. So ever time I put it up, I have to go around here and take some to everbody, I take some to the Rev. Autry Lily, bless his heart, his wife is sick in the bed, and I take some over to Rhoda just naturally, everbody takes her things the way you used to take them to Granny Younger, and besides I had this wart on my hand that I wanted took off, and then I'll take some to my son Bill, that is one of them black-headed twins, whose wife is too feisty to cook good. So I had put up pickle lilly the night before, and I had my day all cut out for me.

This is the way I put it up if you have to know. I take me about a peck of green tomatoes, and a peck of string beans, and a good-size bunch of little old onions and green peppers, and I get me some red peppers too, and two big old head-cabbages, and I chop it all up and put it in the pot. Then I pour in my vinegar to cover, and I add my sugar and some pickling spice, and then I boil it down. It takes about two hours to boil it down.

My mama used to say tomatoes was poison, she wouldn't touch a one. Well, some things change.

And some don't. I was a-crossing Grassy Creek—coming back from Rhoda's with a poultice on my wart—on the foot-path in the early morning dew, I'd left Harp at home a-laying up in the bed, when all of a sudden I felt a cold wind rise up on me out of noplace, and it July. I said I felt that wind rise up. And then the hair on my arms rises straight up too, and I got goose-bumps all over. I knowed I had felt that way before, and it twenty-five years gone. But you don't forget a thing like that, nor how you felt. I quick-looked all about, wasn't naught to be seen but the little flowers and the ferns and all down by the creek, and the fog how it hung by the shady bank, and the sun coming down through the trees. But I felt as cold as death. I looked up the holler toward the Cantrell place, which you just could see if you tried, but wasn't no sign of life up there nor a thing to remark in particular.

Lord knows what-all goes on up there anyway, as I said it that morning to Rhoda who laughed the way she does and says "Nothing much." "Nothing much!" I says. "I would not call it nothing with one girl pregnant and going around like she's having some kind of a spell, with a crippled boy lagging after her, and the little girl sick, and that Jink that takes so after his daddy when he was that age, always slipping out and mooning around."

"It's a fact, he does," Rhoda said, kind of surprised-like, and her daughter who's tetched in the head rolled her eyes back and said, "Does what?" and Rhoda said, "Take after his daddy," and then Rose set in to crying again. Rose was trying to braid her hair.

"Here, now," Rhoda told me. "You keep this on it a hour or so, and then when you get home, I'll tell you what you do. You take this off, and you let it bleed some, and you put the blood on a penny and lay the penny in the road, and when somebody picks it up, the wart will go away." Well, we've all gotten old now and that's a fact, but Rhoda has wrinkled up in the face like a pecan nut with her eyes still as blue as the sky. I call her Rhoda myself, seeing as how we growed up together so, but there's lots of others just calls her Granny. And anyway you take her things when you put them up, just like you did Granny Younger, you know how you do. They was a Ramey girl over there that morning, in fact, bringing Rhoda some beets. Beets! Harp wouldn't eat a beet if he had to. He'll eat anything else in this world.

"They's a curse on the holler," Rose says, follering me to the door, "and on all them pretty girls." Rhoda just smiled her little smile, I'd give a lot to know what she thinks sometimes of what Rose says, and Rose's eyes burned out like cinders in that ashy pale face as she braided her long gray hair. Lord, we're all of us getting so old!

But I'm no fool, I'll tell you, and when I crossed back over that creek is when I felt that cold air rise and then directly I heard that laugh which there wasn't no mistaking even if I hadn't heard it for twenty-five years. I was over the creek by then, and let me tell you I took off as fast as these old legs would carry me. And still I heard that laughing, it was like it come down out of the trees, and then it was right on my heels, or it'll move up ahead on the path, and me just a-freezing to death and moving as fast as I'm able. I see that big pine tree up ahead where I'm fixing to turn to get to Bill's, and I'm thinking well, thank the Lord, when all of a sudden there starts up this barking at my heels. But of course there wasn't no dog! No, it was Almarine's ghost-dog, the one that never come back after he kilt that witch, and this ghost-dog consorts with her now and follers wherever she'll go. It was a good thing for me I started saying the Lord's Prayer out loud then, and I said it as loud as I could.

It's a wonder I ever made it to Bill's in one piece. I knocked and knocked on the door until finally she came to open it, that Susie, and I see at a glance she's been back in the bed, with him already up and gone to the mine. That's Bill. And that's that lazy Susie.

"Why, what's the matter, Ludie?" Susie said, acting just so sweet like butter wouldn't melt in her mouth when you know that's not really her nature, and she helped me to a chair and got me a drink of water. Then I told her all about the witch a-coming to hant me in Hoot Owl Holler and how that ghost-dog barked at my heels. Then I felt so weak-like when I was through that I had to lay down in the bed myself, I had plumb give out. And I slept like a log that whole afternoon, waking up just in time to hear the tail-end of her telling Bill and the boys about it when they got home.

Bill scratched his head and turned that hat with the light on it around and around in his hands. "Well hell, Susie," he said. "What you want me to do about it?"

"She just wants me to wait on her hand and foot," Susie said, which was a lie, and I sat up and said so to her face.

"I have seed a ghost," I told them all, "and I have lost my wart poultice, and I have been chased by a ghost-dog. I am not in bad shape considering," I said, and then I laid back down and told it.

Now Bill Jr., who is the eldest grandson, was standing there so still, listening, with the coal dust ringing his eyes, and when I was finished he said, "That puts me in mind of something, Mamaw. You know last Christmas when Donny Osborne fell offen the mountain and broke his leg over there on Snowman where them big white rocks is? You-all remember that? Well, he swore it was a dog chased him offen the clift but he didn't never see no dog. He said it like to drove him crazy barking." Bill Jr.'s eyes went around at us all, and you know he's so honest since he has got saved.

"Hellfire," Bill said, and then he told Susie to heat up some beans to go with the pickle lilly.

"You can't stay but a day now," she said to me while the men was outside washing. "Or who'll take care of old Harp?"

"I tell you it was *her*," I said, "and that infernal dog, and I don't care if you'll listen to me or not, there's a-plenty that will," I said, and there is. Believe me, there is.

At the Smith Hotel

Later today this room will be hot, too hot for a boarder to stand it even if there was a boarder here to do so, which there is not, times being hard as they are. Come three o'clock, it'll be like an oven in here. Justine Poole will close it off then, and she'll close off the three other rooms which get the sun. She'll sit on the porch drinking tea. But right now it's nice up here. Both the windows are open wide, shades up, and the breeze comes in and moves the soiled muslin curtains which flutter like moths, and noise comes up from the street. Car horns and the occasional clip-clop of a mule-wagon going past, and the women's voices twittering to and fro, in and out of hearing, beneath the windows. Men's voices too, more men than you'd hear if it wasn't hard times and so many out of work, men's voices low and halting, with sometimes a hoarse shout of laughter. The union man has a high-pitched voice, and a different accent. "Absentee money," he says—you can hear him above the rest—and "work like dogs," but you can't hear what-all he says. Anyway it's Saturday, day after payday for those lucky enough to be working, close to noon, and the breeze comes up in the windows blowing the curtains and now Blind Bart has started up on his harmonica over there in front of the court-house, playing "Saro Jane" low and sweet, to suit the morning. Later on when the Busy Bee opens up down the way in the house where the Astons lived, and they start selling beer at Old Man Long's and Loretta's Place, why then Blind Bart will change his tune and Justine Poole will switch from tea to bourbon on her porch, awaiting the rivet salesman from Bluefield, as the town cranks up for Saturday night. But it's still early now, still cool up here, although the sun is bright as it shines through the turning dust in the air, showing up all the gray smudges on the white wallpaper between the violets, falling in a solid golden block across the twisted white sheet on the bed.

Aldous Rife, naked, lies flat on his back with his bandy legs spraddled out so the breeze can get to his vitals. Justine Poole lies on her stomach with her bare ass stuck up in the air and one foot stuck up too, bent at the knee, tracing circles in the sun with her small, surprisingly pretty little foot with its red, red toenails. She props herself up on one elbow now, and starts to fool with the tangled gray hair on Aldous's sunken chest.

"Cut that out, honey," Aldous says like he always does, but he knows she won't. Justine is all the time brushing off your lapel or squeezing a blackhead or doing her own nails or smoothing your hair down in back. She's got to be doing something with her hands. Now this is a trait that Aldous might not have liked in another woman—say, one of his wives—but he likes it fine in Justine. Justine is a busy woman, always was. You know she's got things to do. So when she sighs all of a sudden, a big long sigh like she's lost the last friend she ever had or hoped to have, and rolls over on her back and lets her arms flap down at her sides, this surprises Aldous. It's not a bit like Justine.

"What's the matter?" he asks her.

"I was just thinking about that boy from Richmond, that Richard Burlage," Justine said. "You know this used to be his room."

"Did it?" Aldous is surprised. First they use one room, then another, depending on what time of day it is and which rooms Justine has rented out. They've been at this for twenty years.

"He kept it the whole time he was here," Justine said. "September to January."

"I know how long he was here," Aldous says drily. "In fact I am still surprised that I got him out of town in one piece. I wrote his father quite a letter, Justine, did I tell you that?"

"Letter saying what?"

"Saying that Richard had sowed his oats in the wrong field, basically, and advising him never to come back here again."

Justine sighs and crosses her arms behind her head.

"Well, what have we here?" old Aldous asks, raising himself up so he can see her face. "I believe you were a bit sweet on him yourself, Justine, if the truth be told."

"Oh shit," Justine says, her mouth in a plump round pout.

"Yes?" Aldous asks, in a grotesque parody of the manner he adopts when his few parishioners come to him with their problems. "Yes?" he prompts again.

"Shit yes," Justine says. "He was a sweetie, Aldous, he really was. I mean he was so polite, he was always *thanking* me for something, even if I hadn't done a thing. He was always saying please. You know how he was."

"I know," Aldous says.

"And he had that little look on his face, like he thought you were going to give him a present, or like he thought he was going to learn something."

"Which he did not," Aldous interjects.

"Like he was waiting for something good to happen," she goes on. "That's what it was. And then he used to *worry* so much, too. Well, you know how he was."

"Yes," Aldous says, laying back to stare at the billowing curtains, "By God, I do," realizing he had never liked the boy precisely because he knew all too well how he was, a young man a lot like himself, thinking back to when he had been that young and that idealistic, that capable of obsessive love, and thinking too of the women he'd spent it on, wasted it, the first one who used to undress in a closet and the second who sewed all the time and snapped off her thread with her teeth. Good women both. He had picked them himself out of his various congregations, out of some obscure sense of what was fitting, what was right. Thank God there had been no children. It had been wrong all along, the second as wrong as the first. Perhaps this was why he had not stepped in when he learned that the boy had sent for Dory, that the boy had decided to take her back to Richmond with him. Let him have her, Aldous had thought then, even if it's not fitting, by God! Let her go. But then she had not come! to his great surprise, for Dory—as he well knew—was a girl who had been doted on all her life, a strong-willed girl, he thought, who knew her own mind, and it still surprised him that she had not come. Yet it would be better in the end, he was sure of that, better at least for the boy. Aldous smiles up through the turning dust in the sun, smiling at nothing, as he tries to remember how it was to be young like that and torn up all the time over something. He remembers a time on a trip with his first wife when he had strode furiously out to a gazebo (where had they been?) where he paced and smoked for half the night, flinging his cigarettes over the railing into the roses, but he cannot now recall the quarrel. Nor can he recall how he felt then, or why he was so upset. He's glad it's behind him now.

Justine is at it again, holding one arm straight out and clutching at the drooping flesh of that upper arm with her other hand.

"What are you doing?" he asks.

"I read it in a magazine," Justine says. "See? Looky here. That means you need to go on a diet."

Her upper arm dangles and Aldous snorts. Justine is always dieting, diets she reads in the magazines, but she never stays on them long enough to matter. For one thing, she's such a good cook. Justine is soft all over, white freckled skin so fair she'll bruise if you give her a pinch. Now she turns to him and begins to stroke his penis, pull it a little, and Aldous lies back and looks up and lets her work. They both know he probably won't manage an erection again; once is enough for an old man, but it feels good and she likes to do it. *She likes to do it*, this is what Aldous can never get over about Justine. Her rolls of fat bunch up at her waist and her breasts slide sideways, all of her companionable, as she leans up on an elbow and does it now.

When Justine says, "He was a fool, he couldn't of parked a bicycle," they both know who she's talking about, and why she seems so mad.

Aldous keeps his eyes shut tight as she keeps on. Eventually he says, "He was not a fool, Justine, not exactly, I think. He was something much more dangerous, to my mind, a total innocent."

"You know what I think?" Justine giggles now, whatever vestige of whatever it was she still feels for the boy apparently gone, "I think you're full of shit, all that talking you done. You are just as full of shit as he was," and she laughs—she will never be too old to laugh, Justine won't—and Aldous smiles: of course she's right.

"I do think there's a curse on the Cantrells, though," she says. "All you have to do is look right on the face of it, you don't need any fancy supposing. Like you take Almarine, shot to death, and you take them three sons of hisn, scattered off God knows where. And you go back and take that crazy girl, and he kilt her—"

"We don't know that," Aldous says.

"Well, we just as well as know it," Justine says. "And then that first young wife he had, the one with the gypsy blood . . ."

"She wasn't a gypsy," Aldous says. "Her name was Pricey Jane."

"Well, whatever! Anyway, where is she now, answer me that, and her little son dead with her, not to mention Paris Blankenship or that sick little girl they've got up there right now or what Ludie Davenport saw on the trace, or Harve's Clovis, or whoever else you want to name. There's something up there, Aldous. You ought to go on and say it, honey. You're the one that believes in the spirits."

Aldous is erect now. "What spirits?" he asks.

"Father, Son, and Holy Ghost, I reckon," Justine says. "The big three. I reckon they're spirits too."

"Mmm," Aldous says.

"Listen, I think that old thing is gonna *work*," Justine says. This time she gets on him, the whole satisfying weight of her, and after they're through, she lies back and starts up again. Justine on a subject is just like a dog on a bone.

"Well, you can't say there's *nothing* up there," she says, punching him. "You can't go telling me that."

"Ludie Davenport is a still-healthy woman saddled with a sick husband," Aldous answers her finally, dragging his mind back up from a place near sleep. "Maybe she needs some excitement."

"Excitement, my hind foot!" Justine says.

"Look, Justine. You could make up something about anybody up in any of those hollers, and you know it. Take the Skeens, and that fire they had last Christmas and three of the children burned up, or the way Mavis Rife had two babies to die in a row, just up and died in their cribs with no reason Doc Story could find to ascribe to it. Or take the Harmons—"

"Oh my God!" Justine rolls over giggling. Everybody knows the Harmons are the ultimate sight, God threw out the book when he made up the Harmons, intermarried for eighty years and half of them wall-eyed with short little necks and all of them so backwards that town kids come to gawk whenever they come down the mountain to Black Rock.

"Or any number of other people. Take Rhoda Hibbitts's daughter Rose, for instance."

"Well, Rose is just touched in the head," Justine says reasonably. "Everybody knows *that*."

"I know it," Aldous says. "Everybody knows it, you're right. But somebody could have started up a tale about her—this is the point—only she started up a tale about Almarine instead. And once it starts, it just goes on by itself, it takes on a life of its own no matter who may be hurt in the process. It's ignorance, is what it is, and by God I see no end to it, to ignorance and darkness. I can't see that it does any good to preach false hope or promise some kind of golden hereafter, some happy heaven that people believe in only because the things of this world are so goddamn bleak they can't stand it if they don't have that to fall back on, or that to look forward to, some spurious golden robe."

"Well, for goodness' sakes, Aldous!" Justine stretches lazily. She gets bored when he starts all that. It's getting hot in here now but the sun feels pretty good, as a matter of fact, it's a shame that women can't take the sun, but it has been shown to cause wrinkles. Anybody that can read a magazine knows that. Aldous goes on and on. He's like a clock if you get him wound up on his favorite subject, which God knows she never meant to do. He's a crank, she thinks: *old crank*.

"Listen here now," she tells him finally. "It makes people feel good to go to church."

"Oh my God." Aldous strikes his forehead with the back of his hand, a gesture she's seen before.

"It makes *me* feel good, so there!" she says, and that's that, but isn't it crazy how she's the one who believes in God, and the preacher's the unbeliever? or says he is, but he's said it so much now, it gives her a thought.

"You're just tormenting yourself," she says, "just like a man, and you're old enough to know better, you old fool. If you didn't believe anything, you'd just shut up about it, don't you know that?"

Aldous quits beating his forehead to stare at her.

"I been thinking about moving down to Florida," Justine says. "Sell this place."

"What?"

"Or maybe Kentucky." She stretches in the sun like a big white cat. "Go to the races," she says.

And Aldous, who has decided to leave Black Rock once a day for the last thirty years, is dumbstruck. He knows she *means* it, if she says so; she really might move.

"I ought to get on down there," she says, meaning the kitchen, "and see what-all they've got into now."

"Florida," Aldous says.

"If I could get a good price for this place, I'd move in a New York second," Justine says, "which I can't, the way things is now." But also she knows she likes it, the daily contact with her boarders, the in and out of people, the hiring and firing and knowing what happens in town. Jake, bless his heart, did the only smart thing in his short sad life when he died and left her this. Because she was always a lot like Jake's daddy anyway, a mover and a shaker, a woman that had a way with a dollar bill, it was a funny thing, a daughter-in-law that took after Old Man Poole. And Jake smiles, standing there in his new blue suit, an absolutely still point in the middle of Justine's mind, a boy-man, not ever going to age or get fat or get sick.

Aldous zips his high-waisted dark gray pants—"preacher pants" is what Justine calls them—and then he leaves, an old man in preacher clothes, but he'll be back in a week or so for another cup of coffee. That's how he puts it: going over to the Smith Hotel for a cup of coffee, that's what he says. But what he wants now is a drink.

He leaves, and Justine rolls over to feel the sun on her back but it's getting too hot now for sure, women can't take the sun, and she's starting to sweat. Wonder if that rivet man is going to come? Sometimes she thinks it's all she ever does, just pleasure men, but then there's not a hell of a lot else to do either. Fucking is fine as far as it goes. But it's nothing more than a prick in your belly and that quivery flash and a man's hot breath in your ear. Forget the particular man. It don't matter who the man is, nor what it means to him, nor what he *thinks* it means. Don't none of that matter, and it's fine as far as it goes, but it don't mean a thing in this world but a man and a woman clamped together in a bed behind the closed door having nothing to do with all the rest of it, with death or fate or sudden sorrow, with the rivet man's daughter, for instance, who has taken to acting so funny, he says, and how she'll talk in a different voice from time to time, nor with Aldous and how he sleeps with a handker-chief all balled up in his hand, he has to have it to sleep at night, nor with Jake, for instance, that time at the fair in West Virginia when she wore her new red dress with the patent belt and he shot the gun and won her that paper-weight with the little blue flowers blooming inside. Justine wonders where the paperweight is now. Lost someplace in the jumbled closets of this big house or more probably sto-

len by boarders. They'll take anything you don't tie down—
Justine sits up and squares her shoulders and swings her legs
off the bed, thinking of boarders—they'll eat you right out of
house and home.

Jink Cantrell

First I got up in that sycamore where I like to get but then I
knowed—knew—they could see me up in it when they
started coming in for the hog-killing, they could of seen me
for a country mile. Yet still I was up there when the sun
come up. Lord it was cold too, and black as hell that morning
when I woke up and snuck outen the house and went down
there. I don't need no light. I clumb up in the cold black
night and oncet I got up there hit commenced to changing,
the sky did, it growed from black to pearly white in no time,
and these little slippy clouds just running acrost it to hide
behind Hoot Owl Mountain. That's what I was after—hiding—and yet those little clouds could fly and I could not. It
weren't that long ago I thought I could. I used to sit up in
that same tree and say the words—I made them up and it
was long, a long piece I made up in my head—and it was so
long I never could get it right but I thought if I ever did get
it right I would fly. I swear I did. It weren't—wasn't—but
two years back. Seems like it was a million years ago now,
seems like the dinosaur days. So I sat up there in my thinking place in the top of that tree while the day come on, no
way I could of stopped it any moren I could fly. But then
after while I commenced to get taken with it.

The pearly-white sky set to changing before my eyes,
glowing pink like it had a light behind it, like how the sun
came in those colored windows the time he brung me with
him into Black Rock and we went in the old man's church.

The whole sky started glowing pink, and them little clouds still running acrost it as fast as they could go, and the wind blowing cold and so hard that my thinking place was blowing back and forth too, and me still up in it, away up high. I leaned my head back—I was leaning into that part where the branches come together and make like a kind of a seat, I call it the mother-seat, don't ask me why—I was leaning way back looking straight up, and the thinking place was blowing, and it was like I was the one flying acrost that rosy sky while all the rest of the world stayed still. It was just like I was flying. And the way I was leaned back into the tree put me in mind of a picture in the poem-book he had, of Wyncken, Blynken, and Nod in that boat, sailing off through the stars. Of course they wasn't no—any—stars by that time, nothing but the moon like a ghost-moon, fading away in the full pink light which growed ever minute I looked. Rosy-finger dawn, he said. He read it outen a book. It was eating up the moon and I was glad.

Old ghost-moon nearly gone, and nearly full, I knowed it without even looking. That's why we was—were—killing the hogs. You don't never want to kill a hog on the new of the moon, Mamaw says, or you wouldn't make no lard. And if you kill on the new of the moon, the meat'll blow you till you can't hardly cook it. But if the moon is shrinking, the meat'll shrink, and you won't get but half of what you orter. You got to kill on the first cold day in late November when the moon is right, and this was it. I set up in my place and wished I'd die. Because this was the year I had to help them, Mamaw said. She said it was high time to stand up and be a man, she wasn't keeping no lily-livered fancypants around her house. She said I'd have to go this time, and I knowed it was high time too. Some of me wanted to go and some did not, but didn't none of it make any nevermind with me leaning back in the mother-seat and flying all out through the dawn. The little clouds started taking on that pink color too, then, like it was somebody coloring them in with a crayon, and then some yellow streaks come shooting through, and I sat up straight in time to see the whole round sun come right up over the top of Snowman Mountain, all huge and pink

and dignified, it put me in mind of a sweet old man. It
seemed like there wasn't a thing in the world but me in the
top of a tree and that big fine round new sun.

Up at the house I seen the smoke arising bigger from the
chimley, and I knowed—knew—Mamaw was up, and then
directly I seen another line of smoke come up behind the
house and I knew she had gone out there and started that fire
too, the one in the dugout under the hog drum. Me and
Mary and Dory had to haul the water for it the night before.

And then the sun was coming on for sure. It switched
from pink to silver white till it looked like a big old electric
light-bulb set right on top of the mountain, and then it took
on orange, and then it was shining all over the place. Ice
down on the creek shined out like new money way below. I
wished it *was* new money, I'd of clumb down that tree and
grabbed it up and gone. Well it wasn't, of course, and I knew
it, and neither did that sun have any warmth. It's crazy how
a day can sparkle so and stay so cold. Mamaw says you've
got to have it cold so the meat won't spoil.

Then all of a sudden I could hear them, coming up the
trace. I heard the Ramey boys holler out, acting the fool I
bet, and I heard Little Luther too. They was not but a hoop
and a holler away. I got down that tree lickety-split and took
off for my summer place at the bend of the creek, where that
rocky-hill pooches out into kind of a overhang and you can
get under there, can't nobody see you either. The ground
was all spewed up with frost. When I run acrost it, it made
this little crackle-crackle noise neath my feet. When I was
little I used to think it was hollering out, like my feet was
hurting it. I used to think everything could talk then but it
can't.

"Jink! You Jink!"

Mamaw was hollering out the front door.

Then I could hear all of them, talking and laughing, and I
could hear the horses neighing out and the mules, and
stomping their feet where I knew they'd hitched them in the
piney-trees, and if I was still up in my sycamore I would of
been right on top of them nearabouts. Then I felt like I *was*
still up there, like I could see it all, the horses' breaths com-

ing out white in the air, and everbody milling around and starting up the mountain. I knew Wall Johnson was wearing his hat and his big black coat, and some of the big gals was helping Granny Hibbitts along now she's gotten so stout, and I knew the women was carrying food. And more and more of them coming afoot that had parked down there where the hard-road quits. I knew the women would go in the house and get some coffee outen the big pot Dory'd have on, and they'd be gooing and gaaing over Dory's babies, them little twins, and putting the food out, and pulling off their wraps and settling in, like chickens ruffle up and calm when they go to roost. I knowed all of it. And then the men would be out back by the hog-drum watching it boil, and hunkering and talking, and taking a little nip, but wasn't nobody made any liquor to equal ourn, everybody said. Of course they is some of it left. Mamaw made me and Dory go out and bury it all along by the fencerow, it's froze down in there solid now. Except for the liquor in the jugs, now that don't—doesn't—freeze. Alcohol doesn't freeze, he said in school. So the men would be taking a nip, passing it all around, and by then old man Harve Justice was whittling, I'd say, cleaning off the gambling sticks for stringing up the hogs, and they'd have another fire built too, to warm by. It was like I was right up there and down at Grassy too, and I looked around, at the rocky-jut hanging out over my head, and the black creek singing a little old song, in and outen the ice. Tadpoles in it of a summer, and fast green lizards so pretty it hurt you to watch them.

"Jink."

It was Mary, all wrapped up in the brown coat that used to be Dory's, her face peeping outen the hood. She was coming along the creek, picking her way, and biting her bottom lip so as not to fall. It would kill you to watch Mary coming, how careful she is, and the way she sets down her feet like the ground might just give out at any minute. Mary was the only one who knew about my summer place. Still, I was mad she had come.

"What are you doing down here?" I throwed a rock and broke some ice. "You ain't got no business out here in the cold. Mamaw'll kill you," I said, and Mary smiled that smile she's got, it goes all over her face.

"Mamaw's killing hogs today," she said. "She ain't got time to fool with me."

I allowed as how that much was true, anyway, and got to grinning myself. It tickles me when Mary gets around Mamaw, how sometimes she'll be so sly, like the time when Mamaw locked me down in the root cellar for lying and Mary brung me food for two days solid and then swore it on a Bible she had not.

Mary sat down and her breath went out white like a cloud around her, she looked like she was in a cloud herself and if she took off that coat, she'd be all in white like a holy angel.

"Get on up to the house," I said.

"I ain't coming till you do." When Mary sticks her lip out like that, they is no reasoning with her, she's just like a snapping turtle that won't turn loose till it thunders.

"All right," I said, and I got up, and we went up the mountain together, slow because of Mary. She had these red spots on her cheeks by then, from the cold.

Mary went on in the house but I stayed out in the yard with all the other kids, where Red Rover was breaking up, and Johnny Ramey was crying his arm was broke, he always says that, and then Lute come around for hide and go seek. "Eeny-meeny-miny-mo," he said. "Catch a nigger by the toe, if he hollers let him go. One-two-three spells out goes he." Ray was it. He throwed himself down in the yard with his eyes hid on his jacket sleeve and commenced to counting, and we all took off like a house afire. "10–11–12—" I run around the house and smack into Hester's Billie, who slapped me one time good acrost the butt and said for me to watch out who I was running into. I thought I'd get under the house, but Darlene and Kenny and Hank was already there, and wouldn't a one of them scrunch over. "15–16–17—" I run out to the woodpile, and they was two kids there too, and by then Ray was on "19," so I run back and stopped by them cedar trees and got behind that old rotted-out bench out there. I knowed—knew—Ray could

see me if he come that way and looked good, but I hoped I'd
be long gone by then. I was having a real good time by now,
in fact I was glad that Mary had brung me home.

"Twenty!" Ray yelled out, and he was coming. My heart
was bumping, bumping in my chest. I laid real still and
heard them shoot the firstest hog. Then I heard Ray yelling
and Cindy squealing and Ray said "Dang it," and I knew she
had gotten home. Home is the hollered-out rock in the yard
that the rain sets in, what Dory uses for washing her hair. I
thought about eeny meeny miny mo and what you'd do with
a nigger if you caught him by the toe. What you'd do with a
nigger anyway. They used to be slaves, he said, but that was
immoral. I seen a nigger once, but not close up. They sent a
bunch of them over here from the prison farm where they
was building the hard-road, and ever morning they'd bring
them in, and ever night they'd carry them back out in a
prison truck. We won't have no niggers in this county after
sundown, that's for sure. Everbody went down there to see
them work, you'd take a lunch, I went with Dory and Ora
Mae, and Nun throwed a rock at them and the straw boss
looked the other way. That was immoral.

Ray was coming, and he seen me, and I took off. I might
be little for my age but I can run fastern wind. I took off
alongside the fencerow, running over top of all them buried
jugs of liquor, and zigzagged around the garden patch, and
run down the little creek from the springhouse, wasn't no
way Ray could catch me in the world. All the other kids was
yelling out and running home. "Goddamn you, you little
piss-ant," Ray said, way behind, and I lit off acrost the yard
for the other kids all yelling out and jumping up and down
around that rock. I made it.

"Home free!" I hollered, grabbing out so hard for home
that I got my sleeve wet in the water cotched in that rock.

"No, you ain't," Peter Paul Ramey said, hauling me up by
the seat of my britches. "This year, Vashti says you're coming with me," and before I knowed what was happening, he
had got aholt of my arm and twisted it behind my back and
he was taking me off real fast-like around the house where

they were out there killing the hogs. So I didn't have no choice, and I had to go out there with them, and hunker down around the fire, and watch.

They had shot the first hog in the back of the head and cut its neck, and the blood was pumping out and running all over the ground.

"You got to stick him right in the goozle," Wall was telling me, but I couldn't stop looking at the blood and how red and pretty it looked in the sun, and worrying too because I'd thought *pretty*.

Soon as the bleeding slowed, they drug him over to the drum and hove him up and over into the water. Then they hauled him out and scraped him, and Wall said "Come on, boy, get to work," and I saw I'd have to go and get my knife. "You get right on back here, now," Wall said, and I said I would. Mamaw was out there working along with the men, she always does, and looking at me out the side of her eye. The older Mamaw gets, the more she looks like a Indian.

When I got up to the house, Dory give me a great big piece of divinity fudge. "Here, honey," she said, and popped it right into my mouth. She was holding one of them twins—I can't never tell if it's Pearl nor Maggie—in her arms, and her hair was curling all around her face again, not pulled back the way she had wore it so long, and she looked real pretty. "Have another," she said, and she give me another, and I felt better when I went back out.

At least she was smiling again. For a long time there it was like somebody else had come in and took over her body, or else it was something like that, and she'd go all day without a word, getting bigger and bigger, and never say a thing to Little Luther nor any of them others who'd try to come by.

Before she got so big, there was three or four or maybe more of them coming around, Mamaw said they all of them had an eye on Dory. And Mamaw wanted her to take up with one of them, any one, she didn't care which, she said, and give that baby a name. But Dory said her baby didn't need no name. Me, I liked it when they was all of them coming around, they used to bring stuff to me and Mary, like jawbreakers and marbles and rubber bands. But Dory wouldn't have no truck with a one. She'd smile sometimes, real sweet-like, and she was still pretty enough in spite of how she pulled back her hair so tight then, it made you remark those gold earrings right off, but it was like she was someplace else in her mind. In her mind, she'd gone off from us all. Sometimes she'd go around humming, or nod her head up and down exactly like she was agreeing with herself about something, and she wouldn't eat a bite for Mamaw. In fact she wouldn't do a thing Mamaw said, which tickled me and Mary, but Mamaw liked to rode her to death, telling her what was good for her. And Dory all the time smiling a little, and cocking her head like she was listening to somebody else. So them fellers stopped coming one by one, you couldn't fault them a bit.

Although they told it different, Lute says, up and down the hollers and where he lives over at Tug.

Lute hears everything right off, his daddy runs the store. Lute says that when these fellers come a-courting, soon as they'd start up the mountain they'd hear a woman's voice in their ear that said to turn back and not to go any farther. "Leave, leave," they said it sighed in their ears as they came, and it was like they could feel a woman's hot breath on their cheek but when they turned to see, wasn't nobody there but them and the empty night, and a kind of cold shaky mist in the air.

Now I give Lute a bloody nose for it. It's crooked yet, and going to be crooked the rest of his life. I don't give a damn neither. We're friends again, I guess, we cut our fingers and mixed the blood and swallered some to prove it, but I can't hold with them telling lies like they tell about Dory. It's immoral is what it is. I wanted her to take up with Little Luther, cripple-leg and all. I swear I did. Shut all of them up, and then I wouldn't never have to hit Lute and crook up his nose for life, nor hit any of the rest of them, like I had to do now. Sometimes I wished it was just Dory and Mary and me and him off someplace, someplace pretty, and all the rest of them dead as the dead in the tales they tell, like Lute and those damn bloody bones he'll tell about, that man and that lady that ate up their girls and the bloody bones come to hant them. I wished it was Dory and Mary and me and him in a little house in that grassy bald where the fine grass grows all around in a perfect circle, up top of Hurricane Mountain. I wished it was me and them.

Dory give—gave—me another piece of divinity and sent me back out the door.

I knew I was in for it now. At least Wall had gone and got Lute and had him scraping too, so I could get over next to him and do it. Then they hauled up the hog and throwed him in it again, and then we got him back out and scraped him again. You can't leave him too long in the water, Mamaw said, or the hair will set instead of loosen. Wall took the ax and cut off his head, which rolled a little way and then fetched up against a rock. Its eyes was looking at us. Here came Old Harve with the gambling stick, while Wall cut the hide offen the back legs till the leaders come clean, and they stuck the stick in between the leader and the leg on both hind legs and strung him up on the pole they had put in the trees.

"I don't feel too good," Lute said to me, low-like so nobody else could hear. I didn't feel too good either by then— for one thing I hadn't had nothing to eat since I got up so early except for that divinity, but I wasn't going to allow it, so couldn't nobody use it agin me later. Garner Blankenship, on my other side, was all perked up listening to hear what I'd say. So I never said a thing—it was going on ten o'clock by then, I'd guess—and the Rameys shot another hog while Mamaw made the first cut in the one they had strung up. She slid her eyes over at me first to see if I was watching, and when she saw I was, she cut him. I looked the other way real quick, like I heard something off in the woods, and by the time I looked back, the innards was all in the tub and they was already soaking the liver in the bucket by the spring. Garner had had to take it over there and throw it in. Then they started stripping the first hog, and chopping it up, and they had the second one down in the water, and then they hauled it out and set us to scraping again.

"That's good work, boy," Old Man Justice said to me

when he come by. It made me feel so good, I swear, I quit
listening out for the kids playing down in the yard and
wishing I was there instead of here. I quit looking off in the
woods.

Little Luther, who had been scraping with us, put down
his knife and wiped his hands and went over and got his
guitar. "Rabbit up a gum stump, possum up a holler. Fat gal
down at Sudie's house, fat as she can waller." I laughed
along with the rest of them. Little Luther is kindly a natural
antic, so what if he's not good-looking. I knowed the men
didn't take him serious, though, and not because of his leg.
They was something about his face, I think, the way he
didn't have no chin to speak of and his adam's apple stuck
out in his throat, and something soft around the eyes.
Everybody *liked* him, but you didn't expect much out of
him, I couldn't tell you for why. The way he was follering
Dory around was not a thing, for an instance, that any of
them other men would do. I knowed—knew—it and they
knew it, but I don't know if Little Luther knew it or not. It
was like he was bound to love her, didn't matter what she
did or how she felt about it, there was something there that
rubbed me the wrong way and Mary too. "Head in the
clouds," Mamaw said about Little Luther. She wouldn't give
him too much credit. Me neither, but I liked to hear him
sing.

"If ever I marry in this wide world, it'll be for love, not
riches. Catch a little girl about five feet high and fuck her
through the britches," Little Luther sang.

Lute's eyes went big and he poked me in the side. "You
hear that one?" he said.

Little Luther went on singing a whole bunch of stuff you
don't hear him sing when the womenfolks and girls is
around, now that don't count Mamaw of course nor Granny
Hibbitts. Some of the time they was—were—out there at
the hog-killing and some of the time they were up at the
house getting ready to put up the meat.

While they were up there, Little Luther sung, "Ring-a-
ding-a-doo, Now what is that? Something soft and warm

like a pussycat. With long black hair and split in two, now that, my friend, is the ring-a-ding-a-doo."

Lute punched me in the ribs so hard I liked to drap my knife. I could tell my face was getting hot out there despite of the cold. All the men was looking at us and laughing. Lute's daddy was getting the leaf lard outen the gut and throwing it into the pot on the warming-fire where it set to hissing and popping, rendering is what Mamaw calls it, and afore long I knowed we'd pour off the lard to save it up and then we'd eat the cracklins. My stomach got to hurting, that's how bad I wanted them cracklins, it was like I could taste them already, and Little Luther set in on the verse.

> Lulu the schoolteacher
> Went out West
> To take up fucking
> 'Cause she liked it the best.
> The boys come and the boys went
> The price went down to fifty cent.
> When over the hill from Bare-Ass Creek
> Come the bald-headed bachelor
> Known as Pisspot Pete.

I kept looking down and scraping, with my face not working right. I hated that part about the schoolteacher and also I hated the way Little Luther's little old chin would wobble when he sung, and how he'd grin, the idea of him singing all them dirty words and then making eyes at Dory. I kept looking down and scraping, had no place to lay my eyes. I didn't want to look at Little Luther, nor at none of the other men who was looking at me, nor at Lute, nor most of all at that hog-head fetched up agin the rock.

> Pete had the claps
> And the blue-balls too
> But he took a shot
> At the ring-a-ding-a-doo.

I got to grinning despite of myself. Then I got to laughing, and before I knowed it, I was singing along with the rest.

Ring-a-ding-a-doo,
Now what is that?
Something soft and warm
Like a pussycat.
With long black hairs and split in two—
Now, that, my friends, is the ring-a-ding-a-doo!

I finished up singing loudern Lute. They poured off the lard and all of us got some cracklins. They were the best thing I ever ate in this world, I thought right then while I was eating them, you never tasted nothing so good. I ate them cracklins till I liked to bust, staring that hog-head straight in the eye. Then they sent me up to the house with a bucket of trimmings for the womenfolks to put in the sausage-pots.

On the way up there I walked right through the middle of the kids, still playing all over the yard, and I thought how little they were and how a man don't have time to play. When I got in the kitchen I seen that they had set some of the biggerunses to working in there, grinding up the meat and canning the sausage, and I was glad I didn't have to do that no more neither.

"Mary's been asking for you," Dory said, elbow-deep in sausage in a washtub on the table.

"I got to go right back out there," I said. "I brung you some more trimmings," and I set the bucket down next to the washtub and picked up the empty one to take back with me.

"You orter go in and see Mary," Dory said. "She's doing poorly again."

When Mary does poorly she has these little spells, like a kind of conniption-fit, she'll fall right out in the floor and then wake up and not know a thing about it afterwards. She'll be real tired too, and have to lay down on her mattress-tick, which is what she was doing right then. The fire was going and they had pulled her right up by it to stay warm. Wasn't nobody else in the room except Old Man Little fast asleep and snoring real loud like a engine, and a Davenport girl nursing a baby, and that crazy old Rose Hibbitts over in the corner, talking to herself. I didn't like it a bit for her to be in there with Mary. But I had to get back out.

"Howdy," Mary said when she saw me, and I said howdy back. Then she closed her eyes, it was like she went back to sleep. I couldn't see but her head, she was all tucked in under the bear-paw quilt. So I started backing off.

"Wait," Mary said. She has the littlest voice after she's had one of her falling-out spells. She said something else but I couldn't hear her.

"What?" I said, coming closer.

"Ooh," Mary said. "What-all have you got on your pants?"

I looked down and seen the blood and hog-hairs on my pants legs, where I'd been wiping my hands.

"I've been out there working," I said, "and I've got to get on back."

Rose Hibbitts started talking out loud to herself then, the wildest stuff you ever heard. I was getting too hot from the fire and I started feeling kindly sick-like too, I guess from eating all them cracklins. I didn't see how Mary could stand it to be so close to the fire all wrapped up like she was. It looked to me like she would be burning up. I felt like I had to get out of there fast.

But Mary said, "Read to me, Jink."

"What?" I said, moving back from the fire.

"Read to me," Mary said, and I knew I was stuck for sure. So I went and got Tom Sawyer—Mary loves it about the cave—but when I come back, she had turned her head to the side of her pallet and fallen fast asleep. She breathed in and out, in and out through her open lips, just like one of Dory's babies. I was glad. I was about to die from the heat and I wanted to get on back. So I made for the kitchen lickety-split and run smack into Old Rose Hibbitts, liked to scare me to death, too. I never seen her move from her corner afore I run into her.

"Listen here, boy," she said, "You Almarine." Up close her breath smelled like something that had been dead a week and her eyes was bloodshot and terrible. She couldn't never keep people straight, like the way she thought I was my daddy.

"Now I just got a phone call," she said, "which you orter know about."

Despite of me feeling so hot and sick, it was all I could do not to laugh. We'd all been hearing about Rose Hibbitts and her phone calls, they'd told it from yan to yonder. Seems like Wall Johnson, Lute's daddy, let Old Rose talk on the telephone one time down at the store in Tug, and she taken a fancy to it, and now she thinks she gets these phone calls all the time. Of course she ain't got no phone, and we don't neither.

"I have just received a phone call," she said, old eyes burning into mine, "that you might be interested to know about."

"I got to go," I said, but I couldn't pull loose from her fingers, like sharp little claws fastened into my jacket.

"It was a phone call from hell," said Old Rose. She was breathing right into my face. "A phone call from hell," she went on, "from that red-headed Emmy, that witch you took such a shine to."

"Well, what'd she say?" I asked, since I couldn't get loose and I couldn't think of nothing else to do. Besides I thought I could tell Lute about it, I knowed he would bust a gut laughing.

"She says Dory's the one she has loved all along, and she claims her for sure, and she don't give a damn for a man!" Old Rose spit it out in my face.

Now this taken me aback, it weren't—wasn't—funny at all like I thought. I hate it when folks start up all that stuff about Dory. It made me mad as fire. So I brung up my leg and I kicked Old Rose in the back of her knees, which laid her out face-down on the floor.

"You shouldn't ought've done that," said the Davenport girl.

"Done what?" I said. I had to get out of there. I left with Mary still asleep and Old Rose Hibbitts crying and grubbing around on the floor, I wished she'd of up and died.

But then when I got back out there, the men was telling ghost-tales too. It was like I couldn't get away from what I had to, nevermind which way I'd turn.

"I recall one time back in aught-nine," said a Little, I
disremember which one, and he told about how two witches
got in his cattle and how they acted, how they kicked his old
lady in the side and broke two of her ribs, and then they give
down speckled milk. I wished they would all of them shut
up and get Little Luther to sing some more nasty songs. Little Luther must of gone on up to the house, though, or anyway he wasn't out there when I got back. And Parrot Blankenship had got here now, dressed up fit to kill, the
talkingest man you have ever seen, and they was most of
them gathered around him. I couldn't help but go listen,
myself.

Now Parrot Blankenship was the man who come up here
to court Ora Mae. It surprised us all to death when first he
come. I never thought about Ora Mae ever getting sweet on
anybody, or even about Ora Mae being a girl, which of
course she was, afore Parrot showed up. I thought about Ora
Mae like I thought about Isadore and Nun, say, something
you've got to contend with, or even less than that, like some
walking part of Mamaw that wasn't hooked on, I guess, but
not like a girl like Dory. Wasn't nobody else thought of her
like that neither, nobody around here that is, but Parrot
Blankenship, he was a foreigner, didn't know no better, or if
he did you couldn't prove it. Anyway he was a foreigner,
wouldn't say where he'd been raised up, but he'd tell you
the names of places he'd been, Wheeling and Charleston and
Dayton, Ohio, and Detroit and Cincinnati, he'd roll off them
names so fast like he was a train rolling right through your
head, and his eyes just sparkling. You could not pin him
down to a thing. Nor would he say what he had done for a
living, nor where he bought all them fancy clothes.

"I've got irons in the fire," he used to say, and Mamaw
would snort and spit. She didn't think much of irons in the
fire. But when Parrot talked, Ora Mae stared at him like he
had fallen down offen the moon, it was like she couldn't
never look her fill. Now *she* didn't talk, *he* did. And Ora Mae
would sit there big-eyed, listening. Not a soul could see
what a man like that saw in Ora Mae, and they talked it
around and around. Because Parrot Blankenship was the

kind of man you'd feature with a yellow-haired woman eating in a restaurant someplace, but not here. And he was the only man that had ever come up this mountain and not been taken with Dory. Dory thought Parrot was funny. She'd laugh and laugh when he talked, but Ora Mae didn't crack a smile, just sat real still like a rock which made Parrot talk faster and faster.

So the men were telling ghost-tales, and Parrot had come, and now the men were gathered around him because he was the kind of man that other men just naturally take to. Me too. I liked Parrot, everbody did. You couldn't hardly help it, even if you never knowed a thing about all them irons in the fire.

"Well now I'll tell you about witchery," Parrot said. "Hit was a hot hot summer one time I was working over in Doran, West Virginia. I took a room with a widder lady reputed to be a witch. But I was young then, and full of piss and vinegar, and I thought not a thing of that." Everbody nodded, and Lute and I was back to scraping, and I nodded too. "I was too young to listen to what I should've," Parrot went on. When Parrot tells a story, you can't help believing it's every word true, like the way he'll throw off on hisself instead of building hisself up bigger, and look you in the eye, and grin at how dumb he was. You can't help liking a feller like that.

"Now I did notice that the widder lady's horse was acting right peculiar. When I come there he was a big old roan horse, full of spirit, liked to kicked the side outen the barn and used to gallop around the pasture. But the longer I stayed with the widder lady, the more tuckered out he commenced to look, and come the time he couldn't hardly make it around the pasture one time. Nothing but a shadow of what he was, and the light had gone from his eye. Well, I didn't think nothing of it at the time, just remarked it, and I went on about my business."

Which was what? I wondered, but I kept quiet, and Parrot went on.

"Then one day I was coming home from work and I seen a big lump out in the pasture, and I went over there to look, and sure enough it was that big roan horse laying dead with the flies all over him. When I got close up, I seen what I could not see before—he was down to naught but skin and bones, the skinniest horse I ever laid eyes on, and I marveled at how he had lived as long as he had. Then I looked up— there was one pine tree out there, in the middle of that pasture—and seen three black crows sitting on a single limb of that tree watching me. 'Shoo!' I hollered then, but they never moved, and I have to tell you, that spooked me for fair. So I took off, and went on back to the widder's house, and never said a word about what I'd seen. I went right on straight to bed and I slept like a rock the whole night long.

"Well, boys, the next morning I woke up, and I hurt so bad all over, it was all I could do to get outen the bed. Seemed like my arms and my legs was so heavy I couldn't hardly move 'em, and I was still dead for sleep. So I got up and went along to work anyway, but I wasn't worth a damn all that day nor the next, when the same thing happened over again. But the third night, I figgered it out."

Parrot Blankenship had every one of us right in the palm of his hand by then. The women were hollering out the door for more trimmings, but wasn't nobody about to answer nor to fetch them any till Parrot was through.

"I went to bed early, same as usual, I was so tired by then, but then I woke up in the middle of the night with the awfulest ache in my side, I thought I might have the appendix. But when I looked at my side I seen it was a horse's side, and they was a woman's foot kicking bloody spurs into it."

"Aw, shoot, Parrot," Peter Paul said, but Parrot grinned and went on.

"And then I commenced to notice I had four legs instead of two, and that they was horse's legs, and the reason I couldn't seem to catch my breath atall was because they was somebody on me riding hell-for-leather up a rocky mountain trace, and kicking my side all the way. So then I pricked up my ears—I had these big old horse ears, you know—and I heard more horses galloping behind me, and I swiveled my head around to look, and sure enough here come two more horses and riders behind me, the riders all dressed in black and bent low to the saddle, and my rider sawed back on the bit, liked to broke my jaw, and hit me across the flanks. 'Git on,' come the voice, and then I knowed it was the widder on my back.

"Well they urged us on till I just about drapped in my tracks, and finally we come up to a cave in the mountain and they reined us in at last. My legs and my flanks was quivering so I couldn't hardly stand, but I took enough notice to see what it was that they was a-doing, and why they had rode us here.

"They had two saddle-bags apiece, and they swung them down now offen us and placed them in the cave, and by the weight of them and how they clanked I could tell they was full of money. So I just snorted and pawed at the ground, and acted like I didn't notice, and after a while the three of them come back outen the cave. The other two was men, as mean a-looking men as ever you hope to see, one with a scar come all the way acrost his face like this"—Parrot drew a scar acrost his face—"and the other one missing three fingers on his left hand. So they all mounted up and rode us home. And the next morning, fellers, when I woke up I was stiff as a board and I knew she'd kill me before she was through if I couldn't do naught to outsmart her.

"So I laid out of work that day and went downtown to get my breakfast, and while I was in there eating, I heard them all talking about the bank robberies taking place in that section, and how they'd had three in a row so far, and the sheriff with nary a clue. Well, I didn't say a word to that, mind you, or act like I was interested atall, I just ate my ham and biscuits with nary a word, but I was turning it all in my mind and before I knowed it, I'd come up with what I was going to do, fellers, I'd made me a plan."

Lute and I were so busy listening we'd forgot to scrape.

"Well, they never come that night, nor the next, nor the one after that, I slept like the dead for the next three nights, and then on the fourth night when I woke up with that piercing pain from them spurs digging into my side, I was fit as a fiddle and ready."

"What'd you do?" Lute asked.

But Parrot held up his hand and said, "Son, I'm getting to that. I wanted that money, you see, I wanted to know how to get back there, and so all the way up the mountain that night I made out like I'd gone lame and I stumbled, and the widder woman cursing me every step of the way, but what she didn't know was that I was blazing the trail with my hooves, kicking over rocks and stripping the bark offen bushes and trees, so come morning I could find my way to return. Well, we got up there and sure enough there was the cave, and sure enough they all jumped down and pulled off the saddle-bags and ran in the cave. And I was determined to mark the spot. Now how can I do it, I thought to myself, so I can be sure to find it come daylight? Because that cave was fairly hid in the brushy-thicket, you couldn't even tell it was there if you didn't know. The only time you could see it atall was when they pulled back the brush, you could see the opening. I knowed I could never tell it without no mark.

"So I thought to myself, and I thought to myself, and I thought, 'Parrot, now how can you mark this spot?' and then I got an idea. I screwed up my vitals as hard as I could and laid a big old pile of shit right there outside that brushy thicket and then I worked loose from where she had tied me and I trotted over there to the brushy thicket and pushed through with my nose until I had got my head inside that cave. And you won't believe what happened next."

"*What?*" I don't know if it was me said it, or maybe Lute said it, or maybe we said it together. Wasn't nobody saying another word, everbody crowding right around Parrot to hear what was coming next.

Parrot made his voice go real low and scary, you had to cock your head to hear what he said.

"I stuck my head in that cave like I said, and it was hot in there, which surprised me, and it had a funny smell to it, and it was black as the blackest night you have ever seen or ever imagined in all your life. And then I heard this voice, this real loud voice hollering at me. It said"—Parrot hollered too— "Parrot Blankenship, Parrot Blankenship, you'll be sorry for what you done!

"And then I woke up, boys, and I was in the widder's bed

with my face in her crack, and I had done benastied my-self!"

It took me a minute to get it, and then I started laughing so hard I drapped my knife. All the men was—were—fit to be tied, laughing and slapping their legs, and Wall was fanning his face with his big black hat. This went on for a while, and it took a while before we got back to the hog-killing. We were on the last one by now, the Davenports stringing him up.

"Now boys." Peter Paul Ramey went and stood in front of the last hog—the hog was still so hot from being scalded in the drum that he was throwing out steam from his whole body, steaming out white in the cold air—"You come on over here, boys," Peter Paul said, and me and Lute got up and went over there, and I didn't know what was fixing to happen.

Peter Paul stuck out his hand with the hog knife in it, handle turned to me, and said, "You cut this one, boy," and he told Lute to catch the innards in the tub and to scrape out what did not come natural. I knowed I was fixing to disgrace us all, and be sick or fall out on the ground like Mary in one of her fits, and I looked around quick but thank God anyway Mamaw was up at the house. They must of been ten or eleven men between me and the house, so there wasn't no running thataway, and nothing behind me but Hoot Owl Mountain and I guess I knew already I couldn't go up there and stay for good like I'd thought about for so long, me and Dory and Mary and him. All the men were breathing out white in the air and grinning.

"Start right here," Peter Paul said, pointing, and I knew there was nothing for it but to do it.

So I drawed in my breath and got the knife around the handle with both hands and raised my hands above my head and jabbed it in as hard as I could and pulled it down as far as I was able, and all of them innards came tumbling and quiling out and the men were hollering and laughing, and Lute cotched them up in the tub. Then Peter Paul grabbed up a piece of innards and throwed it around my neck like a rope and one around Lute's neck too, it was hot as fire and

smelled awful, and I got mad then and yelled out and
throwed it straight back at Peter Paul. I didn't care what
happened. Lute throwed his down on the ground and
stomped on it, and then the men were whooping and slapping us both on the back and we all started drinking liquor.

I tipped my head back and took it down like it was water,
and it felt like it burned a path right down my gut, or like
somebody had slit me right down the middle the way I had
done that hog, Old Man Justice said he had never seen a
cleaner cut. I must of got drunk then, I don't recall too much
of the rest of the afternoon, but Lute and me and the other
men drunk some more and finished off that hog and then
some of them went home and some of them went on up to
the house to eat. I was on my way up to the house too, last I
remember, it was well-nigh dark and I was walking up that
way when I had to piss so I went off in the woods and then
the first thing I recall, I woke right up in the pitch dark with
no notion of where I was, nor who I was, nor whether it was
night or day, nor nothing. Then I heard Mamaw calling my
name, so I knew who I was, and then it all come back to me
and I leaned over and puked till I liked to puked up my guts.
I got up—my legs were still real wobbly, the way a foal is
the first time it stands—and made my way outen the woods
and on up to the house.

"Jink! You Jink!" Mamaw hollered out the back door, but
I never answered her back. I went around to the front and
walked in where they had a fire and some several still there
sitting around it, and Little Luther strumming on his guitar
and Dory sitting close by him.

"Everbody's been looking for you, Jink," Dory said to me
when I come in. "Honey, where you been?" But Dory never
took her eyes offen Little Luther, and I could tell she didn't
care where I'd been, and I could tell she had softened up toward him now.

So I went on up to the loft and looked at Mary, fast asleep
on the tick next to mine, it was kindly dark up there but I
still could see Mary's face, and leaned down to see was she
breathing, she looked so poorly. Mamaw was yelling out my

name, but I would of died before I'd of gone down there now.

I hated them ever one. I laid down and looked out through the dark and the firelight shadows up in the beams and then I got up after while and looked down and Dory and Little Luther was kissing, or I thought they was but the fire had got so low you couldn't tell, or I couldn't, I guess I was crying too, and me a man, and I hated them ever one worse than ever and I could see all their faces out there in the dark and they was ever one of their faces black. So I got up and went over in the corner where I had it wrapped up in a old torn shirt stuck down in the tore-up bed tick. It was dried as hard as a rock but I could feel the little dents in it all over and I knowed—knew—it had come from Florida in the South, and in the dark I made like it was still bright orange, as orange as it was when he give them out, as orange as the sun when it come up that morning and as round as Dory's belly used to be, as round as the whole big globe of the earth he had, and I thought to myself how I'd up and leave here after while, me and Mary we'd up and leave and strike out walking as far as we could get acrost the big round world.

Ora Mae

If I hadn't of been like I am, Parrot never would of loved me, and if I hadn't of been like I am, he never would of left me neither. And I don't know to this day which one was worse—the loving or the leaving—and I don't care. He picked me a-purpose to fit his needs, never knowing he fit mine, too. But you do what you have to do, I say. It's not a lot of choices in the world.

I wisht I didn't know what-all I know, nor have to do

what-all I have to. Seems like it's been that way ever since I can remember, I've been working my knuckles straight down to the bone taking care of Cantrells.

Since I was a little girl and I come here with Mamaw, all them years ago but it don't seem that long to me, I swear it don't. It's like you close your eyes and its five years gone, and you blink again and it's ten.

But I remember that day just as plain. We come up the trace and it was raining, and I started hanging back. "Come on, Ora Mae," Mamaw said, yanking at my hand at first and then switching my legs when I wouldn't come. So I come on—nothing else to do, me naught but a little girl—and the farther I come, the more I felt these mountains closing in, and by the time I got up to the house it was like they had closed up in a circle around me. Even before he opened the door and I seen him, I knowed we was there to stay. I knowed I would never leave, and I won't, I'll be right here to the end of my days in Hoot Owl Holler. I know what I know but I wisht I didn't, I've got the gift you don't never want to have. Rhoda said it when I was not but nine or ten, and she was right. I didn't want it then and I don't now. There's folks think they've got it, like Ludie Davenport, say, but by and large they don't know a thing.

Rhoda called me to her oncet a long while back when she was laid up in the bed sick and there was a baby up on Snowman Mountain that had the thrash.

"That baby has not been able to suck for three days running," Rhoda said. "Its mouth is naught but a sore."

"Don't tell me," I told her, but Rhoda said, "I am. I have knowed you since you was a girl, Ora Mae, and we both of us knows what you know. It's high time you got a move on. Now I am a-laying here in the bed with a foot swole up like a punkin, and somebody has got to go on up there and do it. Its daddy is waiting outside."

I went over and looked out the door and sure enough he was out there, smoking cigarettes and stomping his feet in the mud with his horse tied up to a tree, didn't look hardly old enough to have no child.

"Get Rose to go," I said for meanness, and Rhoda said,

"Don't talk like a fool." Rose was in the next room slobbering and mumbling, Rhoda had to keep her in the house by then.

I walked around looking at Rhoda's house and all the stuff people bring her, and looking out the door at that boy by the tree. Rhoda had a little old monkey that smoked these trick cigarettes, somebody had brung it back to her from a trip. Another thing she had was a red velvet cake, which I have always been partial to. I got me a piece and sat down in the chair by the bed and ate it.

"You are a hard one, Ora Mae," Rhoda said, watching me eat that cake. Then she sighed a long rattling sigh, trying to make me feel sorry for her, but I was wise to her tricks, I know all the tricks there is, from dealing with Cantrells. I got me another piece of cake and some apple cider.

"If I *was* to go up there," I said, "just supposing I was, what-all would I have to do?" Of course I didn't have no intention of going.

"It takes a woman that never knowed her daddy," Rhoda said, "and that is you, and you breathe in its mouth while you say the three most powerful names, and that'll get it. It ain't hard."

"And I ain't a-gonna do it neither," I said, getting up. "And don't you send for me no more, neither. I ain't a-gonna do it now and I ain't a-gonna do it never," I said. "You can just forget it." And I went over and yelled out at that boy he could ride on home. He whooped and hollered and said his baby would die, but I said it wouldn't. "You can just relax," I said, and when he wouldn't leave, I closed Rhoda's door and locked it for good measure, and finally he rode on off, and it didn't die, neither, just like I said. But I wouldn't of gone if it had.

When I went back in where Rhoda was, she was sitting straight up in the bed with little old spots of red on her cheeks like rouge on a whore.

"Sit down," she said, and I said I had to go, and she said it again and I sat.

"You are courting damnation," she said. Old Rhoda was a pitiful sight sitting up in the bed with her veins showing blue in her forehead. "You know what Jesus said of the talents," Rhoda said.

"Don't talk religion to me," I said. "I don't believe in no heaven, or no hell. I don't believe in a thing," I said, and Rhoda said, "Then I'm sorry for you. Because you'll end up one of the damned, Ora Mae, as sure as we're a-sitting here in this room. Now listen to me. If you've got a gift and you don't use it, it'll turn on you, mark my words. If you keep it inside it'll eat you alive from the inside out."

"You're a crazy old woman," I said. "I know where Rose gets it now."

"May God have mercy on your soul." Rhoda rolled her eyes up to the ceiling like she was dying, but I know every trick in the book.

"Ain't no God," I said. "Because ain't no God can account for Rose nor Mary, nor what I have to put up with day by day. What-all I have to do."

"Ora Mae, Ora Mae!" Here old Rhoda got all wrought up and stretched out her hands to me over the covers. "You're *young*, Ora Mae, you're just a girl, and you're a pretty girl, too"—that was a lie, Dory was the pretty girl—"and it ain't never too late to change. Honey, come here," Old Rhoda said, but I throwed my apron up over my head and run straight out of the house, wouldn't say another word to Rhoda from then on until she died. Because already I knowed what I knowed, and I knowed what I had to do. If it wasn't for me those Cantrells would of fell apart years and years back, and Mamaw couldn't of made it without me, she's said it again and again and it is true, I'm the only one she favors, you see why. Still, in my dreams some nights I'd see old Rhoda holding out her hands and saying "Honey," and I'd wake up all in a sweat and directly I'd git mad as a wet hen.

Rhoda didn't seem to understand that I had my hands full. Parrot, come to think on it, didn't neither.

I had my hands full of Cantrells.

You might think it was Mary, since she was so sick, or Jink who was naturally bad, but it was Dory that was the worstest one of them all. Dory was born without a lick of sense and I'll swear it, I don't know what would of happened to Dory if I hadn't come along, not a brain in her head. And stubborn! You can't tell Dory a thing and you never could. In one ear and out the other! All you can do is foller her around and pick up the pieces, all you ever could do. Not a notion of how the world is, or people, I've told her a million times. Took up with that schoolteacher, and I said not to, and look where it got her. Two loaves of bread in the oven, I said, and the cook is out to lunch. Ha! I said, but she never listened, or anyway she never listened to me, and now her and Little Luther's got two more besides and she won't listen to me any moren she ever has, I don't know what she'd do if I wasn't here to help out. Spoil them rotten I reckon, giving them bubblegum and painting their toenails, and taking up with whatever comes by wearing pants, like she always has, and expect Little Luther to put up with it which he always does. It makes me sick.

"You've got a good man," I told her the other day, she wasn't even listening, looking down that road, I'll swear she's a sight in the world.

"If I had a husband like him," I started, and all of a sudden she fired back right sharp.

"You could of."

"What?" I said. We was stringing beans out on the porch in the late afternoon, over at her and Luther's.

"Yes, you could of," Dory said. "You could've married Parrot and don't say you couldn't've, you know it's true, Ora Mae."

She turned to me then with the beans in her lap and her eyes got so blue they were awful. Mostly it's like Dory's got something else on her mind all the time, no matter what-all she's doing. "Why didn't you?" Dory asked.

Just like her!

Parrot asked me the same again and again. "Why not?" he'd ask over and over. People like Parrot and Dory don't know a thing. *Why not?* they say, instead of *Why?* They don't understand that there is some people in the world that can't just go around doing whatever the hell they want to. It's like I said to Rhoda, way way back: it's not any heaven, and it's not any hell. All it is, is what you have to do, and you have to do what you have to.

But Parrot—Lord God. I've been thinking on Parrot ever since last week when we was stringing them beans and she brung him up again outen the years between now and then, where he'd be better off kept.

Well, Parrot. Things was not clear in my mind before Parrot, in a crazy way it is like he done me a favor and now I know what it was. Anyway when I met Parrot I was twenty-four years old, no spring chicken by a long shot, and every day was like the one before it and the one that would come after that, and it suited me fine. Almarine dead, and the boys gone and Dory pregnant—I didn't want no more surprises. Oh, I knew they'd come along anyway, Cantrells being what they are, but right then I had my hands full taking care of Dory, and me and Mamaw was working the garden, we had too much to do already.

I went down to the store for seed and there he stood.

Parrot Blankenship was the unlikeliest-looking man, you never saw the beat of him. When I come in the store, he was leaned up against the counter with a catalogue open between him and Old Man Poole, talking a mile a minute. Old Man Poole was rubbing his glasses on a rag and shaking his head *no*, well you might as well have said no to the wind.

"Let's just ask this little lady right here!" Parrot said.

I didn't have time to take in a thing but that curly yellow hair and the mustache that didn't hide the crooked mouth, nor all of them teeth, you never saw so many white teeth on a white man.

I stopped dead in the floor where I was.

"Howdy, Ora Mae," said Old Man Poole.

I started to turn around and go right back out that door, but Parrot had grabbed me by the elbow and gotten me over to the counter where the catalog was.

"Now if this store was to carry a real pretty line of ready-to-wear," Parrot said—he had a voice just like a preacher—"wouldn't you come in here and buy something from time to time?"

"He means dresses and such, Ora Mae," said Old Man Poole.

I didn't say nothing. Parrot and me was as different as night and day. I looked down at that catalog and saw those fancy ladies in fancy dresses and one of them, I'll never forget it, down in the right-hand corner standing with her hand on her hip in her underwear! And Dory made all of our clothes.

"No," I said, "now let go of my arm or I'll shoot you." I made like to go in my purse.

"This is Ora Mae Cantrell and I guess she means it," said Old Man Poole.

"Pleased to meet you," said Parrot.

"Let go of my arm," I said, and he let go but he throwed back his head and laughed that big laugh like he didn't give a damn. And then he turned and watched me go, I could feel his eyes drilling holes in my back all the way out the door, I was mad as fire. I knew he'd come courting me as sure as I was born, and he did.

He come up the mountain the next day bringing me some flowers—did you ever see the beat of a man like that?—and Mamaw a calendar, and Dory a green glass necklace, and the kids a sack of rock candy. You could tell he'd found us out from Old Man Poole. I took the flowers and throwed them to the hogs, I said, "You'll have to do better than that." Which he did. The next time he brung me a brand-new hand mixer. "It's better than nothing," I said. Oh I was just as mean as I could be. "You'll not make a fool out of me," I told him right to his face, and ever time he'd come, I'd have something I had to do, I wouldn't talk to him hardly, or talk to any of them people he sent up here to talk to me. Why you would of thought Parrot was born and raised up right here, the way he settled in and took up with them all. Talk? Talk you to death. Wore a checkered suit and a yellow tie.

Finally I took a walk with him just to shut him up—it was getting spring by then—and we went up Grassy into the woods and when we got up there far enough he grabbed ahold of me and started kissing me like crazy, that mustache

all over my face. I knowed what he was after, all along. I
didn't care by then, neither. At least when he was kissing,
he'd shut up. I hadn't ever had a man then neither, or not
really a man, you can't count Nun and Bill and how you just
fool around, nor even Hutch that time on the hayride over at
the Breaks and he didn't know which hole to put it in. I
didn't know neither.

Well, this was not a problem for Parrot. We laid down by
the bend of the creek and he went right to it, and it weren't
too bad nor was it nothing special, and when we got done, I
said, "Well, I guess you got what you was after. I guess you
can go on back to wherever you come from, and get on back
to doing whatever it is you do, and quit bothering me to
death."

"Hell fire, Ora Mae." Parrot sat up and started putting his
clothes on. He had real white skin with freckles all over, and
thought he was God's gift to women. "Don't you feel a
thing?"

"Nope," I said. This was not quite true, but I was not
about to let on to Parrot.

"I can have any woman I want," Parrot said. He was
stomping all around like a bantam rooster, getting dressed.
"I don't have to fool with you."

"Then don't," I said.

"Goddammit, I won't!" he hollered, and took off, but you
know he kept coming back.

I was the only one that didn't want him, he told Wall. He
said to them all that he'd never get over me. This was why
he was so taken with me, and the only reason, because Parrot
Blankenship had had women all over the place and I was the
only one he'd run acrost he couldn't have. Oh I fucked him,
I'm not saying that, I liked to fucked his eyes out as a matter
of fact, but it didn't mean to me what it means to most and
that riled him up. I came around some, I got to where I liked
it alright, but I would just as soon not do it as do it, and he
knowed that.

"You're driving me crazy," he said. We was up in the
room he rented from Mrs. Smoot and she was in Bluefield at
a Baptist Ladies Auxiliary Convention. It was pouring the

rain outside, June rain, steamy, it smelled like grass. "You know that, girl?" Parrot said. He laid in the bed smoking and I just laid there. "It's like going on some kind of a trip with you."

"What kind of a trip?" I said. Parrot had crazy ideas, they just popped out all the time he talked so much.

"The kind of a trip where you keep going and going and you never get there," Parrot said, and then I understood. I know a lot more than I want to, I said it already, it's true. And I knowed that Parrot Blankenship had got so took up with me because he was a traveling man, and I wasn't going noplace. As soon as I got it straight I turned my face to the wall in Mrs. Smoot's house and starting crying. For one goddamn time in his life, Parrot didn't say a thing. He put out his cigarette and rolled over to me and kissed me all over my body.

"Come on and go to Charleston with me," Parrot said after while, still kissing me. "I've got some irons in the fire over there," he said. He said he had to see a man about a prospect—Parrot was always dealing in prospects—"Let's get out of this hick town," he said. "I'll get you some clothes."

I kept on crying because it was like I seen the mountains all around me open up there for a minute, and I seen Charleston, and me over there with him and all dressed up, I knowed I could go if I wanted. I knowed he would take me, he really would, but iffen I'd of gone over there with him, I knowed he would leave me later, as sure as the world. I hate what-all I know. I kept on crying, but I laid there just as still while he kept kissing me on my shoulders and my breasts and my belly, every damn place, I laid there just as still while he did it, and every kiss burned like fire on my skin, I can feel them kisses yet if I've got a mind to.

Which I don't. I've got my hands full of Cantrells who can't do a thing without me. At least since Mary died and Jink left, it's two more gone. But I've got plenty left to contend with. Mamaw down in the bed, poor Little Luther down in the mine, and Dory off down the road half the time with whatever the cat drags in, those children would of been

dead by now if it wasn't for me and that's a fact. And
Mamaw now she's so old acts just like a baby again, big
strong woman like she was, you wouldn't believe it. Poor old
thing has gone as mealy-mouthed as the rest of them. Lays
in the bed and I have to bring her everything, she has to
have a glass of water right there on the night table just so, if
you put it on the wrong side she'll yell and you have to get
up and go move it. And if you fill it up too full you have to
get up and go pour some out. Well I could go on but I won't,
you have to do what you have to. But it seems like it's no
time passed since she was out there killing them hogs and
working the field, and not a streak of gray in her long black
hair. Nobody fooled with Mamaw then, and nobody fools
with me now. That's the way it is. And Parrot Blankenship
is someplace loose in the world, and he never got over me. I
know it, but knowing it don't help a bit. Still sometimes I
think and I wonder, well what if I *had* give Dory that note,
and what if she had gone off to Richmond? She wouldn't
have had her such a fine husband she don't deserve, for one
thing. Or what if I had gone off with Parrot, even knowing
what I knowed? Who would of took care of Mary and
Mamaw and all the rest? I'm all they've got.

Richard Burlage Discourses Upon the Circumstances Concerning His Collection of Appalachian Photographs, c. 1934.

I parked my automobile carefully in front of the bank,
wrapped my new English scarf about my neck and put on
my hat, adjusting it in the mirror. The scarf and the hat

were important to me, affording—or so I thought—a kind of disguise. The mustache helped, too. And the mirror pleased me because of its frame, the way it entrapped my image and framed it so nicely, reassuring me again that here was a new man, a confident man, so different from the boy who had left here ten years back. Even my eyes were different: no longer startled and wild, but melancholy and wise in the mirror's frame, betraying a knowledge beyond my years. And why not? I mused upon the singular pain to which I had been privy in these hills. Now I returned as a mature man, an artist, having in that interim deserted literature for the relatively new field of photography—this vocation, in fact, having occasioned my present visit. For I wished—foolish notion—to capture a bit of the past. I checked my film, my lenses. I stepped out into the cold clear light of early mountain spring, and turned to lock the door.

A crowd of little boys had gathered around my automobile, giggling and poking at each other, yet retaining still that judgmental solemnity I always found so unsettling among the mountain youngsters.

"Hey mister," one of them said. "Hey mister, how much you pay for that car?"

Glancing up and down the narrow, rutted street, I noted then that mine was the only new automobile among all those parked cars and battered muddy trucks which lined it. The pale sunlight glinted somehow obscenely off the outstretched wings of the silver eagle on the hood.

"Hey mister, you gotta nickel?" The boys kicked at my tires. I considered asking them not to, yet refrained from so doing when they were joined by several older friends, lean and hard-faced, who hung back against the bank's streaked marble façade and gathered beneath the green-striped flapping awning of Stinson's Pharmacy next door. The possibility of an unpleasant incident dawned on me. I smiled uncertainly, I hoped disarmingly, in the general direction of them all, checking my camera again, for these fellows were nothing if not picturesque.

"Hey mister, take my picture! Hey mister, looky here!" The little boys went into a frenzy.

"You'll have to stand very still then," I told them, focusing, relieved to have diverted their attention away from the automobile. "Stand still," I repeated.

"Like this?" one said, pushing another, so that three of them fell in a struggling heap until one sat up bawling, with a bloody nose.

I snapped the shutter.

This photograph caught the boy sitting flat in the muddy street, legs stretched out straight before him so that one can plainly see the hole in the sole of his shoe and how it has been patched with cardboard—"Hoover leather," they call it—the boy digging one fist into his face crying, his expression one of anger and loss so extreme as to be obviously inappropriate to the momentary injustice which occasioned it, blood running down from his torn nose into his mouth and dribbling back out the corner of his mouth, his other hand with its pudgy fingers splayed childishly in the dirt. I captured this boy in the foreground, sharp relief: even the patches on his overalls stand out. Behind him, blurred and grinning, stand the other boys and the shiny new automobile, an incongruous, ironic juxtaposition!

The other photographs I made that day captured beautifully, I feel, the essence of that mountain town in those depressing times, including, as they did, the following:

—The older boys, bashful and hateful, in a sullen row before the bank with its boarded-up windows and doors. A skinny rat-faced dog walks out the side of this photograph, one of the boys kicking at it but kicking with his foot only, body stiff and unmoving, no expression on his face except for that ominous squint they all have, squinting straight into the sun.

—An old man, stooped and worn, leaning on his cane in front of the new monument to the WWI dead which the V.F.W. had put up in front of the courthouse. The monument, white and shining, the old man gray, shades of gray deepening to the final dark blur of his face beneath the lowered black brim of his hat.

—A store window empty except for a glassy-eyed naked

doll, rampantly blond, with one eye wildly open and one eye flatly closed with its uniform black-brush lashes lying flat against its dimpled cheek, several pieces of chipped, flowered china, a messy pile of clothes in the corner, and a sign that says "Out of Buisness" (sic!).

—A young mother sitting patiently on the curb waiting for somebody as if she has all day or perhaps all month to wait, which perhaps she has, a filthy squirming barefoot baby on her lap, her plaid dress torn at the armpit, her eyes huge and dark and tubercular and staring straight into the camera, her lips parted slightly as if to utter something she cannot articulate, something which I feel I captured, nonetheless, in this photograph.

After I had knocked for at least five minutes—the place still looked open, at any rate, if run-down—Justine Poole herself unlocked the door. Justine had grown hugely, grossly fat in these lean years, shrewd eyes nearly hidden within their bulging pouches of fat, a series of chins cascading down into some kind of billowing Chinese robe. The lobby behind her lay furred in shadow, drapery drawn, the desk empty.

I stood stunned, blinking in the light on the threshold.

"Richard," Justine said promptly. "You haven't changed a bit." I confess I was taken aback!

I professed gallantly, "Nor have you," as it seemed the thing to say, but she threw back her head at this and laughed uproariously, the old Justine, and flung open the door.

I seated myself on a maroon velvet wing chair I remembered, terrible tufted imitation velvet, and took the liquor she brought me in a glass which looked none too clean although it was difficult to tell, the lobby being so full of shadow, and the room itself seemed larger than it had been. Emptier. Yet I felt we were not alone; indistinct murmurings reached my ears from time to time, muffled footsteps above. The light was of course insufficient for me to make photographs and I felt suddenly disoriented, or perhaps it was the effect of the liquor after the long hard drive. Justine spoke at length of what had happened since I left.

"You'll hear folks say hell, it don't make hardly no difference"—she referred to the Depression which she had already characterized as "old Hoover's fault"—"and for them
in the hollers it's true, I reckon, you know how things was
up there all along"—I nodded in agreement—"but down
here in town it's a different story. You see them banks
closed? and such as that? I could tell you stories after stories,
like old Ludie Davenport whose husband, God rest his soul,
finally died after lingering all those years, and so she sold the
farm hit'll be two year ago come April, and got a pretty
penny for it, all that bottom land, and then she come into
town and put every cent of that sixteen-hundred dollars into
the Miners and Merchants Bank, and two days later it closed
down flat, there's lots of stories I could tell you, Richard. . . ."

In the gloom, Justine's rustling form billowed and spread
on the chaise longue, growing larger and larger, it seemed to
me, while her voice grew more and more indistinct and
seemed to be floating away. I wondered if she was drunk.

"Ah," she said finally, after telling me that the best she
could do these days was to give hobos a room in exchange
for chopping wood, and telling me how she had to cook rab-
bits and how she had to make coffee out of roasted sweet potatoes, information so first-hand as to make me—I admit
it—distinctly uneasy, as, indeed, this whole conversation
made me uneasy what with the occasional murmuring
sounds and a girl's high sudden giggle coming from nowhere
out of the stories above us and then nothing, a hush, except
for Justine's whispery recital of hard times.

"Ah," she said, pouring more whiskey into my glass then
leaning forward, a monstrous effort, "you want to know
whatever happened to Dory Cantrell."

I felt the liquor flaming up inside me, burning out my
whole stomach suddenly so that I was unable to speak. I felt
again exactly as I had felt then, caught fast in the grip of
something I had thought (hoped) was dead. It seemed that
the years burned away to reduce me to what I was then,
red-hot flame and ash, awful and elemental: I fought to
maintain my carefully wrought control.

"Oh, not necessarily," I said.

Justine Poole laughed her huge and genuine laugh. *"Not necessarily!"* she mimicked me, and for an instant I hated her, and became unreasonably frightened of her, and offended. I stood to take my leave.

I had opened my mouth to say something appropriately chilling, something to the effect that I am happily married thank you to the daughter of an Episcopal bishop, a woman wise and warm and intelligent beyond my wildest dreams, that I am the father of two handsome children etc., when I heard loud deliberate steps descending and I turned, hat in hand, to see who it might be. A coarse-looking man of about fifty, wearing overalls and a thick dark suit coat, walked heavily through the dim lobby and out the front door. He did not speak or nod to Justine or myself.

Disconcerted, I sat back down abruptly.

"She married Luther Wade, Richard." Justine's voice came to me through the wake which I imagined the man had made through the lobby's still, dusty air. "She's a wife now, with a husband better than most, and children, and you are not to go up there and bother her any more. They live in the Blackey coal camp up in the holler that used to be Granny Younger's, if you want to know that. Now you can go on back to Richmond and stay there." Justine's words hung in the air like the dust. Of course she was right. Still, I had thought I might give Dory some money perhaps, and I had hoped—oh God, what *had* I hoped? I felt as much of a fool as ever. I had been inspired to make this trip by a passage from *Ecclesiastes.* Oh God!

Justine struggled to heave herself up from the chaise longue. Her ankles, I saw, remained as white and tiny as ever, and I wondered how they could possibly support her.

"Take care of yourself," she enjoined, enveloping me in a hug from which I feared I might never recover. She was so huge and soft it was like embracing a cloud and sinking down and down into it; she smelt of liquor, nicotine, and cheap perfume and powder—loose powder, the kind one finds for sale in dime stores. I broke free at last and gave her soft fat hands a final squeeze, wondering, queasily, if I would bruise them. She sank back onto the chaise.

"Oh yes," I said, turning back at the door. "Aldous. Do you think I could find him at home right now?"

Justine laughed low in her throat; I fancied she had misunderstood the question.

"Aldous," I said, louder, and Justine said, "Dead."

"He's been dead for seven years now," she said in her whispery voice, "and if you go out the way he went, you'll be a lucky man, Richard—a lucky man."

Thus I departed, shaken, buoyed out the door on the wave of her ghostly laughter. *Dead!* I shook my head to clear it and gulped cold air, astounded at the brightness of the day and at the very fact that it *was* still day, still February, after all. Dead. Full of fiery unmanageable energy then, I adjusted my camera and clicked away rapidly, framing everything:

—The peeling door as Justine closed it, her puffy fingers visible around its edge, the rest of her a great unseen burgeoning presence within the dark slit which is all that is left now of the interior of the Smith Hotel, façade merely, in this photograph of the door.

—A blank bottom-story window with its shade drawn tightly down, white woodwork and white shade in the pale flat glare of the sun.

—The corner porch viewed from an odd angle so that the hanging swing appears to be in motion, although empty. An overturned flowerpot spilling earth in the foreground on the corner of the porch. And Justine's foolish forsythia, wildly ahead of its time, blooming enthusiastically in the muddy dirt by the front steps, the only intricate thing and in fact the only living thing in this photograph of flat surfaces, square angles, diminishing planes.

—And finally, the long view, which I gained from a vantage point in the middle of the busy street where I was almost (twice) run down while I made this picture: the whole of the Smith Hotel, the Gothic lettering on the small sign in its window still an anomaly, promising something quaint or charming, something clearly not present here, the whole hotel rising flat and white up from its tiny wrecked yard, porch on the side like an afterthought, a joke perpetrated by somebody who had once been somewhere else, the illogical forsythia down in the corner of the photograph, Black Rock Mountain behind, no sky—and then, on the second story, the surprise: that far left window with the shade momentarily raised and the two girls in their white slips pressed giggling against the glass, their breasts flattened against it, their bare white shoulders indistinct in the gloom behind them.

I confess I leaped for my magnifying glass when, upon development, these girls emerged! They were quite a shock to me, validating somehow my theory of photography if not life itself: the way a frame, a photograph, can illumine and enlarge one's vision rather than limit it. Frankly, I find in this theory an *apologia* for the settled life, for the lovely woman I have married who manages things so well yet understands the worth of my artistic pursuits.

This photograph, one of the best, I entitled "Whorehouse, c. Hard Times."

Although it was three o'clock already and I knew all too well how soon the sun set there, I found myself unable to leave without photographing, at least, Hoot Owl Mountain, and the schoolhouse at Tug, and the store (although I had no desire to encounter Wall!), Grassy Creek perhaps: I was obsessed by capturing these scenes. It proved slow going, however, the road treacherous, wide enough for only one vehicle at a time, but, thank God, there was truly a road, at least! Everything that had happened to me seemed to have happened a million years ago, or seemed to be, in some inexplicable way, *still* happening, over and over again as it has, I suppose, been happening on some level ever since these events took place, *as all events that ever happened always do, are never ever over,* I realized, surprised, jerking the wheel so the automobile veered suddenly off onto the shoulder of the road in the dark patch through the pines. Shuddering, I gripped the wheel again with sweaty palms and steered the car back onto the unpaved road, still ascending. I saw the sycamore tree.

—The sycamore stands hugely white and stark against the

dark mountain beyond it, the lowering sky. The Cantrell homestead, nestled high among the three mountains, has a snug dreamy other-worldliness; a ribbon of mist clings to the peak of Snowman Mountain.

—The store at Tug, added onto now in several different directions, squats on its patch of litter-covered bare clay like something built by ignorant children out of whatever came to hand, the people around it stopped dead in their tracks to stare at the camera and beyond it with their habitual resigned distrust, their old wariness.

I found myself astounded by the changes along the road. Tiny ugly frame houses and makeshift shacks had mostly replaced the log cabins I remembered; or those cabins had been fronted and boarded out of all resemblance to the kind of homemade simplicity I used to love. Nothing had been done with thought or care of consequence, I noted—lumber stripped and the land left, machine parts everywhere rusting, trash and refuse out in the yards in front of the homes, if you could call them that, and children—children everywhere, ragged and dirty, in the road and in the filthy bare yards along it. Even the creek itself looked different, brown and swollen, trash along its banks where evidently it had flooded, and not so long ago. I drove slowly and deliberately up the hazardous hairpin turns of Hurricane Mountain; rounding a final curve, I found myself on a kind of overlook from which I could make wide-angle shots of the Blackey Coal Camp which occupied now the entire holler where the old woman named Granny Younger used to live.

I had never seen anything like it. The lumber companies had stripped the timber out all the way up the mountain, on both sides of the holler. They were doing it, I recalled, logging this holler, even while I was here, the logs on the narrow-gauge line going down to the Levisa River, filling it bank to bank, the loggers waiting for high water to raft them down to Catlettsburg, Ky. Somehow I had thought nothing of it at the time, which caused me to wonder what else I might have missed! what else might have made no impression. I did not enjoy the uneasiness which this idea produced, nor the way this holler made me feel, this coal camp.

One mountainside was layered with small identical company houses, rickety coal-blackened flimsy squares each with its door in the middle, its two windows giving out onto the porch, the porch itself on stilts as the houses were set back against the steep mountain. Dogs and chickens, sometimes children, could be glimpsed beneath the houses. The houses appeared to be in imminent danger of falling off the mountain. The unpaved roads leading up to them were muddy, full of potholes. Trash, rusting machine parts, and bodies of cars lay everywhere, along that road, in all the yards (where no grass grew!). At the bottom of the holler stood a structure of yellow bricks—the company store—surrounded by other cement-block and frame buildings which appeared to be offices. Behind these, the jumble of trucks and equipment, the railroad, the coal cars, and the giant black hulk of the tipple hanging over it all. The air was acrid, sulfurous. Looking up beyond the tipple to the top of the mountain, I saw the hulking slag heap, black and vast and smooth and slightly smoking, always on fire. The sulfur came from there.

My vantage point on the hairpin turn of Hurricane Mountain, facing this coal camp, made me feel omniscient: I could view it all and view it whole, the people tiny, not real people, not at all, the cars and trucks nothing but toys. I was taking wide-angle shots when the man approached me silently, the way they always come, and hunkered down to watch me for a while before he spoke.

"You got some business here, buddy?" The voice was flat and nasal, absolutely without intonation.

I whirled, almost dropping the camera.

The man hunkered silently, watching. He was so still he looked of a piece with the mountainside, rock cropped bare and left there weathering, his face seamed, the telltale black circles of coaldust ringing his pale colorless eyes so that he resembled, I thought, some giant ominous raccoon. Before I could stop myself, I was giggling wildly! Cold sweat prickled under my arms.

"What's so goddamn funny?" The man stood up slowly, then advanced. "Nothing," I said finally. "Nothing." I stood poised by the automobile, my hand on the door.

The man looked at me. "You'll be one of them government fellers, I reckon," he said.

Christ, yes! "W.P.A. Administration." I fell into it quickly. "From Charleston."

The man came closer, squinting at me. "Then I'll tell you some things," he said. "I'll tell you some things. We been eating wild greens at my house since January this year, greens that the goddamn pigs eat. The children needs milk and we can't get none of it, you hear me mister? None of it."

"But surely," I protested, "at the company store . . ." I gestured toward Granny Younger's holler.

"Store, my ass," the man said. His voice was so flat that he might have been saying "It's going to rain": he might have been saying anything. "I owe that store so much I ain't never going to pay it, I'll die owing the company everthing I got. You got to buy your powder from the store, see, you can't blast coal without no powder, and you can't get it no-place but the store, and it keeps going up on you—then they pay you by the ton, see, and then they have went and gone up on the ton too." The man fell silent, looking out at the coal camp.

"You can't win for losing," he said.

I confess I have never been able to hold my peace when I should.

"But the union," I protested. "This new man, Lewis, don't you think—"

"I don't think shit," the man said. "Ain't nobody paying me to think."

"I guess not," I stammered. "I mean, I guess so."

"Hell, they talk big," the man said, "but they ain't done nothing yet. The only thing they done so far is get Mr. Blossom all riled up so he's got him some Gatling guns and a bunch of Pinkertons up here. Hit's coming on fer a bad time," he said, almost as if to himself, then suddenly grinned a wide feral grin, exposing his yellowed broken teeth. "You heard enough?" he asked. "You want to hear some more?"

"I have to be on my way," I responded quickly. "Perhaps I could ask you, however, do you know the family of Luther Wade? I'm told they live up here someplace."

"That second row of houses over there," the man said, pointing. "The one on the end," he said. "I reckon you come up here to hear him sing. You gonna write it down or what?"

"Something like that."

"They was some other fellers up here already, doing that."

I remained silent, vastly relieved.

"Didn't none of them have a car like thisun, though."

I got into the automobile and locked the door.

"Didn't none of 'em have such a fancy car."

The man pulled a gun (!) out from somewhere—shoulder holster?—and looked at it, turning it in his hands. The gun was black and seemed to absorb the sunlight. The man looked at it carefully, blew in the barrel.

"Look, you want money?" I said—I think I said. "Is that it? Here." I struggled with my overcoat.

"I don't want nothing you've got."

Carelessly, grinning, the man lifted the gun and shot out the rearview mirror attached to the car on the driver's side. Glass splintered against the car and down onto the packed red clay.

The sound of the gun ricocheted deafeningly from the mountain wall.

The man grinned.

I threw the car into gear and screeched off down the narrow road into the holler, not the way I had intended going, not at all, but the man stood behind me there in the middle of the road still grinning so I could not turn the car and I had simply no choice at all.

Children ran beside me as I drove past the company store; everybody stared. I drove on, ascending now, at last almost within shooting range of the house I knew to be hers, then braked and turned and put the automobile out of gear and leaned out for a couple of quick shots.

By this time, the light was nearly gone. This series of

photographs has an indistinct, grainy surface, as if coal dust were blowing palpably through the air.

The first photograph shows the house itself with the clothes flapping on the line beside it, children out playing in the dirt of the yard, such as it is, beyond the fence, children taking a trip of their own in the rusted-out Dodge or part of a Dodge in the yard.

—Then two lovely girls, apparently twins, holding hands as they come down the steps, frail and angelic: they've got no business here in this darkening yard. The twins, their dresses, and the wringer washer on the porch all seem to glow in this photograph; the yard, the house, the other children blurry and dark.

Finally Dory herself appeared in the lighted rectangle of the door.

"You girls!" she called. "Sally! Lewis Ray! Billy! You all come on, now."

I drew my breath in sharply, clicking away.

But these pictures did not turn out because the light had gone by then! because Dory, at the door, picked just that moment to turn her head. She was reduced to an indistinct, stooped shape, the posture of an older woman—they age so fast in those mountains anyway—or perhaps it was simply the angle of her head and the way she stood at the door, her head a mere bright blur.

Even when I blew it up, there was nothing there.

I drove for most of the night, beyond Claypool Hill and Tazewell to a hotel outside Christiansburg, desperate to put as much distance as possible between myself and the mountains. When I awakened the next day, in the late morning after seven hours of deep black sleep, I felt exhausted, drugged. Driving on, I was suddenly struck by the way my splintered rearview mirror fractured the noonday sun and sent it out in a splatter of light: like a prism, in all truth. I stopped the car and stared into this phenomenon until I was nearly blinded, and when I looked back at the rolling landscape of Lynchburg around me, it appeared all different, all new, as if cleansed by a silvery wash. I felt as I had felt several years ago upon hearing the news that a ninth planet

—Pluto—had been found revolving around the sun, a planet that of course *had been there* all along: oh God! I thought. Nothing is ever over, nothing is ever ended, and worlds open up within the world we know. I was anxious to rejoin my family. Yet I sat there for quite some time, just east of Lynchburg, looking out at the first faint springing green on the earth's wide rolling field.

Pricey Jane + Almarine Cantrell
- Eli ~ 1899
- Dory ~ 1902

Vashti Cantrell + Almarine Cantrell
  Ora Mae-1895
- Isadore-1903
- Bill-1904
- Nun-1906
- James-1914
- Mary-1916

Dory Cantrell + Orvil Luther Wade
- Pearl } 1924
- Maggie }
- Sally-1926
- Lewis Ray-1928

Ora Mae Cantrell + Morris Blankenship
- Billy-1925

IV

Sally

There's two things I like to do better than anything else in this world, even at my age—and one of them is talk. You all can guess what the other one is.

A while back, Roy and me were in the bed—that's my husband, Roy—and I said this out loud to him it is something I have thought to myself for a while.

"Roy," I said, "when you get right down to it, honey, there's not a lot worth doing, is there, outside of this and talking?" and Roy wrinkled up his eyes in that way he has, and thought for the longest time, and then he said, "Well, Sally, I guess there's sports." Sports! I laughed so loud.

But that's Roy for you. He'd roll over and die if he missed a bowl game on TV. One time he didn't get up from that recliner for seven hours solid and his knees went right out from under him when he stood up when the news come on.

Roy has a good time, that's the thing I like about Roy. He's a lineman for the Appalachian Power and he likes that job fine, no complaints, turned down a promotion because it meant he'd have to wear a tie and spend half time at the office.

"Count me out," was what Roy said.

Roy likes his sports and he likes my kids and he likes pepperoni pizza and he likes to have some beer of an evening—I do too—and he'll grow him some tomatoes every year out there by the garage, he likes tomatoes, and he likes engines better than any man you ever saw. Any kind of engine. He made Davy the cutest little dune buggie, and got him a helmet to go with it. Roy likes cars and boats. And Roy can fuck your eyes out, Roy can, and talking all the time. "Talk to me," he says. Well I like that.

My first husband came from a family up in Ohio that

didn't believe in talking to women and he never said one word, just roll over and go to sleep.

I didn't run into Roy until I was over the hill—I had this other husband first, as I said—but by God I know a good thing when I see it.

I jumped right on it.

Because him and me we are two of a kind and sometimes when we're there in the bed it's like it all gets mixed up some way, like you kind of forget where your body stops and his starts or who did what to who and who came when and all that. I said we are two of a kind.

Another way we are, Roy and me, is *down to earth.* I've always been like that basically and so has Roy, even before we took up with each other. Sometimes we play a little poker with Lois and Ozell Banks and sometimes we go to Myrtle Beach. We don't want the moon.

Not like Almarine, who is all the time trying to get us to go into the AmWay business with him and Debra. The more people they get, see, the closer him and Debra get to being a diamond distributor, or a ruby or a emerald distributor, or whatever the hell it is he wants so bad.

"I'll buy your soap," I said, "and I'll buy your oven cleaner," I said, "but by God that's it and you might as well take all those cosmetics right out of this house."

I am not about to go fooling around with any soap cosmetics.

I told Almarine that, too, right to his face.

"I don't buy a thing but Mary Kay," I said. "Now get that straight." Roy was laughing and laughing. Lord, I love the way that man can laugh. And Almarine leaning forward, just so serious, he was sitting right there on that couch.

"Tell me your dreams," he said. Almarine learned that at the AmWay convention, they tell you to say that and write them down.

"I dreamed I went to a demolition derby in my Maidenform bra." Roger said that—that's my grandson, Roger, with the smart mouth. We were all in here in the family room looking at Almarine sitting on the couch with all that soap and air fresheners and nail polish and God knows what-all spread out around him like he was a regular store. And putting on weight, too, I noticed—Almarine used to be a tackle in high school and now he's got this real big neck.

"No, I'm serious." He held his pencil up in his hand like he was back in tenth grade, taking a spelling test. "Tell me your dreams," he said.

"Shit, Almarine," Roy said. "Come on."

So finally Almarine got up and went home. If he had any sense he would of known he'd never get anyplace with me and Roy who are the only people on our street who haven't ever planted any grass in our yard so we won't have to mow it. That's how we are.

But Almarine is always telling people that if they go in the AmWay business their life and their marriage will improve.

"It's a couples business," Almarine says.

Shows you how much he knows.

But my whole family is like that. People say they're haunted and they are—every one of them all eat up with wanting something they haven't got. If it's not being a double ruby it's something else. Roy says that watching my family carry on is better than TV. They've *always* been like that—not Ora Mae, of course, but she's another case altogether, and not Pappy, that's Luther—any more since he's gotten so old and crazy he's forgotten what it was that he wanted so bad although all the rest of us remembers it real well as you might imagine. But the rest of them, Lord!

When Roy fell off of the truck about a month ago and got his knee smashed up so bad, I told him the whole story, I never had told it before, Roy sitting home in a leg cast so he couldn't do anything else *but* talk.

"Listen," I said, and I got him a beer, "I'll start at the beginning," I said, which I did, and although I told it the best I could, I'm still not sure I got it straight. It took me a day to tell the whole thing.

I've always said this: either a person loves their mama or they don't. And either a family will work or it won't, that

may not be the way it is everywhere, and especially not now
with women's lib, but that's the way it was here, when I was
growing up.

You've been in those houses too, the ones that don't work,
and you know what that's like, the kind of house that makes
your blood pressure go up just to put one foot inside the
door, everybody yelling and snapping off each other's heads,
breaking stuff, running off in all directions, and once the kids
are gone they never come back, oh they might send a
Christmas card or something but that's it, couldn't wait to
get the hell out of Dodge, and who's to blame them? or else
it's the kind of house you go in there and it's so quiet and
you can hear a pin drop all the time. Everything happens the
same way every day, same time, you know you almost die
you get so bored. Nobody has got anything to say to anybody else.

This is the kind of house my friend Lois Crowe grew up
in, you couldn't even open the Frigidaire Lois said between
meals and you had to sit on plastic on the chairs. The end of
that story is the way her mama, who was such a house-
keeper, got at the last, how she took to washing her hands
about twenty or thirty times every day, but then every time
she got them clean, she'd just stand in front of the sink and
holler for Lois or Ozell or one of the kids to turn off the
water because she couldn't stand to touch the faucets, see,
she had gotten her hands so clean.

Well, there is houses and houses, I guess.

Sometimes I'll be driving along over to Black Rock or up
to Richlands or something, and I'll pass by a bunch of company houses—the kind we used to live in, at the Blackey
camp—and I'll get to looking real close, and wondering what
kind of families live in each one and what all they do, what
makes them tick, you might say, or not tick as the case might
be and often is, I guess—all those houses just alike, and all
the families inside them different, but those houses still exactly the way ours was then, that porch on stilts and the cool
dark place beneath it where we played, wringer washer on
the front porch, the front room where the sofa was and the
lamp from Ohio with tassels, and Mama and Pappy's bed,

and the back room where all the rest of us stayed except for Lewis Ray, the baby.

Pappy made him a little bed in a box by the kitchen stove when he was born, and even when he got bigger, he slept in there. Once Lewis Ray set his mind on something, he just had to have his way. Our house was like the rest. And we were like the rest, too, I guess, us children, snot-nosed and sniveling, and hungry half the time, playing games we made up straight out of our heads.

I remember us all getting in that old Dodge out in the yard and taking a trip to the West. "Where the cowboys are," I'd say. And Billy used to tell us over and over how much Tom Mix had been hurt: blown up once, shot twelve times, hurt forty-seven times in the movies alone which didn't even count stuff, Billy said, like knife cuts. "Turn left," I'd say, "for the Grand Canyon." "I don't wanna go in the Grand Canyon," Lewis Ray'd start hollering. He was so stingy and contrary we never let him play if we could help it. "I wanna go out West," he yelled, "where the cowboys are." "The Grand Canyon *is* West," I had to tell him, so he'd shut up, and Pearl and Maggie sat on the back seat folding their hands like ladies and giggling.

I remember those times we'd go with Pappy over to the fiddlers' convention at Matewan and sit under the big old shade trees along the banks of the Tug, and Pappy'd walk off with all the prizes.

And sing! He sang to us by the hour in those days. Songs he made up or the old songs, songs he just naturally knew. Such as for instance "Barbary Allen," or "Fair and Tender Ladies," or—this was my favorite—"Down in the Valley."

I can still see it all so plain, us of an evening, sitting out on the porch, and Pappy on the steps with his guitar or his dulcimore across his knees, and all of us sitting around out there on the porch in the dark or out in the cool dark yard.

"Down in the valley, valley so low, hang your head over, hear the wind blow," Pappy would sing, his voice so pure and true at that time it was like it never came out of him at all, it was like it was something he called up out of the dark green summer air and out of the mountains themselves—

"hang your head over, hear the wind blow." The neighbors used to come over too, you could see the end of Horace Stiles' cigarette shining red by the corner of the house where he stood, and the women's dresses light in the shadows of the porch.

It's a funny thing but I don't know now whatever happened to Horace or any of all those Stileses.

Way up on the side of Hurricane, where the slag heap from the coal camp was, you could see the red glow of the burning slag, which never went out, and when the wind was right you could smell it, a sweet-awful smell that doesn't smell like anything else in the world but it's got a little sulfur in it somehow, enough sulfur anyway so that every time I peel a boiled egg nowadays it takes me right back there in a flash, just like I never left, like we are all still sitting around there listening to Pappy sing. "Send me a letter, send it by mail, send it in care of the Birmingham jail." He had the prettiest voice, he could go up high if he wanted just like a woman, or down real low, he could almost whisper and still be singing. I've heard it said a million times that Pappy could of made a mint if he'd of wanted to, if he had ever written down those songs he made up or if he had gone to Nashville and got on the radio. I believe this is true. But Pappy didn't want any more than he had, I think—or I'll say it this way—he already had everything he wanted.

Which was Mama.

Now the funny thing about our family at that time was how the whole thing turned around her. It's like the kaleidoscope we got that year for Christmas that Lewis Ray took such a fit over, and wanted to hold all the time and not share, and got his way, of course, like he always did.

But I remember looking in that kaleidoscope too, and how it had a bright blue spot in the middle of all the patterns, one spot that never moved no matter which way you turned it or how many pretty bright patterns came and went all around. Our family was like that, with Mama at the center, not doing anything particular but not *having* to either, and all the rest of us falling in place around. Whatever she was doing, it was like Mama was *waiting* somehow, caught up in a waiting dream. Mama was so beautiful then, and she never raised her voice. I said, she didn't have to. There are some people like that, you know, where the whole world just gets in line to help them out. And if it's that kind of person, you don't mind being in that line.

Most nights, after supper, and after *Amos 'n' Andy*, I'd get the lantern and Mama would get the bucket, and if it was winter I'd put on Pearl's winter coat which was the warmest, and we'd go out to the sidetrack which ran down the mountain close by the house, and after the train came by, striking sparks off the rails, we'd go along the track picking up the coal it spilled along the track. They used to overload them at the tipple on Hurricane.

"Mama, we've got enough now," I'd say finally, but sometimes she didn't seem to hear, walking head down into the wind. "Mama!" I'd say. A lot of times, it was like she was listening to something couldn't none of the rest of us hear. I'd run to catch up piling handfuls of coal into her bucket, and I'd pull at her hand until finally she turned back and then we'd walk the dark track together, home.

I would have done anything for Mama, and did. She called me her little right hand and swore she couldn't get along without me, and it was true, no matter what Ora Mae thought.

Ora Mae would not leave us alone. Mama seemed to draw her too like she drew the rest of us, around and around, the only difference being that Ora Mae didn't want to be that way, and all the rest of us did.

I grew up with Ora Mae there like anything else we had to contend with, like the flash floods that came in the spring, or how they kill your favorite hog to put meat on the table, or how they would up and lay people off at the mine without telling them first not so much as a by-your-leave.

I grew up with Ora Mae like some kind of a natural aggravation.

I didn't care, then. We had a lot to put up with in those days and we put up with all of it and didn't care. We were

happy. This is why Billy—that's Ora Mae's son—he wanted
to live with us instead of her, and most of the time he did.
Ora Mae couldn't hardly get him to go home at all.

Billy was curly-headed and blond, like that daddy of his
we never saw nor ever heard much about, either. And he
was smart. But flighty, lots of ideas and no real sense (I'll
say it—I was the only one with any sense, out of all us children, I mean. It's true. I was. And I was the one who was
good, which may be the reason that when I turned bad, I
went so far the other way. But in those days, in a way I
never liked, I was the one who took after Ora Mae, which
may be the reason I hate her so much and won't let her in
my and Roy's house—I wouldn't let her come in here if she
begged me, which she won't. I've got her number, old Ora
Mae, and she's got mine). So Billy was flighty and silly and
giggled a lot, a kind of a sissy almost, and afraid of the dark.
He used to wet his bed instead of get up and go to the outhouse, even after he was a big, big boy. It seemed like me
and Mama were all the time boiling sheets whenever Billy
had been at our house.

Billy as a boy reminds me of a wire strung out in the
wind, like those highwires Roy works on sometimes that
scare me to death. When the wind blows real hard they start
whining, a high-pitched terrible whine. Billy was like that. I
used to think he might just fly off any day and disappear in
all directions over the world.

Which he might have, if it wasn't for Maggie, who was
everybody's favorite next to Mama. Maggie looked the most
like Mama, which was probably part of it, real pretty, but
also she was sweet. If Maggie didn't have something good to
say about something, why then she just never said a thing.
Some people like that can drive you crazy, but not her, because all of it was *natural.* If it's not natural, it pisses you
off. Maggie used to keep Billy calmed down, she was not a
thing like Pearl, even though when they were little, folks
called them identical.

Well those twins were not identical, they were just as different as night and day. It's funny the way I think of the

twins, even now, like I was their big sister instead of it being the other way around. I was just so *good* then—well I said that.

But Pearl was out for blood. I mean never satisfied, not for one minute, always worrying, whether it was over a coat she thought didn't look good on her or somebody she thought didn't like her. If I think of Pearl even right today, with her now dead and gone, what I see in my mind is those thin pretty white hands of hers grabbing and grabbing out at the air. Pearl was the worst one for wanting, of all of us. And the biggest fool. You could see it in her eyes, pretty eyes, blue eyes, exactly the color and shape of Maggie's, but while Maggie's eyes were like a pool and it was restful looking into them, Pearl's eyes were glittery and jumped around. They looked wet and kind of *smeared.*

Poor Pearl, she always wanted to know what everything *meant,* God knows why, she couldn't sit back and take life as it comes. I remember the first time Mama caught her stealing—it was cut-glass earrings from old man Poole's—and Mama caught her with them and held them up and said, "Why Pearl! Whatever do you want with these?" They were made to look like little diamond baskets, they sparkled and caught the light. Pearl was eleven years old. *"I need them,"* she said, and from the way she said it with each word coming out so sharp like it hurt her, I knew it was true, and I knew myself well enough by then to know that I would never understand what in the world Pearl needed them *for.*

Pearl had so many ideas. She used to sit and look at magazines by the hour, everybody around here saved them for her, and she'd cut out pictures and hide them away. Not only pictures of models in pretty clothes, either, the kind you make paper dolls out of. Pearl cut out weird pictures—a photograph of a storm is one I particularly remember, out of *Life* magazine. It was a farm in the midwest, plain white house with the black clouds hanging down low over it, and a wind so strong you could almost see it blowing everything down, sending chairs across the yard and lifting the roof— you could see it—off of the chicken house, and whirling a man around like a top right outside his own front door. Pearl smoothed that picture out flat on her knees and stared at it for the longest time. I was watching her.

Finally she looked up at me.

"Imagine that," she said.

Another picture she had was this picture she cut out of the *National Geographic* at school, which of course you're not supposed to do. I couldn't see what in the world she wanted with it either. All it was, was this 110-year-old lady in some foreign country who by then looked a lot like a prune. She looked terrible. Her eyes looked like holes in her head.

"That lady has been alive for a hundred and ten years," Pearl said.

She said this several times.

"So what?" I said.

It was the only thing to say to most of the stuff Pearl came up with.

What Pearl wanted—I've always thought this—was several lives. One was just plain not enough. Even when she was tiny—going back before the magazines and back before Lewis Ray was born—she used to go out behind the house with a cup and a gourd and dig for China.

"Whoever told Pearl about China ought to be horse-whipped," Pappy said.

"Why do you want to go to China, Pearl?" Mama asked her, and Pearl said because she wanted to see all the funny hats.

Funny hats! Nobody could make her stop digging, she must of dug for a week with that gourd and that little cup, and cried for another week when she didn't get there.

And what about me, back then? Roy asked me over and over, laying on the couch with his foot in the cast stretched out on a kitchen chair, he couldn't fit it together with the way I am now. I can see why, too.

This is me, at say twelve, big-boned and gawky, looking a lot more like Pappy's daddy, old man Luther Wade with his big nose sticking out in the daguerreotypes, than like Pappy or Mama either one. I sure didn't look a thing like Mama, and still don't, which is probably a good thing and the only reason I'm still alive. Anyway some of the boys said I looked like a chicken hawk. This made me cry, not because I liked boys then, I hated them every one, but because I wanted to look like Mama and I did not. Her little right hand, she said.

I'd get up in the morning and put the water on to boil—Pappy would of poked up the fire that much earlier, before he went out to the mine—and then I'd get Lewis Ray up and get him dressed before the rest of them got up, because it used to take so long. Lewis Ray wouldn't do a thing for himself, he'd stick his arms out straight like little poles for you to put on his shirt, which made it that much harder, he refused to tie his shoes till he was eight. By the time Mama got up, I'd have us some coffee ready, and Mama and I'd sit in the kitchen and drink it together, taking our time, while Lewis Ray threw corn to the chickens or rolled on the floor at our feet and everyone else slept on.

I drank coffee with Mama every day from the time I was six years old, strong coffee with lots of sugar and lots of Carnation poured in it out of the can.

I can taste it still on my tongue. There we'd be, Mama in her blue chenille robe and me already dressed in my jeans, sitting in that kitchen not saying much while it grew full light outside till you could see what kind of day it was going to be.

Now there was a lot of big things that happened in those years—when Billy fell in the well, or Lewis Ray getting born in the front room bed for instance and me right there to hold him first, Pappy so nervous he stayed over at the Stileses' drinking liquor the whole night long. Or the disaster of 1933, that's what they called it, when fourteen men got trapped in the Number Two shaft and it was eleven hours before they dug them out, and one of them was Pappy. We stood out on the hill with the rest all night and waited. Five men died in the Number Two mine and Pappy wrote a song about it named "Buried Alive," you can still hear it sung today. Or the time Billy trained a bluebird to come to your hand, or we got those patent leather shoes from the Mountain Mission, or Pearl broke her arm and we got the insurance money and took a trip to Cherokee to see the Indians, or when Vashti finally died and we had to stay up all night at the wake, even the children, and Billy took a fit when they made him kiss her.

A lot of big things happened, is what I'm saying. It's funny how you don't remember those, though, how after the passing of so many years what you hold to is what you never thought about at the time, like Pappy out on the porch singing or me and Mama having coffee so early in the morning.

I think, even then, I had a sense that it wouldn't last. I think, even then, I knew we had Mama with us on borrowed time, she was so clearly waiting—and patiently, too, not troubling us at all—but a place inside her was empty that we couldn't fill. This made Maggie nicer than nice, it made Billy sissier than ever, Pearl wilder and Lewis Ray more contrary, it made Pappy sing louder and play the fool, and me? It made me work as hard as I could—I was a little girl like an old, old woman, that is probably why I turned into a woman too much like a girl—I wouldn't for instance, for years and years defrost the refrigerator until it just killed you to see it, or make up the beds.

Anyway, whenever Mama disappeared, I'd cover up. She used to go walking, see, not so much in the first years but then more and more as time passed and we all got older. Sometimes she'd be gone for two, three hours, and sometimes more like a day. I don't think she planned it either. A lot of times she'd be right in the middle of something like hemming a skirt, and all of a sudden she'd take off her thimble and lay down the skirt and walk straight out the door. Then I'd finish up whatever it was she was doing, and if anybody asked where she was, I'd say she had to go up the holler to sit with old Margie Ramey, or I'd say she had to go over the mountain to Johnson's store, or something. But I didn't know where she went either, most of the time, although when I followed her once or twice just to see, it was noplace special, down the spur line most likely, just walking along by the tracks with her head cocked a little bit like she might be listening out for the train.

I know they whispered about my mama, said things. I

guess we all knew it, even Lewis Ray. Nobody ever *came right out*, I mean, but there's things you know. It's like they seep into your head the way water collects in a basement, coming from noplace at all in particular. Still, in spite of that sense of biding time, or even maybe *because* of it—I just thought of that—we were happy. There was a kind of life that went on in that house that was better than most, the whole time we had Mama.

Which wasn't too long.

And I knew it was coming. I knew it all the time.

She died in 1937, when I was thirteen years old. She fell—or laid down—on the spur line, and the train cut off her head.

Everybody knows that.

This is why folks came from all around to stare at our house, for months and months after it happened, whispering and pointing, I guess they thought we were as good as Cherokee or Grandfather Mountain or Blowing Rock. They'd fill up the road of a Sunday. They'd take pictures of first one and then the other, pointing at our house.

We were a tourist attraction.

This is why, finally, we all moved over to Ora Mae's, to the Cantrell homeplace in Hoot Owl Holler.

I can see I'll have to start again. It's hard, you know, to find the beginning. This is not it either, of course—nothing ever is—but this is where we'll start. It was summer. Let's start here. Mama was putting up stewed tomatoes. She had a big black kettle full of them which she had been cooking since morning. When Mama cooked, the stove heat made her yellow hair come loose and curl up all around her face, it made her face flush pink and she was just so pretty. She had me in there by late afternoon, boiling the Mason jars. Pearl never helped, of course, and neither did Maggie. Lord it was hot in the kitchen. It would of been hot enough in that house already, without all the cooking. Sweat was just pouring off of my face in a half an hour, but you've got to can tomatoes, you know, when they're ready to can. You can't wait for some cool day. We had put up twelve pints, two batches, when the thunder came.

The thunder rolled so hard it shook the house.

And all of a sudden outside it got dark, so dark it was just like night, and a cold wind came up out of nowhere straight in the back screen door where we were, and blew all around the kitchen.

I was taking out the Mason jars one by one.

"It's fixing to storm," I said.

The wind flopped the towels by the kitchen sink. It felt good, that wind after all the heat. You could smell the funny sharp smell in it like you get in a summer storm, a mostly chemical smell. "Mama?" I said. "It's fixing to rain."

When I turned back around, she was gone.

She had left the pot of tomatoes boiling on the stove, steam coming up in a funnel. She had laid the big spoon down right by it, dripping red tomatoes all over the stove, and the sugar jar was out too where she had left it, top off, beside the stirring spoon. That was the first thing I had to deal with, whether or not she had put in the sugar yet or whether I ought to put it in. So I had to get me a spoonful of tomatoes, and blow on it to cool it off, and taste it, and then add the sugar and some salt and cook it down before I could put it in the jars. All the time the wind was rising, and the storm was coming on, and I had an awful empty space in my stomach because I knew that something was wrong. Finally I finished canning the tomatoes that had been cooking, sealed them and turned the jars upside down, and left the rest of the ripe ones in the basket on the floor.

It was just about dark by that time. Right after the rain hit, Maggie came running in the door with her hair blowing every which way, pulling Lewis Ray along by the hand. I fixed him a peanut butter sandwich. Maggie and I sat in the kitchen chairs at the table while Lewis Ray ate and the rain came down. Maggie got up to turn on the light but I said not to, that lightning might hit. You know how you turn everything off in a storm. It got dark in the kitchen and every now and then the lightning flashed and then we'd hear the thunder.

"Must have hit someplace over on Snowman," Maggie

said, meaning the lightning. You can count from the time the lightning flashes to the time you hear the thunder rolling right afterwards. You count slow—one boy scout, two boy scouts, three boy scouts—and however many boy scouts you get up to before it thunders, that's how many miles away the lightning hit.

"I reckon," I said. I sat there feeling awful, tracing the pattern on the linoleum on the table even though it was too dark to see it—roses that used to be red, climbing over a brown fence that ran in squares all over the table—the linoleum on the kitchen table is the first thing, I think, that I remember, so I didn't have to see it to trace it out.

"When did she leave?" Maggie said.

I had never talked about Mama and how I felt we had her on borrowed time, or how she took off walking, with Maggie or anyone else. I had covered it up as I said. But when Maggie said that, I knew that she knew, too. Maybe they all did. I felt so stupid, Mama's little right hand that worked so hard and couldn't do anything, really, to help. In a way I was glad that Maggie knew. I looked at her across the table, couldn't hardly see her there in the dark, but she was the spitting image of Mama, I knew that, and I could feel her there like something warm across from me.

"Upwards of an hour ago," I told her.

We sat in the dark and the rain came down, making the awfulest racket on our tin roof—when it rained just a little bit, I loved to hear it, and still do, which is why I made Roy put a tin roof on our bedroom addition in spite of how funny it looks—but that rain was loud and terrible. We put the dishpan in the corner to catch the leak and then we kept having to get up and empty it. Pappy came in after while and sat—they had let them off early, afraid of slides—and Billy came in and went and got in somebody's bed which is what he always did when it stormed, and then Pearl came back too from Lucy Rasnake's house sopping wet with her blue eyes glittering.

"Lucy and me are going to peroxide our hair," she said, and none of us said a word.

Pappy hadn't even bothered to wash up, he sat in a chair with his hands folded tight in his lap and hummed one little tune over and over.

"I said we're going to peroxide our hair," Pearl said. She went whirling around the kitchen like a dancer in a ballet— storms always did get her all wrought up.

"Watch out for that basket of tomatoes," I said.

Pearl stopped dancing.

"What's the matter with you-all?" she said.

Lewis Ray started crying.

Pearl started dancing again. "Creek's on the rise," she said to nobody in particular. The rain drummed down like bullets on the roof. Pearl went around and around with her pale skirt flying, and I traced the pattern I couldn't see. Lewis Ray was crying and nobody cared.

"Honey," Pappy said, "sit down."

Pearl sat down then and shut her mouth, and we all just sat there, and that's the way we were sitting when we heard the train whistle down in the valley, and then the squealing brakes.

When Mama was buried up on the mountain, folks came from all around, the same kind of folks I was telling you about who came later, of a Sunday, to look at our house. Strangers. We were going to bury Mama on a Saturday morning, as I recall, and by dark on Friday night both sides of the road to Tug and on up past Hoot Owl Holler were jammed with cars and trucks and folks in them, waiting. They had brought their food and liquor with them, they planned to stay the night. I remember one whole family, all of them fat, sitting in the back of a pickup truck, laughing and eating fried chicken. I think I remember this so well because the man had on an Hawaiian shirt, and it was the first time I ever saw one.

Then on Saturday morning, real early, old Eustis Hubie, the sheriff, showed up at the door with five or so of his boys. It was just getting light outside, and drizzling.

Ora Mae opened the door and stood there.

"Howdy," Eustis Hubie said. He touched his hat.

I was looking at the back of Ora Mae's head, the black hair pulled tight in a knot, and it never moved. Her back was poker-straight. Nor did she say a word.

Eustis Hubie cleared his throat.

"Is Luther around?" he said.

"He ain't good for a thing," Ora Mae said. "Won't do you no good to talk to Luther, he won't talk back."

"Now listen here, Miz Cantrell," Eustis Hubie said louder. "My boys and me, we aim to shut this holler off to all them that's camped down there on the road below, and all the others we hear is coming. Now your daddy was not always straight with the law—we all know that—but it did seem to me and the boys that you all ought to be able to go and bury your dead in peace. Anybody ought to be able to do that. So me and the boys, we aim to cordon this holler off—"

"What's that?" Billy hollered from inside, where we were. "What's that word?" he said.

"Cordon," said Eustis Hubie. He was getting red in the face by this time and kicking his boot straight down in the dirt. "Unless of course you folks are too goddamn ornery to—"

"Now, hell, Eustis," Pappy said all of a sudden—he had not spoken for two solid days while his brothers built the box and then while she laid out in it. Now Pappy came slithering around Ora Mae like a little snake. He was so skinny his pants half-hung on his waist, and barefooted, so you could see the twisted foot which looked so white. Both of his feet were so white. I had to turn my head away then, it set me back to crying. I wished he wasn't crippled, I wished he had had on his shoes.

"Well, Luther, I sure am sorry," Eustis said. He was a decent man I know in spite of his rough way of speaking, he'd have to have been to have come up there.

Pappy hitched up his pants and hung his head, and Ora Mae stood still.

"I guess it's nothing to say," said Eustis Hubie, and Pappy said no, there was not. Then a long silence came down on them all during which you could hear Eustis's boys mumbling and something like a string of firecrackers going off down the road.

Eustis Hubie jerked a thumb back over his shoulder. "You see what I mean," he said. It was raining harder by then. Eustis's boys ducked their heads and shuffled their feet in the rain.

Pappy gave one dry little sob like a baby's hiccup, which sounded so funny it got me and Billy and Pearl and Maggie to laughing, we couldn't stop.

"Go on and do it then," Pappy said to Eustis. "We'll be beholden."

"I guess this is the first time the law ever came up here to Hoot Owl Holler and got told to stay." Eustis Hubie was trying to joke.

All of us were holding our hands against our faces to try and stop.

Pappy shuffled his little white feet. It set us off again, I'm ashamed to say but it did.

"Well," Eustis Hubie said. "We'll be for doing it, then," and he turned and left.

"My God," Pappy said. "My God in heaven," he said, and still holding onto his pants he turned back from the door and Ora Mae closed it against the rain. I hoped it would stop before we went out in it, up the mountain to bury Mama, even though we had a road halfway up. Mama was in the back of the Branscombs' truck already, they were carrying her up there now.

Ora Mae stared hard at us all.

I had crammed the end of the blanket into my mouth but it didn't help. We couldn't stop.

Ora Mae looked at us.

"You all ought to be ashamed," she said.

Maggie got the earrings, which Pearl wanted.

I don't know who decided it, finally—Pappy probably, and he was right, Maggie took after Mama the most—but a lot was made about those earrings later, and who got them, after what-all happened. Anyway Maggie got them, and they looked real pretty on her, and Pappy bought Pearl some fake gold hoops at the store in Roseann, to try and satisfy her. ("I wouldn't have them!" Narcissa Ramey said to Maggie right on the street in Black Rock, in front of the bank. "I wouldn't touch them with a ten-foot pole!") Maggie just smiled at her, she had a sweet smile, like an angel, I'm sure she put Narcissa Ramey to shame. Maggie chose to be beyond the gossip, and all the talk of bewitching. Pearl, too, who was always so busy with her magazines anyway, or reading some book, but Billy fought on Snowman Mountain with Harlan Estep over something he said about Mama, and Harlan broke Billy's nose which stayed crooked the rest of his life. You can imagine how bad that got to Billy, whatever it was Harlan said, for him to up and fight, which wasn't like Billy at all.

Lewis Ray went into a shell of a kind, serious and pig-headed as ever. He's still in it if you ask me! Anyway he packed his own lunch, for instance, even though I would have done it. I packed everybody else's. He went off to school every day like a little businessman going to work, and saved all his money in a sock under his bed-tick and got it out and counted it every night. He never mentioned Mama once and hasn't since in all the years, so far as I know. Would not let you touch him, either. Once when I put my arm around him—we were out by the garden, I think, but I forget exactly what we were doing—he jumped back like he'd been licked by fire. I didn't do it again.

And what about me, you might ask, like Roy did—old chicken hawk? Mama's little right hand?

At first I tried to keep on doing like I had, even though we were living on Hoot Owl Holler and everything had changed. But you hold—you know you have to hold—to what you know. So I'd get up early to start the breakfast but Ora Mae would have it going before I got up. Oatmeal. Ora Mae had a thing for oatmeal, she said it stuck to your ribs. And after she made Lewis Ray start dressing himself and tying his own shoes was when he took to doing it *all* for himself and wouldn't accept any kind of help. Ora Mae made Pearl and Maggie work too, around the house, and wouldn't let me lay out of school like Mama had. We had to go to bed when Ora Mae said and nobody laughed around our house anymore, not like in the old days. I tried to talk about it to Pappy one time, but he wouldn't talk much. "Sally, Sally," was all he said. "You've always been a good girl. Don't start up on me now." So what I knew was gone, and I went around with a big empty hole in my stomach and couldn't concentrate in school enough to do long division. I got real skinny and looked more like a chicken hawk than ever. When a boy from Tug—Miles Looney—asked me to go out for a date one time, to the movies over in Black Rock, I laughed in his face.

A year had gone by then, and we were back to canning. I was in the kitchen helping Ora Mae, who had a fine garden like she had always had, and we were putting up sweet peppers. Maggie and I had cut them in rings and piled them all up in the center of the table. They were real pretty, red and green. Then Ora Mae would blanch them, and we'd put them in the jars. Pearl was boiling the jars on one side of the stove and we were blanching in the big black pot on the other.

"I know!" Pearl said. "Let's put the rings in layers, like a red layer and then a green layer, you know, like that, all the way up the jars. Wouldn't that be pretty?"

Ora Mae, who was blanching the peppers, snorted.

"Oh, come on, Ora Mae!" Pearl said. "It would be so pretty, and besides we could give them to people for Christmas."

"Give them to *who?*" Ora Mae asked. Now Mama used to make a real big deal out of Christmas—or any occasion or any holiday—and sometimes we all forgot.

"Oh, I don't know," Pearl said. "Just . . . anybody!" She cocked her head and giggled.

"Waste of time," said Ora Mae.

Pearl stopped giggling. Without another word, she pushed the pile of red pepper rings—which she had just started separating—back into the pile with the rest.

I took off my apron and left, I didn't care if the screen door banged. I ran off the mountain down toward the creek, almost falling a couple of times I was crying too hard to see. I ran along the edge of the creek to this special place nobody knew about, this place I had that was all my own where the rocks hung out and made like a kind of a cave and you could get in there and no one could see you. The whole creek was alive that day, buzzing with summer, mayflies blue and shiny skimming over the water. Queen Anne's lace grew by the front of my cave. It really *did* look like lace, too, I remember I stopped crying long enough to look at it, but like anything pretty it put me in mind of Mama and then I started up again and cried until I guess I lost my head entirely, I think that's what they call it, and I came to stretched out full length on my stomach in the dirt, with dirt in my mouth and my nose, couldn't hardly breathe.

Now I'm no fool.

Even at that age, I knew I couldn't go on acting like *that*.

So I laid there a minute tasting the dirt. Then I got up and pushed the Queen Anne's lace aside and walked out of my cave and straight into the creek and laid down on my back on the shiny little rocks where the water was maybe eight inches deep. It ran over me in little ripples and I laid my head back and let it run over my face. It felt so good, and cold! Grassy Creek comes out of a spring on the top of Hurricane Mountain, or so they say, I've never been up there myself. Anyway it felt good. By and by, I sat up on my elbows and let the sun dry off my face, and then I got up out of the creek and went back up the mountain and called up Miles Looney and said I thought I'd like to go to the movies after all, if he still wanted me to.

Roy stopped me here. "I don't get the connection," he said.

I looked at him. "Connection?" I said. "Well I guess there's *not* one. That's just what I did next."

"Honey," Roy said. "There's always a connection."

"No there is not," I said. "Sometimes things just happen, is all," but Roy shook his head and ate some more pimiento cheese—I guess he has to believe in connections, being a lineman and all, but I don't. I think what I please!—and I went on and told him how it was not much later than this, that same summer, that Pappy moved off of his bed on the porch and started sleeping with Ora Mae. I came in from a date with Miles Looney and Pappy was in bed with her, and she was snoring. Sounded like a mule.

That was all there was to it, and things went along this way for a while.

You can get used to anything.

So this is how we lived then, and how we all grew up. It wasn't so bad either. There's worse, I guess. I never liked Ora Mae, of course, but I wasn't around much either. I dropped out of school at fifteen and got a job at the fountain in the Rexall drugstore in Black Rock, I used to ride over there and back every day with Mr. Bristol from up on Hurricane, who worked in the men's store. I think we all called him Mr. Bristol because he was always dressed up, because he worked in the men's store. I don't remember what his first name was. Anyway I worked at the Rexall, and sometimes if a traveling man came through or a mine inspector or somebody else I took a fancy to, I might go upstairs with them, over at Justine Poole's, but I never took money for that.

Mr. Bristol used to give me lectures on the way to Black Rock, it would be real early in the morning and he'd smell so strong, like after-shave, and he'd tell me how a smart girl like me ought to finish high school and then go over to Radford or someplace and learn a trade. He said I could improve myself. At least you could learn to type, he said. Or find you a husband, he said that too, one of the nice town boys. I sat real still in the car—or sometimes I'd do my nails on the way—and listened to what he said. Mr. Bristol didn't understand that the nice town boys didn't want to go out with me, or that I couldn't leave Hoot Owl Holler either. Somehow I could leave enough by then to go off and work but still not leave them entirely, even though I hated Ora Mae, as long as there was something left of the way it used to be.

I couldn't go and I couldn't stay.

I remember Mr. Bristol, all fresh-shaved except for his neat little beard, pink-cheeked and smelling *awful*—Mr. Bristol looked exactly like a gentleman, even if he was not,

which was why he was so good at running the men's store—
Mr. Bristol giving me more of the same old advice one
morning in December—he looked like Santa Claus anyway—when there was ice on the road and even in the car it
was so cold that your breath hung like clouds in the air.

"Little lady," Mr. Bristol said—he always called me
that—"You ought to make something of yourself." His
words seemed to hang in the air like his breath, all the way
into town, the same way I was hanging myself between
what I might do and what I was doing, between Hoot Owl
Holler and leaving these hills, and I was wrapped up in it all
like the fog of his breath, like the fog that hung on the side of
Black Rock Mountain which I used to look at of an evening,
sitting on our porch.

Pappy was making music again by then. Billy never
sang—he was moving away by degrees then, the same way I
was—but Maggie and Pearl did, and the neighbors would
come over and still it was not the same. It was not so I could
leave it, but still it was not the same.

This is the way it went until Ora Mae got pregnant and
Maggie got polio.

Ora Mae got fatter and fatter, and when I finally mentioned it to her she patted her stomach stretched out big and
tight beneath her old black skirt and said "Hunh!" like she
was real surprised to find a baby in there. Pappy acted silly,
he was tickled pink, you could tell it, and he always did have
a silly streak. He told Mr. Bristol he bet Mr. Bristol didn't
know he could still cut the mustard, did he. Stuff like
that.

Ora Mae was real big when Maggie got polio. "Polio!"
Roy said when I told him. He shifted his leg on the kitchen
chair. You remember polio—nobody gets it anymore, and
didn't then either as I recall except way off someplace in the
newspaper and you'd read about it—but Maggie got sick her
senior year in high school and the day she went back to
school after being sick, she leaned over to get a drink of
water out of the water fountain and couldn't stand back up.

For a long time we all thought she'd die. I will never forget the time when she was back home from the hospital in

Richlands—she was in and out a lot—and she was in Pappy and Ora Mae's bed in the front room and Pearl had been reading out loud to her.

"That's enough now," Maggie said. "Thank you, Pearl." Maggie was so thin her face looked almost *blue* somehow against the white pillow, and the quilt barely rose at all over her body beneath it on the bed. That was the bear paw quilt—the old, old one—her favorite. Maggie loved all the old songs, and all old things.

I was real glad when Maggie said that because Pearl had been reading poems, which I hate. Pearl was the salutatorian. "Do you all want some ice tea?" I asked everybody, and Pearl and Ora Mae said they did and I went to get it.

"Actually," I heard Maggie say when I was halfway into the kitchen, "I wouldn't mind if you read to me out of the Bible, Pearl," and something about the way she said it stopped me dead in my tracks.

I knew then she was going to die.

I knew then it was what I was waiting around for.

I got the ice tea like a robot while all the rest of them scrambled around like crazy looking for a Bible, which of course we did not have.

"That's all right," Maggie was saying when I got back in with the tea. "That's all right," she said, and she held one thin hand up like a blessing, and then she let it drop.

I held the tea for her so she could drink.

"I guess I'd better get ready," Pearl said. She was going to the Key Club Awards Banquet, it was the end of school.

"Wait," Maggie said, so faint you could barely hear her. "Just a minute, Pearl."

Maggie reached up and took out her earrings, Mama's old gold hoops, and handed them over to Pearl. "I want you to have them," she said. "You can wear them tonight."

"Oh, I couldn't," Pearl said, but her hand was already out and her eyes were glittering.

"For me," Maggie said. "I want you to keep them."

Pearl took the earrings and ran straight out of the room.

"Luther!" Ora Mae said suddenly, grabbing the arms of her chair.

"Luther, I think it's time," she said, and Pappy got up and got her bag and I helped him get her down the mountain to the car, which was not easy, the pains coming close together and Ora Mae such a stout woman anyway, and no spring chicken either. I'll swear they looked just about comical— Ora Mae so tall and fat, and Pappy like a little bug or something, hopping all around her. "Just take it easy, honey," he said.

"You take it easy," said Ora Mae.

I stayed with Maggie while they were gone.

The baby as you know was a big healthy baby, not Mongoloid at all like the woman at the County Health had said he might be, and since we all thought Maggie was dying, they let her name him.

Maggie named the baby Almarine.

"Not hardly!" Ora Mae snorted when she heard, but for one time Pappy stood up to her and said if that's what Maggie wanted to name him, then by God that was that. He said Maggie could name him whatever she wanted. Ora Mae said if that was the case, why then she'd call him Al.

Ora Mae went out on the porch where I was and smoked three Lucky Strikes and then she came back in and nursed Al.

Pearl came out on the porch with me.

At the Honors Banquet, she had been named Most Artistic. I was stringing beans.

"I don't think I can stand it," she said. She wore Mama's earrings all the time.

"Stand what?" I went on stringing beans and looking out at the mountains.

"Ora Mae and that baby," Pearl said. "Her in there nursing him like that."

"Well, Pearl," I said. "He's got to eat."

"Oh, but it's just so *gross*," she said. She was holding tight to the porch rail, I could see her veins through her hands.

"It's just natural," I said, which was true, but I never liked Ora Mae much myself as you recall. I couldn't bring myself to stand up for her.

"Well you *would* say that," Pearl snapped out at me. "I know what you do."

I went on stringing beans. I knew what I did too. But whatever I do, or ever have done, it is right out in the open, for one and all to see.

What could I say?

"Listen, Sally, I've got to leave here. I'm going ahead and start in summer school, start now instead of fall"—Pearl had this full scholarship at East Tennessee State—"and I know it leaves you with a lot on you"—she meant Maggie dying— "but it's all I can do. I want . . . I want . . . " Pearl burst into tears then, big old horrible gut-wrenching sobs, and came over and threw herself down on the porch floor and buried her head in my lap, beans and newspaper and all.

"What do you want, Pearl?" I asked.

"I don't want anything to be like this. I want things to be *pretty*," Pearl said. "I want to be *in love*."

I kept on stroking her hair, and two weeks later she left.

I'm going to speed this story up now.

Oh, I could go on and on—draw it out, you can draw anything out—but when I was telling it to Roy, it was the middle of the afternoon by then and I knew if I wanted to finish by dinner, I'd have to move right along.

We hadn't even gotten to the part Roy really wanted to hear about anyway—the only part he knew, about Pearl and the high school boy.

Here's what happened.

All of us grew up and left.

Maggie did not die at all. She got well and married a visiting evangelist, John Diamond, who has been perfect for her. They had four kids right off the bat and she has never been sick a day in her life since, that I know of. She lives in Marietta, Ga., right now in a brick house next door to her husband's Baptist Church, but they move about every four years.

Pearl went to East Tennessee State where she made the Dean's List every time, majoring in art, and then she got a job teaching high school in Abingdon. Lewis Ray went into

the Army and then to two years of college at V.P.I. He runs
an insurance agency in Pikeville, Ky., and does real well.
Married—I never see him. I bet he's still stingy and mean as
a snake.

Billy went to technical school at Radford and then he
went in the Army—that's where Lewis Ray got the idea, I
guess, since Billy went first—and then he started an electrical supply business and married a stuck-up bitch from Richlands. Her daddy was a surgeon and she had a pool in her
backyard. That's where their wedding was, around the pool,
and my Davy who was three then was the ringbearer. I had
to buy him a little white three-piece suit to be in the wedding, cost me an arm and a leg, and then he cried at the last
minute and refused to do it at all! The surgeon never
thought Billy was good enough for his daughter, and neither
did she. I don't know why she married him. She had been
married once before, and I guess she was tired of being single in a little town like Richlands where everybody is just
naturally married, and drinking gin and tonic with couples
at the country club gets old real fast. Billy was already bald
then, and picked at his fingernails. But he wanted to move
up in the world. Trouble ahead, you could see it. I said as
much.

"Trouble ahead," I told my husband right at the wedding,
and he agreed. I looked down into the pink champagne
fountain they had put up there by the diving board, at the
bubbles coming up and how they popped when they got to
the surface. Those bubbles kept coming, and somehow I was
reminded of Billy the time he fell down in the well.

That pink champagne gave me the creeps.

Of course it was trouble ahead for me too.

I forgot to say I ran off to Florida with a disc jockey from
Gate City, Tennessee, who came in the Rexall one time. I
did this soon after Maggie got well. I won't say too much
about it—this part is Pearl's story, not mine, from here on
out, and I'll get to her in a minute—but I had a hard time
down there. Things were not like I thought, and I still have
this scar on my leg to prove it. I won't even tell the disc
jockey's name because he didn't last long, and neither did

any of the others. I stayed down there a long time, until the day I was leaning over the side of some old scummy falling-down bridge in North Florida, didn't ev . have grocery money that day, and I was pregnant, looking out over this flat white water with the trees standing up in it. Some planes went by overhead and I was wondering a little bit where they were going, Miami or where, and then I started back to the trailer.

It was so hot, it was always so hot down there. The heat would beat in on your head. When I was almost to the trailer, two big black birds rose up out of noplace, right out of the swamp grass in front of my feet it seemed like, straight up out of the swamp, flapping their wings and screaming like cats. They almost scared me to death. I stood there shaking and watched them fly away over the water, thinking about my baby.

I went back home. Not to Pappy and Ora Mae's house in Hoot Owl Holler—or not for long—I got me and Rosy a two-room apartment in Black Rock over the Western Auto store, where I got a job, and then I took over the books and then I got a job at the bank as a teller, and by and by I married old Ding-a-ling and we had Davy.

I shouldn't call him that. But he married me to *save* me, or so he said, and I married him because I wanted to be saved and make something of myself—"improve my condition" as Mr. Bristol had told me, all those years ago. Have a respectable life.

We had it, too. I wish to hell it had all worked out. I mean, we were married for years and years. But all we did was work and come home from work and as I said we never talked. We didn't have much to say, and you'll think that's funny coming from me, the way I run on, but it's true. I didn't have anything to say and neither did he. What scares me now is that we might have gone our whole lives like that. Plenty of people do. Not knowing anything better but knowing a lot about worse, you know they really do.

What happened was I met Roy.

"You weren't worth saving," my husband said the day he left. All those years I had gone to church with him and been in the Home Extension Club which I hated, and done the best I could.

"I guess not," I told him, which was true. I was glad to hear it. I was happy I didn't have to be saved anymore, tired of putting up a front. You can put up a front for years until it becomes a part of you, you don't even know you're doing it. I was glad it was over with.

Pearl did that too, I guess. It's her story from here on out—hers and Pappy's and Ora Mae's, some of it Al's too.

I should say now that Al turned out to be the joy of Pappy's life. I guess it's a good thing he *got* some joy, finally. Al was a rough-and-tumble baby from the word Go, a cut-up, a clown, a go-getter. Pappy taught him to play the guitar when he was not but six. Pappy and Al had little Western shirts and string ties and cowboy hats exactly alike, they used to go and play at hoedowns and UMW meetings and political rallies. "Bunch of foolishness," Ora Mae called it. She never went with them. But I bet she kind of liked it, all the same. She liked anything Al did. I was not around then but I've seen the pictures—Pappy and Al, cowboy hats cocked at exactly the same angle, grinning. Pappy and Al performing was the most embarrassing thing that ever happened in the world, according to Pearl. She said she could not stand even the thought of it, and didn't go to see them when they played at the Miss Claytor Lake Contest right outside Bristol, not two miles from where she was in school. They said it hurt Pappy's feelings real bad.

Pearl grew more and more high-falutin.

She wouldn't associate with the rest of us, except Billy a little bit, and during all that time I lived over the Western Auto store she never once gave me the time of day.

Which is why I was surprised that day when I was still married to old Ding-a-ling, who saved me, and Pearl showed up at my front door. No phone call, no warning, no nothing. We lived out of Black Rock on Potter Street then, by the nylon hose company.

The doorbell rang and there she was.

I was still in my bathrobe. Davy, who was about six

weeks old at the time and had the worst case of colic you
ever saw, was asleep. I never slept at night, it seemed like. I
was always so tired with Davy. I had taken a two months'
maternity leave from the bank to have him. Anyway I
squinched the venetian blinds apart to see who might be
ringing my doorbell in the middle of the morning, and
looked out there and saw her. I remember it was August,
you could see the heat coming up in waves from the cement
road in front of my house.

Pearl looked as cool as a cucumber, though. She had on a
white frilly dress and white shoes and looked like she was
fixing to have her picture taken at Olan Mills. Red lipstick
and bubble hair.

It got all over me, the way she looked. I was still wearing
Kotex from having Davy. Still bleeding. I had back pains
and looked like hell.

She rang the doorbell again.

Finally I opened the door.

"Sally!" Pearl said in the breathy way she'd taken up
since she had gone to college and gotten so arty. "I guess
you're surprised to see me."

"I guess I am," I said.

"Oh, and I've brought the baby a present, where *is* the
baby?" Pearl asked, and when I pointed at the bassinet over
by the recliner she went over and pulled back his blanket
and looked at him.

"Oh, he's so *little!*" she said. "Ooh, look how little he is!"

"He's not but six weeks old," I said.

"Are you sure his head's OK?" Pearl asked. "I mean it's so
pointed and all."

"That's forceps," I told her. I got a cigarette and lit it.
Pearl was making me nervous.

"Well, is it *normal?*" Pearl said. "To be that pointed?"

"Hell, yeah, it's normal," I told her. Davy was just ador-
able. "What's the matter with you?"

Then to my complete shock, Pearl sat down hard in the
recliner and started wringing her hands. She looked like she
was fixing to cry any minute already—wet eyes shining with
tears to come—with Pearl you always felt like there was a

nervous breakdown right around the corner anyway, right beneath those slick blue shifting eyes.

"What's the matter?" I asked again.

"I *don't know*," Pearl said. She looked around and around my house, at the pile of diapers folded and the other pile of diapers not folded on the floor beside the recliner, at Davy in his bassinet, at the picture I'd gotten with Green Stamps and hung up over the couch, at the antimacassars which my husband's mother had crocheted.

I saw my house for the first time through her eyes, I knew what she thought. I was trying so hard then, too. Then I got mad. It made me mad, what I thought Pearl thought. *I don't give a damn*, I said to myself. I put the present she had brought me, still wrapped, on the coffee table in front of the couch. I sat on the couch and lit another cigarette.

We both looked at the present—wrapped in blue, with a bow and a rattle, you know she had them do it at the store—sitting there on the coffee table. Neither one of us said anything. The air conditioner switched on.

Pearl was twisting her hands. Platinum nail polish, that's what she wore—

"What do you want?" I asked.

Pearl took a deep breath. "You may find this hard to believe, Sally," she said, "but I want us to be friends. I want to talk to you." She seemed to be making this decision in spite of the way my house looked.

"Why?" I asked. I wasn't going to let her get away with anything.

Davy twisted and sighed in sleep. I knew he'd wake up before long.

"Well, as I said, you may find this hard to believe. But I've always admired you, Sally, and I feel like although we've taken different paths in life, we still have a lot in common."

Pearl is the only person I ever knew who said things like "paths in life" out loud.

"Such as what?" I said.

"Mama," Pearl said then, and I jumped like I'd been shot.

It was the only thing she could have said that would have kept me from running her straight out the door.

Pearl took a deep breath. "I'm going to get married," she said.

"Well good," I told her. "I guess."

Pearl looked like she didn't know whether it was good or not.

"I feel kind of funny about it," she said. "I thought I'd come and ask you . . . " Her voice trailed off to nothing and she licked her red lips. I waited.

"Listen, it seemed to me," she said, "it always seemed to me when we were girls like you knew some kind of secret I didn't know, I didn't even know what it was *about*," Pearl said. "You always knew what to do around the house and all. You always knew what you were doing, you always did what you wanted to." (Now this, as you know, is not true. I didn't know what I was doing any more than anybody else does. I just did what I had to, which goes for most.) Anyway, Pearl went on. "I mean the way you just up and quit school, and the things you did, and the way you ran away to Florida and then how you came back and had Rosy—it was like you always knew what you wanted and you always did it whatever the consequences, and I always admired that, Sally, I wanted to be like that, Sally, I wanted to be like that, I wanted to be *you* in fact and run off to Florida with a disc jockey, but you scared me too which is why I hated you then, although I didn't really, I never really did. I went the other way, you know, as far as I could get from all that. And everything is just so right for me now but I still feel like there's something I missed, something somewhere that you had ahold of."

Pearl was so upset by then that her language was slipping from the fancy way she'd come to talk, she sounded like a mountain girl again, like me. "I've done my best to better myself, to get away, to have a new life—"

"Listen, Pearl," I surprised myself by saying. "Honey, there's no new life." (Now where did that come from? I guess deep down inside I knew that already, in spite of being saved and listening to Mr. Bristol so long ago.)

"What?" Pearl said. "What?" She was all wrought up.

"Forget it," I said. "Go on."

"Anyway, I feel like we went about it different ways—me doing what I had to do to get away, and you doing what you had to, but now you're all married, and you have this cute little pointy-headed baby, and that's what I'm fixing to do, too, get married, and as you know it's all I ever wanted"— (HA! I thought, but I held my peace.)—"and now I just don't know. I mean, you had something else there for a while, something wild, you did whatever you wanted and never cared a minute what anybody else thought"—(Is that true? I thought. My problem is, I can't decide, looking back, what is true and what's not.)—"and now you're married, and you have a daughter and a husband and a baby, and you're just like anybody else, and I just thought I'd ask you—"

"*What?*" I said.

"How you like it."

I started laughing so hard I couldn't stop. "Pearl, Pearl," I said.

"I mean, what else is there?" she said. "Or is there?"

Nobody else would have asked it out loud.

"Listen," I said. "Who knows?"

Not me, and not then, that's for sure. They say experience is the best teacher, but I'll be damned if I know what it teaches you. I'll be damned if I know.

"Well!" Pearl sat up straight in the recliner and then fell back again like she was having what they used to call a sinking spell. She closed her eyes and let the cool wind from the air conditioner, which she was right in front of, blow over her face.

"It's not like that, is it," she said without opening her eyes. I didn't even answer. I think she didn't expect me to. "What I keep thinking is that there's something else, you know, something that Mama knew about and never told us, something she was going to tell us when we got old enough, she said that one time, but then she died, and everything that comes up, I think well is this it? Is this it? but the thing is, you never know."

I smoked another cigarette. Davy whimpered like a puppy in his sleep.

"It's all about love," Pearl said.

The air-conditioner wind barely moved her hair, she had sprayed it so high and tight.

Davy woke up and started hollering and I changed his diaper and let him nurse. There is something about a baby's pull on your nipple that puts you in mind of a man, but it is entirely different from that—it's different from everything else. And there's a lot of things, like that and what Pearl was saying, you can't explain.

Pearl powdered her face and drew on some new red lips. "Who is it you're marrying?" I said.

"Earl Bingham, he's an upholsterer in Abingdon, he does the most beautiful work. He's twenty years older than me, he just adores me," Pearl said. "He just loves me to death." But she seemed absent-minded, fishing around in her purse.

"There was something else," she said and then trailed it away. She stood up, smoothed down her skirt. "I'm sorry." She hugged me suddenly so hard I almost dropped Davy.

"Pearl, Pearl," I said—and again I surprised myself, I didn't realize what I was fixing to say—"You'd better watch out," I said.

Pearl hugged me again and left me there in my six-room respectable house on Potter Street near the nylon hose company with Davy and Rosy and Ding-a-ling, doing the best I could. Which wasn't so hot at the time!

I watched through the venetian blinds as she went down the walk on her white high heels and got in her car—pale gray Buick, Pearl was so goddamn tasteful—and left. *Watch out, watch out*, I thought. This is the closest thing to a premonition which I have ever had to the kind of ESP like you see nowadays in *The National Enquirer*. Of course it might of been purely post-partum depression. But the air conditioner clicked up a notch—it was hot that day, as I said—and the way it droned sounded suddenly awful to me, like war planes across the sky.

When my husband left me and Roy moved in, some years after that, Pearl called me up on the phone.

"Hello?" I said, kind of frazzled. It had been a snowstorm

going on, lines down all over the place, and the phone had been ringing off the hook for Roy who had not had but three or four hours of sleep a night in the whole past week.

"It's me," she said.

Trust Pearl to say "It's me" and expect you to know who it is.

"Me who?" I asked.

"*Pearl,*" she said.

"Long time no see," I told her, grinning. I was back to being myself then, from living just that long with Roy. All that time of working so hard and trying so hard and not talking had passed away like a dream.

"I'm sorry about you and your husband," she said. "Ora Mae told me about it when I called to tell her the news."

"Well, I'm not sorry," I said. Then I said, "What news?"

"I'm going to have a baby," Pearl said, "like you."

Not like me, I wanted to scream. Not like me at all, you fool, no one is ever alike, I thought, don't say that.

"Well, that's real nice, Pearl," I said.

"Why did he leave you?" she asked me with that high strained note in her voice that I knew from before. Obviously she had not heard the whole story. "You had his baby and then he left you," she said. "Sally, why?"

There was never any way to tell Pearl that there are things you cannot ask about, or things you can't explain. No small talk: that was one of her problems.

"It's a long, long story," was all I said. "But I'm lots better off, believe me."

"I thought you had decided—I thought you had made your—" Pearl was crying, I think, but the connection went bad then too and all I could hear was static. I hung up the phone, imagining the long black wires strung out across the snow and all the snowy mountains between my house and hers where she lived with that poor old upholsterer who loved her to death—in a way, I guess, like old Ding-a-ling had loved me, but sometimes that's not enough, and for Pearl I knew already that nothing was ever going to be enough. I thought about the long black wires, and Pearl over there, the night coming on, and Roy out in the middle of it somewhere, working on the power lines. I did not—maybe I should have—call her back. Instead I thought about Roy some more, and ran another load of wash, you know how kids change clothes about five times a day when it snows, and made some potato soup.

The next time I saw Pearl was two or three years after *that*, when her little girl Jennifer was, I guess, maybe three, and this time I went myself to see her because Billy had called me up. This is the only part that Roy already knew, and he thinks it's funny and it is, but it isn't really. Billy calling me up was unusual to say the least. Oh, Billy stayed in a kind of distant jittery contact with all of us, I guess, not much more than Christmas cards but *that* at least, better than Lewis Ray. I think Billy just kept in touch so he wouldn't get caught by surprise. Anyway, Billy said that a man from his electrical supply house went over there to put in a chandelier which Pearl and her upholsterer had ordered for their new house, and while he was over there, Pearl came halfway down the stairs wearing nothing but a see-through blue nylon nightie and holding a box of Kleenex, and she sat down right there on the stairs and cried into the Kleenex and wadded them up one by one and threw them down over the banister. The electrician from Billy's company didn't know what he ought to do, as you can imagine. He went on working on the chandelier for a little while, getting more and more nervous, as you can imagine, and then at noon when the upholsterer came in with the little girl, Jennifer, and they started hollering at each other, the electrician packed up his tools and got out of there.

"You can't blame him," Billy said, and I agreed. Then Billy said maybe I ought to go over there and see what was going on, since I was the only one as far as he knew that Pearl might think to talk to, and he himself didn't need any more gossip and innuendo and tales circulating around about him and our family, there had been too goddamn much of *that* already. I knew what he meant, of course. I knew Billy was harder pressed than ever to keep that wife of his satisfied, and be a member of the country club and everything else I knew they did because I read about them in the social column of the *Mountain Gazette* all the time.

Billy himself had a hard row to hoe.

So I went.

Part of it, I'll admit, was curiosity. I wanted to see how Pearl, who had been so high-falutin and arty, how Pearl lived. I also went because I was happy by then and that made me nicer, I guess. And Pearl had laid that claim on me way back, the time I told you about when she said, "Mama." Maggie was gone, and there was nobody else to see about her. Blood *is* thicker than water, when you get right down to it: it *is*.

Pearl had the damnedest new house you ever saw. It was exactly what I expected, and I wouldn't have had it myself for a million bucks. Just dusting would take you two days. A long curved driveway out front, winding up to the house itself which was set up on one of those rolling hills they have over there around Abingdon, not like here where the mountains are so high and so close together that the sun won't come up until ten o'clock. Anyway this long driveway curved up to the front, where they had kind of a big paved parking area with shrubs all around it, and around the house, which had a big porch on the main section of it, and columns. Columns! I thought I'd die. Two wings spread out on either side of the main section with the columns.

Pearl's house was huge. It looked like the Old South Motor Inn in Roanoke, where Roy and I stay sometimes when we go over there to the Tech football games.

I rang the doorbell and when nobody came, I rang again. I knew somebody was home because a pale-blue Lincoln was parked in the drive.

Finally I heard a noise from behind the big Spanish-looking door, and then Pearl's voice saying "Who is it?" Only it didn't really sound like her voice.

"It's Sally," I said. "Now you open up," and after another wait, she did.

This time I looked pretty good—a chicken hawk will age well—and Pearl was the one who looked terrible. She was wearing a kind of a long housedress, or housecoat, which under normal circumstances she would not have been caught dead in. She was skinny as a rail, with white blotchy skin, and no makeup. It was the first time I'd ever seen Pearl without makeup since we were thirteen or fourteen years old. She stood there twisting Kleenex into a tight little ball in her hand.

"Sally," she said, with no feeling at all in her voice, exactly like she might have been saying "five o'clock" or any other damn thing.

"Well, it's me," I said. Now that I was there, I didn't know what to say.

Pearl looked at me. Her eyes were bloodshot, old.

Somehow they put me in mind of Ora Mae.

Somehow they gave me the creeps.

"Let's go sit down, honey," I said, and turned to the left, but Pearl said, "No, this way," and I went with her in the other direction. She had all these living rooms, all of them naturally gorgeous. It looked like nobody lived there.

I sat down on a tufted brocade loveseat with about a million little buttons in it, I wondered if Earl had done it himself.

"Some house," I said.

Pearl blew her nose.

"I wouldn't keep on teaching high school if my husband could set me up in a house like this," I said, which was not true at all, I was just trying to think of something to say. Now that I'm an accountant and work out of the house I wouldn't give it up for a thing, I like to have funds of my own. Mad money, Roy calls it. I'm glad I've got it and so is he.

"Well, Sally, that's not the point," Pearl said. She blew her nose again.

"What is the point," I said. "Pearl, honey, what's going on?"

She stared off into her empty dining room.

"They fired me," she said next.

"Who?" I was so surprised.

"The high school," Pearl said. "You don't know what-all

has happened." She started crying into her little wadded-up ball of Kleenex again.

"Now honey—" I didn't know what else to say.

"Don't honey me," Pearl said. "I'm moving out, packing. I'm in the process of packing right now." For a minute she sounded like herself again, that "in the process of packing."

"Well where are you going?" I was thunderstruck.

"Back," she said, "back up on Hoot Owl Holler, back to Pappy and Ora Mae. Where do you think? Where else can I go? Me and my poor little baby Jennifer." This "poor little baby Jennifer" set her off crying again.

"Whoa, Pearl," I said. "I don't know what's going on here, but if I was you, I'd think twice before I left my husband and this perfectly beautiful house."

"It's not paid for," Pearl said. "He can't pay for it, he's going to have to file for bankruptcy he says, he says he just built it to try and make me happy and it didn't work."

"I guess not."

"You see that loveseat you're sitting on? He did it himself," she said.

"Well, it looks like hell," I told her.

For the first time, Pearl smiled. "Piss and vinegar," she said. "That's what they used to say about you."

"Who?" I asked.

"Oh, everybody . . . " Pearl let her voice trail off.

"Pearl," I said. "What's happened?"

Pearl leaned back in her wing chair—crewel work, you know it cost her a mint—and brought her knees up to her chin and tucked her housecoat in around her feet. She looked like a little old woman, with no makeup, like Granny Hibbitts used to look. Granny Hibbitts used to wear a housecoat all the time.

"I fell in love with a high school boy," she said, back in that no-tone voice. "Or at least he fell in love with me. With one of my students. That's awful, isn't it."

"Well it doesn't sound too good," I admitted. "Right on the face of it. But you know I am the last person in the world to go pointing a finger, or say anything is awful, or say anything about anything anybody ever does. The very last in the world. Tell me about it."

"He was in my art class," she said, "and he's just the most beautiful boy. Real shy. And talented, real talented in art, but he spent all his time down in the shop with Mr. Pegram, had terrible grades. He wanted to be a carpenter, was what he said."

"Well, that's all right," I allowed.

But Pearl went on like she hadn't heard me. "A carpenter! Can you imagine? With all that talent? He could have been a real sculptor, Sally, or anything else he wanted. So I got him to stay after school two days a week for some extra art classes with me, and there we'd be in the art room with the sun slanting in the window on all his curly hair, and nobody else around. Sometimes you could hear the sound of band practice away off in the other end of the building, but it was just him and me."

"Then what?" I asked.

I couldn't believe it!

"He looks like a Greek god," Pearl said. This didn't tell me a thing. "Oh, I know how bad this sounds!"

"Go on," I said, "Get to it."

"Well one afternoon we were in there, just the two of us, and—you've got to believe me, Sally, I never laid a finger on him before that day—oh this is not but two weeks ago, it seems like years—anyway, I went up to him and laid my hand on his shoulder and he turned around and stood up and kissed me."

"Lord," I said.

"You think that's something? That's nothing to what came next," Pearl said. "Mr. Robinson, that's the assistant principal, just happened to come along the hall right then checking a fuse, or that's what he said, and looked in the door of the art room and said 'Aha!' and then it was all over." Pearl bit at her bottom lip.

"All over?" I said. "Sounds to me like it hadn't started."

"It goes on from there," she said. "Mr. Robinson called Paul Fuqua, that's the principal, and then called the boy's mother who is a terrible, terrible woman, I just can't tell you the things she said to me, the terrible things she said when all in the world I ever intended to do was just give him a taste, one taste of the finer things in life, show him what it was like, I never meant to touch him at all."

"Then why did you?" I said. "What's this boy's name anyway?" I asked.

"I *don't know* why I did it," Pearl said. "It was like a voice told me to do it and I did. I couldn't help myself," Pearl said, "any more than fly to the moon.

"His name is Donnie Osborne," she said next.

"Anyway, that night Earl took Jennifer and went over to his sister's to spend the night, he said he was ruined, and I was unfit, I was distraught as you can imagine. I was just *beside myself.* Then there came this ringing of the doorbell and when I opened the door there stood Donnie Osborne with a suitcase and his mother's car out in the drive. Only he wasn't supposed to drive it, he just had a learner's permit."

My God, I thought. "Well what did he want?" I said.

"What do you think? He wanted me to go away with him, he said he didn't care what his mother or anybody else thought, it was all his fault for kissing me, he was packed and ready to go."

"So what did you do?"

Pearl looked straight at me.

"I went," she said.

"Oh Pearl." It was all I could manage to say and you know me—I'm not one to be at a loss for words. "How long were you gone for?" I asked.

"Two days," she said. "But I want you to know one thing, Sally. *I* was the one who made us come back. I'm proud of that. I mean, the police were looking and all, I found that out later, but I was the one," she said. "I'll never forget the moment it all came home. We were in a Howard Johnson's—" (this is Roy's favorite part)"—and he ordered a hamburger and French fries, which is all he'd had to eat on the whole trip so far, and I said—you won't believe this, Sally—I said, Donny, you know you really ought to order some vegetables. You know you're a growing boy."

"Jesus," I said.

"So then I knew I had to bring him back and I did."

"I guess so," I said.

"You know what he told me?" Pearl had gone back to crying again. "He said, 'I will always love you, Mrs. Bingham, and you're the best teacher I ever had.' "

I stood up. "Pearl, let's get your stuff packed," I said. "I'll drive you and Jennifer home."

I wish I could have stopped the telling there. Because that part—that last part, Roy's favorite—*is* funny, even though it is also bad, and the rest of it is just bad. Sometimes it's hard to tell the difference.

It's not hard from here on out.

And most of this is so bad I'll have to tell it real fast, the way I did Mama dying. I had to tell it real fast to Roy that day anyway, we were pushing suppertime by then.

When I got up to Hoot Owl Holler with Pearl and Jennifer, Pappy listened to what I had to say with his little head cocked to one side like a robin, and then he turned his face away, over toward Snowman Mountain.

"She can come in here, I reckon," he said, "but she's none of my get and never was. I don't give a damn what she does."

Well!!! You could have knocked me over with a feather when he said that.

"You're kidding," Roy said. "You mean you didn't know?" And then Roy told me that half the county knew that or at least suspected. He said he had heard it himself, he thought, and then forgot. Something about a school-teacher—came and went.

Nobody had ever told *me*.

After Pappy said it, a lot of things made more sense to me though, like Pearl's smart ways. It took me a long while to get over the shock of it, I might not be over it yet. I really might never get over the way you live your life, I mean, and not know what a lot of it's all about. Connections, Roy said. Well, he's a good man, but sometimes you can make those connections and sometimes you can't.

Anyway Billy got a divorce and had a nervous breakdown and came home too, not long after Pearl, and sat in the rocker out on the porch and rocked all day long and half the night. And then Pearl was pregnant, and had the baby premature and never got over it—Pearl died of complications—and when the baby died, Ora Mae buried it herself up on the mountain or so they said. Nobody ever saw that grave.

And then, of course, you know about the murder.

Everybody knows about that.

How Billy was sitting out there on the porch in the rocker drinking ice tea when all of a sudden here comes Donnie Osborne, Pearl's high school boy, at ten o'clock in the morning, walks straight up to Billy and takes out his father's pistol and shoots him point blank in the face. Billy never even had a chance to stand up from his chair. If he *would have,* I mean, which I have had my doubts about all along. Billy was looking for that bullet as sure as it was looking for him, if you ask me. Especially since Pearl was gone. Anyway, Billy pitches forward out of the chair and falls half off of the porch. Blood and ice tea all over the place, and that rocker rocks back and forth.

Now, who knows what Donnie Osborne thought?

Who knows what went on in his head?

Some said he was jealous, and had got it in mind that the baby was Billy's, not his—and who knows but it might've been? When you get right down to it, who knows? Life is a mystery and that's a fact. Anyway, most said he was crazy with grief at Pearl dying, and he was just a high school boy to begin with, and you know he was crazy period. Life is one big mystery, as I said.

The murder took place one month to the day after Pearl died of complications.

Now Pearl's was the saddest burial I ever went to, and the smallest.

Pearl was buried on a February Sunday, cold and cloudy, up on Hoot Owl Mountain. That little Jennifer was not there—Ora Mae had sent her right back to the upholsterer, and I must say I can't blame her—and the upholsterer was not there either. We stood out there in the wind, me and Roy, all hugged up tight together, and the wind blew so slow and steady it was almost like you could see it, like it was a real, gray *thing* sweeping across that flat wet grassy bald. The clouds had covered all the mountains, had filled the gorge. They rolled in gray and scary out of Kentucky. A young minister none of us knew—he was in the Junior Toastmasters with Al—said the words, and when it was over, it started to rain. Not a thunderstorm, or a *good* rain, the kind you don't mind being out in, but a slow rain like the saddest rain you ever saw. They put Pearl next to Mama, which was fitting. The clouds from Kentucky had rolled in so far that you couldn't even see the graves on down the hill at the edge of the burying ground next to the cliff, even if you knew who was buried down there anyway, which I don't.

And don't care!

I held on tight to Roy.

It was Pappy and Ora Mae, Al and Debra—Maggie couldn't be there, it cost too much to fly, and Billy wouldn't get out of the rocker—and Roy and Davy and me. Lewis Ray, of course, couldn't make it. And Donnie Osborne's mama would not have let him come.

After the preacher said the words we went back to the cars, and that was it. The preacher had a pickup truck and he and Roy got to talking about trucks, or something, and then Davy came up to say he was ready to drive Ora Mae and Pappy down the mountain—them being, of course, naturally too old to drive by now—but they couldn't find Ora Mae.

"Can't find her!" I said. "Well, where could she be?"

There's noplace in the world beyond the grassy bald at the top of Hoot Owl Mountain, there's nothing left but sky.

"You keep Pappy in the car," I told Davy. "Don't let him out in the weather and get sick. I'll find her," I said.

Then out of the corner of my eye I spied something moving down at the cloudy edge of the cliff near the gorge. I knew in my bones it was Ora Mae, and I also knew, right after I thought of it, that she would never jump. It's not in her to jump, I thought. She thinks she's too important. Crazy old woman! But I was dying to see what she was up to. So I just took off down the burying ground, ruining my shoes entirely if they weren't already ruint by then, I guess they were anyway, and snuck up on Ora Mae from behind.

In her long dark coat she looked right spooky, there in the clouds at the edge of the cliff. She looked like a rock or a tree, something that belonged there.

Ora Mae! I was just about to holler, but I did not.

Something made me stand still and watch her. Ora Mae was fishing around in one of the pockets of that big dark coat of hers—I'll swear she's had that same coat, and this is no lie, for fifty years.

I stood still and watched her.

She pulled something little out of the pocket, pulled it out slow and painful, the way she does everything, and then she let out the awfulest low sad wail I ever heard. It did not sound like a person at all. It sounded like something right out of the burying ground, some rising up of age and pain. She fiddled with what she had—I'd guessed what it was, by then, and I'll bet you have too—and she got one of them in each hand and held them up, I watched her, for a long, long moment, to her own ears. That old, old ugly woman! It was just about the worst and saddest thing I ever saw. And I've seen some things. Then she slung both arms straight out and threw the earrings into the swirling clouds in the gorge and they went down, down, I guess, to the river so far below, and I guess that's where they are now, thank God.

Gone.

Ora Mae had the right idea.

But she stood there with her arms flung out, like a big black statue in a church or something, for the longest time.

She gave me the creeps.

Then she lowered her arms real slow, and while I watched, she shrank back from whatever she was to old Ora Mae again, so old she can't even drive. I took her arm and helped her back up the burying ground to the cars and she didn't say one word, never mind thanked me, her eyes rolled kind of back in her head like she was in a trance, both of us soaked through by then from the rain.

"It beats all, don't it," I said to Roy, "her holding them up to her ears?"

"It does and it don't," Roy said. Roy is getting stoop-shouldered now, his hair gone gray, but he's the finest figure of a man I ever saw. And the nicest, a man like an old sweater, the older it gets, the more comfortable.

"Is that all?" Roy said.

"Well, it's time to eat," I told him—I'd been fixing a pot roast, cooking while I told it—"so I guess it is."

And just as soon as I got it on the table, wouldn't you know in came my grandson Roger, the one with the smart mouth, he eats over here all the time. Roy gets a kick out of Roger. So Roger ate with us, and then he left, and finally I got Roy where I wanted him, alone in the bed with me after the ten o'clock news, and I propped his cast up real nice on three pillows and we were just fooling around when all of a sudden Roy busted out laughing. He's got this big, big laugh.

I was a little put out.

"What's so damn funny?" I said.

"Well, if you didn't laugh you'd have to cry, it's like you said," said Roy, "and all of that, and now it's all come down to Ora Mae and Pappy and me and you and Al and Debra and those three kids of theirs, the only ones connected, still around I mean. Good Lord, Sally. You've had a life, old Sal."

"Well, it's not over yet!" I said.

Roy started laughing. He likes to get a rise out of me.

"That's the *past*," I said. "It's nothing to talk about now. Now it's you and me. It's what happens after this, and if Roger gets into college or not, and if Rosy ever gets married again, and if Al gets to be a double ruby or whatever the hell else it is he takes it into his mind to do next, or if those men buy the land and put that ski run up Hoot Owl Holler, or who knows what will happen in this world? It's not over yet," I said.

"And you?" Roy said. "Old Sal?"

He reached over and put his hand on my breast where it fits.

Then he got real tickled.

"Tell me your dreams," said Roy.

Pricey Jane   +   Almarine Cantrell

           ⌐ Eli — 1899
           ⌐ Dory ~ 1902

Vashti Cantrell   +   Almarine Cantrell
⌐ Ora Mae - 1895
           ⌐ Isadore - 1903
           ⌐ Bill - 1904
           ⌐ Nun - 1906
           ⌐ James - 1914
           ⌐ Mary - 1916

Dory Cantrell   +   Orvil Luther Wade

           ⌐ Pearl   } 1924
           ⌐ Maggie
           ⌐ Sally - 1926
           ⌐ Lewis Ray - 1928

Ora Mae Cantrell   +   Morris Blankenship
           ⌐ Billy - 1925

Ora Mae Cantrell   +   Orvil Luther Wade
           ⌐ Almarine - 1940

"Now I've got one more I want you to hear." Little Luther cackles out from the swing as if from a dream, as if none of that had really happened at all, not Jennifer coming or Al going up the holler to get the tape recorder and coming back all shook up. "Wait'll you hear this one," and he starts strumming, but Ora Mae rises up white and definite on the steps.

"You hush up, you old fool," she spits at him. "It's way past your bedtime anyhow."

Jennifer stands up, clutching the tape recorder tightly in both hands. "Well, I guess I'd better be going," she says in a high strained too-sweet voice. "Thank you ever so much, Grandmother—"

"Thank you ever so much." Al mimics her from the door. "Shit." He comes out drinking a beer. Jennifer finds herself backing down the steps but she won't let him know how she feels, he's her uncle after all, she won't let him know she feels scared. The wind is still rising, it whips her hair around her face and into her eyes. But Jennifer holds her ground.

"What happened up there?" she asks him. "You never did say."

Thunder rolls softly over the mountain while Al drains the last of his beer.

"Oh, nothing much," he says finally, affecting elaborate scorn. "That chair was just rocking, that's all, nothing much, all by itself in there, and when I went by it to get that thing—" he walks over and jabs at the tape recorder in Jennifer's arms like it's something awful, and she grabs it before it drops—"when I went over there to get that thing, I felt a cold chill come over me and I got goosebumps all over."

"*I can't wait to hear the tape,*" *Jennifer says.* "*Dr. Ripman will be so excited.*"

"*I need me another beer,*" *Al says, turning to go, and Jennifer starts to feel better. The rain is coming now, big drops that ring like marbles on the tin porch roof.*

"*You ever hear the one about the three dogs and the pussycat?*" *Little Luther asks.*

"*I said hush,*" *says Ora Mae.*

She turns to Jennifer. "*Now you take that thing, and you go on. Go on. He never had no business saying you could come over here in the first place.*" *Ora Mae is talking out now from that place inside her where she knows things.* "*I reckon you'll find plenty of banging on that tape, everything you want to hear,*" *she says.* "*You take it and go on, and don't you ever come back here no more with no tape recorder because if you set it going up there, you'll likely hear what you don't want to hear.*"

Jennifer feels cold all over. The rain has slowed now, drumming softly on the roof. "*What will I hear?*" *she asks.*

But Ora Mae has said her piece. She puts her arms across her bosom and goes inside. "*I need to lay down,*" *she says.*

"*Thanks so much for the delicious dinner,*" *Jennifer calls out after her, her hands on the tape recorder have gotten so sweaty. But Ora Mae doesn't look back. Somewhere inside the house, Debra is giggling.* "*Serves you right, you damn fool thing,*" *she says.* "*You ought to know better.*"

"*Jennifer, honey, you come back real soon, you hear?*" *Little Luther calls from the swing.* "*And if you was to put me on that tape recording machine, why that would be all right with me.*"

"*Yes sir,*" *Jennifer says. She goes back and gives the old man a kiss on his hard wrinkled cheek, recoiling as she encounters tears. Tears? And close up, he smells terrible: body odor, tobacco, something else. Maybe it's just old age. Maybe you cry from old age. He's still on the porch, still strumming the dulcimer, when Jennifer walks back across the yard to her car. She's surprised to find her uncle Al there, leaning up against her little Toyota like he has all the time in the world, like it's not even raining. Al lights a cigarette and when the match flares up behind his cupped hands, Jennifer can see the gleam of his eyes and the long curl of his lip under the blond mustache.*

"Thanks so much for everything, Uncle Al," Jennifer says. "It's been real nice getting to know all of you, and I especially appreciate your going up to get the tape recorder for me. I'm sorry it was such an ordeal for you."

Al snorts. "Ordeal, hell," he says. "Nothing to it."

"Well—" Jennifer feels very tired and kind of light-headed out here in the soft wet dark. The tree frogs are singing so loud. She sticks her hand out to shake hands with Al, but he does not take it although Jennifer is sure he can see her do it even in the shadow of the van. When Jennifer tries to move past him to get in her car, he's blocking the way.

"I want to tell you one thing," he says, "Short and sweet. Don't you come back here with that thing anymore, you hear me? Mama is having one of her spells now but she's dead right on that one. So don't you do it. We are doing all right around here. We are doing just fine, you hear me?"

Jennifer starts to cry. "I don't understand what's going on," she says. "I mean, I don't see why she's so mean to me—your mother—or why Little Luther is crying, or why nobody will tell me why my cousin Billy sat in that chair for so long."

Al leans over her, big and dark, breathing beer down into her face. "Because nobody knows, *that's why. People don't know everything. But I'll tell you one thing. It was your own mother had to do with it, and that high school boy, and it wasn't from pneumonia your mother died, neither.* Hell no."

"It wasn't?" Jennifer hears herself say this from a long way off, like somebody down in a cave.

"Almarine?" Little Luther's voice carries across the yard. "Almarine?" he calls.

"Go on," Jennifer whispers. Each word bites into the dark. "Tell me. I want to know."

But *Al throws back his head and laughs and laughs.*
"Well, it might *have been pneumonia." He is talking real*
loud now. "Hell, maybe it was *pneumonia. Or maybe it was*
complications. There's people die of complications all the
time. Anyway, you can't take all that too serious-like. You
take that tape recorder on back now and I hope you get a
hundred on it. You come back sometime and see us again.
And drive careful now, you hear?"

This makes Jennifer feel a whole lot better. But when he
opens the door of the Toyota for her, just before she can get
in, her uncle Al grabs her right up off her feet and kisses her
so hard that stars smash in front of her eyes. Al sticks his
tongue inside her mouth. Then before Jennifer can even
think what is happening to her, Al lets go of her and she
drops back against the open door. "Drive careful," he says.
He walks across the yard and helps his daddy inside, and
then they all are gone. Jennifer backs up so fast she slams
into the bumper of Al's van. Then she's gone too, off down
the holler like a streak, crying and crying and wiping her
eyes with the back of her hand.

But by the time she gets back to the college, Jennifer has
stopped crying and gotten a hold on herself. She has
changed it all around in her head. Al is nothing but a big
old bully, a joker, after all. They still live so close to the land,
all of them. Some things may seem modern, like the van, but
they're not, not really. They are really very primitive people,
resembling nothing so much as some sort of early tribe.
Crude jokes and animal instincts—it's the other side of the
pastoral coin.

Jennifer's tape, when she plays it, will have enough bang-
ing and crashing and wild laughter on it to satisfy even the
most hardened cynic in the class. Jennifer will make an A
for the course. Jennifer will marry Dr. Bernie Ripman the
summer after she graduates from college, and her step-
mother will give a dramatic reading from the works of
Kahlil Gibran at the ceremony. Jennifer will not send a
wedding invitation to any of her real mother's family in
Hoot Owl Holler: not to Ora Mae, or Al, or Debra, or even

to Little Luther. And even though in later years her husband will urge her to go back there and take him, and even though in a way she intends to, Jennifer will never get around to going back over there, and then when she and Dr. Bernie Ripman move to Chicago, it becomes clear that she never will. Jennifer will never see any of them again.

Eventually, Debra will have a hysterectomy. Roscoe will win a Morehead Scholarship to the University of North Carolina; Troy will start a rock group; Sally and Roy will buy a retirement house at Claytor Lake where they will continue to live out their long and happy lives; Suzy Q will marry young; old Richard Burlage will write his memoirs and they will be published, to universal if somewhat limited acclaim, by LSU Press; Little Luther and Ora Mae will get sick one by one and then die. Donnie Osborne, institutionalized for years, will grow older and older fashioning the dowels he especially loves to make in the prison workshop, the smoothly rounded, tapering, perfectly symmetrical beautiful wood. Al will be elected president of the Junior Toastmasters Club. Then he will make a killing in AmWay and retire from it young, sinking his money in land. He will be a major investor in the ski run which will be built, eventually, on the side of Black Rock Mountain. The success of this enterprise will inspire him to embark on his grandest plan yet: Ghostland, the wildly successful theme park and recreation area (campground, motel, Olympic-size pool, waterslide and gift shop) in Hoot Owl Holler. Ghostland, designed by a Nashville architect, will be the prettiest theme park east of Opryland itself, its rides and amusements terraced up and down the steep holler, its skylift zooming up and `rwn from the burial ground where the cafeteria is. And the old homeplace still stands, smack in the middle of Ghostland, untouched. Vines grow up through the porch where the rocking chair sits, and the south wall of the house has fallen in. It's surrounded by a chain link fence, fronted by the observation deck with redwood benches which fill up every summer night at sunset with those who have paid the extra $4.50 to be here, to sit in this cool misty hush while the *shadows lengthen from the three mountains—Hoot Owl, Snowman, and Hurricane—while the night settles in, to be here when dark comes and the wind and the laughter start, to see it with their own eyes when that rocking chair starts rocking and rocks like crazy the whole night long.*

About the Author

LEE SMITH is the author of nine novels, including *Black Mountain Breakdown*, *Oral History*, *Family Linen*, *Fair and Tender Ladies*, and *The Devil's Dream*, and two short story collections, *Cakewalk* and *Me and My Baby View the Eclipse*. She won the John Dos Passos Prize for literature in 1988 and has twice won the O. Henry Award. Her most recent novel is *Saving Grace*. She lives in Chapel Hill, North Carolina.

Lee Smith

Published by Ballantine Books.
Available at your local bookstore.
Or call toll free 1-800-793-BOOK (2665) to order by
phone and use your major credit card.
Or use this coupon to order by mail.

____BLACK MOUNTAIN BREAKDOWN	345-41031-9	$11.00
____CAKEWALK	345-41042-4	$11.00
____THE DEVIL'S DREAM	345-38291-9	$10.00
____FAIR AND TENDER LADIES	345-38399-0	$10.00
____FAMILY LINEN	345-41060-2	$11.00
____FANCY STRUT	345-41039-4	$11.00
____ORAL HISTORY	345-41028-9	$11.00
____SAVING GRACE	345-40333-9	$11.00

Name_____
Address_____
City_____ State_____ Zip_____

Please send me the Ballantine Books I have checked above.

I am enclosing	$_____
plus	$_____
Postage & handling*	$_____
Sales tax (where applicable)	$_____
Total amount enclosed	$_____

*Add $4 for the first book and $1 for each additional book.

Please send check or money order (no cash or CODs) to
Ballantine Mail Sales, 400 Hahn Road, Westminster, MD   21157.

Prices and numbers subject to change without notice.
Valid in the U.S. only.
All orders subject to availability.